The story of Josephine Cox is as extraordinary as anything in her novels. Born in a cotton-mill house in Blackburn, she was one of ten children. Growing up, her life was full of tragedy and hardship – but not without love and laughter. At the age of sixteen, Josephine met and married her husband Ken, and had two sons. When the boys started school, she decided to go to college and eventually gained a place at Cambridge University. She was unable to take this up as it would have meant living away from home, but she went into teaching – and started to write her first full-length novel. She then won the 'Superwoman of Great Britain' Award, for which her family had secretly entered her, and this coincided with the acceptance of her first novel for publication. Over the years, her gritty and inspirational stories, taken from the tapestry of life, have become *Sunday Times* bestsellers, and they continue to enthral readers everywhere.

Praise for Josephine Cox's compelling and emotional family dramas:

'Driven and passionate' *The Sunday Times*

'Cox's talent as a storyteller never lets you escape the spell' *Daily Mail*

'Another hit for Josephine Cox' *Sunday Express*

'Josephine Cox brings so much freshness to the plot, and the characters . . . Her fans will love this coming-of-age novel' *Birmingham Post*

'Impossible to resist' *Woman's Realm*

'Another beautifully spun family epic' *Scottish Daily Echo*

'A surefire winner' *Woman's Weekly*

'A born storyteller' *Bedfordshire Times*

Also by Josephine Cox and available from Headline

Queenie's Story
Her Father's Sins
Let Loose the Tigers

The Emma Grady Trilogy
Outcast
Alley Urchin
Vagabonds

Angels Cry Sometimes
Take This Woman
Whistledown Woman
Don't Cry Alone
Jessica's Girl
Nobody's Darling
Born To Serve
More Than Riches
A Little Badness
Living A Lie
The Devil You Know
A Time For Us
Cradle of Thorns
Miss You Forever
Love Me or Leave Me
Tomorrow the World
The Gilded Cage
Somewhere, Someday
Rainbow Days
Looking Back
Let It Shine
The Woman Who Left
Jinnie
Bad Boy Jack

JOSEPHINE
COX

THE
GILDED
CAGE

HEADLINE

First published in hardback in 1999
by HEADLINE PUBLISHING GROUP

First published in paperback in 1999
by HEADLINE PUBLISHING GROUP

This paperback edition published in 2023
by HEADLINE PUBLISHING GROUP

1

Cataloguing in Publication Data is available from the British Library

ISBN 978 1 0354 0928 0

Typeset in Times by Avon DataSet Ltd, Alcester, Warwickshire

Printed and bound in the UK by Clays Ltd, Elcograf S.p.A.

Headline's policy is to use papers that are natural, renewable and recyclable
products and made from wood grown in sustainable forests. The logging and
manufacturing processes are expected to conform to the environmental
regulations of the country of origin.

HEADLINE PUBLISHING GROUP
An Hachette UK Company
Carmelite House
50 Victoria Embankment
London EC4Y 0DZ

www.headline.co.uk
www.hachette.co.uk

I know some of my readers were already aware that there was a new baby on the way. Well, I'm thrilled to tell you that Amelia Jane arrived, on 22 May 1998. By the time this book is published, she will be almost a year old, God willing. Thanks to our son Wayne and lovely Jane, Ken and I now have two darling little girls to love and cherish.

All of you who have been fortunate enough to have had a new baby added to your family will know how I feel. And for those of you who are still hoping, I'll be thinking of you.

P.S. Here's a snippet of information that might bring a smile to your face. Having a few minutes to spare while in town, I went into a very busy shop and tried on a pretty blue dress; unfortunately it wasn't me, so I got dressed and made my way out of the shop.

I was almost to the door when I heard the assistant call me back. Thinking I'd left something in the changing room, I returned to the counter; only to be told, between giggles, that I'd gone off not knowing that the hem of my skirt was tucked up in my knickers!

I tell you! After hurriedly untucking myself, I went out of that shop with a face like a beacon . . . through a gauntlet of grinning customers; not to mention the man who was fixing the overhead light. When, later that day, I told my family (who callously fell about laughing), I did manage to see the funny side.

Have you seen the advert where the girl walks off into the sunset, totally oblivious to the fact that she's showing her naked rear-end to the entire world?

Need I say more!

Contents

Part One

WHITECHAPEL
OCTOBER 1888

THE NEWCOMER

Chapter One

The girl sat at the front of the church. White-faced, her eyes downcast, she could hardly believe the events unfolding around her.

Her bright blue eyes were dry now. There would be no more tears, for she had cried them all away. Now the happier memories she held close would have to carry her through the uncertain times ahead.

She had not wanted to come here today, but her mother had insisted. 'People must see you there,' she'd said. 'Even if the thought of being near me makes your blood run cold.'

The girl raised her gaze to the woman beside her; this was the one she called Mother, and yet she was no more her mother than any stranger here. In fact, any stranger might have been more compassionate, more loving, and less cruel than this one.

Recalling everything that had happened, the girl could not suppress the fleeting sense of hatred that took hold of her. For *here* was a monster, while there, only an arm's reach away, dead of pneumonia, lay the soul of kindness itself. Why is it, the girl wondered, that the good are taken while the bad live on?

She watched the woman for a moment, hoping she might feel some measure of pain at her loss, yet thinking that she never would. Oblivious to the girl's attention, the woman sat rigid, playing her part to perfection . . . pretending to care, when all the time she was giving thanks. For what she had done, the girl could never forgive her.

Suddenly the congregation was rising. 'Move yourself, girl!' The hissing voice persisted in her ear. She felt the woman's bony finger in her back and, in a moment, was ushered out of the church . . . into the brightness of a sunny day.

Brushing shoulders, the people filed out. Some, not knowing the woman's true nature, gathered round to comfort her. Others, who knew her only too well, kept their distance.

'She helped put that poor man where he is!' one brave woman remarked, and, glancing to the girl, murmured to her neighbour, 'It's Sally I feel sorry for. I can't bear to imagine what her life will be like now.'

Discreetly, the pair observed her. 'She's such a pretty little creature, and so quiet,' said the second woman. 'But then, I don't suppose she's been allowed to have much of a say . . . not with a mother like that.'

Along with everyone else, they went to the girl and spoke of her loss, and asked how she would cope. 'You and your mother must look after each other now,' someone suggested kindly.

Sally nodded. They don't know the truth she thought. They don't know what it is really like.

On foot, the funeral party made their way to the woman's house, she leading the way. Tall and straight with hard features, she made a formidable sight.

The girl followed. Small and dainty with sad eyes bluer than summer skies, she won everyone's sympathy.

Along the route, passers-by showed respect; men raised their hats and women nodded their heads, before hurrying on their way.

Soon they were filing into the humble little house in Whitechapel. 'Tea in the parlour,' the woman said, and they rushed to quench their thirsts.

When Sally made to follow, she was taken by the arm and pressed against the wall. 'Not *you*!' the woman told her in a harsh whisper. 'You're not needed here.' With a spiteful flick of her arm she pushed the girl towards the stairway: 'Stay in your room until I come up.'

Knowing what was to come, Sally went with fearful heart.

Hating the loneliness of her room, she sat at the top of the stairs for what seemed an age. From the parlour, she could hear the gentle clatter of cups on saucers and the quiet drumming of voices. Thoughts of the man who had lovingly raised her stole into Sally's heart.

'Oh, Daddy, I wish you were still here,' she murmured. Heart-broken, she bent her head forward and covered it with her hands. 'I miss you so much. You were always there, and now I don't know what to do.' What *could* she do? She wasn't yet fifteen. She had nothing to call her own, and now, God help her, she was at the mercy of a mother who hated her.

It had always been that way, ever since she could remember. 'Why can't she love me?' she asked softly. 'And why was she so cruel to *you*? What did we ever do to make her hate us like that?'

Whatever the reason, their lives had been hell on earth.

When, some time later, the visitors could be heard preparing to leave, Sally softly got up from the step and went on tiptoe along the landing. Like the house itself, the landing was small and dark; her room too. Simple and hard-wearing, the furniture all over the house was made from sturdy, old oak. The walls were damp and the carpets frayed and sometimes, when it rained very heavily, the roof leaked.

It wasn't a pleasant place, but it was all the home she had known. When her father was alive, he had brought sunshine into it. He created laughter and made everything seem worthwhile. Now the house had lost its soul.

Letting herself into the bedroom, Sally climbed on to the bed, her back to the wall and eyes focused on the door. 'Don't let her hurt me,' she muttered over and over. 'Please don't let her hurt me.'

A short time later she heard the front door close. There was a span of silence, then a sound that struck terror into her heart – the slow, heavy sound of footsteps climbing the stairs.

Her heart pounding, she waited.

With a resounding crash, the door was flung open and there the woman stood, a dark, evil smile creasing her leathery face. For a long moment she stood, legs apart, the whip in her hand softly flicking the floor. 'They've gone,' she murmured. 'We're all alone now.' Her eyes were like those of a wild woman.

'Leave me alone,' the girl pleaded, 'I haven't done anything.'

Suddenly, the smile slipped away. Closing the door, the woman turned the key and dropped it into her skirt pocket. Then without a word she went across the room and drew the curtains halfway over the windows.

When she turned to see the girl scrambling off the bed, her laughter rang out. 'There's no escape,' she said, 'nobody to help you now. He's gone. It's *my* turn now.'

Desperate, Sally rattled the door handle although she knew it was futile. 'Why do you hate me?' she asked. 'What have I ever done to you?'

'Ruined my life, that's all. You're not my child . . . nor were you *his* . . . for all he doted on you!'

'I don't believe you!' To be told he wasn't her father was the worst kind of punishment.

Satisfied to see how distressed the girl was by her words, the woman smiled. 'You were brought to this house over fourteen years ago, a babe in arms . . .' Her voice shook with emotion. 'A bastard!' All these years she had told no one, but now the truth poured out in a rush of venom. 'I hated you right from the start.

But he didn't, oh no. He took you in his arms . . . in a way he had never taken me, and he loved you from that very first minute.' While she talked, her eyes were closed. 'I would have given anything to give him a child of our own, but I couldn't, you see. I don't know why.' Her warped mind going back over the years, the woman went on: 'You were my brother's bastard . . . got by some common streetwoman!' Hatred trembled in her voice. 'Oh, he paid us well enough . . . a small fortune. You'd think the money would have given me the life of a lady, wouldn't you? But not when my own husband thought more of somebody else's child than he did of his own wife.'

She took a step forward and Sally flinched, her arms over her face.

The woman laughed. Then, just as quickly, the laughter stopped. 'I was given a pittance,' she snapped, 'while the rest was hidden away . . . "It's for the child," he said. "For when she grows up."'

Taking another step forward, she continued bitterly: 'Can you imagine what it was like . . . cleaning and feeding you, when with every bone in my body I wanted you dead? I might have strangled you with my own bare hands, but he was always there. The day after you were brought here, he stopped going to work and made his office in the parlour. It was *me* that had to deliver his ledgers, and collect them again. Maybe he didn't trust me alone with you. He'll never know how right he was!'

The hatred on her face was ugly to see. 'I couldn't even blackmail my own brother. Here I was . . . married to a clerk and raising a bastard, while my brother had properties and riches I could only dream of! But he hadn't made all that for nothing. Oh no! He was a clever, devious man. When he brought you here, he brought a legal man with him. We had to sign a paper saying that we were paid handsomely and that the solicitor had acted as go-between. We agreed never to be in touch with Leonard again.'

7

She shook her head. 'I should have known we could never hurt him. He even told me that if I should ever ask for more money, he would send his "people" after me, and they would show me no mercy.'

A look of fear trembled on her face. 'He would do it too. Leonard was always cruel, even as a child.'

When she began to advance, the girl cried out: 'I didn't know! Please . . . I'll go away. I'll do anything you say.'

The woman stared at her with disbelief, the tears rolling down her sorry face. 'Will you give me back all those wasted years?' she asked simply.

There was one, brief moment when Sally thought she might be spared. But the moment passed. Now, as the woman raised the whip, there was no mercy in her heart.

Some time later, the woman prepared to leave. She placed a tapestry bag on her bed, then from her wardrobe chose only a few items, and laid them reverently beside the bag: long black underskirt and camisole, with other, neatly pressed undergarments, a small, frilled black jacket and skirt to match, and a pair of best brown boots.

She then gathered together a number of toiletries, which she packed along with everything else. There were no jewels, nothing of any value. 'I have money enough to buy whatever else I want,' she murmured. 'And no one to please but myself.'

Snapping the bag shut, she stretched out her left hand and stared at it for a while, all manner of thoughts going through her tortured mind.

Slowly, she slipped the wedding ring from her finger and slung it on the bed. 'I'm done with all that now.' For a moment longer she stood there, gazing round the room and wishing with all her being that she had never seen it. Not this room, nor this house, and certainly not that girl. 'May the devil take her!'

Grabbing the tapestry bag, she went out of the room and down the stairs. In the parlour, she closed the door behind her and crossed to where the desk stood in the far corner.

Pushing the desk to one side, she fell to her knees, groaning with discomfort. Then she gave a small laugh. 'I may not be so young as I was, but I'm richer, and that's all that matters.'

Kneeling beside the desk, she turned back the rug and lifted the loose floorboard. 'You thought I would never find it, didn't you?' Chuckling insanely, she drew out a small wooden chest. 'It took me all week, but I found it. If it had taken me a year and I had to tear the house apart, I would never have given up.'

Clutching the chest to her body, she took a moment to savour the feeling. 'I've waited so long . . . a lifetime. And now, it's all mine!'

Having previously opened the chest, she removed the broken lock and raised the lid. Peeping inside she saw her fortune nestling there. She had seen it only twice before . . . once when it was placed inside the chest on the night the girl was brought here, and the day before his funeral, when she had searched high and low until finding its hiding place.

Tipping its contents on to the floor, she watched, mesmerised, while all manner of documents tumbled out. Spying the house deeds, and the fat wad of banknotes, she grew excited. 'Mine!' Furtively, she snatched them up, and rammed them in her travelling bag.

With trembling fingers, she then began sifting through the documents. There was the will and that wretched letter, signed by each of them that night, but little else of benefit to her.

She concentrated her mind on the will. Rolled and tied with a blue bow, it made a pretty sight. She didn't yet know its contents.

Untying the bow, she laid the document out on the floor, but what she read only served to fire the loathing that had eaten away at her all these years:

To whom it may concern:

I, Edward Hale, of 14 Victoria Street, Whitechapel, do hereby bequeath all my worldly goods and possessions to my daughter, Sally Elizabeth Hale.

In here is the sum of fifty guineas, which is to be given to her at ten guineas on my demise, and the remainder to provide a regular income at her disposal . . .

The deeds to 14 Victoria Street, Whitechapel, are enclosed with my will, the house and its contents to be given to the said Sally Elizabeth Hale.

I ask only one thing in return, and that is for my dear daughter to show compassion to my wife, Anne Polly Hale, of the same address.

Out of the goodness of her heart, I ask that she will allow my wife to end her days in the house, and I pray that, in the fullness of time, they might somehow become friends . . .

'Never!' Shaking with rage, Anne took the will into her hands and tore it to shreds. 'You fool! It isn't *me* who'll "end her days" here . . . it's *her*!'

Glancing up at the ceiling, she dropped her voice to an awesome whisper. 'You see, I've done something I should have done long ago, and I don't regret it . . . not for one minute!'

She gathered the torn paper and, taking it with the chest to the fireplace, set it down there. Quickly now, she went into the kitchen, returning a moment later with matches, and a folded newspaper, which she crumpled, then spread over the firegrate. 'Burn them,' she kept whispering. 'Burn them all!'

She laid the documents over the newspaper. First the will, then other papers relating to his work . . . private things in which she had no interest. Only four items in that chest had warranted her attention: the letter, the will, the precious house deeds, and that wonderful wad of banknotes.

One by one, the contents of the chest were torn asunder, before being thrown into the firegrate and set alight.

Last of all was the copy of the letter. 'That was when it all started,' she muttered, her hard gaze scanning the words written there. 'My own brother's bastard . . . given over to me, as if I was a wet nurse. Oh yes, he may have paid out a handsome sum of money . . . but it was never mine . . .' She chuckled, 'Until now, that is.'

Tearing the letter from top to bottom, she flung it into the grate. The fire was slow getting going, so she fanned it with one hand until the flames began leaping from the back. Taking the travelling bag into her fist, she stood there, watching with delight while the flames licked high.

She waited long enough to satisfy herself that the damning will was burned to a crisp, and now the letter too was engulfed in flames. Her heart soared. She'd waited so long for this day.

Unable to stay one minute longer in that house, she quickly left. Not even pausing long enough to make sure the front door was closed behind her, she went at a fast pace, down the street and on to the bus-stop, where she boarded a bus for Baker Street.

On arrival, she went straight to number sixteen, the office of a gentleman named Andrew Slater.

'I thought you might have changed your mind,' he said, ushering her inside.

'I wouldn't do that,' she said, seating herself before his desk. 'Have you the money?'

'I have.' Beaming with satisfaction, he revealed, 'My client deposited the money with me two days ago . . . soon after you approached me.' Adopting a more serious mood, he asked guardedly, 'And have *you* brought the necessary proof of ownership?'

'Of course.' Triumphant, she took the house deeds out of her bag and placed them before him. 'It's all here.' Opening her purse, she took out a long brown envelope and offered it to him. 'I have his death certificate,' she said. 'I am the only relative he had. The house is mine now.'

There was something about the way she said it. As though she had won a long, hard battle. He stared at her for a moment, noting the haggard face and the twitching hands, and the way she constantly glanced towards the door. There must have been a time when she was a handsome woman, he thought curiously. Even in her mourning clothes, she had a certain appeal. Her eyes were darkest brown and her hair shone like that of a younger woman. And yet she looked so very old, as though all the light had gone from her life.

He didn't know why but, in spite of her arrogant and peevish manner, he pitied her.

'I don't have time to waste,' she said, guiltily shrinking before his gaze.

'Of course not.' Pinching his nose with spectacles that were painfully small, he perused both documents. 'It seems we can do business,' he said presently.

She visibly relaxed.

Ringing a bell on his desk, he brought a harassed-looking clerk rushing into the room. 'Are you ready for me to witness, sir?'

The other man nodded. Addressing Anne Hale, he pointed to the relevant line. 'Sign each one,' he said. 'My clerk will countersign.'

Heaving a great sigh, she took up the pen.

In no time at all, the transaction was complete. 'You haven't forgotten, I've sold the furniture and contents,' she pointed out. 'As I have already explained, these will be collected in the next few days. Your man can take possession only after that.'

He nodded. 'Of course. As we agreed, I have taken a note of it all.' Only when she rose to leave did he offer his condolences:

'I am sorry about your husband,' he told her reverently. 'It must be a great loss to you.'

Her smile surprised and shocked him. 'I think I have gained far more than I lost,' she answered, and swept out, leaving him to consider her odd remark.

Twenty minutes after arriving at the office, Anne Hale emerged from it, far wealthier than she could ever have imagined. In her bag she carried a small fortune. I must get to a bank, she decided. London is not a place in which to be carrying so much money about.

Torn and bleeding, Sally took a moment to realise what had happened to her. For what seemed an age, she lay on the floor where Anne Hale had left her, astonished to be still alive, though she knew she was badly hurt.

The silence was ominous. She tried to remember . . . what had been said? Why had she been so brutally punished? Her mind began to focus . . . something about not being their daughter?

Opening her eyes she recognised familiar surroundings. They brought no comfort. Fear trembled inside her. Was she alone here now, or was there someone else in the house? Was Anne Hale waiting to finish her off? She hardly dared breathe. Listening, she could hear no sounds from downstairs; only the silence permeated the house. Somehow, the silence was more frightening than anything she had endured so far. 'Have to get up . . .' But even the slightest movement made her cry out.

She lay a while longer, growing weaker as the blood trickled away. When it soaked deep into the rug, leaving a crimson stain, she knew then how truly desperate her situation was. 'Have to get help . . .' She tried to turn over but the pain was excruciating. 'You can do it, Sally,' the words shouted in her mind. She opened her mouth to call for help, but no sound came out.

She lay a while longer, her senses coming and going, and her mind alive with terrible images . . . the church . . . her daddy. No! *Not* her daddy. And the woman . . . *not* her mother. Oh, the hatred, that shocking hatred . . . all her life. But why? Of course . . . now she remembered. That was why she had to be punished.

She listened again, so afraid. It was all right now. There was no one in the house but her. Mustering every ounce of strength, she made herself turn over. The pain was unbearable. It felt as if the whole of her body had dried in one position and to move just one inch tore it wide open. But she couldn't stay here and die. She had things to do. People to find!

Determination took hold and, bit by bit, she edged along the floor. Somehow she had imagined she was near the door, but then she remembered . . . When the whip came down again and again, she was rolled along the floor like a top, until now that same door was so far away it seemed impossible to reach. Inch by agonising inch, she pulled herself along. The door was partially open. With curled fingers she tugged, until it was wide enough for her to creep through.

She never realised the landing was so big, nor the stairs so steep. Lying there, looking down, she feared her life would end then. She called out, 'Help . . . me.' Her voice was pitiful. Falling back, she lay very still, drained of strength; thinking of her daddy. Tears filled her eyes. He would *always* be her daddy, no matter what.

The neighbours had never liked Anne Hale. 'A sly, unfriendly woman,' they called her. Even the passing of her husband had not brought her many friends. Their sympathy was for Sally.

Two women who lived in the street always walked past the Hale house to and from the bus-stop. That very afternoon, they had noticed the front door was not properly closed.

'She's left it open on purpose,' one said, 'in case anyone

should want to pay their respects.' That was the way round here.

'Well, she'll not get *me* paying respects,' the other answered. 'I wouldn't set foot through that door if my life depended on it.' Then she remembered. 'Did you hear the noise earlier?' she asked. 'Shouting and screaming . . . like there was a murder going on?'

Her neighbour shook her head. 'No, but nothing surprises me.'

Moving on to other things, like the price of fish at the market, and how the cobbler's prices were going through the roof, the two women hurried to catch their bus.

It was growing dark when they passed that way again. 'Look there,' said one, 'the door is still open, and the house is in darkness. That's strange.'

In both their minds was the earlier comment about the noise 'like there was a murder going on'.

Afraid to go in by themselves, they went for help. It came in the form of a burly neighbour. On night shift as a cab driver, he slept through the daytime.

'I thought I heard a row earlier,' he recalled. 'It woke me up, but I didn't take much notice. Well, you know what she's like . . . allus shouting and screaming at summat.'

Pushing open the door, he carried his lantern along the passageway. Keeping a safe distance, the two women followed. First they looked into the kitchen. The door held fast at first; most doors in these old houses were badly warped. But there was no one in there.

'Hello!' he called upstairs. There was no answer. 'That's funny,' he remarked, 'why would she go out and leave the door undone?'

'Yes, and where's the girl?' The question was on all their minds.

'We'll check in there.' He led the way towards the parlour,

tripping over something on the way. 'What the devil's this?' Shining his light down, he saw it there, curled like a snake, its tongue reaching out to the front door, the shaft close to his feet where he had tripped over it. Bending to pick it up, he gasped, 'My God! Look at this . . . it's a *whip* . . . covered in blood too.' Grimacing, he dropped it to the floor, wiping his hand where the blood had stained it.

Raising his lantern, he shone it into the parlour. The small, twisted shape by the fireplace was just recognisable. The woman saw her first. 'Oh, dear God!' she cried, pushing forward. 'It's the girl!'

And she was barely alive.

Gently they carried her to the ambulance.

Outside, the neighbours watched and prayed. 'Did you see her?' they asked each other. 'Did you see what that evil woman did?' For there was no doubt in their minds that it was the work of Anne Hale.

The nurse was kindness itself.

For over a week, she had watched over Sally, soothing her, bathing her scarred back, and talking to her about everything in general that might stimulate her mind. But still the girl was not ready to talk. She just lay there, white and sad, and racked with pain in spite of all the efforts of the hospital staff.

On the tenth morning, when the girl was able to attempt a light breakfast, the nurse brought her an envelope. Inside was a charred piece of paper. 'It was clutched in your hand when they brought you in,' she explained. 'You were holding it so tight, we thought we should keep it. If it's nothing, I'll dispose of it straight away.'

Intrigued, the girl smoothed out the torn paper. In a whisper, she read out the name, 'Leonard Mears . . .' Funny . . . Mears was her mother's maiden name. Her *mother*! Repulsed, she looked away.

'Leonard Mears.' Repeating the name, she tried hard to work out why that name should be on a charred scrap of paper. There was something else too, but it was barely readable. Part of a street name, and a town. She whispered the words, 'P-e-ton New Road . . . Blackburn . . .' The rest was beyond recognition.

She remembered crawling into the room where she saw the smouldering paper. Instinctively she knew the woman had been burning something important . . . evidence, perhaps, to do with her, and her real parents.

She looked at the name again, saying it softly, 'Leonard Mears . . . her brother. *My father*.' Bitterness flooded in. 'The one who signed me away.'

Carefully studying the scrap of paper once more, she asked the nurse, 'Where is this place . . . Blackburn?'

Delighted Sally was beginning to recover, the nurse smiled. 'Somewhere in the North, if I'm not mistaken. But then, I'm a cockney born and bred. I've never strayed from these parts and never wanted to, so I could be wrong.'

'How long before I can leave here?'

'Well now, that depends on you.'

For the first time in many a lost day, Sally smiled: 'Then it won't be too long.'

Because suddenly, she had a purpose.

Part Two

BLACKBURN
FEBRUARY 1889

THE TRUTH

Chapter Two

James Peterson took off his boots and hurled them into the cupboard. 'Leonard Mears is the worst kind of bastard. If I had my way, he'd be run the length of the high street, with a cat-o'-nine-tails licking his cowardly back!'

'Hey! You mind your tongue, my boy!' Maureen Peterson had an Irish temper and a set of rules that she stood by come hell or high water. There were two things in life she would not tolerate: one was a man who thought woman was put on this earth to serve his every need, the other was violent language. 'I'll not have you cursing like that in my house,' she warned sternly, 'and I'll thank you not to fling your smelly boots in my cupboard like that! By! Like as not you'll send them right through to the other side, so you will!'

Rushing across the room, with auburn hair flying and her small hands bunched into fists around the wet dishcloth, she looked ready for anyone.

Feigning terror, James smiled behind his arms as he crossed them over his face. 'I didn't mean it,' he cried fearfully. 'Leave me be.' He could never keep a bad mood, especially when his mother was about.

Maureen laughed out loud. 'Give over, you silly divil!' Slapping him over the head with the dishcloth, she urged, 'Wash

21

that work-muck off, and sit yourself at the table. I've got stew and dumplings, and a jar of best ale for afterwards.'

Standing to full height, James reached down to kiss her on the cheek. 'I don't know why I put up with you,' he quipped, 'unless it's your stew and dumplings.'

'I spoil you, that's the trouble.' Yet she loved spoiling him. Maureen could never imagine this cosy little place without his big, familiar figure lumbering about in it.

Sniffing the air he gave a sigh. 'What man could resist an aroma like that?' Making his way to the stove, he lifted the lid from the pan and peered inside. Chunks of meat and fat, juicy vegetables bubbled in a sea of rich, dark gravy. 'It's a wonder every manjack for miles round isn't clambering at the door.'

Maureen's answer was to give him another slap with the wet dishcloth. 'Less of your cheek, young fella-me-lad!' she warned. 'And you'd best move yourself, or your dinner will be cooked to a cinder.'

She went away, quietly chuckling. 'It's good to be appreciated,' she murmured, and broke into song.

Tall and well-built, with smiling eyes and an unruly mop of thick dark hair, James was her only son, and she adored him. But, though she consulted him on every matter and respected his sound judgement, there was room for only one master in this household, and that was her.

From past experience, Maureen had learned you had to keep the men in check, or they'd run rings round you at the first opportunity: husbands, men-friends and sons alike, it made no difference.

She had suffered a madly possessive husband for too many years before pneumonia took him. Now, at long last, she was enjoying her hard-won independence. Life was good, and she was happier than she had been in a very long time. Deep down she knew she had James to thank for that because, in truth, he was her strength and inspiration.

* * *

A short time later, the two of them were seated at the table: Maureen with her homely face flushed from the cooking, and James, fresh and handsome in a forest-green shirt and a pair of dark trousers. While his mother dished up the food, he sat head bowed, his troubled thoughts back at the Mears' house, with the lass he had loved since he was ten years old.

'You don't look too happy,' Maureen remarked. 'What's Leonard Mears done now, eh?'

Ruffled, James looked up. 'What does he *ever* do?' he replied. 'He has a talent for rattling me, that's for sure.'

'Hmh!' Depositing a ladleful of meat on to his plate, she eyed him curiously. 'Was it the lass?' she wanted to know. 'Did he catch the two of you together, is that it?'

James smiled at her, but it was a pained smile, betraying only a little of the heartache he felt. 'I'd give anything for that to be the case,' he confessed, 'but we could never be together. Besides, if she was even to look my way, he'd flay her alive, that's the kind of coward he is!'

Maureen sensed his anger, and it frightened her. 'I don't like you working for Mears,' she told him. 'You don't have to stay there . . . torturing yourself.'

'You *know* why I have to work there,' he reminded her.

'You mean, it's Mears who puts the roof over our heads and the food in our stomachs, is that what you're saying?'

His handsome features hardened. 'Well, isn't it the truth?'

'Yes, I'm not denying that.' Maureen's thoughts rolled back over the years, to the day Edmund Peterson had brought her here as his young bride.

'I've lived in this house since I was first married . . . just a wee young thing . . .' she smiled. 'Eighteen years old I was, and just wed to your daddy.' Reaching out she took hold of his hand. 'Two years later you were born, and I was never happier.' Except

23

when Edmund started showing his jealousy of the boy, and life began to get difficult. 'Your father was employed by the Mears family all his working life, and now, here you are, twenty-two years of age and just as tied to them as he was . . . as we *all* are.'

'It won't always be that way, Mam,' he promised.

'It needn't be that way *now*!' she argued. 'Think about it, James. We could break the mould . . . leave the area. A man like you would always find work, and I could help out until we got settled. I've cleaned and skivvied before. I can do it again.'

'Not while *I've* got two strong arms, you won't!'

'Don't you be so proud!' There he goes again, she thought defensively, protecting me when there's no need.

'Sorry, Mam. I know how independent you can be, and I respect that,' he apologised. 'But, don't you see, there's no harm in a man being proud? Especially not if proud means being ambitious.' He laughed softly. 'Oh, Mam, I have such big plans.'

'I know.'

'I mean to have my own business.' His dark eyes glittered with determination. 'There'll come a day when I can stand against Mears and come out a better man than he'll ever be.'

She looked at him and her heart swelled. 'I don't doubt that for a minute, son,' she admitted. Maureen had always known he had fire in his blood.

'I begrudge every minute in that man's employ,' James confided, 'but, for the moment at least, we *need* Leonard Mears. We need the security he offers.'

'All the same, it might be good for us to start up somewhere else.' Though, God only knew, it would be a terrible wrench for her.

Groaning, he thumped the table in frustration. 'You're right, Mam,' he acknowledged. 'I *know* we could start up somewhere else, and yes, I would find work anywhere, I know that too.'

'But it doesn't fit in with your plans, does it, son?' She knew him too well.

He shook his head. 'Look, Mam, I've worked the overtime, and I've been careful with whatever money came my way. But it's nowhere near enough. Besides, there's so much more I have to learn. I won't be satisfied until I've mastered every skill – from sorting the best timber, to haggling the price. I know a wheel-wright's trade well enough to secure the strongest wheel. I can beat a delivery date by a week if needed, and still turn out the best-quality wagon anywhere in the country.'

He was proud of his achievements and had a right to be. 'I get on well with the men; they respect me because I treat them like human beings. The only thing I haven't mastered yet is the actual building of a wagon and carriage, and then the selling of 'em.'

Maureen winked. 'I've no doubt you'll soon put that right an' all,' she said.

Smiling wickedly, he leaned forward. 'Leonard Mears heads one of the wealthiest families in this county,' he imparted softly, 'and I won't be satisfied until I've toppled him from his lofty perch.'

'You're talking strong stuff, son.' Yet she never doubted he was capable of unseating that arrogant man.

His eyes twinkled with excitement. 'Aye, and I'm not fool enough to think it will be easy. Taking him on will try me to my limit, I've no illusions on that score.' He took a deep, invigorating breath. 'I *will* do it though, Mam. But look . . . it will take time and planning, and I can't afford to make any mistakes.'

Leaning back in his chair he smiled at her. 'Trust me,' he said. 'I'm obliged to tolerate Mears a while yet; for many good reasons.'

For a long moment she observed him. Then: 'You haven't told me everything, have you, son?'

Lowering his gaze to the table, he hesitated, struggling within himself. Eventually, he glanced up. 'I've never lied to you, Mam,' he reminded her fondly, 'and I never will. But there are certain things a man has to keep in his own heart.'

Maureen nodded. 'I understand what you're saying,' she replied, 'and I won't press the matter. But if you feel the need to talk, I'm always here, you know that, don't you?'

His dark eyes smiling, he merely touched her hand and returned to his meal.

He didn't have to say what was in his heart, because Maureen already knew. One of the reasons for staying at Mears' was the lass. She had known it for years, ever since a pretty little child with chestnut-coloured hair and rich, blue eyes had wandered into their garden twelve years ago.

It was James's tenth birthday, and they were having a small party to celebrate. There was just the three of them – James's daddy, herself and James. The sun was shining and they were having a great time and, for a few wonderful minutes, before her brutish father came rushing in to take her away, the lass was part of it all.

Maureen recalled how James seemed lost after the lass had gone. It was as though the soul of the party had gone with her.

Now, stealing a glance at his face, she saw how troubled and distracted he was, and it broke her heart.

Later, when the crockery was cleared away and the two of them sat beside a cheery fire, he lounged in the armchair, long legs stretched out and one arm hanging over the chair-arm to stroke the lazy dog at his feet.

Suddenly, he surprised her by revealing, 'She smiled at me from the window again.' He looked up, half-smiling. 'Like a bird in a gilded cage.'

'You're asking for trouble, you know that, don't you?'

'Hmh! I only wish it were that easy. If I could get her out of there and only have "trouble" to contend with, I'd do it this minute.'

Oh, the hours he had thought about it, and each time he came to the same conclusion: force was not the answer. 'There are too many issues at stake here, not least of which is the fact that Leonard Mears might be all kinds of a monster, but he is her father after all, and who knows how strong the bond is between them . . . flesh and blood, and all that.'

'Then there's the *mother*,' Maureen commented, 'that pale, wretched little thing who trembles if you say good-morning to her. I'm sure the children would never leave her to that man's mercy and, if I read the woman right, she would never dare to defy him and leave with them.' Thanking her own lucky stars, Maureen shook her head. 'It's a sorry affair, and that's for sure.'

His mind was still on the lass. 'Isabel was eighteen last summer, did you know that?'

'I thought she might be about that age.' Casting her mind back to that day of James's tenth birthday, she guessed the lass had been about six years old at the time.

James had kept this to himself, but this evening he was in a mood to confide. 'The party was going on as I walked past the garden gates. Isabel had on a blue dress and her hair was loose about her shoulders.' The image had stayed with him ever since. 'She looked beautiful, Mam . . . but kind of sad.'

'Did anyone see you there?'

Noting the look on his mother's face, he hastened to reassure her. 'Don't worry. They were all too busy to worry about me. I recognised a few of our bigger customers, huddled in quiet conversation with the big man himself.' He snorted with disgust. 'No doubt he invited them, hoping to get an increase in their next lot of orders!'

'I'm sure you're right, son. He's not one for missing any opportunity to line his fat wallet.'

'If you ask me, it wasn't so much a birthday party, more a showing-off to impress the businessmen. God knows there were enough of them there, long-faced, sour-looking individuals.'

Maureen chuckled. 'Can't say as *I'd* like to attend one of his parties then.'

'Oh, they had entertainers there, and the trees were festooned with bunting and such. Oh, and he hired entertainers, would you believe? And the food!' He blew out his cheeks. 'You've never seen so much grand food – fit for royalty it was – all laid out on long tables, with white cloths and huge, floral displays.'

'Oh, aye! The gentry know how to put a good show on, you can't deny that!' All the same, Maureen was not impressed. 'But then, they've got the means, haven't they?' she pointed out. 'I dare say we could all lay out such a grand spread if we had the same money, and as many servants.'

'I only had eyes for Isabel,' he confessed. 'She was sitting on a bench over by the shrubbery.'

Curious, he brought the picture to mind. 'She was with a younger lass, fifteen . . . sixteen maybe, small, with long fair hair. They were deep in conversation. I wondered if it might be her sister.' The deep sigh seemed to come up from his boots. 'I stood at the gates for a long time, hoping Isabel might look my way, but she didn't. Oh, Mam! She looked so sad. I have to get her away from him.'

'She may not feel the same way you do. Have you thought of that?'

'You wouldn't say that if you could see the light in her eyes when she sees me. I *know* she feels the same way. I know it by the way she smiles at me when I pass by, and last summer, when she was walking the garden alone, she came to the gates and said how much she looked forward to seeing me. All that week, she waited at the gate and we talked a lot, about all kinds of things.

She even remembers my tenth party, when her father dragged her away.'

His expression darkened. 'Apparently she got out of their garden by crawling through a gap in the hedge. Isabel told me her father had the gardener dismissed. She was locked in her room for a week. Her mother was forbidden to go anywhere near her, and the only person she saw was the maid. Even then she wasn't allowed to speak.'

Maureen was shocked. 'She told you all that?'

'She told me a great deal more; about herself and her own feelings, and how she could never see a future for herself outside his control.'

'Did she mention her mother?'

'She never talks about her mother, and I never ask.'

Having opened his heart, James went on, 'The last time she came to the gate, we kissed through the railings.' Shyly, he glanced at his mother. 'I know . . . I know!' he intercepted her protest. 'It was a rash thing to do, but I've never regretted it.'

Wisely, Maureen chose not to pursue it. James was usually a private young man, who did not easily share his feelings, so, thinking it best to let him talk, she kept her silence.

He stared into the flames, his mind going back to the lass. 'I think her father must have stopped her from walking the gardens alone, because after that day she was always accompanied by a woman – the governess I should imagine. Anyway, she never came to the gate again. Instead, she watches from the window. We look, and smile, and I know she's been waiting for me.'

Moaning like a man in pain, he leaned forward, running his two hands through his mop of hair, as he did when agitated. 'I'm telling you, Mam . . . it's driving me crazy!'

Aching for these two young people, Maureen only confirmed an idea he himself had been toying with. 'Then you must walk home another way, for *her* sake as well as your own.'

His reply was simple and heartfelt. 'I can't.'

Daring to mention what was on her mind, Maureen told him sternly, 'I'm sorry, son, but you *must* realise no good can come of it. You know how obsessed Mears is with shutting his family away from the world.' In her heart she suspected Leonard Mears must be out of his mind. 'It's like he's the jailer and they're his prisoners.'

James shook his head. 'Dear God! What kind of man is he?'

'He's a man you must never underestimate,' she warned. 'I worked up at the house long enough to know what he's capable of. Leonard Mears rules his own family the same way he rules his empire – with a hard heart and an iron fist. I saw things first hand at that house, shocking things that don't bear thinking about. Your father too; many were the times when he'd come home with terrible tales of how the men were treated.'

James nodded, having seen at work the kinds of things his father had seen. 'The men could never do anything about it, not then, and not now.' His jaw set hard. 'But I'll change all that, you'll see.'

'It won't be easy, son.' Pride mingled with fear. 'Don't fool yourself you can change things all on your own. Leonard Mears is a law unto himself. Politicians, businessmen, anyone who makes money out of him and his enterprises – he's got them all in his back pocket. He knows there's no one to touch him.'

'Mebbe it's time he was taught different!'

She watched his fists clench and unclench, and fear struck deep inside. Keeping outwardly calm, she told him, 'You could be right, son. Maybe he *does* want teaching different,' she conceded, 'but if by that you mean to give him a thrashing, it wouldn't solve anything. It wouldn't free the lass, and it wouldn't do *you* any good either, not if you want to play him at his own game. Or are you beginning to think you're not capable of pitting your wits against him?'

Her strategy worked. 'What! You just give me half a chance, and I'll finish him once and for all! They say he built his fortune up from nothing. If he can do it, so can I!'

Relieved, Maureen spelled it out. 'You've got the right ideas . . . *use* him. Watch and learn, isn't that what you said?'

Fired with the challenge, James reiterated his plans. 'I've thought about it a lot,' he confided. 'Learn his strengths and weaknesses, then turn them against him, steal his kingdom bit by bit. Until he's got nothing left but the clothes he stands up in!'

'Be careful, son. He'll make a powerful enemy.'

'It isn't the *man* who's powerful,' he answered quietly. 'It's what he controls—' Closing his hand into a tight fist which he then clutched in the air, he spoke in a soft, trembling voice. 'First of all, there's his wretched family, his own flesh and blood, treated little better than servants; *worse* in fact, because the servants at least have a measure of freedom. Down in the factories, there are the God-fearing men who suffer his spite, so as not to lose their livelihood, which is a pittance when measured against his. Then there are the others: fat, greedy men who, like him, make a fortune on the backs of others. *That's* what he controls, Mam – a kingdom that's rotten and corrupt.'

Settling back into the chair, he dropped his arm to stroke the dog, who had lain loyally at his feet the whole time. After a moment James gave a long, withering sigh. 'I can promise you this, Mam,' he told her. 'I won't rest until I've finished him, for good and all.'

She knew he would not be deterred, but she had to warn him: 'If he caught wind of what you were up to, he could break you like a twig.' Leaning forward she spoke in a hushed whisper, as though afraid even the walls had ears. 'Remember what I said,' she urged, 'Leonard Mears will make a powerful, deadly enemy.'

'You're right, Mam,' he conceded. 'He will make a powerful

enemy.' He looked into her eyes, and for one awful moment she didn't recognise him. 'But so will I, Mam,' he murmured. 'So will I.'

A few minutes later, James put on his coat and slipped the lead over the dog's head. 'Come on, Jake,' he said patting the animal's neck, 'I reckon we could both do with a breath of air.'

From the parlour window, Maureen watched them go. 'By! If it isn't one thing it's another,' she muttered. 'Taking a fancy to Leonard Mears' lass – dear God above! It's asking for the worst kind of trouble.'

Dropping the curtain, she turned away and went to the mantelpiece. Here she took down a small, oval-framed photograph of a dark-haired, handsome man. A man in his late forties, a man who bore the same strong features as his son, James.

Holding the photograph in her hands, Maureen took a moment to gaze on it. With the warmth of the fire on her face, and his eyes looking up at her, she began to feel nostalgic. 'Do you remember how it was when we were first wed?' she asked him, a little smile lifting the corners of her mouth. 'When you brought me here to this lovely cottage, and I said I never wanted to leave it?'

Sadness clouded her eyes. 'We were so happy then, before James was born and you got the idea into your head that I loved him more than I loved you. Oh, Edmund! How could you think that?'

She wiped away a tear. 'Nothing was ever the same again. One thing followed another. First, you moved into the spare room, then it wasn't long before you accused me of having an affair with anything in trousers.' She gave a soft, gentle laugh. 'It would have served you right if I was! But, as God's my judge, I was never interested in anyone but you, Edmund. Even when you made my life miserable with your silly suspicions, I still loved you. I love you now, and I always will.'

As if he could somehow hear her, she bared her soul to him: 'In spite of everything, I know how much you loved us, always there, strong and sure whenever we needed you.' Her voice broke with emotion. 'Oh, Edmund! I could do with some of that strength now,' she confided quietly, 'because there's trouble brewing for sure.'

Holding the photograph close to her breast, she walked across the room, her fond gaze roving across everything familiar. The pretty floral curtains she had made herself, sitting up night after night, sewing in the light of the lamp. And there was the very same lamp, standing proud on the sideboard, slim and tall, with a stained-glass shade above.

Her gaze encompassed everything, from the black horse-hair settee to the piecework rag-rug before the hearth. 'I love this place,' she murmured, 'and it would break my heart to be wrenched from it. All the same, I've a feeling before too long, there might be some difficult choices to make.'

Momentarily closing her eyes, she leaned her head back and took a great, withering sigh. Who knows? she thought. Maybe we won't even *have* a choice!

Disillusioned, she replaced the photograph. 'So there it is, Jack,' she concluded. 'Whether we like it or not, God help us, our son has taken a liking to Leonard Mears' daughter. On top of that, he has the man himself in his sights, and there is nothing I can do about it.'

Except to pray his ambitions would not see them on the street, with all their possessions gone.

The idea made her blood run cold.

A short time later, having rolled back the rug to protect it from soot and cinders, she placed the small, domed guard around the hearth, and closed the curtains. 'By! That's a cold, dark sky out there,' she commented. The wind was tumbling an old newspaper along the cobbles.

Now, as she listened closely, she could hear the strengthening wind rattling the front door. 'I shall have to ask our Jamie to take a look at that door,' she remarked. 'It's looser than Tom Tuttle's front teeth!' Turning away, she gave a chuckle. 'Poor old Tom.'

Tom Tuttle was the chimney-sweep round these parts, and sometimes, when you were in the middle of an earnest conversation, he'd laugh out loud and his front teeth would fly across the room. After a while, you'd find yourself more interested in the antics of his teeth than in what he was trying to say. Laughing aloud, she turned down the lamp on the table and collected the smaller lamp from the sideboard. With a backward glance she satisfied herself that all was secure, and made her way up the narrow, closeted stairway.

Turning out the light, she snuggled down in her bed, her eyes drawn to the moonlight through the window. 'It's a funny old world and no mistake,' she whispered.

In the next minute she was fast asleep and loudly snoring; the kind of snoring that James light-heartedly called orchestral music. The kind of music that shook the timbers and set the birds to flight. But Maureen would deny it to the last. 'Me? Snoring?' she'd say. 'Away with you!'

James had no intention of following the lane to the big house, but he found himself headed that way all the same. 'Don't you start barking at shadows,' he instructed Jake, 'or you'll have somebody coming at us with a shotgun!'

The Mears' residence was a grand old place. Situated at the end of a long, winding lane, it was protected by high walls, to keep both family and possessions protected from the outside world. At night, prowling the darkness, were two ferocious dogs.

Aware of this, James took up position far enough away not to alert the dogs, but near enough to have the house in his sights.

Through the lighted downstairs window, he could see the

room where the family would gather together. It was immense: high ceilings and panelled walls, and each wall adorned with large, beautiful paintings of landscapes and people, and all finished with fancy gold frames. Arranged round the large, ornate fireplace were wide settees and high-backed chairs in the softest of colours. In the far corner was a grand piano, dressed with candelabras, tall, elegant lamps and what looked like silver ornaments.

With the enormous tapestry curtains drawn right back, James could see it all. Taken aback by such splendour, he gasped with astonishment. 'Good God Almighty, how can I ever compete with that?' Never before had he come along here of an evening, and so had no idea. Now, the scene illuminated before him, he was made to wonder. 'I don't know as I'd be comfortable in such a grand place,' he told the dog. 'Not even if I had money enough to buy it. We're worlds apart, me and her,' he murmured. Disillusioned, he turned to go. 'Happen it would never work between us after all.' But he loved Isabel so much, he couldn't envisage a life without her. 'Maybe love itself won't be enough to overcome our different backgrounds,' he mused. 'When it comes right down to it, happen I'd be doing her no favours at all.'

He had taken only a few steps when some slight movement made him pause. Glancing back, he saw that Leonard Mears and his family were coming into the room.

Softly, he withdrew to the shadows. Watching as they went towards the fireplace, he sought out Isabel, and suddenly there she was, seated with her face to the window and her eyes sweeping the night, as though wanting to escape. Dressed in a dark blue, off-shoulder gown, with her long chestnut hair brushed loose, she looked so beautiful it took his breath away.

Beside her sat a younger girl. Fair-haired and pretty, this was Isabel's scatterbrained sister, Hannah. Wearing a white blouse and dark skirt, she fidgeted incessantly, constantly looking to Isabel for confidence.

To their right, on the broader settee, sat Leonard Mears and his wife, a tall, slim woman with mousy hair and a nervous demeanour, made that way through years of humiliation from him.

The two sons remained standing. Robert, the elder, was the taller of the two; brown-eyed with fair hair, he was painfully thin and more nervous than his mother. Possessed of a slight stoop, he was gentle-natured and kind, though his father saw such virtues as being cowardly and useless, especially when he had put his elder son in charge of his larger and more productive factory. All the same, in spite of his father's disapproval and because of his good nature and sound managerial skills, Robert was well-liked and respected by everyone.

Jack was so different from his brother, anyone could have been forgiven for thinking they were in no way related. Thick-set and of medium height, he had strong blue eyes and a slick of dark hair. His nature was bitter and unforgiving. He worshipped and adored his father as a beaten dog will fawn at the feet of a cruel master.

Seated in the armchairs were two men James had never seen before. The older man was grey-haired and red-faced, with a round, pock-marked nose.

'That one likes his booze,' James muttered. Curiously, he had taken an instant dislike to the man who, in his late fifties, had a devilish arrogance about him.

The other, younger man was probably in his mid-twenties; with brown hair and of medium build, he appeared to have more to say than the others. Whatever it was, they seemed intent on listening; all but Isabel, whose gaze kept returning to the window, though she could have no idea that James was out there in the darkness. Intrigued, James watched a while longer.

Nervous in her master's presence, a maid entered with a tray of drinks. When, impatient as ever, Leonard Mears dismissed her with a wave of his porky hand, she scurried thankfully away.

Desperately willing Isabel to look out and see him there, James stepped forward, though still far enough away not to set the dogs barking.

Yet he was not the only one with eyes for Isabel. Much to James's irritation, the young man beside seemed to be making a deliberate play for her attention, chatting and laughing, and even touching her hand with an intimacy that had James wondering how well she knew him. It pleased him, though, to see how discreetly she rebuffed him. Leonard Mears, only a short distance away, seemed not to notice the young man's unwanted attentions. Or *had* he noticed and chosen not to intervene? And if so, what would be his reason? James wondered.

Suddenly, his mind cleared. Of course! There was only one reason why Mears would sacrifice Isabel, and that was if he stood to gain either money or power!

His attention returned to the young man, and how he continued to bother Isabel. 'Bloody jackal!' he scowled. 'He can thank his lucky stars I'm not in there, because so help me God, I'd have him out that bloody door before he knew what day it was!'

Incensed, he kicked out at a piece of wood lying on the ground. The wood shot forward and hit the fence, and suddenly all hell was let loose. Not only did the two dogs inside start barking, but so did the dog beside him. Torches appeared in the distance; there came the sound of running feet and raised voices, and a command for James to 'Stay where you are!'

'I think it's time we made ourselves scarce!' Grabbing Jake into his arms, he went down the lane at a run. 'If they think we're staying to be a dog's dinner, they're out of their tiny minds!'

Once out of reach of his pursuers, he put Jake to the ground and went at a fast pace towards home. The laughter began as a wicked little smile, then it grew, until suddenly he was laughing out loud. 'By! We must have looked a comical sight,' he wagged a finger at the forlorn creature trudging along beside him. 'And you're getting too fat and heavy,' he warned. 'As from tonight, you're off porridge, and no arguments!'

By the time he reached the cottage and let himself in, the laughter had given way to serious thought. 'What have I got to offer her against someone like that?' James asked himself.

He wondered about it while he settled the dog in for the night. Maureen had already gone to bed, and up in his room James paced the floor and went over the evening's events. He searched his mind and heart for an answer, and could find none. He found little sleep either, because one minute he was catnapping and the next he was back on his feet and staring out the window. 'He could never love you as much as I do,' he murmured. 'But he could give you everything else that matters.'

Then he remembered how Isabel had rebuffed that young man, while he himself had always been given encouragement. The smallest of smiles lit his dark eyes. 'Maybe I do have a chance after all.'

Chapter Three

'Come back 'ere, you thieving little devil!'

The man's cry rang out across the market square, but it didn't stop the girl. After weeks of being on the streets, desperation had taught her well. Now, her blue eyes laughing, she ran like the wind.

'Look at her go!' A fat woman buying cockles urged her on. 'Go on, gal!' she cried, but the child needed no encouragement.

Barefoot, she fled over the cobbles, a vibrant creature with an energy that belied her waif-like appearance. Dodging and dipping, she emerged from the other side of the market, unsure now of which way to go.

Behind her, the market trader's cry told all and sundry, 'I've been robbed . . . stop that girl!'

Curious passers-by paused to see what all the fuss was about, but they made no attempt to stop her. As long as they were not inconvenienced, they were happy to go about their own business. After all, one more street urchin stealing from a barrow was nothing new.

'Pretty young thing though.' The customer was middle-aged, a worldly man with an eye for the girls. 'If she'd asked me I might well have found her some work in my house.'

'Oh aye?' The stallholder laughed aloud. 'In your bed, don't yer mean?'

'You'd better watch your tongue,' came the sharp retort, 'or I'll have you for slander.' Digging into his pocket he produced a handful of coins. Choosing the right change, he threw it across the stall. 'If I find one bad orange in this little lot, I'll be back. Make no mistake about it.'

Smiling, the stallholder doffed his hat. 'Tell you what I'll do, guv,' he offered slyly. 'If you find one bad orange there, I'll give you a whole new bagful for nothing. How's that?'

The fellow didn't answer. Instead he wandered off, casting a withering glance backwards as he went. Behind his back, the burly stallholder made a rude gesture.

'You're a bloody fool, you are!' His wife was a fat, idle woman with her claim to beauty long gone.

'What d'you mean?'

'*You!*' She'd long known he didn't have much of a brain. 'Shouting "Police" at the top of your voice. D'you *really* want the rozzers to come poking their noses in?'

'That little devil robbed me, you know she did!'

'Oh, aye? And what about you then?' she demanded. 'Where did them two crates of cabbages come from? Don't tell me they were paid for, because I know they were got underhand. And what about these, eh?' Grabbing a ripe beetroot from a box, she held it under his nose. 'Took from a barn the other side of Preston. Seems to me, you've been doing a bit o' robbing yourself.'

'Somebody did me a favour, what's wrong with that? Anyway, it's a different thing altogether. I've got a living to earn.'

'Aye, happen you have, you artful old sod. But that lass has to keep body and soul together, and by the look of her, a few apples past their best won't do it. A bag o' bones, that's what she was, poor little sod . . . a bag o' bleedin' bones.' Dropping the squashed beetroot, she clapped him round the head.

'Hey, that hurt!' He was a born softie.

'It's too bloody thick for it to hurt,' she scoffed, 'and in future you'd best think twice afore you start yelling for the police! Or I might take it on meself to tell 'em a thing or two.'

'You never would!'

'Don't count on it, matey.' Observing him closer, she got a bit of a fright. 'Whatever's that?' Tentatively reaching up, she wiped her hand over his head. 'My Gawd!' Rubbing the red stain from her fingers, she told him, 'You're bleeding bad, luv. You'd best get off to the infirmary right away.'

When he began to panic, she laughed out loud, and only then did he suspect her hoax. 'Why, you old bugger—' Taking a closer look at the red liquid running down his forehead he exclaimed, 'It's beetroot juice!'

'More's the pity,' she said, and there followed an almighty row, much to the amusement of the other stallholders.

'At it again they are,' said the flower seller. 'Never a dull moment with them two.' With all eyes focused on these two, the urchin with the stolen apples was soon forgotten.

Sally ran until she could run no more.

Exhausted, her feet rising with blisters, and one knee skinned where she'd fallen to the cobbles, she came to the canal. Carefully scooping the water into her hands, she bathed her torn knee. That done, she sat on the lip of the bank and dangled her sore feet in the water. It was bitterly cold, but pleasantly soothing, yet when the blisters popped the pain was like knives cutting her flesh.

She looked about. Seeing a sign not far off, she read aloud, 'Penny Street.' She gave a sigh of relief. The man she'd asked had said Leonard Mears had factories down this way. At long last she was close to finding him.

A few more steps and Sally knew her searching was over. For

there was his name and business, larger than life, above a factory entrance:

LEONARD MEARS

WAGONS AND CARRIAGES

MADE TO ORDER

After all the hardship, and the long, cold winter when she didn't know from one day to the next where the trail would lead, here he was, just an arm's reach away. Relief flooded through her. There was no holding back the tears now, and so she let them fall, and somehow they eased her sorry heart.

She wondered how she might approach this man who was her true father. If he didn't want you fifteen years ago, why should he want you now? she asked herself. Not for the first time she began to doubt the wisdom of tracking him down. What if he sends you on your way? Always the same nagging questions.

But there was no one else and, no matter what he had done, Leonard Mears was her only flesh and blood. Her only hope.

She thought of that other man, the gentle soul who had raised her as his own, and her grief was painful. Then she recalled the woman who had beaten her within an inch of her life. Were they alike, the woman and her brother? All her young life went before her. All the memories, good and bad, came back to haunt her. But she had not come all this way and endured hardships not to see her quest through to the end.

Glancing down she realised how filthy she had become, and so very tired. She couldn't see him like that, and she had to sleep for a while. Then she would find somewhere to wash, maybe earn the price of some clean clothes. She looked about, wondering where she might lay her head.

Seeing her there, and being let off his chain for the first time in a week, the dog came at her from a distance, teeth bared and out to kill.

Behind him, the owner saw the danger and chased after him. 'Monty! Get back 'ere . . . back, I say!' The dog paused to glance back, wanting to run yet knowing he would be punished if he did.

His moment of hesitation was Sally's opportunity, and she took it. Scrambling up, she set off at a run, initiating the dog's disobedience. In great bounds he covered the distance between them. When he leaped on to the girl's back, fighting her to the ground, it seemed he would tear her apart. As she fell she caught her head on a loose paving slab. The scent of blood excited the dog into a frenzy, and the man became afraid she would be killed. 'Monty! Get away, you mad bastard!' Taking hold of the dog's collar, he lugged him off.

'Are you crazy, or what?' His anger was for the girl. 'It's your own bloody fault! If you hadn't run off like that, he would never have got so excited. Weeks of hard training, and you've ruined it all. By God! I should have let him tear you limb from limb!' Enraged, he snatched the dog away. 'Bloody tramp! If I see you round these parts again, I'll have the authorities on you!'

Cursing, he stormed off, spitefully yanking at the dog's collar until the poor thing was lifted from the ground and almost choked to death.

Behind him, Sally wondered at his words. Indignant, she called after him, 'I'm as good as you any day, you miserable old sod!' Fear, and weeks fending for herself on her journey north, had hardened her.

Her earlier misgivings about her appearance had been confirmed, but fortunately through weary eyes she saw a small, timber building not far off, some way from the Mears' factory and standing far enough back for her not to be disturbed. She decided it was as good a place as any to rest and recover.

Wincing with pain, she touched the cut on the back of her head, and wiped away a small trickle of blood. 'Not as bad as I thought, thank goodness. I'm lucky he didn't kill me.'

She was so tired that when she glanced at the hut again, it seemed a million miles away. Cautious, she made her way towards it. Through the open factory gates she could see men at work. 'And to think the owner is my father,' she mused. The thought gave her no pleasure. Only the memory of that other, gentle man gave her pleasure.

Being careful not to let anyone see her, she slunk along by the wall. When she reached the hut, she quickly opened the door and slipped inside, where it was surprisingly warm, considering it was February and remnants of snow still lay on the ground. Going to a darkened corner, she drew an old sack over her, and settled down to sleep. 'An hour, that's all,' she murmured, 'then I'll be . . . good—' No sooner had her head touched the floor than she was fast asleep.

Only a few feet away, Leonard Mears was inspecting the pile of rejected parts.

'I want this lot out of here,' he told James.

Efficient as ever, James called over two men to help shift the offending articles.

'Not now!' Leonard Mears ordered the men back to their work. 'The mayor needs his carriage by this evening, You can shift this little lot outside later. I'm not giving factory room to rubbish like this.' Kicking out at the pile of cut timbers, he screamed at the men, 'Now, get back there and make sure that carriage is finished on time!' As they hurried off, he told James, 'Right! You keep them at it, while I arrange to have this pile of junk collected.'

Muttering to himself, he went away. 'It'll be the last time they send rubbish like that to *my* factory!'

Behind him, the men gave vent to their feelings. 'There's nowt wrong with them timber cuts,' one man said. 'They're as good as any I've seen.'

The other man agreed. 'He's in a bad mood, that's all.'

'Huh! One of these days, somebody might take it into their head to bump that bugger off, and it'll be good shuts an' all!'

Their grumblings stopped when James came along. 'The quicker you get that job done, the sooner we can shift these parts,' he told them, 'then they'll not be here to antagonise him every time he walks past.'

Knowing they could trust this man, they pointed to the departing carriage. 'Look! He'll be on his way to the timber yard. The poor buggers don't know what they're in for.'

When James reminded them that he wouldn't be long gone, they bent their backs to their work.

'I wouldn't mind,' said one, 'but the miserable old sod wouldn't know a good piece o' timber if he fell over it.'

The other man agreed. 'If it wasn't for James Peterson, this place would have folded long since,' he said. 'It's *him* that's built up the name and quality, and Leonard Mears knows it!'

James, overhearing this, knew it too.

Chapter Four

Silent and proud beneath the onslaught of her father's words, Isabel did not flinch, nor did she show any emotion.

She was not afraid of him, and he knew it. That was why he resented her so. It was why he loved to hurt and humiliate her. It was also the reason why there could never be anything between them but bitterness.

His voice grated on her ears, always demanding, ever angry. 'Answer me, girl!' Pausing, he waited for her response. When it was not forthcoming, he rushed across the room and, taking her by the shoulders, shook her violently. 'So! You mean to go on defying me, do you?'

Her calm answer took him aback. 'I've already told you, Father,' she reminded him, 'I have done nothing wrong and, in spite of what you say, I have no man-friend.' Cynicism crept into her voice. 'In fact, I have no friends at all.' And if you have your way, she thought sadly, I never will.

'You're lying.' He held her very still, a sadistic thrill running through him when he felt her trembling in his hands. 'You *want* him, don't you?'

'*Who*, Father?'

'The young man I saw you watching from the window.'

'You're mistaken.'

'I am *not* mistaken.' His brow furrowed. 'Who was he?'

'I don't know. Maybe you could tell me?'

Anger darkened his face. 'Be very careful, my dear,' he warned. 'I am no fool. Unfortunately I did not move quickly enough to see who delighted you so. But I suspect it was a young man. I will ask you once again – who was he?'

Knowing how cunning he could be, Isabel wisely said nothing to antagonise him further. Instead, she looked him steadily in the eye, choosing not to grace his prying questions with a reply.

As always, her confidence only served to enrage him more. Red in the face, he addressed her in a low, harsh growl: 'I saw you at the window. You were smiling and happy. I *know* you were waving at a young man. I want his name. And don't lie to me!'

Guiltily, she lowered her gaze.

Suddenly, his manner changed, his voice shivering with emotion as he told her gently, 'It hurts me to punish you. You've always been my favourite, do you know that?'

Shocked, she looked up at him. 'But you've always *hated* me.'

'No, my dear.' He shook his head. 'It's you I love the most . . . right from when you were a tiny infant. You always had a smile for your daddy . . . always brave, while the others shrank from me.'

'I'm sorry, Father.' Instinctively, she took a step back. 'I don't understand what you want from me.' For a long time she had suspected him of unspeakable things. But though he was cruel – and, she was certain, slightly mad – he had never laid a hand on her in that way.

After a time she had come to realise that his thoughts were not incestuous, but insanely possessive. Obsessed with the idea that his family must never be exposed to the outside world and its evil influences, he had acquired a house fit for royalty, but, to those incarcerated there, it was *not* a home in which to be content, but a prison that fostered in them all a futile and desperate need to escape.

Over the years, Leonard Mears had been successful in keeping first his timid wife, and then his children, under his thumb. Now they were older and becoming restless, the iron hand with which he had always ruled was even harsher. With his two daughters on the verge of womanhood, he was like a jailer, always watching, alert to their every mood.

His sons were allowed only slightly more freedom. He knew they would one day inherit the business and he harnessed their energy for work. Yet he was a terrible taskmaster. They were paid pitiful wages, and treated far harsher than any other sorry employee.

Beneath his eagle eye, their every move was monitored, every word noted, and if they showed signs of becoming too independent, he used any devious means to rein them back under his control.

Like their sisters, they were hopelessly trapped. Fed and clothed, and given a roof over their heads but little money of their own, they had no independence at all. Stripped of self-respect, they were held there for many reasons, good and bad, not least of which was the love and concern for their mother.

Isabel was the wilful one, the one who stood up to her father when no one else would. He respected her for that. But he saw that respect as a weakness in himself he must never let her use against him; so in order to disguise his fondness for her, he treated her with a firmer, crueller discipline, which inevitably earned only her dislike of him.

'What do you mean?' he demanded now. 'How can you *not* understand what I want from you? Haven't I told you time and again, and still you make me punish you.'

Her cool, sapphire eyes bathed his face, quietly taking note of his repulsive appearance: the fat jowls and small, pea-like eyes peering through layers of baggy flesh; and he raised in her a kind of loathing. 'Some day, Father, I shall leave this house and never return,' she promised bravely. 'You can't hold me here for ever.'

Wonderingly, he gazed on this child of his – a wilful young woman who carried his own defiant spirit, but in a different way. For he was ruthless, while she knew compassion; he was greedy of nature, while she was giving. They were like two sides of the same coin, and from the day she could speak he was intrigued and fascinated by her.

He had always known that men would want her. With her long, chestnut hair and sincere, sapphire-blue eyes, she was stunning; but she had a deeper kind of beauty too. A soft, caring beauty that smiled from within. 'Promise me,' he urged, 'you will never let yourself be spoiled by an unsuitable man. You're a valuable woman, a prize for the right man, and I will decide who he is to be.'

'If being "unspoiled" means I can never know the love of a man I love and respect in return,' she said quietly, 'then I'm sorry, Father, I cannot promise, for that is what I want more than anything in the world.' Into her quiet mind came the image of James Peterson. Thinking about him, and the way he secretly smiled at her, gave her all the courage she needed. 'You find it hard to accept that one day I mean to control my own life, but it will happen, Father. *That* is my promise. The only promise I can make to you.'

Her rebellious words had such a profound effect on him that Isabel instinctively took a step back.

'Defiant, is it?' Grinning wickedly, before she could move he grabbed her by the hair. 'Defiant little bitch!' Jerking her face close to his, he growled menacingly. 'Always defiant!'

Knowing what was to come, she told him, 'Punish me if you must, Father. But remember this . . . I mean to leave this house, *and* you, and to make a life with a husband of my choosing at the first opportunity.' Her quiet calm and dignity shamed him, but he knew no mercy.

'Then I shall have to make doubly sure you are not given such an opportunity.' Clutching his fingers about her arm, he led her away.

At a quickening pace, he propelled her across the large, beautifully furnished drawing room, then down the hall towards the servants' quarters, and beyond, where at this late hour the corridors were dimly lit by gas lamps.

From here, he took her along a small, dark passage and on into the darker recesses of the house. At the end of a long dark corridor he paused before a narrow door. The door straddled the width of the passageway, so there was no way out either side, and no way out behind because she knew when he returned along this route he would lock every door behind him.

The door now blocking their way was already padlocked. Holding Isabel securely with one hand, he used the other to locate the bunch of keys hanging from his belt. After unlocking the door, he turned to her. 'Before we go any further, I have a question.'

Isabel waited.

'Are you afraid of the dark?'

'No.'

'Or of being locked in the watch-tower?'

Isabel shook her head. 'No, Father.'

He stared at her, desperately needing to break her spirit, but knowing he never would. 'Are you afraid of *me*?'

She shook her head once more, this time the merest of smiles on her face. Her voice was cool. 'I will *never* be afraid of you.'

When the blow came it was with such force that it knocked her back. When, defiant, she held her head high, he hit her again, this time harder, the spittle flying from his mouth as he screamed, 'I swear to God, you try my patience too far!'

Her quiet dignity made him pause. Trembling with excitement, he chided her. '*Now* see what you made me do?' he accused. Wiping a gentle hand over her bloodied face, he whined like a spoiled child. 'See how you make me lose my temper.' Brushing her tumbled hair aside, he told her pitifully, 'Don't you see, child, you always seem to bring out the worst in me?'

Raising her gaze, she looked him straight in the eye, silently condemning.

Unnerved, he began to stutter: 'We'll . . . talk again, when you begin . . . to see sense.' Stepping aside, he beckoned to the open doorway.

Taking a pace forward, she went through and, without a backward glance, mounted the stone stairway. Behind her, he cursed and moaned and urged her on. While they progressed ever upwards, Isabel made not a sound; she knew the futility of it. Instead, she kept her dignity, and prepared herself for the vigil ahead.

At the top of the stairs was a square, stone landing, just large enough for him to stand beside her. 'Have you anything to say?' he asked.

Isabel gave no answer.

'You stubborn little fool! You could have avoided all this unpleasantness by making me an apology . . . together with the promise I asked of you.'

Still she gave no answer.

Suddenly, from somewhere in the far distance could be heard the chiming of a church clock. He listened while it tolled the hours . . . one . . . four . . . seven . . . and so it went on, striking into the silence and making the moments seem like hours.

'There!' Taking out his pocket watch, he glanced at it in the half-light of the gas wall bracket. 'Midnight!' Tutting, he replaced the watch. 'My word,' he remarked casually, 'I had no idea it was so late.'

Selecting a long iron key from the wad of keys on his belt, he unlocked the door and, continuing to hold her secure, he flung open the door to reveal a tiny, darkened room.

'It's such a pity I had to have the windows blocked up,' he complained. 'There was a time, before you children came along, when I sought sanctuary in this pretty watch-tower. Through those portholes, I could imagine the whole of Lancashire at my feet.' He sighed wistfully. 'That's why I had the tower built, to escape from the hectic world about me. Oh, I would sit here for hours – reading, contemplating, planning my empire.'

Roughly, he thrust her inside. 'Now, thanks to the defiance and corruption that surround me, the watch-tower serves a better purpose!'

Growing accustomed to the darkened room, Isabel rubbed her eyes. Suddenly the door was slammed shut; the soft arc of light from the lower hallway was snuffed out, and not for the first time she found herself alone there.

Isabel had been imprisoned in the watch-tower many times over the years. Except for the faint chink of moonlight easing in between the warped window frame and the timber covering the pane, she was closeted in darkness, but, even without that small relief, she knew every inch of the damp slimy walls, each dip and rise in the flagstone floors, and every changing, choking smell. It was not a pleasant place. Before her lay a cold, lonely vigil – behind her a locked door, and no escape.

Until *he* came to let her out.

She had lied when he asked if she was afraid of the dark. Because of him, the dark had always held terrors for her. And yet, there was something strangely comforting about being closeted here, away from his tyranny, for a time at least.

Here in the dark, she was free to think and imagine. No one

could see her. No one could read her thoughts or witness the pleasure on her face as she thought of *him* . . . the handsome young man she was watching when her father caught sight of her at the window.

But he hadn't seen her yesterday, or the day before, and so he knew nothing of their distant gestures of affection. All he saw was that one occasion today, when she waved from the window. He caught sight of James striding away, but there was not time enough for him to recognise the man who worked for him, and she would never tell, so their secret was safe.

'Thank God he didn't see who I was waving at,' she murmured. 'If he *had*, then James would have been out of work, and his mother out of house and home.'

A smile covered her lovely face. She could whisper his name here, and no one would know. 'James . . .' the soft sound of her voice gentled round the room. No one to hear. No one to punish her. 'James.' It felt good to say his name and not be afraid.

She leaned on the wall for a while, eyes closed, picturing him in her mind. 'If only we could get to know each other properly,' she sighed. 'I do like him so, and I *know* he likes me.'

She thought about the way their strange friendship had evolved over these past months. Every day, at the same time, he would pass the house on his way to work, and every evening he would walk by again. And each time she would wait by the window, hoping to catch a glimpse of him, and not once had he disappointed her.

Lost in her thoughts, she had little sense of time. The same clock that had chimed before, chimed again, now striking the first hour of morning. How long will he leave me here this time? she wondered. One hour . . . two? A day?

Shivering, hunched on the floor, with her head forward, she thought of James, and smiled.

* * *

Satisfied with his night's work, and feeling the need to gratify himself, Leonard Mears made straight for the whisky tumbler. After swigging down a considerable measure of the comforting liquid, he began to feel a warmth about his loins. 'I need a good woman under me,' he chuckled. 'Pity . . . I'll have to make do with that useless bag o' bones upstairs.'

Licking his lips with relish, he went out of the room and up the stairs, though his footsteps were unsteady and once or twice he swayed dangerously as he climbed. 'Bugger it!' Taking a moment to compose himself he caressed the bulge in his trousers. 'Be patient,' he sniggered. 'Not too far to go now.'

A few moments and he was outside the bedroom door. Another moment and he was inside. Finding his way by the glow of moonlight coming in through the open curtains, he made his way towards the bed. 'Frances?' Twice stumbling against the furniture, he called her name. 'Frances, can you hear me?'

Falling clumsily across the bed, he leaned over and touched the woman lying there. 'Frances, m'dear, are you awake?'

With her back to him, his wife lay quite still, eyes half-closed, her heart beating with fear. The sound of his voice in her ear, the touch of his hand on her, was nauseating. Silently praying he might go away, she pretended to be asleep.

Taking off his trousers, he persisted. 'For God's sake, woman, what's the matter with you? It's your husband – wanting some attention.'

Softly trembling, she lay dormant.

When he seemed to go away, she gave a silent prayer of thanks. Her joy was short-lived, however, for suddenly the bed sank beneath his considerable weight. 'Roll over, damn you!' Locking both his hands round her waist, he tugged her round towards him. 'I'm feeling lustful,' he said, with a drunken laugh. 'Don't spoil it now.'

Knowing he would persist until she succumbed, Frances

opened her eyes and peered at him in the moonlight. 'Ah, ha!' Jubilant, he tore at her nightgown. 'So! You were awake the whole time, were you?'

Appealing to any decency he might still have, she pleaded: 'Not tonight, please, Leonard. Let me sleep.'

The only answer she got was a hard slap across the face. 'Sleep!' Tearing away the remnants of her nightgown, he then threw the bedcovers on to the floor. 'You can sleep later,' he told her. 'Right now, I'm in the mood for some fun.'

Shaking off his undergarments, he fell on top of her, laughing and giggling like a silly schoolboy. 'Though why I shouldn't be out looking for a woman more endowed than you, I will never know!'

Raising himself to his knees, he pointed to his proud member. 'Look at that!' Taking hold of her hand he placed it there. 'Do you think you're woman enough to satisfy it, do you, eh?'

Having her there, naked before him, legs spread-eagled and that look of fear on her timid face, only excited him all the more. Snatching a pillow he rammed it under her buttocks and, with a cry of anticipation, thrust himself into her. With each thrust he raised and lowered himself, his mouth wiping her neck with ceaseless dribble, his hands all over her body.

The more excited he got, the more she hated him. Over the years she had learned to endure his unwanted attentions, and now, like always, she lay passive until he was done with her.

Grunting and panting, he worked himself into a frenzy. His cries and moans could be heard all over the house, but he was oblivious to all that, wanting only to satisfy himself on this poor, wretched woman whose crime was to have taken him for her husband, and then to have borne him four children.

When she thought she could bear it no longer, he gave a muffled cry and collapsed his whole grotesque weight on to her. Then, when she tried to slide from beneath him, he grabbed her by the ears and held her tight. 'Keep still, bitch!' he growled. 'I'm not finished yet.' So she stayed, wishing him dead, but believing in her heart that he would long outlive her.

When, a while later, he climbed off and went away, she heard him in the bathroom, coughing and spluttering, emptying his bladder and softly laughing as he finished. 'If only I had the courage,' she whispered, 'I would be gone before morning.'

'But even if I had the courage, I still would not have the means,' she reminded herself. 'And he will make sure I never have.'

Frances was in no doubt but that her miserable existence would end here, in this house, with Leonard Mears. And, however daunting, it was a likelihood she had reluctantly come to accept.

Breakfast time in the Mears' household was run like a military operation. At precisely 8.00 a.m., the maid would bring in the morning newspaper and place it, neatly ironed, beside the master's plate. She would then call him from the study where he had been ensconced for the past two hours. On her announcement that breakfast was ready, he would emerge, full of his own importance, before strutting along the hallway with the air of authority, sweeping all before him.

The servants were like flies around him, fetching this, taking that, and making sure he wanted for nothing. Once the master was seated and eating, the rest of the family were notified, and would file into the breakfast room. Mrs Mears first, then the children in order of age: Robert, Jack, Isabel and Hannah. Only this morning, Isabel was nowhere to be seen.

Odd glances went from one to the other, but nothing was said. Nothing was questioned. Nobody dared.

Breakfast was eaten in silence. The ordeal was only over when Mears strode out of the room.

'Where's Isabel?' Hannah was the first to voice the question. 'Why isn't she here?'

No one knew, but they suspected. 'It's her own fault!' Jack had heard something last night. 'I expect she's been disobedient again, and he's confined her to her room.'

Just then the housekeeper came to oversee their needs. Tall and slim, with brown, tied-back hair and kind eyes, Mrs Flanagan was not much to look at, but she had a good heart and she adored the family – with one exception.

Frances called her the salt of the earth, and had confided in this dear woman on more than one occasion. She addressed her now, softly, in case *he* was near. 'Mrs Flanagan, have you seen Miss Isabel this morning?'

'No, ma'am,' came the answer, 'but I have an idea where she might be.'

'Go on—' Then, when the woman glanced fearfully towards the door, Frances urged, 'It's all right.'

'I think she's being punished.' Something in her face said what she could not bring herself to voice.

Frances nodded and Mrs Flanagan scurried away.

'I *knew* it!' Jack was sure. 'She's been confined to her room.'

Hannah guessed different. 'No, she hasn't! He's locked her in that horrible little prison above the servants' quarters.'

Terrified in case her husband returned, Frances quietened them. 'Isabel is her own worst enemy. She knows how he hates to be defied, yet she will go on doing it.'

Robert had been silent until now. 'Whatever she's done, it can't warrant being shut away in that dark little room!' He knew more, but wasn't saying.

Suspecting he was keeping secrets, Frances gave him a curious glance. 'Do *you* know why she's being punished?'

'How should *I* know?' He blushed a gentle pink.

'Because you and Isabel are very close.'

Jack had always envied the relationship his brother had with his sister. 'That's right! She *tells* him things.'

Hannah giggled. '*I* know why she's being punished.'

Everyone gave her their undivided attention. 'Oh?' Jack thought she was a pain sometimes. 'And why is that?'

'I expect Father has found out.'

'Found out what?' He enjoyed a juicy bit of gossip.

'That she's fond of a certain young man.'

Robert was horrified in case she should blurt out the name. 'Hannah! That's enough!'

Jack persisted: 'Who is he . . . this certain young man?'

Digging her fork through her sausage, Hannah peeked at Robert's worried face. 'I don't know,' she shrugged. 'I never saw him.'

Disappointed, Jack resumed his breakfast. 'The truth is, you silly girl, you don't know *anything*.'

Herself troubled, Frances intervened. 'That's enough!' Lately Jack had been on edge, too quick in rising to an argument. 'Wherever she is, Isabel will come to no harm.'

Frances knew her elder daughter was the favourite – rebellious and strong-minded, the girl had no fear of her father. It infuriated him to know he could never break her spirit. Time after time she had stood up to him and paid the price. Yet, rather than emerging from her period of punishment with a sense of defeat, she came out as she had gone in – quietly defiant.

'Be quick and finish your breakfasts,' Frances advised her sons. 'He'll be down any minute. Don't let him catch you loitering.' Addressing Hannah, she said, 'You had better make yourself ready for the governess, child.'

'Yes, Mother.' Like the others, Hannah loved her mother dearly.

Still concerned for his sister, Robert had a question for

Frances. 'If he *has* locked Isabel in the watch-tower . . . how long do you think it will be before he lets her out?'

Frances too had wondered about that. 'I have no idea,' she answered truthfully; 'if only Isabel would learn to appease him, he wouldn't see cause to keep punishing her like this.'

'Huh!' Jack spoke what was on *all* their minds. 'She'd rather *die* than appease Father!' Slamming his cup down he looked from one to the other. 'If you ask me, she deserves every bit of what she gets!'

'Don't talk stupid, man!' Robert flew to her defence. 'She's the only one with the guts to stand up to him, and he can't abide that. Besides, what sort of monster would shut someone away in a place like that, especially when they're terrified of the dark?'

'We've *all* suffered the same punishment.' Embittered because he had never found a way into his father's affections the way she had, Jack held little regard for Isabel. 'Anyway, she brings it on herself.'

Hannah rounded on him. 'You're jealous of her,' she accused. 'You always have been.'

'Hmh!' Hurt because she had put her finger on the root of his discontent, he demanded, 'Why on earth should I be jealous of Isabel?'

'Because he thinks more of her than *any* of us.' Hannah was always one for speaking her mind. 'It doesn't bother me, nor Robert, because we love her, whereas you want to get in Father's good books so badly, you'd crawl on all fours if he asked you.'

'Like hell I would!' But he *would*, and they all knew it.

'Anyway, I for one am glad Father keeps a closer eye on Isabel, because then he's not watching *me* all the time.'

'And *should* he be watching you?' Jack had his suspicions about Hannah.

Sorry she hadn't yet learned to keep her mouth shut, Hannah retaliated. 'Oh! You'd like to know I was defying him in some way, wouldn't you, eh? Then you'd be able to report *me*, and who knows? You might even get a pat on the back.'

Robert gave her a sideways glance. 'Hannah! I think you've said more than enough.'

Up to now, Frances had been deep in thought, wondering how she might tackle this problem of Isabel. What if Leonard kept her locked away for longer than usual? What if Isabel should die of cold in that awful place? And how dare she approach him about it? She had tried to intervene in the past and received a brutal punishment, which helped her children not one bit.

Now, with Robert's quiet warning, she realised things were getting out of hand. 'I think you've *all* had far too much to say,' she told them. 'For goodness' sake, haven't we got enough problems in this house, without the three of you arguing amongst yourselves?'

Yet again, Hannah had something to say. 'It wasn't me, and it wasn't Robert!' she protested. 'It was Jack . . . being petty as usual.'

'Ssh, child.' Replacing her napkin on the table, Frances pushed away her chair and stood up. 'No more bickering,' she warned, 'or your sister won't be the only one to earn a punishment.'

Her warning drove home, because, shortly after Frances left the room, Robert and Jack departed for the factory. Soon after that, Hannah reported to the governess.

As they swept out of the dining room, Mrs Flanagan swept in. 'The man has them frightened out of their wits, so he has!' she muttered to herself. Standing by the window she watched the two young men climbing into the carriage. 'Treats the whole family like dirt under his feet. If it was up to me, I'd have him put down like the mad dog he is!'

She almost leaped out of her skin when his voice boomed across the room. 'You! Where's the mistress?'

Spinning round, she was horrified when her skirt caught the edge of a small figurine on the dresser. When it fell crashing to the floor, she gave a cry of horror. 'Oh dear!' Bending to pick it up, she cried out again, 'Oh dear, I *am* sorry, sir. But it isn't broken, thank goodness.' Trembling uncontrollably, she turned the figure over in her hands. 'Well I never . . . not a scratch nor a chip in sight!' With his beady eyes on her, she could hardly stop herself from fleeing out the door.

'Dammit, woman!' Striding into the room, he glared at her. 'Are you deaf? I asked you a question.'

Red in the face and anxious in case he had heard her mutterings just now, she answered with as much dignity as she could muster. 'The mistress has gone to look for you, sir. Miss Hannah is with the governess, and the young masters have already left for their duties.'

Casting an eye over the untidy table he snapped, 'Get this lot cleaned away. Quickly!'

'Yes, sir.'

Stepping aside a meagre half-pace he gave her very little room to squeeze by, but she managed it with only the lightest brush of his arm in the process. 'Sorry, sir. Excuse me, sir. I'll have cleared it in no time.' Breaking into a frantic kind of trot, she set off for the kitchen.

By the time she flung herself through the kitchen door, poor Mrs Flanagan was in a terrible state. 'Where the devil have you been?' she asked the startled maid. 'You should be in there clearing the breakfast table . . . in fact you should have been in there ten minutes back.'

'I'm sorry, Mrs Flanagan, only I . . . oh—' She burst into tears.

'Sorry? That won't do, I'm afraid.' In full sail, Mrs Flanagan strode across the kitchen and cornered the poor girl against the range. Wagging an angry finger, she told her, 'Thanks to you,

I've been brought to the master's attention, and he's not best pleased, I can tell you that!'

Alarmed, Cook intervened. 'If you want to blame somebody,' she invited, 'blame me, 'cause it were me as asked her to help in the kitchen. I thought the family were still at their breakfasts.'

'Well, you thought wrong!' Deeply wounded, Mrs Flanagan was not easily won over. Still panting and with one hand spread over her heart, she took a moment to compose herself. 'The master is in the worst mood I've ever seen him,' she informed them, 'and, God help me, I was in the wrong place at the wrong time, so I was.'

''Tweren't my fault,' the maid wailed. 'Like Cook said, it was her who asked me to stay in the kitchen.' At times like this she wished she was home with her dear old mam.

'Don't you dare answer me back, miss!' Recovered enough to give her the length of her tongue, Mrs Flanagan chided, 'Take yourself in there a bit sharpish and clear that table the fastest you've ever done . . . or we'll all be out of work before you can bat an eyelid.'

The young lass lingered, unsure what to do, with a dishcloth in one hand and a half-washed pan in the other. Mrs Flanagan yelled, 'Well? What the devil are you waiting for?'

When the girl dropped what she was doing and ran past her, the kindly housekeeper put out an arm and stopped her. 'I'm sorry,' she apologised, 'but he's put my nerves on end, so he has. The master is out for blood, so you watch your step, there's a good girl.' Yet it wasn't only that which had unsettled her. *There were other more personal matters she must never speak of.*

The girl hurried away. 'Ah, bless 'er,' said Cook. 'Look at her little legs going . . . she looks like a sparrer in flight.'

Mrs Flanagan wasn't in the mood. 'Tell me, Mabel . . . you wouldn't have a drop of the good stuff hidden away, by any chance?' she asked furtively.

Cook was cautious. 'I might have,' she said. 'Why? Who wants to know?'

Mrs Flanagan gave her a reassuring wink. 'I wouldn't mind a little tipple, if you know what I mean? All this business has upset me.'

'I thought you never indulged while on duty?'

'Not as a rule, no.' Smiling meaningfully, she asked, 'There's no harm in me taking a ten-minute break though, is there?'

'None whatsoever.' Grinning all the way, Cook went to the big pine dresser and opened the bottom cupboard. 'Not a word to anyone?' she said, plonking the big earthenware jar on the table.

Intrigued, Mrs Flanagan peered at the label on the jar. 'But look here . . . it says turpentine.' Curiously regarding the other woman, she went on hesitantly, 'Now then, Mabel Arkwright. I know we've had our differences in the past, but you wouldn't be trying to poison me now, would you?'

Cook laughed out loud. 'Give over! What a thing to say!'

'But it *does* say turpentine on the label.'

Mabel didn't have to look at the label, for she had put it there with her own two hands. 'Aye, that's what it *says* all right.' Ambling over to the dresser for a second time, she took down two pretty rose-china teacups. 'But it don't mean to say there's turpentine *inside* the jar, does it, eh?'

'Whatever do you mean?' Mrs Flanagan was probably the best housekeeper in Lancashire – maybe even the world. But when it came to important matters like being sneaky, she was positively naïve.

'Trust me.' Popping out the cork, Cook put her nose to the mouth of the jar. Taking a long, deep sniff she chuckled, 'Cor!' Rolling her eyes with pleasure, she sighed, 'Nectar of the gods, that's what this is.' Wiping the tip of her finger round the lip of the jar, she sucked it clean. 'Mmm . . . wonderful!'

Mrs Flanagan got the picture. 'Why, you little devil,' she giggled. 'Turpentine! I should have known.'

'Well, you know now.' Cheekily raising one furry grey eyebrow, she asked, 'Still fancy a drop, do you?'

'What do *you* think?'

'Right!'

First, she poured herself a measure, then she took a sip and sighed again. Then she poured a smaller measure for Mrs Flanagan, who promptly took a sip and licking her lips took another. 'Here's to you.' Holding out her teacup she waited for Cook to pour her a second measure, which Cook did, though somewhat reluctantly.

Not to be outdone, Cook then poured herself as much again and raised her cup to make a toast. 'Here's to you, Mrs Flanagan,' she giggled, 'and here's to me.'

Mrs Flanagan was not as cunning as Cook. 'Why does it say turpentine particularly? Why not methylated spirits . . . or something even more obnoxious?'

'Because I'm the only one allowed to use turpentine in this 'ere kitchen, so I should be the only one as ever touches that jar.'

'I see.' A full minute passed before Mrs Flanagan had another question. 'If you don't mind me asking . . . why are we drinking out of teacups instead of proper glasses?' Mrs Flanagan came from a respectable home.

'Use your common sense, lass.' Cook had a no-nonsense way with her. 'We're drinking out o' teacups so's folk might think we're enjoying a cup of tea, instead of summat stronger, of course!' Tutting aloud, Cook shook her head. 'You like to think you're a cut above the likes of me and them . . . but I'll tell you this, Mrs "Irish" Flanagan, when it comes right down to it, there's a lot you've to learn yet.'

'Is that so?' Full of 'gin-tiddly' and feeling rather pink with it, Mrs Flanagan wagged her authoritative finger. 'Don't you speak to your betters like that, my dear!' Suddenly she was giggling. 'I don't mind if I do,' she said, holding out her cup yet again.

Cook obliged, but this time it was only a drop because, 'You bugger, you've nearly emptied the jar.'

'Ah, but I've enjoyed it so I have.' Emptying the last dregs in the teacup, she licked her lips and stood up, ever so slightly swaying, then went at a rather peculiar gait across the room, with Cook watching, bemused.

At the door she paused and, not trusting herself to turn around, told Cook with a giggle, 'You're a woman after me own heart, so you are.'

Holding on to the door-jamb, she steadied herself and continued down the hallway. 'Stand up straight, Eliza Flanagan!' she told herself. 'You have an example to set in this house.'

Whereupon she tripped over a kink in the carpet. Lying prostrate on the floor, she was horrified when the parlour-maid came running out of nowhere. 'Go away!' With great difficulty, she struggled to her feet. 'Anybody would think you'd never seen a woman go arse over tit before!'

When the maid stifled a giggle with the flat of her hand, Mrs Flanagan gave her a withering look. 'Get back to your work,' she told her, 'and don't be so silly!' though, halfway to her own quarters, she saw the funny side of it all.

Smiling happily, she set about sobering herself with handfuls of cold water over her brow. Composed and sober enough to carry on, she patted her hair and straightened her blouse, and walked to the door. Then she paused, her quiet gaze going to the wardrobe.

Retracing her footsteps, she went to the wardrobe and opened the door. Taking an old shoebox from the bottom shelf, she placed it on the bed and sat beside it.

At first she could not bring herself to lift the lid, and when she did lay the contents bare, her eyes swam with tears. 'So long ago,' she murmured sadly. And yet it was like only yesterday.

Taking the picture into her hands, she held it ever so gently, as though afraid it might crumble at her touch. Gazing down on the face of that young woman was like looking into a mirror, and there before her was her whole life. With her smiling Irish eyes and that mess of brown hair, she hardly recognised herself in the picture. So young and innocent she had been. So gullible. She smiled sadly. Even *he* had not recognised her. 'Thank God for small mercies,' she whispered.

Against all the teaching, she had let her heart rule her young head and, soon after, had given birth to a child – a beautiful little girl with bright blue eyes the colour of a summer sky. 'Oh, dear God, why did I let it happen?' All these years later, and the memory was still too painful to bear.

Now, with the tears tumbling down her face, she cried out: 'I couldn't keep her. *He* wouldn't let me keep her.' Afterwards he had found her a job in another big house – out of sight and mind. But now she'd followed him here, hoping to find out the truth.

The tears stopped and her face hardened. 'If only I had been stronger. But I was all alone. I never had anyone to talk to. Oh, little girl, I hope you never know what it's like to be so alone. It's been so hard,' she confessed, 'and after all this time, I'm *still* alone.'

Then she remembered, and softly smiled. 'But I think I've found a friend in Cook.' This time her smile was brighter. 'Oh, I *do* hope so.'

Tenderly, she laid the picture on top of the other documents and slid the lid back on. She then replaced the box in the wardrobe and departed, head high, smart as ever, and ready for anything.

And, though her day would bring her into contact with many members of this turbulent household, there was not one among them who could guess at the heartache she was hiding.

Chapter Five

'Good morning, son.' Maureen was cheered by the sight of James as he wandered into the kitchen. 'You look like you're ready to tackle anything.'

James smiled at her. Even a rough night had not diminished the light in his dark eyes. Well-built and handsome, with his hair brushed back, James always looked good.

'Morning, Mam.' Leaning over the table, he kissed her soundly on the cheek. 'Sleep well, did you?'

'Well enough,' she answered, 'and you?'

Drawing out a chair he sat opposite her. 'Off and on,' he laughed. 'Lizzie's cockerel kept me awake half the night. One of these days I'll wring its bloody neck.'

'Language! And you know very well you'd never do such a thing,' she tutted. 'You're too much like me . . . don't like hurting things. And you're far too fond of Lizzie.'

'You might be right.' Pouring himself a mug of tea, he recalled something Lizzie had said. 'Anyway, I thought she were planning to get rid of the damned thing?'

'Oh, you know what Lizzie's like,' she answered with a smile. 'Sure, she'll never get rid of that cockerel, not in a million years. A law unto herself, that's what she is. Seventy years old at least and still running that smallholding. Honest to God, I don't know how she does it – out in all weathers, summer and winter alike – tending to her vegetables and looking after her animals.'

Chuckling, Maureen related an incident from yesterday morning. 'Running full pelt across the field she was, after some hungry fox who'd been at her chickens.'

Laughing, James could imagine it. 'Pity it didn't get that damned cockerel.' He shook his head. 'I take that back,' he said sombrely. 'No animal should be torn apart like that.'

Fond of the old woman though he was, James had someone else on his mind. A lovely young creature whose wings had been cruelly clipped. 'Look here, Mam,' he began hesitantly, 'this business with Leonard Mears. I don't want you worrying.'

Maureen knew what he meant. 'As long as you know what you're doing.'

'Whatever I do, you can be sure of one thing,' he promised. 'I will never bring trouble to *your* doorstep.'

Maureen nodded. 'I know that, son.' The smile fell from her eyes. 'All the same, be careful. You're all I've got.'

Winking, he assured her, 'I have my plans, and they've been too long in the making for me to make any mistakes. Trust me, Mam. I'm not about to throw caution to the wind. Now I'd best be off.' Itching to catch a glimpse of Isabel, James had prepared to leave early and spend a few minutes watching for her.

Maureen guessed his intention. 'Not before you've had a good breakfast.'

Glancing at the panful of eggs and bacon sizzling on the stove, James's stomach turned over. 'Go on then, you've twisted my arm . . .'

Before he could change his mind, Maureen got busy. In no time at all, she placed the plate in front of him. 'That'll put hair on your chest,' she teased, and taking up the saw-bladed knife, sliced him two chunky helpings of newly baked bread. 'Straight out of the oven this very morning,' she declared proudly, slapping on a generous measure of freshly churned butter.

By the time James had eaten he felt like he'd never fit his trousers again. 'You'll have me waddling all the way to work,' he joked. 'I'll be finished before I start.'

Laughing at the pained look on his face, Maureen told him, 'Away with you! By the time you get to work you'll have walked it off, and be hungry all over again. I know you. You've an appetite like a horse, and always have had. That's why you're such a fine young man an' all.' Her smile was a delight to see.

Maureen was not a proud person by nature. But, whenever she and James walked the streets of Blackburn, she felt privileged to be alongside him. Head high and her heart glowing with pride, she wanted the world to know that here was her son, and hadn't she done a fine job in raising him.

Cleaning away his plate, James poured them both another round of tea.

'I'm going into Blackburn town this morning,' Maureen informed him. 'I've got my eye on a new hat, and Lizzie said she saw a beauty in Dickens' shop window.'

'Want some money, do you?' He began to dig in his trouser pocket.

Maureen stopped him. 'You give me more than enough,' she chided. 'Don't forget, I earn a few shillings on my own now, helping Lizzie sell her wares door to door.'

Talk of the devil and he's sure to appear, because at that moment Lizzie thrust her head through the kitchen window. Thin-faced, with a head of wild grey hair and a cavernous smile, she was a frightening little sight. 'Come on, you two!' she cackled. 'You ain't got all bleedin' morning to sit on yer arses. Not when there's work to be done.'

James leaped from his chair. 'Right. I'm off.' With a quick

cheerio to both, he was away down the lane, whistling a merry tune.

'He's a grand lad.' Lizzie carried two large wicker baskets, one laden with winter produce from her back garden, the other piled high with pretty, crocheted table squares made by her own hand. She set them to rest on the flagstoned floor. 'Is there a spare cuppa tea in that there pot? I'm that parched I could lick the sea dry.'

Maureen stifled a smile. 'I thought you said you were in a hurry?'

'Allus got time for a cuppa.' Settling herself into the chair she drew her shawl tightly about her. 'You ain't got a bit o' fried bread and a pair o' juicy eggs, I don't suppose?'

This time Maureen let the laughter out. 'You're a sly little devil,' she said, 'but if you want eggs and fried bread, that's what you shall have.' She thought the world of old Lizzie.

'Only if it ain't no trouble.'

'Right then.' Feeling mischievous, Maureen sat down again. 'I'll not bother.'

'You better had, you cheeky so-and-so!' the old woman cackled. 'Stop your teasing and be quick about it.'

Going to the stove, Maureen reheated the pan. 'How do you want your eggs?' She might have known the answer, because it was always the same.

'Wobbly in the middle and crispy on the edges.' She rubbed her bony hands together in gleeful anticipation.

It was only a matter of minutes before the fried bread and eggs was put before her, together with a huge mug of hot tea. 'Take your time,' Maureen told Lizzie, 'I've a few chores to be getting on with while you tuck into that.'

'Wait on a minute, lass.' Old Lizzie beckoned her to sit down. 'I've an idea I want to talk over with you,' she revealed.

Curious, Maureen did as she was bid. 'What idea's that?'

Lizzie didn't answer right away. Instead she lapsed into thought, happily chewing on the bread and turning it over in her toothless mouth for all the world to see.

Just when Maureen thought she might have forgotten all about her, the old woman looked up. 'Well, you see, I've been thinking,' she began tentatively. 'Would you say we work well together?'

Maureen nodded.

Displaying her pink gums in a toothless smile, the old woman went on, 'And would you say we've built up a tidy little round?'

Maureen was beginning to wonder what might come next. 'You *know* we have, Lizzie,' she answered. 'What's this all about, eh?'

'I'm coming to that, lass.' Tearing another great chunk out of her bread, she dipped it into the runny yolk. 'Am I right in thinking folks have come to trust us an' all?' Without waiting for an answer, she thrust the bread into her mouth. 'I mean, we've never let 'em down, have we, eh? Not even when it were a foot deep in snow?' With the back of her hand she wiped the dripping yolk from her chin.

'*Lizzie!*' Frustrated, Maureen threatened to get on with her chores. 'Tell me, right now, what's going on in that devious little mind of yours—'

'Eeh, you've no bloody patience, have you?' Her crooked smile was oddly comical. 'Right then!' Clapping her hands together, she leaned forward, oblivious to the fact that the tip of her shawl was bobbing in her tea. 'What I've been thinking is this. I've a tidy sum put by, and I reckon it should be put to good use.' Looking very pleased with herself, she leaned back in her chair, then realising the corner of her shawl was dripping with tea, she popped it in her mouth and sucked it dry. 'Now then, lass, what I want to know is this: how do you feel about getting a barrer?'

Maureen couldn't believe her ears. 'A *what*?'

'A barrer!' Tutting impatiently, the old dear insisted, 'You *must* know what a barrer is!'

'Well of course I do, but why would we want to spend your hard-earned money on buying a barrow? It's not as if we ever have more than two baskets to carry between us.'

Looking very smug, the old woman informed her, 'Ah, but what if we *doubled* the size of the round? What if we had *four* baskets to carry? What then, eh?'

Maureen shook her head. 'What's got into you?'

'Eggs.'

'What?'

'You've said yourself our best seller is the fresh eggs, and so I've decided to buy a dozen more laying hens. It'll be money well spent, you'll see. Then, when they're past laying, I'll wring their scrawny necks and sell 'em for Christmas. That way we'll make even more money, so the barrer will soon pay for itself.'

Amused, Maureen told her, 'You've saved *your* money, Lizzie, and you must spend it as you please.'

Lizzie was delighted. 'Right, that's settled. Now let's get off, afore we miss the best of the morning.'

'I'll have to do my chores first!' Maureen liked to leave a tidy house behind her.

'The chores can wait,' Lizzie argued. 'When we've got rid of this little lot, you can help me choose a barrer . . . a good, strong 'un.' She laughed aloud. 'With four wheels instead o' two . . . in case one of us gets tired and the other has to wheel her home.'

'Ah!' Maureen wrapped her shawl about her. '*Now* I know what you're up to, you crafty monkey.' Placing the guard in front of the fire, she glanced about before leading the way out and locking the door behind them. 'You're after *me* wheeling you home – admit it.'

Lizzie wasn't listening. 'You know what, lass?'

'*Now* what?'

'I've *allus* wanted a barrer of my own, ever since I were a little lass.' Pausing, she took a deep breath, as if gathering strength. 'My dad had a barrer, he used to sell chestnuts and hot potatoes on Blackburn boulevard.' Her voice broke, but she quickly regained composure. 'One night he were coming home along King Street. Some cowardly thugs set about him, they stole his takings and left him for dead.' Tears filled her eyes. 'He never regained consciousness. They found his barrer all broke up and thrown in the canal.' She gave a small laugh. 'He loved that barrer – washed and polished it every Sunday, he did – allus said as how it would be mine after he'd gone.' Lost for words, she walked on.

Maureen's heart went out to her. A barrer seemed such a petty thing when a man's life had been taken, but she tried hard to imagine how Lizzie must have felt. 'I'm sorry.' More sorry than she could say.

Lizzie brightened. 'I've a lot to thank you for, lass.'

'I can't think how.'

'Thanks to you, I've got a bit o' money behind me. It were *you* as said I ought to sell my crocheted bits, and the vegetables I grew in the garden. I never would have made money if it hadn't been for you.'

'You work hard, Lizzie. You deserve to do well.'

'Fancy though!' With a winning smile, the old woman gave Maureen a nudge. 'Aren't we coming up in the world?' she chuckled. 'Our very own barrer.'

'We'll write your name on it too,' Maureen suggested. 'Lizzie Tamworth . . . in bright lights.'

Blushing to the roots of her hair, Lizzie gave a little, embarrassed smirk. 'Give over, you're having me on.'

'No!' Maureen could see it now. 'We'll wash and paint it, so it looks smart, then we'll put your name on it for everyone to see.'

'Well, I never!' The old woman's voice shook with emotion. 'What would my old dad say, eh?'

Maureen could have told her how pushing a barrow would be much harder than carrying a basket or two, especially in the bad weather, and over the hills, where their trade took them. But everybody had their own heart's desire, and if owning a barrer like her daddy's put the light of joy in the old lady's eyes, then who was she to say anything?

In silence they trudged along, down Scab Lane and on to the canal. They were old friends and could be silent with each other when their hearts were full.

But, when their hearts were sore, they could confide in each other too, and that's what Maureen did now. 'I'm worried James might be getting into trouble,' she murmured.

'What sort o' trouble, lass?'

'He's taken a fancy to Leonard Mears' lass.'

'What makes you think that?'

'He told me.'

'Good God, he mustn't get tangled up with that lot, or he *will* be heading for trouble.'

'There's nothing I can do, Lizzie. He won't listen to anything I say. He's head over heels, he means to have her for his wife.'

'His *wife*!' Lizzie was so shocked she stopped in her tracks. 'The young fool, he doesn't know what he's saying.'

Maureen walked on, head down, her thoughts in a whirl. 'He seems to have it in his head that she's taken a fancy to him as well.'

'Playing him along, more like. These wealthy folk get pleasure out of using such as us.'

'He says she waits at the gate for him, and sometimes they talk – though I can't think what they'd have to talk about, coming from such different backgrounds. But she did tell him her father locks her up, and she'd do *anything* to get away. What if she sees

James as a means of escape? What if she's desperate enough to put him at risk?'

Seeing the concerned look on Maureen's face, the old woman reassured her. 'Don't you worry about that,' she said. 'Nothing will ever come of it, you'll see.'

Changing her heavy basket to the other arm, Maureen quickened her step. 'I hope to God you're right,' she whispered. 'Because if Leonard Mears knew he had an enemy in his ranks, my son's life would be worth nothing.'

James took the wall at a leap. With his eyes peeled for a sight of Isabel, he strolled along the footpath skirting the big house. A rambling Tudor house with high, beamed gables, pretty, crooked windows, and the more recent addition of a charming watchtower, it was one of the grandest in the area. Rumoured to have been built by a wool merchant and later sold for the princely sum of four guineas, the house was a splendid sight to behold. Flanked by chestnut trees and rhododendron bushes, it provided James with an opportunity to stand where he himself was unlikely to be seen.

From the corner, he had the garden in full view, the same garden where Isabel loved to walk, and where he often set eyes on her. This morning, though, she was nowhere in sight. 'Too early yet,' he murmured. 'She's probably still dreaming.'

He chuckled. 'Happen that's just what *you're* doing,' he told himself sharply. 'Dreaming about something you can never have.'

But, as always, his determination rose to smother the doubts. You mustn't lose sight of what you want, he thought. A man can make *anything* come true if his heart is big enough.

He walked on, momentarily pausing at the gate where they had talked on that wonderful day. Raising his eyes to the upper windows, he saw how the curtains at each window were open, but there was no sign of anyone. 'Best get a move on, James Peterson,' he reminded himself, 'or they'll have the law on you for a peeping Tom.'

Through the narrow chink in the window-boarding, Isabel saw him there. Twice she almost called through the chink, but changed her mind at the last minute. 'I mustn't let him know I'm being punished,' she decided wisely. 'It would solve nothing.'

She watched him for a moment, wondering if she would ever be able to say the things she wanted him to know. Yet in a strange way she felt he knew what was in her heart. Now, seeing him there, she wondered how he felt towards her . . . how he *really* felt.

In that short time last summer when they had stolen a few moments together at the gates, she had learned about his mother, and how his father had died some time ago. She had seen the look of affection in his dark eyes when he gazed upon her, and felt the same affection in her own lonely heart. But she couldn't be sure, and it wasn't enough to build a future on. For now though, because of the way things were, it would have to be enough.

With a heavy heart she returned to the darkest corner where, sliding down against the wall, she sat cross-legged on the hard floor. 'It won't be for ever,' she murmured. 'Sooner or later, *one way or another*, I will have a life of my own.'

Comforting herself with the knowledge that James had come looking for her, she bent her head on her folded arms and gave herself up to thoughts of him.

The night watchman was a short, round creature with a red face and pock-marked nose, got from too much of the good stuff. He was on the point of leaving, when James approached.

'Morning, son.'

'Morning, Arnie.' James liked the old fellow; drunk half the time, but amiable all the same. 'Off home, are you?'

'Aye, an' not afore time neither.' Loudly blowing his nose, he stuffed the grubby handkerchief back into his jacket pocket. 'It's been a damned cold night, I'll tell yer that.' He glanced towards the hut. 'I were half-tempted to sneak in there and take the fire with me,' he chuckled. 'Only if *he'd* caught me, I'd have been thrown out and told not to come back.'

'That cold, was it?' James didn't envy the fellow his job.

'Cold enough to freeze the balls off a pawnshop sign.'

'How old are you, Arnie?'

'Forty-two.'

James laughed. 'And I'm ninety.'

'I'm fifty-three come next birthday, that's how old I am.'

'Have you asked Mr Mears for a job inside, like I told you?'

'Yes, and he told me to think meself lucky I'd got a job at all, seeing as how I weren't no good to man nor beast.'

'He can be a wicked sod.'

'Aye, well, if it gets cold tonight, I might just kip in that there shed and be buggered to him.'

James glanced at the small timber hut. 'I wouldn't count on being comfortable if you did,' he warned, 'there's all manner of rubbish and stuff in there – rats too, I shouldn't wonder. In fact I don't know why it hasn't been shifted long since.'

The old fellow wasn't listening. 'Right! I'm off to my bed.' When he smiled, as he did now, he was surprisingly handsome, in a leathery kind of way.

'Why did you never marry, Arnie?' James had always wondered.

Arnie laughed out loud. 'Because no woman in her right mind would have me,' he said. 'I like a tipple and I like to do as I please. I'm untidy, I work all night and sleep all day, and happen I don't wash as often as I should.' Squaring his shoulders, he chuckled heartily. 'Happen I wouldn't mind cuddling up against some fat, warm little thing of a cold night, but it wouldn't work. I'm too set in me ways now. I don't know as I'd want some woman telling me what to do.'

'You're impossible.'

'Aye, lad, that's what I am – impossible – and I don't give a bugger.' Picking up his snapbox and billycan, he rammed them in his khaki bag and slung it over his shoulder. Then a quick warm of his hands over the brazier and he braced himself for the long walk home. 'I'm not sorry to see the back of another shift,' he confided. 'I hate the cold – allus have.' With his back hunched against the cold, he scuttled off.

James laughed, 'Then you've picked the wrong job, Arnie.'

'Story of my life,' came the far-off reply. 'Picked the wrong job: no missus, no kids, no money. I work for a man who thinks I'm dirt under his feet, and I've a landlord who puts up the rent every time he claps eyes on me. Why do I bother, that's what I want to know.'

Chuckling, James watched him go. For a long, quiet moment he stood, soaking in the atmosphere in this old place. The canal had a nature all its own – sometimes dark and mysterious, other times dappled by the sun, winking and smiling, quietly taking the many loaded barges on their way. Blackburn without its canal was unthinkable. Part of industry, it fetched and carried, providing men with a living, and a town with a soul.

Behind him were the warehouses and factories, mostly owned by Leonard Mears, or others of his kind. Work was hard and poorly paid, but it was work all the same, and gave a man his pride.

Oddly disturbed and not knowing why, James lingered, wanting to go in. *Not* wanting to go in. His heart was back there, with Isabel.

With his thoughts far away, he wasn't sure if he had heard

something, a kind of groan – a scuffle of sorts. 'Who's there?' Taking a step towards the old storage shed, he called again, 'Is there someone there?'

'It's a bad thing when you start talking to yourself.' The voice was young and impatient, like its owner. 'What the devil are you up to, Peterson?' Jack Mears appeared in the yard.

'Oh, good morning, Mr Mears.' It rankled having to address a young pup with such respect. 'I thought I heard something.'

'Rats!' Taking a pace forward, he regarded James through narrowed eyes. 'The whole canalside is riddled with them.'

'I dare say.' And of course it was true. Only last week the rat-catcher caught upwards of a hundred right inside the factory.

Jack Mears seemed to read his thoughts. 'If you ask me, it's a waste of good money having the rat-catcher in. But Robert *would* have his way. I told Father it was money down the drain. However many vermin the rat-catcher takes, there's always more waiting to move in.'

He glanced up at the factory clock on the outside wall. 'You'd better go in,' he snapped. 'It's bad for the men to see a supervisor late.'

James looked him steadily in the eye. 'No fear of that with me, Mr Mears,' he answered solemnly, 'I've never yet been late for work. I'd rather be early than late.' He too glanced at the clock. 'It's a good ten minutes before the whistle goes,' he reminded him. 'I'll be in long before that.'

Resenting the other man's attitude, Jack Mears nodded stiffly. 'If you value your job, you will!' With an arrogant smirk, he made his way towards the factory entrance. Once there, he afforded himself a backward glance, curious to see how deep in thought James was. 'I'm watching you, Peterson,' he mumbled. 'One wrong step and I'll have you, so help me.'

James had too much on his mind to worry for long about the short exchange of words between them. All the same, he was no fool. I'll have to keep my wits about me, he thought, because if I'm right . . . that little bugger is another Leonard Mears in the making. He's petty-minded and jealous of my standing with the men.

Agitated, he dug in his pocket and took out a packet of cigarettes and a match. Striking the match on the sole of his boot he lit the cigarette and took a long, satisfying drag. Two more, then he stubbed out the cigarette, flicking it into the murky water.

Again, he thought he heard a strange sound.

Taking a moment to listen, he cocked his head on one side, wondering whether it was just the usual sounds of another day starting. Morning, noon and night, there was always noise around the canal: water splashing, barges creaking, and occasionally the sound of someone throwing stones in: it had even been known for a body or two to be dumped in the canal overnight and found in the morning, pale and bloated.

He listened a moment longer, but there was nothing. 'You're beginning to hear things,' he said. 'Best go inside and get on with your work, before that little twerp Jack finds an excuse to send you packing.' James knew he would too, given half a chance.

Quickly now, he hurried to the arched entrance of the factory, situated at the largest and busiest end of a long run of buildings. To the right of him was the entrance, ahead of him the factory floor with all its paraphernalia, and to the left a narrow stairway rising to the office.

Standing at the window of the office was Jack Mears, a man of low morals, who, like his father, took sadistic pleasure in surveying the workers from a superior height. Knowing he was under scrutiny, James wisely kept his eyes averted.

Suddenly, the shrill sound of the factory whistle sliced through the morning air, and the men appeared from every corner. Half asleep and long-faced, they shuffled in one behind the other. James stood watching as they filed past, the section leaders keeping a tally of their men. As soon as all were accounted for, James began his rounds. Every morning he walked from one end of the factory to the other, making himself available if needed, and satisfying himself that every man had all he needed to do a good day's work.

The first stop was the timber barn. A high, vast place at the side of the main building, it was open-ended to allow weathering and so bitterly cold in winter and unbearably hot in summer. Here, all the timber was delivered and off-loaded from the supplier. It was then kept ready for distributing round the many workshops inside the factory. Part of James's duties was to maintain stock levels, reporting to one of the Mears brothers whenever an order was needed.

Remaining at the mouth of the barn, James looked across, his observant gaze roving the numerous bays. He was so engrossed in making mental notes, he didn't hear the other man approach.

'Morning, James.' It was Leonard Mears' elder son, Robert. 'How are we doing?'

'Morning, Mr Mears.' James liked Robert; unlike his brother Jack, he knew how to treat the men.

'You look like a man with a lot on his mind.'

'Much like yourself, I shouldn't wonder,' James replied, leaving the man to take the remark as he would. 'I'm just about to walk the bays,' he added. 'But from where I'm standing, it seems we're all right for the most part, though I reckon we might need another delivery of floorboards.'

Robert smiled. 'If that's what you think, then that's what we need.' Robert was under no illusion where this man was concerned. What he didn't know about the running of this place wasn't worth knowing. Every man looked up to him, including Robert himself. The truth was, James had taught him a lot. Besides maintaining stock levels and carrying responsibility for the smooth running of the workforce, James also made the wheels for both carriage and cart alike. This was a skilled, creative job, but like everything he did, James took it all in his stride. Being a wheelwright gave him a sense of deep pride, and it showed in his work.

And as if that wasn't enough, he regularly came up with ideas that had saved Robert's father both time and money over the years.

Robert made mention of it now, as they walked on. 'This system of yours was a godsend.' He gestured to the line of bays, which ran both sides of the building. Reaching up to the rafters, they measured some fifteen feet wide, each one hung with a sign depicting its specific contents. 'Before you suggested separating the timber into these large bays, there was little or no order at all,' Robert went on. 'One batch of timber would be mixed with another and God only knows how many man-hours it took to sort it when needed. I don't know why my father didn't see it before.'

'I'm sure he would have seen it eventually.'

'I don't think so, James.' Robert admired James's ingenuity. 'It takes a man with vision to see the smaller details. My father is only interested in the end result – *money*.' He pointed to the ledger hanging from each bay. 'That's the kind of thing I mean, a stock book for each different kind of timber, so simple yet look at the time and effort it saves. Instead of ploughing through a huge book to work out what stock we need, here we have an individual record of delivery and stock on *every* grade of timber we use.'

'Makes for quicker, easier work, sir.'

'That's exactly what I mean—' Robert wagged a finger at him. 'And don't call me sir. Mr Mears will do.'

While James took stock, Robert walked with him. 'You should have your own factory,' he said, to James's astonishment, '*that* would give Father a run for his money.'

'Aye, and it takes money to set up on your own. More money happen than I'll ever see in a lifetime.'

Robert nodded. 'Pity though,' he mused. 'You're a born businessman, there's no doubt about it.'

James thought it wise to make no reply. After all, though different in nature, Robert Mears was still his father's son.

Another voice intervened. 'Father's on the rampage.' Jack came rushing up to Robert. 'He wants you . . . *now*!'

Giving him a cool, angry glance, Robert told him, 'I'll be along in a minute.'

'He wants you *now*!'

'Tell him, I'm talking stock with James.'

Jack was pink with anger. 'He won't like it.'

In a quiet voice, Robert insisted, 'Just *tell* him.'

Throwing a seething glance at James, the younger man went off in a rush.

Robert shook his head. 'Jack's got a lot to learn,' he said. 'Unfortunately, he's only interested in being more like Father.'

Again, James kept silent. There was too much undercurrent here . . . a man could be drowned if he wasn't sure which way to swim.

Realising he might have caused some embarrassment, Robert told James, 'I'd better go and pacify him.' Nodding to the timber bays, he said, 'I mean it though, James, you've got a good head on your shoulders – too good to be wasted here.'

Alarm bells rang in James's mind. 'You're not thinking of finishing me, are you, Mr Mears?'

Surprised he had been misunderstood, Robert reassured him. 'I would never be so foolhardy,' he said smiling. 'I've a feeling, if you were finished, we'd *all* be finished.'

With that, he hurried away.

James watched him go. 'You've never said a truer word,' he murmured, 'but when I do set up on my own, and I *will*, you'll be welcome, and so will the men.'

His face darkened. 'But never them two!' His bitter gaze went to the upper office, where he could see Jack and his father talking. 'I wouldn't give them two the time of day.'

Up in the office, Leonard Mears slated his sons. 'Lazy, idle no-goods!' Pacing the floor, hands behind his back and a face like thunder, his fury knew no bounds. 'I'm surrounded by idiots.' Swinging round he addressed himself to Jack. 'When I arrive at the factory, I expect you to be down there, chivvying the lazy bastards on. Instead, I find you closeted in the office with your feet on my desk, while down there they're getting away with murder!'

Jack was visibly trembling. 'I'm sorry, Father. It won't happen again.'

Saving Jack's punishment for later, he turned on Robert. 'As for *you*, I want an explanation and it had better be good. Not only were you strolling about the place with Peterson – as if the pair of you had all the time in the world – but, when I send for you, you have the bloody gall to make me wait!' Glaring at his elder son, he expected a swift and humble answer.

In a calm and assured voice, Robert replied: 'I was doing the job I'm paid for; the men were already hard at work as usual. James was checking the bays and I was making sure there were no problems. I came back as quick as I could.'

For a long, uncomfortable moment, his father remained where he stood, his spiteful eyes focused on Robert and his mind feverish with ideas of punishment.

Abruptly, he turned away and went to the window, where he surveyed the men below. From here, he could see the whole panorama of his empire. Directly beneath him were the workers who prepared and shaped the timber; in the next area they pieced together the floors; then came the stage where the wheels and chassis were married together.

Shifted from one area to the next on the many huge trollies, the partly finished carriage went through many stages, until finally it arrived at the finisher's, where it was varnished, polished and brought alive. The smell of new wood and varnish permeated the air.

All in all, the making of a carriage was a wonderful thing to watch; a cart and wagon too, though to a lesser degree.

Down there, on the factory floor, there wasn't a man whose heart didn't swell with pride when he saw a magnificent carriage leave the premises. It was to their credit alone that, out of the timber and leather which came in at one end of the factory, they could create such a masterpiece; with nothing more than a few tools, a big heart, and the hands God gave them.

But Leonard Mears was not interested in men or the making; he valued only *money*.

Robert dared to interrupt his thoughts. 'You need have no worry, Father,' he assured him quietly. 'The men won't let you down.'

Eager to please, Jack had his say too. 'I'll make sure they don't,' he bragged. 'From now on, I'll be down there, watching and listening. They won't breathe without me knowing about it.'

Slowly, his father turned. When his curious gaze fell on his younger son, there was wickedness in his eyes. 'That's the best idea you've come up with yet,' he told him.

'Thank you, Father.' Beaming with delight, Jack congratulated himself.

But joy turned to horror when his father instructed, 'Find yourself a boiler suit and get down there among them. Tell Peterson I said you're not to be given a heavy job nor one where you might have to think too much.' He laughed. 'I don't think you have the muscle or the brain to cope with either.'

A nervous smile flickered over Jack's face. 'You don't mean that, do you, Father?' Glancing at Robert he silently pleaded for help.

As always, Robert came to his aid. 'Think again, Father,' he suggested. 'Jack already has a job. He fetches and carries all day long between your two factories. He runs messages to suppliers and buyers, and often has to collect small, urgent implements. Moreover, he helps me no end round this office. You already keep him so busy, he has little time for anything else, let alone taking on a manual job down there with the men.'

'Then *you* must cover his duties.'

'How can I do that, sir? What with checking orders in and out, meeting customers, maintaining a flow of orders in, and delivery out. Mountains of paperwork, working through any problems; and there are always problems to be sorted, you know that yourself, Father. Then there are the men themselves. They need guidance, and naturally a certain amount of discipline.'

Angry at his father's intention to humiliate his own son in such a way, he went on, 'I have my hands full in maintaining the smooth running of this place. I cannot do Jack's work as well as my own. It's a physical impossibility.'

Knowing all that, Leonard Mears remained adamant. 'Let there be an end to this discussion,' he snapped. 'I want him down there – he can be my eyes and ears.'

Realising how Jack would not survive such an ordeal happily, Robert offered, 'I'll go down in his place. I might not make you a better spy, but you could use the time to groom Jack in other, more important matters.'

Both young men were visibly startled when their father slammed his fist down on the desk. 'Enough!' Clutching a paperweight, he sent it flying across the office towards them. It landed with a thud at Robert's feet and no one was hurt.

'I can't do it!' Jack wailed. 'They'll make my life a misery.' Spying from up here was one thing, but down there, rolling up his sleeves to work with them, that was another.

'Coward!' Grabbing Jack by the lapels, his father sent him

hurtling out the door. 'You heard what I said, now get on with it!'

Turning, he snarled at Robert, 'I have to go out, but I'll be back in ten minutes, and when I am, I expect to see that young devil working up a sweat. As for *you*, you had better watch your step.' His meaning was clear. 'I have a first-class manager at the barrel factory. With a little incentive, I'm sure he could run two factories as well as one.'

When Robert gave no reply, he warned: 'Don't delude yourselves that you have a place for life with me. Sons or not, you have to *earn* privilege.' Crossing the room he came closer, his face a study in cunning as he told Robert in a hushed voice, 'If I think you're getting above yourselves, I'll knock you down so fast you won't know what's hit you.'

Robert stood tall, his gaze unflinching. 'You've done Jack a terrible wrong,' he answered. 'You know he won't be able to cope with the task you've set him.'

'It is not for you to question my decisions,' he replied smartly. 'Get on with your work. I'll be back shortly.'

As he went down the office steps, he didn't even glance at his younger son, who was pressed against the wall, hiding where the men could not see him.

The tears rolled down Jack's face as he realised at long last that whatever he did to please, he would never win his father's approval. For that one awful moment, the love he had for his father turned to an all-consuming hate.

Robert made his way to where Jack was still hiding and took him by the shoulders. 'Don't let him beat you,' he pleaded softly. 'This is your chance to show him what you can do.'

Looking up with tearful eyes, Jack's answer was pitiful. 'I can't do it,' he said. 'I *can't* work alongside these men. I'm made of better stuff than that.'

'I don't want to hear that talk!' Robert had always known Jack was his father in the making, but he had not realised it was happening so quickly. 'These men are hard-working, honest people. They ask nothing more than to be paid for what they do and, God only knows, they don't even get that adequately. But you, Jack . . . you have privileges they will probably never know.'

'I can't help *that*!'

'No, I'm not saying you can, but you have no right to look down on them.' Suddenly he began to see. 'I thought Father was wrong to order you down here, but now I'm beginning to wonder if it isn't the best thing that could ever happen to you.'

Sullen, Jack drew away from him.

'What I mean is . . . it might be good for you to get to know these men, to work alongside them and see them for what they are. They won't make your life a misery as you seem to think. They'll help and guide you. It's their way.'

Jack was afraid, and he admitted it. 'Do you think Father will punish me if I refuse?'

'You *know* he will.'

'He'll throw me out, won't he?'

'Or worse.' There was no point in denying it. 'Truthfully, Jack . . . I don't think you have much choice.'

Jack thought about that for a minute, before drying his tears. 'You're right,' he said, 'it's my chance to show him what I can do, and when he sees me down here, amongst this rabble, he's sure to realise I don't belong.'

Disgusted, Robert chose to ignore his remarks; besides, he had said his piece, and it didn't seem to have changed Jack's thinking. 'Whatever you say, Jack.'

Convinced his father would not humiliate him for too long, Jack asked, 'Will you help me?'

'Of course I will.' Jack was his brother after all.

Turning, Robert discreetly beckoned over James, who had witnessed the whole sorry little scene. 'Jack will be working with you and the men for a time,' he explained to him. 'Can you find him a job that isn't too taxing?'

'I'm sure that can be arranged.' James was no fool; he knew the lie of the land. 'We can always do with an extra pair of hands fitting seats into the carriages. It's a light job, and fairly clean.'

'Thank you. I'm sure he could manage that.' There was something else. 'You might as well know, Jack isn't too happy about it.'

'I understand.'

'It's an idea of Father's.'

James nodded knowingly. 'I expect he wants the lad to learn the business from ground level up, that'll be his thinking, I expect?' He hoped that would clear the air. 'Is that what you want me to tell the men, sir?'

Placing a hand on the other man's shoulder, Robert told him, 'You're a good man, James Peterson. If things were different, I'd be proud to have you as a friend.'

'Thank you.' James had an idea what Robert must be going through, caught between father and brother like he was. 'I consider that to be a real compliment.'

'Look after him.'

'You know I will.'

While Robert went about his business, James began by finding the right size boiler suit for Jack.

'I'm sorry, Mr Mears,' he decided, 'I don't think any of these are suitable for you.' He knew Jack had a mind to be difficult, so tried not to rile him. 'Besides, they've all been used at some time or another.'

'Then *I'm* not about to wear them, am I?' Arrogant as ever.

Unperturbed by Jack's sullenness, James scratched his head. 'Of course!' He didn't need to consult the stock ledger. 'If I remember rightly, there's a batch of new aprons in the shed. If you'll give me a minute, sir, I'll go and fetch them now.'

Aware that he was being observed by the men, Jack turned his anger on them. 'Back to your work, or you'll find yourself outside the doors.'

As James walked away, Jack felt uncomfortable being left all alone there. 'You! Wait a minute.' Scurrying after James, he told him in a loud, authoritative voice, 'Stay at your work, Peterson! *I'll* find the aprons. Just tell me where they are.'

While Jack went outside, James walked back to his work with the whisperings of a smile on his handsome face. 'Little upstart,' he murmured. 'Some people never learn.'

Nearby, one of the men voiced what the others were thinking. 'What's that young bugger up to?'

'Don't you worry about it,' James answered. 'Just do your work and don't ask questions, that's the best way.'

As always, they took his good advice.

Inside the shed, Sally stirred.

Exhausted, and weakened by the blow to her head, she had slept for many hours. Now, coming to her senses, she heard the footsteps approaching. I've got to get out of here! she thought. But how? The footsteps had paused right outside the door. 'Oh, God!' The door was opening.

As it swung open the rush of light was almost blinding. She saw the vague outline of a man. He was peering in. 'Who the devil are *you*?' In two strides he was standing over her. 'You filthy little tramp!' Lashing out with his foot he caught her hard on the shoulder. 'Get out of here!'

When he raised his foot to kick her again, Sally took hold of his ankle; with all her strength she tipped him backwards, sending him flying into a pile of wooden crates. 'You little bastard!' Struggling to regain his balance he shouted all manner of obscenities after her. But Sally was already out the door and away.

Having heard the commotion from inside the factory, James came rushing out. He saw the girl first. Behind her, Jack came staggering from the shed; it was easy to imagine what had taken place here.

Seeing how thin and unkempt she was, James made no attempt to stop the girl. 'Poor little beggar,' he muttered. 'Looks like she's had a bad time of it.'

Jack, however, was not so charitable. 'Stop her, you fool!' he called out to James. James, though, had no intention of waylaying that sorry young creature.

Suddenly, coming at speed, a carriage appeared. The girl stumbled in its path, and James feared she might be crushed beneath the wheels. Rushing forward he heard Jack yell, 'It's Father! He'll deal with the little bitch!'

Clambering out of the carriage, Leonard Mears grabbed the girl by the ear. 'Been thieving, have you?' He yanked her to her feet. 'Been looking to make away with whatever you could find, is that it?' Slapping her hard round the head he warned, 'We have laws to deal with rabble like you, and by God, I intend to make sure you'll never be in a position to rob decent folk again!'

'I *wasn't* thieving!' But the more vehemently she denied it, the angrier he became. Shaking her until her teeth chattered, he kept a tight hold on her, while addressing Jack: 'What was she after?'

While Jack gave his account, Leonard Mears held the girl tight; her distress meant nothing compared with the fact that she was out to steal from him.

'So that's where I found her,' Jack concluded, 'loitering in the store-shed.' He gabbled with excitement, 'She was up to no good . . . or why would she be there . . . on *our* property?'

Beaming with pride, his father told him how pleased he was.

'You've made a good start in your new position. It seems I did the right thing after all.'

James intervened, 'Excuse me, sir, but the girl is obviously hurt—' He pointed to the blood caked on the back of her head. 'Why don't we let her explain what she was doing in the shed?'

Swelling with indignation, Leonard Mears laughed off the suggestion. 'What? So she can lie her way out of it? I think you must have lost your sense of decency. She's a vagabond . . . a tramp from the streets. A thief if ever I saw one!'

Roused by his father's praise and eager to do even better, Jack stepped forward. 'Let me take her inside, Father,' he said. 'I'll tie her up so she can't escape, then we'll send for the authorities.' He smiled from one to the other. 'It's the only way to deal with her sort.'

The smile was knocked from his face when his father reached out with his stick and rapped him hard across the back. 'Have you lost your senses?' he snapped. 'You will *not* take her inside my factory. She must be riddled with fleas and God knows what.' Casting a derisory glance at the girl, he spat on the ground in disgust. 'Stinks to high heaven, she does!'

'What shall we do with her then?' Jack's triumph was short-lived.

'Peterson will return her to the shed and secure her there. Meanwhile *you* get off and fetch the police. Tell them we've caught a thief red-handed, and they're to come straight away.'

Eager to please, Jack thought the quickest way was to take his father's carriage; but the idea was soon scuttled. 'You're not getting in there . . . not when you've been handling *this*.' Beckoning James to him, he handed the girl over, at the same time ordering his son, 'Get off then, you idiot! I want her off these premises and into jail where she can't do any harm.'

When Jack went off at a run, he brushed himself down and clapped his hands as if ridding himself of disease. 'Tie her fast,' he ordered, 'then lock the door. We don't want her escaping, do we now, eh?'

Knowing he was being watched every step of the way, James looked suitably stern as he took the girl away. When he arrived at the door of the shed, he thrust her inside and glanced back, relieved to see Leonard Mears already on his way towards the building.

Smiling to himself, James followed the girl inside. When he closed the door behind him, she cowered in the corner, eyes wild and frightened. 'Please don't hurt me.' The colour drained from her face. 'I wasn't stealing . . . honest to God, I wasn't.'

James smiled. 'That's what they *all* say.' He meant it as a matter-of-fact comment, but she took it differently; in the same way she misjudged his lazy, easy smile.

In desperation, she flew at him, scratching and kicking, and making James fight to keep control of her. 'Whoa! You silly little bugger . . . listen to what I'm saying!' Stretching out her skinny arms, he held her tight against the wall. 'I'm not out to take advantage of you, or punish you in any way.'

'Liar!'

'Look, didn't you hear me plead for you back there? Didn't you hear me ask him to let you have your say?'

'Why did you?'

'Because I felt sorry for you.' His quiet, calm voice had a sobering effect on her. 'I can see how badly you've been treated, and I didn't want him hurting you any more.' He shook his head. 'The trouble is . . . he *enjoys* hurting people. That young man is his own son, and he treats him like dirt, you saw it for yourself.' Anger hardened his features. 'But then, Leonard Mears treats *everyone* like that.'

Visibly shocked, Sally fell back against the wall. 'Leonard Mears!' She could hardly believe it. 'That man is Leonard Mears?'

Puzzled by her outburst, James asked, 'Do you know of him?'

Suddenly she grew cautious. 'No, I've never heard of him.' But she had, and she wished with all her heart she had not. This man *was* her father; every trail and enquiry had led her here, only to discover that she was cursed by her birth.

'When the police come,' she asked nervously, 'what will they do to me?' Shock became fear.

Taking her firmly by the shoulders, James bade her listen carefully. 'If you do as I say, you need have no fear,' he promised. 'You have to trust me.'

'I don't trust *anybody*! Not any more, I don't.' Leonard Mears loomed large in her mind. She had looked for a father and found a monster.

Reaching out, James tenderly ran his finger along the back of her head. Drawing it away when she winced, he observed the blood on his hand. 'You have no choice,' he told her. 'You're hurt and probably starving.' Digging into his pocket he drew out a number of coins. 'There's no time to waste. They'll be here soon, and then I won't be able to help you, however much I want to.'

Pressing the coins into her small fist, he urged, 'Take these, find somewhere to wash, get something to eat, then make your way to Preston Road. Ask for Scab Lane, and search out a lady by the name of Maureen Peterson. She's a good woman. She'll help you. Tell her James has sent you . . . tell her I said to take care of you.'

When she might have questioned him again, he edged her towards the door. 'When I shout, you must run as fast as ever you can,' he warned. 'Don't look back . . . just keep going. Remember . . . Scab Lane . . . Maureen Peterson.'

Inching open the door he peered out. 'It's all clear.' Pushing her out the door, he hissed, 'Quickly . . . go!'

Knowing this was her only chance, Sally took off and was out of sight before he started yelling, 'Mr Mears!' Heading towards the factory, he feigned breathlessness. 'Mr Mears. The little bugger's got away!'

At once Leonard Mears came crashing down the office steps. 'Got away?' he yelled. 'What do you mean?'

Gasping for breath, James made a good show of it. 'She caught me unawares, sir. A split second, that's all it was . . . I turned to get something strong to tie her up with, and she pounced on me like the wildcat she is.' Clutching one shoulder, he groaned. 'I reckon she's cut me deep . . . but it's nothing to what I'll do if I ever get my hands on the little bitch. By! She's a bad lot and no mistake.'

Frustrated and waving his arms, Leonard Mears gave vent to his anger. 'I told you to secure her until the police came, and now you tell me you've let her go? You useless article! I'd be within my rights to kick you bag and baggage out that door!'

'You would, sir.' James could grovel with the best of them, when the occasion demanded. 'I should never have turned my back, not even for a second.'

'Father?' Coming closer, Robert, who stood by, bemused and knowing how James was putting on a show, had a word in his ear. 'If you were to throw James out over a ragamuffin like that, you would be doing yourself a great injustice. James is hard-working and too knowledgeable for us to turn him away. You'd be hard pressed to find anyone else of his calibre. You know yourself, there are any number of factory owners who would be more than delighted to take him on. What's more, you would be a laughing stock for letting him go. It would be more trouble than it's worth, and all because of some filthy little vagabond who means nothing to any of us.' His sympathy lay with the girl, but, like James, he had to play the game.

At first it seemed Leonard Mears would turn on Robert as well. 'Don't presume to tell me my business, young man!' he growled. Yet he did appear to be giving Robert's advice some thought, while behind his back Robert and James exchanged the merest of smiles.

Leonard Mears came to a decision. Addressing James, he said sombrely, 'You did a very foolish thing in letting that young rascal go. I thought I could rely on you to do the right thing.'

'You can, sir.'

'Hmh!' Crossing his hands behind his back, he stood on the step, staring down like the eyes of judgement. 'I hope you realise, you won't get a second chance. In future when I entrust you to carry out my orders, I shall expect it to be done to the letter. Do you understand me, Peterson?'

'Of course, sir, and I really am sorry.' Sorry he had not been the one to find that poor girl in the shed, instead of Jack the coward.

'Against my better nature, I'm prepared to overlook your negligence . . . on this one occasion only! Now, be off with you before I change my mind!'

With James out of the way, he and Robert returned to the office. 'It goes against the grain for me to let him off with a caution,' he admitted grudgingly. 'By rights, I should be making an example of him in front of the men.' Unhappy with his decision, he paced the floor, his beady eyes going occasionally to James, who was toiling away at his work. 'The man is too confident for his own good. Happen he wants taking down a peg or two.'

Concerned that his father might still be thinking to punish James in some way, Robert reminded him, 'You do see how it would have been though, don't you, Father? Letting him go . . . a man the likes of James Peterson . . . we could never have replaced him.'

'All the same, it wouldn't do to let him think he can get away with murder.'

'He would never think such a thing.'

'I have a sneaking suspicion Peterson will have to be watched.

Invaluable or not, I can't allow him to believe he's any better than the others. He works for me and I pay his wages. That's the full measure of it.'

It was like he had been thinking out loud, because suddenly he swung round. 'Peterson is trouble. One step out of line and I'll have him. And I don't give tuppence for what calibre of man he is! Now there are things I have to attend to. I have to stop off at the barrel factory. Then I'm away home. Is there anything you want my advice on before I leave?'

Robert saw an opportunity to tackle something that was worrying him. 'Taylor has been chasing his money again. I kept it back as you said, but now he insists . . . if we don't pay him for that last batch of material for the carriage seats, he means to take action.'

'Tell him to run for his money.'

'I don't understand why you won't let me pay him. The money *is* owed, after all.'

'Do as I say!' Rapping the desk with his stick, he lowered his voice, 'I happen to know that Taylor is already on his way out.' Grinning he revealed, 'I think you'll find that when the new owner takes over, the entry for that material will have conveniently vanished . . . along with a few others.'

'What do you mean?'

'You'll know soon enough. Meanwhile, keep your mouth shut and do as you're told. And when that useless brother of yours gets back, send him to work. Oh, and tell the police how the girl was allowed to escape.' His smile was evil. 'Give them Peterson's name . . . maybe they'll remember it at some future date.'

'Why would they do that?'

'You ask too many questions.'

Robert would have asked a deal more, but Leonard Mears was already on his way out of the building. Looking to cause more mischief elsewhere.

* * *

It was late afternoon. The Mears' household was always quiet at this time of day. With everything done and the dining-table already set for the evening meal, the servants were gathered round the kitchen table, enjoying tea and a slice of fruit cake.

'My heart goes out to that poor girl,' Cook remarked, sipping her hot tea and making a noise like water through a drain. 'It's one thing locking her in that room for an hour, or maybe even two, but she's been up there far too long, and I for one think it's a sin and a shame.'

Mrs Flanagan put down her cup. 'You're right, Mabel,' she lowered her voice to a whisper, 'and if there was any justice, it would be *him* who was locked away. He's a wicked, wicked man and I hope one day he pays for his sins!'

There was such fire in her voice that Cook gave her a curious glance. Mrs Flanagan was a kind and honest soul, and Cook had taken a liking to her. But she had always suspected there was more to the housekeeper than met the eye.

They sat for a moment in silence, contemplating their thoughts; while at the far end of the table, the two servant girls quietly chatted and giggled amongst themselves. Plain-faced and bony with tied-up brown hair, they could have been sisters; they also shared the same room, the same clothes, and fancied the same young man – though the fellow in question had no idea and probably never would.

At that very moment, he was outside, clearing the garden ready for spring, unaware that he was the topic of conversation.

Upstairs, Frances Mears paced her room. Like Cook and Mrs Flanagan, she was thinking of Isabel. 'Why can't she humour him?' she muttered. 'She knows what he's like. Why does she always have to be so stubborn?'

Unable to settle, she continued pacing, growing more agitated by the minute. 'I wish I was strong enough to stand up to him,' she whispered. 'I wish I had the courage to hurt him like he hurts me.'

In all her life she had never known such a feeling as surged through her now. Always obedient, ever patient, she bore her unhappiness in silence. Suddenly she realised how very much she hated him – how much she wanted him dead.

Filled with a sense of terror, she rushed from the room and hurried to the library, where Hannah was still engrossed in her lessons. When Frances entered the room, Hannah greeted her with a burst of excitement. 'Mother . . . did you know that women are now allowed to vote for County Borough Councils?'

Surprised and dismayed that this was the subject of her lesson, Frances addressed the governess, 'Is this what you've been teaching her?'

'It was merely a passing comment, ma'am,' she answered. 'Hannah showed an interest and I thought it my duty to satisfy her curiosity.' A small, trim figure with a look of learning, the governess seemed highly nervous. 'I hoped you might approve. We live in a changing world, with women taking a more important role than ever before.'

'I see.' Taking her aside, Frances advised, 'The master has very strong views about women and politics. He would not be best pleased if you were to stray into that particular area.'

'I understand.' Having spent many hours in this house, she knew the nature of the man. 'But, like I say, it *was* just a passing comment.'

'Of course, but Hannah is very impressionable . . . strong-minded even. You must be very careful not to fill her head with the wrong ideas.'

Going to Hannah, she peeped over her shoulder. 'Keep your mind on your work, my dear,' she said. 'Your father is bound to question you later.'

Hannah looked away. 'Interrogate more like.'

'That's enough, child!' Deeply disturbed by events unfolding about her, Frances hurried away.

Her next port of call was the kitchen. To reach it she had to walk the long, narrow passage. It was a dim, unlovely place, hung as it was with portraits of relatives long gone. But this was the place Leonard admired best, just as he admired the portraits of his ancestors. In their gold and finery, they gave him an inflated sense of his own importance.

In the kitchen, everyone was busy: Cook was already preparing the evening meal; Mrs Flanagan was instructing one of the girls on how to fold napkins properly; and the second maid was ironing.

'Is everything all right?' Frances would gladly have changed places with any one of them.

'Yes, thank you, ma'am.' Looking up from the hot stove, Cook's face was bright pink.

Sniffing the air, Frances remarked, 'I swear it always makes me hungry whenever I come into this kitchen.' Filled with the smells of cabbage, roast pork and stewing apples, the air was deliciously warm and heavy. 'Don't tell me . . .' She sniffed again. 'It's apple pie for dessert.' Apple pie and custard was her all-time favourite.

Cook laughed. 'With thick, creamy custard to make your eyes water.'

'Cook, you're an absolute treasure.' A second glance round the kitchen, a smile at all who looked, and Frances went away to embark on another errand. *A devious errand that could cost her dearly if it was discovered.*

This time she did not turn towards the main house. Instead, she carried on past the kitchen and continued on towards the servants' quarters, then followed the passage until it began to narrow. As she hurried along, her heart beat so frantically she feared it might burst right out of her chest. 'You must be quick!' she told herself over and over. 'You must be quick!'

Soon the main passage forked away. While one way continued to the servants' rooms, the other led up, through the door, to the watch-tower.

Frances stood before it, hardly daring to breathe. Several times she glanced back, before taking the key, which she had removed from her husband's desk, from her skirt pocket. With shaking fingers, she inserted the key into the lock and pushed open the door. Another minute and she had gone up the stairs and was now in front of the door leading directly to where Isabel was imprisoned.

'Isabel?' Pressing her face close to the door, she softly called, 'Isabel, it's me . . . I only have a minute before he comes back.'

Almost immediately Isabel answered, 'You shouldn't have come here. If he finds out, you'll be punished.'

'I had to make sure you were all right. It's too long . . . he's kept you here too long this time.'

'I'm all right. Please, Mother, go back. Don't let him catch you here.'

'Then answer me, child . . . if he comes to let you out, will you promise not to antagonise him?'

'How can I promise such a thing? I want a life of my own, Mother. I need to choose my own direction.'

Frances sighed, 'Oh, child, I'm so afraid for you.'

'Don't be. He doesn't frighten me any more, Mother, not like when I was little.'

'For my sake, Isabel . . . please don't tell *him* that.'

'Go back now, Mother. We'll talk when he lets me out of here.'

'All right, child, but remember what I said.'

'I will.' She meant she would remember the advice, but not follow it.

Softly, Frances went away, and with every step her heart was in her mouth. No sooner had she locked the bottom door and taken half a dozen steps along the passage, than he was there, blocking her way. 'What are you doing here?'

Quickly, Frances had to think. 'I . . . I've been checking the servants' quarters.'

'Why would you do that?' He didn't believe her and she knew it.

'Cook said she's been hearing noises . . . like a rat scratching at the floorboards.'

'Has she now?' He gave a soft mirthless laugh. 'And you thought you'd be brave and chase the rat away, did you?'

With his beady eyes staring into her face, she felt herself trembling. Praying he couldn't tell how afraid she was, she answered coolly, 'I couldn't hear anything. Cook must have been imagining things. I'm just on my way to tell her that . . . put her mind at rest.'

'You're lying.' Snatching at her face, he squeezed her chin between his fingers. 'Where have you been? The truth now!'

'I've already told you.'

'If you think I'll swallow the story about the rat, it's you who are imagining things, not Cook.' Slapping her twice across the head, he demanded to know, 'Do you have a key to that door?' He looked towards the door she had locked only moments ago.

Trembling, Frances shook her head, but unfortunately the lie was alive in her eyes.

Suddenly, he grabbed her to him, his hands raking her skirt, searching for the pocket. When he found it, he triumphantly drew out the key. 'I knew it!' With a cry of rage, he raised the key in his clenched fist, then with the whole force of his weight brought the key edge down on to her face, slicing the skin from ear to mouth. When she screamed out, he callously threw her to the floor. 'Get out of my sight!'

While she lay there, writhing in agony, he stood over her. 'If you should accuse me of this, you will rue the day. Everyone knows what a nervous disposition you have, and a man has to protect his family, even against his own wife.' He smiled. 'It wouldn't take much to convince a doctor that you need to be put away, for your own sake, as well as ours. I mean, look how you hurt yourself just now . . . and for no other reason than you worked yourself into such a terrible temper.' Softly tutting, he wagged a finger at her. 'It only proves what a danger you are. Oh, I do hope you understand what I'm saying, my dear.'

With deliberate calm, he put the key into his pocket and strolled away. Out of the corner of her eye she could see him leisurely opening the door, before disappearing behind it.

When the door was locked from the other side, she pulled herself up by the wall, and went, at a painstakingly slow pace, along the passage; one hand balancing herself, the other clasped to her face. She knew from the rush of blood that he had damaged her deeply.

Hearing a noise in the corridor, Mrs Flanagan came rushing out of the kitchen, horrified to find the mistress doubled up in pain. Frances had wanted to sneak by the kitchen without anyone seeing her, but this was a busy household and not much went unseen.

'Oh, good God above!' Grabbing hold of Frances, Mrs Flanagan called out for help. 'Cook! Come quickly. It's the mistress . . . quickly now!'

Cook, too, was shocked to find Frances with her face bleeding, and her whole body shaking so much she expected to see her faint away there and then. 'Please . . .' Frances pleaded with them. 'Get me . . . upstairs . . .'

Slowly they helped her upstairs. 'Dear God, what happened to you, ma'am?' Mrs Flanagan took one arm, Cook took the other and between them they laid her tenderly on the bed. 'Was it an accident?' She couldn't imagine how such a thing could have happened.

Cook gave her a warning glance and the questions were stilled.

'It's a terrible cut, ma'am.' Mrs Flanagan had never seen worse. Sending Cook for a bowl of water and flannel, she promised Frances, 'I'll have the doctor here in no time.'

'No!' Panicking, Frances grabbed her by the hand. 'No doctor!' she was adamant. 'Bathe my face, then I'll sleep a while. There's no cause for alarm.' The blood ran into her eye, and the pain was almost more than she could bear, but what he had done must never be spoken of, not if she was to remain here to watch over her children. 'I fell—' the tears rolled down her face. 'It was . . . an accident, just as you said.'

Beneath the drying blood, her jaw was already stiffening. It would be many a day before she dared look in the mirror.

Chapter Six

'We were so drunk, we lost our way and wandered into an argument on Bent Street.' Lizzie loved to relate stories of when she was young and silly. 'There were these three men . . . knocking hell and damnation out of each other they were,' she cackled, 'and I'd got this new fella, you see . . .' her old eyes rolled with bliss. 'By! He were a good-looking sort.'

Maureen could imagine it. 'You never married him though, did you?' She knew Lizzie had never married, and often wondered why.

'No, I never married him,' Lizzie chuckled, 'but it's not so surprising after what happened that night.' Gathering her wits she went on, 'As I were saying, there we were, strolling down Bent Street, when we suddenly come across these three fighting fellas. All of a sudden, one of 'em lands a fist on *my* poor fella's chin.'

'How awful!' Maureen could see it all in her mind's eye. 'What happened then?'

Laughing out loud, Lizzie went on, 'Well, what d'you think? He ups and throws himself right in the middle of it, and afore you know it, he's flinging punches with the rest of 'em. I'm standing there, innocent as you please, when suddenly out of nowhere I'm grabbed from the back and trussed up like a chicken ready for the oven!'

Putting her hands behind her back, she demonstrated how it was. 'In no time at all they were everywhere – whistles blowing and all five of us bundled into the cart and taken away.' She was laughing so much her sides ached. 'Three days in jail my bloke got,' she said. 'As for me, I got a good wagging from the sergeant. "You should know better," he said, "a nice young lady like yourself."'

'Sounds to me like you were enjoying it, you old divil.' Maureen never tired of hearing the old lady's tales. 'Was your young man hurt bad in the scuffle?'

'A black eye and busted nose, that's all.'

Maureen laughed. 'That's *all*! Sure it's enough to put a fella in the infirmary, so it is. And it wasn't even his fight, poor soul.'

'Aye, it were a pity an' all. I wouldn't mind, but I'd only known the poor fella a few days. We were just out for a walk, getting to know each other if you know what I mean, and it all finished up like that. Hey! It's a good job we weren't up to no hanky-panky when the scuffling started. But then again—' Rolling her eyes she gave a little 'Whoopee!'

'You're a bad 'un, that's what you are.' Bad and wonderful, Maureen thought.

Wiping the laughter from her eyes, Lizzie shook her head. 'I never saw him again after that. I reckon he blamed me.'

'But that's not fair! You came across three blokes fighting, one of them threw a fist and your fella punched him back. How could he blame you for that?'

The old woman's eyes twinkled. 'Ah, well now, it might have summat to do with the fact that the fella who threw the fist was my old sweetheart. He were jealous, you see, a nasty rowdy sort he turned out to be. That's why I got rid of him.'

'Sounds to me like you've had a colourful life,' Maureen laughed. 'If I'd been a young fella, I think I might have given you a wide berth.'

The two of them laughed and chatted until Lizzie glanced up at the mantelpiece clock. 'Look how the time flies!' she gasped. 'It's gone six. Your boy will be home soon.'

'Oh, there's time enough yet,' Maureen told her. 'James will be the last one out of that factory, as always. You know yourself it's sometimes eight o' clock and more when he gets home.' Though she suspected he spent a lot of his time hanging around outside the Mears' house looking for the girl.

'This might just be the night when he'll walk through the door when you least expect it.'

'Are you trying to get rid of me?' Maureen and Lizzie understood each other.

'Aye, go on,' Lizzie chuckled, 'bugger off and leave me to me memories.'

As always, Maureen gave her a little peck on the cheek before leaving. 'You've made me think,' she remarked sombrely.

Anxious, the old woman looked up. 'Why's that?'

'Well now . . . after what you've just told me,' she said wickedly, 'I'm wondering if it's safe to be seen on the streets with you.'

Lizzie laughed. 'Go on. Be off with you!'

Maureen put the stew on to simmer, then banked up the fire with newly sliced logs. When the logs began spitting and crackling and the room filled with a rosy glow, she gave herself a few minutes to enjoy it. With the old dog beside her, she felt truly content. Spreading her hands in front of the fire she let the heat permeate her skin. She was never happier than when here, in her lovely wee cottage.

Right from the first time she set eyes on it, Maureen had wanted to be no other place in the whole, wide world. When she had suggested leaving, it had been out of desperation, to get James away from the Mears family and all they stood for.

Try as she might to shut it from her mind, she sensed there was some kind of tragedy ahead. All she could do was pray that James did not get hurt.

Now her thoughts were interrupted by a noise outside, she wasn't sure what. Up on his haunches, Jake pricked his ears.

Going to the window she looked out. Already the day was melting to dusk. 'Hmh!' The old cottage was forever creaking and groaning. 'Ghosts in the woodwork, I shouldn't wonder,' she told the dog. 'I bet they've seen some goings-on over the years.'

She was poking the stew about when she heard it again, and this time she recognised it as someone tapping on the door; hair raised and yapping, the dog ran across the room, with Maureen in pursuit. 'Who the devil can that be?' She knew Lizzie's knock, and it wasn't her.

Cautiously she inched open the door, curious to see a slight, somewhat scruffy girl there. When the girl asked, 'Are you Maureen Peterson?' her curiosity was heightened.

'Yes, that's me.' Opening the door a little more she asked, 'How do you know my name?'

'I was told it.'

'*Who* told you it?'

'The man who helped me.'

'And what man was that?' Maureen was concerned that somebody had given her name to this girl and sent her here. 'What was his name?'

'I don't know his name, but he said I was to come here and you was to take care of me.'

Maureen's face opened with astonishment. 'Take care of you, eh?' Damned cheek! 'And what did he look like?' Wondering if this was all a hoax, she smiled and winked. 'Or have you conveniently forgotten *that* too?'

The girl lapsed into thoughtful silence. Presently, she answered, 'He was older than me . . . about twenty-four?'

'I should think that covers half the men in this country.'

The girl thought again. 'He had a kind face . . . handsome too.' The image of James was strong in her mind. 'He gave me money and told me to find somewhere to wash. Then I was to get something to eat, and find you . . . he said you were a good woman, and you would help me.'

Intrigued, Maureen observed the girl more closely. She was too thin by far and, by the look of her clothes, had travelled a long way. And, unless she was mistaken, there were specks of blood in the girl's hair and down her neck. 'I think you'd better come in.' Even if she didn't know who had sent her, Maureen decided it would be uncharitable to send her away, especially when the poor thing looked worn out.

Grateful, Sally followed her into the parlour.

The smell of food and the glow of that cosy fire sent Sally mixed feelings. She felt warm and content, while on the other hand she was reminded of the man who had raised her from an infant. Realising all she had lost, she burst into tears.

Maureen was quickly at her side. 'Hey! I'm sorry if I seemed unfriendly just now . . . I didn't mean to be.'

'No. It's *me* that's sorry.' Sniffing, she turned her soulful eyes to Maureen. 'It's just . . . I've been so disappointed.' With the back of her hands she wiped away the tears. 'I don't usually cry.' Except in private, when no one can see, she thought.

Leading her to the settee, Maureen assured her, 'It's all right to cry, you know. It's like laughing, only the other side of the coin.' She smiled. 'It's all a question of balance . . . it helps to keep the soul upright.'

'That's a strange thing to say.' And yet, it made sense.

Maureen laughed. 'That's because I'm a strange woman.'

'A good woman too . . . just like he said. Otherwise why would you let me in, when I'm a stranger on your doorstep?'

'Because some man who I still don't know gave you my

name.' Sitting down beside her, Maureen asked again, 'Tell me about him.'

'I was caught and he helped me escape. If it hadn't been for him, I would have been turned over to the authorities. Leonard Mears sent his son to fetch them, and the man I told you about, he was ordered to tie me up in the barn until they came for me. Instead, he gave me some money and let me go. He told me to make my way to Scab Lane and that you would take care of me.'

Beginning to realise, Maureen smiled. 'Was he tall and built strong? Did he have thick, untidy hair?'

'Yes, that's right!' Sally pictured him in her mind. 'And the most beautiful dark eyes.' He had the kind of face you didn't easily forget. 'He has a good heart too.' Apart from this woman here, the kindest heart she had met along the way.

'You're right.' Maureen was in no doubt that it was James. 'He does have a good heart.'

'Do you know who he is?'

'I have an idea.'

'If you see him, will you thank him for me?' Sally would have liked to see him again, but not if it meant taking any chances. 'I just ran . . . I wanted to get away before they came for me.'

'What did you do wrong?'

Sally shrugged her shoulders. 'Nothing. I was so tired. When the dog attacked me, I just ran and ran. The shed seemed a good place to hide.' Instinctively her hand went to the back of her head.

Maureen saw her wince. 'Is it bad?'

Sally denied it. 'It bled a bit, but it's all right now.' The cut to her head was nothing compared to what she had endured at the hands of Anne Hale.

'What happened then?'

'When Leonard Mears' son found me sleeping in the shed, he went mad. He called me a thief, but I swear to God I wasn't.

I was only resting there before moving on.' Pausing, she cast her gaze to the floor. 'I needed to get my strength back, because there was . . . someone I had to find.'

She looked so sad, Maureen didn't have the heart to question her further, except, 'What's your name, lass?'

'Sally.'

'Just Sally?'

When Sally gave no answer, she nodded. 'That's all right,' she told her, 'Sally will do just fine.'

Sally's gaze went to the stew pan.

'Are you hungry, lass?'

'A bit.'

'Right! Then we'd best feed you.'

Plucking at the clothes on Sally's back, she asked, 'Would you take offence if I offered you some of my clothes? They might hang on you a bit, but they'll be better than the rags you're wearing now.'

'I don't mind, thank you.'

'What would you like first – food or a bath?'

Sally's eyes went back to the stewpot.

'Right then, food it is.' She glanced at the girl's dirty hands. 'You might want to wash *them* though.' Gesturing with a nod she chuckled, 'You look as if you've crawled all the way here on them hands.'

Embarrassed, Sally hid her hands beneath her skirt.

'The sink's over there.' Pointing to the far side of the kitchen, Maureen told her, 'You'll find all you need in the cupboard underneath.'

She watched while Sally went to the sink. She's just a bairn, she mused. She wondered where the girl's parents might be, and why she was out on the road all on her own.

It took a few minutes to dish up the stew. Jake, too, sat wagging his tail and waiting for his share. 'Don't you go straight into that now,' Maureen put the bowl down on the floor, 'or it'll singe your tongue, so it will.' But the dog knew an old trick or two; whacking it with his paw, he turned the bowl on to its side, spilling the hot food across the cool flagstones. 'You crafty little devil!' Maureen laughed. 'What a mess. You make sure you lick up every last drop.'

While she went about slicing the bread, Maureen could feel Sally's eyes following her every move. 'There you are.' Fetching the plates of stew and bread, she set them down on the table. 'And if that doesn't fill the hole, there's plenty more in the pan.'

Waiting for James to come home before she had her own meal, Maureen sat nearby.

Attacking the stew with enthusiasm, Sally began to feel more human. 'I haven't had a proper meal for so long, I'd forgotten.' Dipping the bread in her stew she gobbled it down. 'I've been sleeping rough, you see.'

'Do you want to talk about it?'

Sally shook her head. 'I don't think so.' Yet she needed to talk to someone. She had no idea what to do next, or where to turn.

'The man who helped me . . . what name does he go by?' She couldn't get him out of her mind.

'James. And I'm Maureen.'

'Does he live near here?'

'Near enough.' She wasn't sure whether the girl would run if she knew James was on his way here. The presence of two people might be more than the nervous child could cope with.

'Why would he help me like that?'

'Because he hates to see anyone hurt, especially if it's Leonard Mears doing the hurting.'

'That Leonard Mears is a wicked man.' And he's my father, she thought bitterly; though no man could ever take the place of that gentle soul she had left in the Whitechapel churchyard.

Answering her comment, Maureen added, 'Leonard Mears

considers himself to be above the law. He's a very influential and dangerous man. Money speaks volumes, as you can imagine.'

'The man who helped me . . . James. He took a terrible risk.'

'He would.' Any opportunity to challenge Leonard Mears' authority, that was James all right.

'Maybe I'll be able to thank him properly.'

'I'm sure.' Sooner than she thought.

'Is it all right if I have some more stew?'

'You can have as much as you like.' Amazed that such a skinny girl could put away such an amount of food, Maureen dished up another helping.

Sally had almost finished mopping up the gravy with her last remaining chunk of bread, when the door swung open and there he stood. 'It's him!' Surprised and shocked by his sudden appearance, Sally looked up, the bread halfway to her mouth and the gravy dripping on her front.

Maureen explained. 'This is my son,' she said. 'When you mentioned Leonard Mears, I wondered . . . then you described the man and I knew it must be James.'

Struck silent, Sally continued to stare at him.

James seemed pleased to see her. 'You made it all right then.' Throwing off his work-bag, he suggested, 'I should eat that bread if I were you. You may not have noticed, but your blouse is swimming in gravy.'

Coming across to the fire he winked at his mother, who had been watching the situation with interest. 'Shame on you, Mam,' he chided, 'I should have thought you'd have taught her to eat properly if nothing else.'

'The lass has been telling me what happened.' While James went to wash, Maureen returned to the stove, where the stew was gently simmering. 'I'll lend her some of my clothes 'til we can find some that fit her proper.'

Stripped to the waist, James listened but said nothing. Instead he concentrated on washing the day's sweat from his body. Reaching out he wiped himself dry, before putting on the clean shirt already laid out over the chair. 'What in God's name were you doing in that shed?' Slipping the shirt over his head he quickly buttoned it up. 'Do you realise he could have had you locked away for life?'

Embarrassed by his bared muscles and by the way he studied her through those intense dark eyes, Sally looked away. 'I didn't know.'

'Well, you know now.' Running his fingers through his hair, James came to the table. 'There are any number of sheds and outhouses along that wharf, and you had to kip down in one belonging to *him*.'

'Leave the lass alone.' Serving his meal, Maureen gave him a warning glance. 'She's been through enough for one day.'

'Aye, well—' Glancing at her, James could see that in spite of the meal she'd had and the warmth of the fire on her face, the girl still looked pale and undernourished. 'She's had a lucky escape, that's all I'm saying.'

Except for the smacking of lips, clatter of cutlery and the occasional slurping of gravy, there followed a long, awkward span of silence. During which Maureen looked at James; James looked at Sally; and Sally fussed over Jake.

The dog had taken to her like he took to no other outside this family. James thought it a pleasant sight to see the girl on her knees and the dog licking her with affection. Jake was his, and James knew how normally he was wary of strangers.

Having finished his meal, James settled back in the chair. 'Thanks, Mam, I really enjoyed that.' The loving wink he gave her was reward enough for Maureen.

Clearing away the dishes, she discreetly glanced behind her, a smile enveloping her features when she saw how James was still looking at the girl. She knew how much he loved that dog, and the fact that the dog had found a friend in the girl was in her favour.

'What's your name then?' James went to the fireplace where he stood with his back to it. 'You have *got* a name, have you?'

She looked up, made nervous by his closeness. 'Sally.'

'Sally *what*?'

There was a long pause when it seemed she might not answer him. 'Sally Hale.'

He sensed the fear in her, and it made him gentle. 'Well, Sally Hale, what brings you to these parts?'

'I don't want to talk about it.'

Nodding, he agreed, 'Then you don't have to.'

During the conversation, Jake had lain very still, his tail happily wagging and his old eyes upturned towards her. Suddenly he playfully pounced and knocked her over. 'Hey, you big lump!' James pulled him off. 'She's not strong enough to play rough like that.'

Laughing, Sally ruffled the dog's coat. 'It's all right,' she said, fondling him. 'You didn't mean to hurt me, did you, not like the other dog?'

Maureen helped her up. 'Is that how you gashed the back of your head?'

'He chased me and I fell, hit my head on the ground.'

'Hmh!' Holding Sally by the shoulder, Maureen stole a glance at the gash on the back of her head. 'That wants washing clean before it becomes infected,' she told her. 'I'd best run you a bath. You can stay the night here.'

'I can't do that. I have to move on.'

Maureen played along. 'Oh? And where are you headed?'

'I have plans.' The truth was, she had no plans now she'd seen what sort of a man her father was, and nowhere to go, but she couldn't put on these good people. They had done more than enough.

'Look, child, I've got a spare bed, and you're welcome to it. I'd feel better if you got a good night's sleep, then tomorrow you can decide what to do.'

'All right. Just for tonight though.' *Then* what would she do? The road ahead seemed long and lonely, especially when she didn't yet know where it would lead.

While they talked, James listened. Now he asked the girl, 'How long have you been travelling?'

When Sally looked away, seeming afraid or unwilling to answer, Maureen came to her rescue. 'James, fetch the bath in from outside, will you?'

Without question, James went out to the backyard. A moment later he returned carrying a long tin bath. 'Where do you want it?'

Turning back the hearthrug, Maureen gestured to the space before the fire. 'Same as always,' she answered. 'Just here.'

'You two get to know each other properly,' Maureen told Sally. 'I need to get you a nightgown and a clean towel.' She liked the girl, and hoped she might stay with them awhile.

Upstairs, Maureen rummaged through her drawers for the smallest nightgown, while down in the kitchen James watched as Sally tried to clean the gravy stain from her blouse.

Conscious of his attention, she kept her back to him, dabbing at the stain with the wet dishcloth and intermittently squeezing it out in the sink. 'Thank you for what you did,' she said. 'I'll be moving on in the morning and, as soon as I find work, I'll pay the money back.'

'Where will you go?' Standing there she looked so small and slight. She had a wide, frightened look in her eyes that made him suspect she had been through bad times.

Sally shrugged. 'Wherever the work is, that's where I'll go.'

'There's work here,' Maureen said, reappearing. 'If you want to stay?'

James laughed. 'I should watch her,' he told Sally, 'or she

and Lizzie will have you signed up before you know what's happening.'

Sally was intrigued. 'Who's Lizzie?'

'Never mind that.' Dragging the bath nearer the fire, Maureen gave James a stern look. 'She could do worse than work with me and Lizzie!'

'Sorry!' Putting up his hands in surrender, James betrayed the tiniest smile, which in turn made Maureen smile and Sally think what lovely people they were, and how she wished she'd had a mother like Maureen.

When the bath was filled and ready, Maureen dipped her elbow in to test the water. 'Just right!' Bringing the towel and carbolic soap, she arranged a chair nearby and spread the towel over the chairback. Drawing it closer to the fire, she explained, 'That'll keep it nice and warm to wrap yourself in afterwards.'

Next, she gave James his instructions. 'Right! You've done your bit,' she rolled up her sleeves, 'you're in the way now, so be off with you.'

'Well, that's gratitude for you,' he told the old dog at his feet. 'Come on, old fella. We don't want to stay where we're not wanted.' Putting on his jacket, he slipped the lead round Jake's neck and led him to the door; with a backward wink at Sally, he went out the door and softly closed it.

'You'll hear him whistling in a minute,' Maureen said. 'Listen for the dog too.'

Sure enough the sound of plaintive whistling filtered back to them. Suddenly there was a second sound – like a train whistle through a faraway tunnel. 'That's Jake,' Maureen laughed. 'He hasn't got it right just yet, but he's getting there.'

Sally couldn't believe it. 'I've never heard anything like that!' She burst out laughing as she hadn't laughed in an age. It felt good. This house and these people felt good. And she didn't want to leave.

'Right then. Get out of them baggy clothes and into the bath with you.' When Sally hesitated, Maureen offered, 'I'll leave you to it, shall I?' Smiling, she apologised, 'I'm treating you like a bairn. I'm sorry.' Beginning to roll down her sleeves, she turned away.

Sally pleaded, 'I've never known anyone so kind . . .' Thinking back, her eyes clouded over. 'Please stay.'

'If you're sure?'

'If you don't mind washing my back? I'd really appreciate that.' She had bad memories of having her back washed. Anne Hale's idea was to take the scrubbing brush and almost skin her alive.

Maureen was delighted to be of use. 'Course I'll wash your back, child,' she replied, rolling up her sleeves again.

Slipping her grubby clothes off, Sally lowered herself into the bath, sighing contentedly when the warm water lapped over her. Maureen noticed the scars on her pale body but decided it was too soon to ask the child what had happened to her.

'How old is James?' asked Sally.

'He's twenty-two, but with an older sense of responsibility. Circumstances forced him to grow up too quick, I think.' Maureen glowed with pride. 'Since his father died, he's been the mainstay of my life. I dread the day when he gets married and moves out.'

There followed a moment of quiet, when each was engrossed in her own thoughts. Presently, Sally asked, 'Has he got a sweetheart?'

'He fancies he has.'

'What does that mean?' Disappointment coursed through her.

'It means he's hankering after something that will never be his, especially not if Leonard Mears has his way.'

'What does Leonard Mears have to do with it?' Just the mention of his name made her shiver.

'It's *his* daughter James intends to wed. Her name is Isabel, a lovely girl by all accounts. But it could never work. They come of different stock, you see. Leonard Mears has more money than folks like us could ever set eyes on in a whole lifetime. They live in a big house with servants at their beck and call. They have their clothes tailor-made, and eat from china plates. Oh, there's nothing wrong with that,' she chuckled. 'I wouldn't mind a bit of it myself.'

She waved her hand to encompass the room. 'But that's them, and this is us. Tin baths in front of the fire and a pot of stew on the table. It's all we've ever known. It's all *James* has ever known. How can he keep her in the way she's been raised? He can't, it's that simple! That's why I say it would never work. But can *he* see that? No, he can't! *Now* he tells me he means to play Mears at his own game, to topple him from his pedestal and build an empire from the ashes.'

Filled with admiration, Sally asked, 'Could James do that?'

'Hmh!' Maureen knew her son when he set his mind on anything, and it did not make her easy. 'When he was small and said he would do a thing, he always did it. *That's* what worries me.'

Remembering how it was when Leonard Mears caught hold of her, Sally had strong thoughts on the matter. 'If you ask me, *somebody* should bring him down.'

'Oh, I couldn't agree more!' Having worked herself into a sweat, Maureen leaned back on her haunches. 'God knows what it will all come to,' she sighed. 'I daren't think.'

Sally's thoughts had gone back to the earlier conversation. 'Does Leonard Mears know? About his daughter and James?'

'Good God no!' Sitting bolt upright, Maureen frantically slapped the soap over Sally's shoulders. 'Though I don't suppose it would worry James too much . . . except he's always afraid Isabel would be punished.' Lowering her voice she revealed, 'He locks them in the watch-tower of his house.'

Sally swung round. 'Who?'

'Leonard Mears. He has two sons and two daughters. Isabel is the elder daughter and the most rebellious child. If any of them defy him, he locks them in the watch-tower, sometimes for days on end, or so I'm told.'

Shocked, Sally was put in mind of Anne Hale, and she hated Leonard Mears all the more. Then it struck her. Of course! They were brother and sister – 'My brother's bastard!' That's what Anne Hale had told her, and now it all made sense. They were two peas out of the same pod. 'Is he mad?'

'Mad?' Maureen thought hard about that. 'I don't know about that, but I do know he keeps a prison for a house. According to the butcher, who delivers there twice a week and has a fancy for one of the maids, the family are asked to account for their every move, day and night. He rules them with a rod of iron.' Unaware that she was actually talking to another of Leonard Mears' daughters, Maureen went on, 'They're not allowed to enter the dining room unless he goes first; he approves the food they eat and the clothes they wear, and sometimes at night his wife's crying can be heard all over the house. It's a terrible shame. She's a tiny, harmless little thing. Nice to everyone, that's what I'm told.'

'He sounds like a monster.' Perhaps even more of a monster than his sister, for she had to raise his child when she didn't want to. No wonder she grew to hate me, Sally thought.

Maureen nodded. 'That's what he is all right. A spiteful, wicked monster.' Taking a jug, she dipped it into the water and poured it gently over Sally's head. 'Is that all right, lass?'

'It feels lovely.' Throwing her head back, she let Maureen swill her hair with another soapy jugful of water. 'It's the first time I've had soap on my hair in a long time.'

The bath was just what she needed. With Maureen rubbing her back with carbolic soap and the warm water splashing over her every part, it felt like bliss. 'I did wash in the brooks,' she told Maureen, 'but I'm always nervous in deep water. I never learned to swim, you see.'

Maureen saw her chance to find out more about this quiet stranger. 'Did you live in a town?'

'Yes. Whitechapel. It's a part of London.'

'There you are then. Townfolks don't bother too much about learning how to swim. They don't have reason to, you see, while here so near the countryside it's second nature. James could swim almost as soon as he could walk. His daddy taught him young. He'd take him down the valley; there's a little hollow where the brook forks away, and this little pool of shallow water. That's where James learned to swim, and oh, it were a wonderful sight, seeing him ducking and diving, and so small you could fit him in your pocket.'

While she reminisced, all the good memories flooded over her, bringing tears to her eyes. 'It seems so long ago now.' Before her husband changed, she thought sadly, before he began to see James as a rival for her affection.

'But there you are!' Taking a deep breath she chased the shadows away. 'I'm going on a bit, and you can't be interested in all that.'

Sally felt her distress and said nothing.

A moment passed before Maureen spoke again. 'How come a young lass like you is wandering about on her own?'

'I'm not so young.' With James in her mind, it was suddenly important to be more woman than child. 'I'll be sixteen soon,' she lied.

'Sixteen, eh?' Maureen smiled. 'Well, I never.'

'I can take care of myself.'

'I don't doubt it for a minute.' After all, she had been on the road for some time by the looks of her. 'But don't you have parents to worry about you?'

Feeling relaxed and safe, Sally told her just a little of the truth. 'My father died,' she said.

'What about your mother?'

Bitterness marbled her voice. 'I haven't got a mother.'

Realising she might have gone one question too far, Maureen washed the lather from her hands. 'I'll fill the jug with clean water to rinse your hair,' she said. 'That should do it.'

Taking the pitcher from the shelf, she filled it with warm water from the kettle; having rested on the trivet for some time, the water had cooled and was now just the right temperature. Returning with it to Sally, she rinsed the soap from her long hair. 'You've got pretty hair,' she observed, 'though it could do with tidying up.' Taking a strand in her fingers, she noted how the ends were split and torn. 'It's time somebody looked after you proper, my girl!'

When the rinsing was done and the water ran clearer, she handed her a towel. 'While you're drying, I'll go and get the spare bed made up.'

Taking one of the lamps, she left Sally in the glow from the fire. The halo of light from the smaller lamp on the table was sufficient on its own. 'I'll not be long,' she promised.

It only took a minute or two; the sheets and blankets were already aired and ready to lay over the mattress. She lit the lamp on the dressing table and checked everything was laid out. There was a silver-backed hairbrush left her by her late mammy; a small round mirror to match – although the dressing table had a big oval mirror of its own. And, laid next to the lamp, a length of blue ribbon she took from the drawer. 'The lass should have pretty things,' she murmured. The ribbon had been her own, but she didn't have much call for that kind of thing these days. One of her prettier nightgowns, blue, with pearl buttons and lace hem, was laid over the back of the chair. 'There! All nice and dandy.'

When she came back downstairs, Sally was dried and wrapped

in the towel. 'It's all there,' Maureen told her, 'in the back bedroom, everything you need.' She glanced at the clock on the mantelpiece. 'It's going on nine,' she said. 'You get yourself into bed. A good night's sleep will put the roses back in your cheeks.' She worried about how pale and thin the girl was. 'If there's owt else you want, you've only to shout out.'

Sally hesitated. 'I can help you to empty the bath and what about the dishes, I can wash them up if you like?'

'Away with you!' Maureen would never allow a guest to help with the clearing away. 'I'll have it done in no time. Besides, I won't be going to bed for a while yet.'

'Oh.' Sally hadn't wanted to go to bed either. She had hoped to stay down until James came back. 'Good-night then.'

'Good-night, God bless.' Going to the far side of the kitchen, Maureen collected a big tin bucket. 'Don't forget now, if you want anything, you only have to ask. Oh, and you'll find a jeremiah under the bed.' Dipping the bucket into the bath, she scooped out a measure of water.

When she looked up again, Sally had gone. 'Poor little beggar,' she mumbled. 'What's going to become of her, I wonder?' If she had her way, Sally would stay here, at least until she had a proper direction. 'But then, I can't tell the lass what to do. She's not *my* lass, or she would never have been wandering the streets in the first place.'

Maureen wondered why Sally had run away. I expect she'll tell me in her own good time, she thought. But then, if she really meant to move on tomorrow, there wouldn't be any time. Maureen hoped Sally might change her mind about that.

Upstairs, Sally was led by the lamplight emanating from the back bedroom. Going inside she found the things Maureen had laid out on the dressing table, and for a moment she just sat there, looking at herself in the mirror and thinking how fortunate she had been to find her way here. If I hadn't stumbled on that factory, I might have gone to Leonard Mears' house and knocked on his door, bold as you like, she thought. She gave a little dry laugh. He would have set the dogs on me for sure, a ragamuffin arriving on his doorstep and claiming to be his daughter.

The more she thought about it, the more she understood there was a certain humour in the tragedy. As realisation dawned she thanked her lucky stars that James had intervened. If it hadn't been for James, I daren't think how I would have ended up . . . not here, that's for sure, she thought.

She looked around the little room, with its homely touches and warm, welcoming atmosphere. 'I've been lucky,' she mused aloud. 'But what next? Where do I go from here?' On her own again, trudging the streets was a frightening prospect.

Spying the nightgown, she plucked it from the back of the chair and brushed it against her face. 'I bet she made this herself.' Looking at the pretty thing, she could imagine Maureen sewing the lace hem to the skirt. 'I wonder if I'll ever be able to sew like that.' She had not been taught these things. Sally regretted that.

Dropping the towel to the floor, she slipped the nightgown over her head. It felt soft and cool. Going to the mirror, she observed the image there. 'You have to be strong now,' she told herself. 'You have to make a new life, find work first, then a roof over your head. It won't be so bad, you'll see.'

Taking up the brush, she admired it for a moment or two, before running it through her tangled hair. As she did so, the dampness formed tiny droplets of water that trickled down her back. Pausing, she looked at herself in the mirror. 'What's going to happen to you, Sally?' she asked quietly. Something in that soulful question made her realise how alone she really was and, despite her determination that she must not let loose her emotions, she found herself shedding bitter tears.

As she cried, the hurt began to ease and with it came a sense of purpose. 'Shame on you, Sally.' Wiping her eyes, she straightened her shoulders and put on a brave face.

'You'll be sixteen this year,' she reminded herself proudly. 'You can do what you like, and go where you please.' The emptiness of that remark made her laugh. 'We'll see.' She sighed deep and long. 'We'll see what the morning brings.'

Outside, Maureen poured the last of the bathwater down the drain. Now for the dishes, then a cup of tea with me feet up in front of the fire, she thought. Leaving the bucket against the wall, she made her way back inside, and was astonished to see Sally standing there, hair tousled and the brush still in her hand. 'Woa! You gave me a fright,' she gasped. 'I thought you'd be fast asleep by now.' On looking at Sally she could see the wet trail left by her tears, though she made no comment on it.

'Is it all right if I stay down with you for a while?'

Maureen smiled at that. 'O' course it's all right,' she answered warmly, secretly thinking: coming up sixteen, you may be, but when you're alone and afraid, what does that matter?

Taking her by the arm, Maureen chatted on. 'Couldn't you sleep, lass?' she asked kindly and, without waiting for an answer, ushered her over to the fireplace. 'You sit yourself there, and I'll make us a brew of tea, and happen a biscuit. What do you think to that?'

Hoping not to offend, Sally gratefully declined. What she needed was someone to confide in. Up in the bedroom she had been so sure she could talk to Maureen. Now, looking her in the face, her courage seemed to slip away.

Sensing her distress, Maureen stroked a comforting hand down Sally's hair. 'Hey, lass, if there's summat playing on your mind, you can allus talk to me. I'll not repeat anything you tell me. I would never do that.'

When Sally was too choked to answer, Maureen gently took

the brush from her hand. 'I'll brush your hair, shall I?' she suggested. 'If you sleep on it like that, it'll be such a mess in the morning you won't get the brush through it at all.'

Before starting, she reached up to the mantelpiece and, taking down the small mirror, placed it on the chair-arm. 'There! You can see what I'm doing,' she said, 'and if I put your parting in the wrong place, you be quick and tell me now.'

Those few precious moments were something Sally would remember all her life.

Sitting there, with Maureen brushing her hair and the warmth from the fire making her sleepy. Sally began to realise just what she had been missing. A father's love was wonderful, but there was also something very special about a mother's love, especially when you were blossoming from child to woman.

When a girl had a mother to talk with, they shared all manner of things that a girl would never bring herself to discuss with her father: dreams and fancies, matters of the heart, and how her life might change when married. Then there were the matter-of-fact things like dresses and hats, and how did she look with her hair done up in a particular way. These were the things a woman knew about, and a girl needed to know.

Through the mirror, Sally quietly regarded the woman. With her long red hair and smiling green eyes Maureen made a handsome sight. Sally deduced that if James was twenty-two, she could be aged somewhere near forty, maybe a little older, but not much. Sally thought she must have been very beautiful when young.

Glancing in the mirror, Maureen saw her looking and was momentarily embarrassed. 'Hey! I hope you're not comparing faces,' she laughed. 'Yours is smooth and pretty, while I've a face that's long past its best.' Taking a look at herself in the mirror, she sighed, 'That's what you get for trudging about in all weathers, your poor old skin comes to look like the bark of a tree.'

'I think you're very pretty.'

'Used to be . . . a long time ago.'

'Did you have lots of sweethearts?'

Maureen giggled like a girl. 'A few.'

'What's it like to have a sweetheart?'

Taking her time to answer, Maureen stared into the flames, the merest of smiles on her face. 'It's so long ago now . . . so many memories.' They still lived on in her heart, still gave her pleasure on a cold night. 'There were only two boys in particular,' she confessed. 'One was James's dad, the other a lad who worked in a travelling circus.'

Her quiet smile erupted in a burst of laughter. 'My daddy found out about that one and gave me a hiding I'll never forget. It came as a shock because he had never once laid a hand on me until that night, and never once after. He was a good father to me.'

Sally was almost tempted to tell her about those two men who were father to her – the one who raised her and the one she had met only that day, but she wasn't quite ready yet.

'My mammy was a quiet, lovely soul,' Maureen went on. 'I was fortunate in having good parents.' She hoped talking about her own background might draw Sally into conversation, but it didn't. So she went on brushing her hair, and neither spoke for a time.

A moment later she was finished. 'You've got such pretty hair,' she said, laying the brush on the arm of the chair. 'So soft and silky.' She smoothed her hand down the length of Sally's long, brown hair. 'In the firelight it shines gold, did you know that?'

'My daddy used to say that,' she revealed unexpectedly, and much to Maureen's delight. 'When I was little, *he* used to brush my hair.'

'Not your mammy then?' When Sally shook her head and fell

silent, she knew it had been the wrong thing to say. 'Sally?' she began after a pause.

Sally looked up.

'Sometimes there are things we'd rather not talk about,' Maureen said softly. 'Things that are too painful even to consider. When that happens to me, I have a good friend in Lizzie next door. She will let me tell her things I could never tell anybody else, and when she listens it doesn't seem so bad after all. Do you know what I'm saying, child? I can be that kind of a friend to *you*. I would like to feel that you could confide in me, so your troubles won't seem so terrible.' Her voice fell almost to a whisper. 'Right now, your troubles do seem terrible to you, don't they, child?'

Something in the gentleness of her voice, or in the softness of her kind eyes, touched Sally's heart so deeply that she could hardly speak. 'I . . . want . . . to tell you everything.'

It was what Maureen had been hoping for. 'And I want to help, if I can. Come on, cuddle up, child, and we'll talk, you and me, eh? If there's summat playing on your mind, it's allus better out than in.'

Knowing that here was someone she could really trust, Sally turned to her.

James always enjoyed his evening walk in the quiet lane behind the canal. In the cool of the evening, with the day's hard grind behind him, he felt a deeper sense of peace somehow.

For the umpteenth time he threw the stick far into the undergrowth. 'Fetch it, boy!' With head high and tail wagging, Jake took off in a leap.

Softly laughing, James followed. 'Don't lose sight of me now, you old bugger,' he called, and, as he burst through the bushes, there stood the dog, proud as punch, with the stick gripped tight between his teeth.

'I reckon it's time we made our way home.' Retrieving the stick, James prepared to throw it in the opposite direction. 'I dare say the women's work is done by now.' A wave of embarrassment washed over him. 'We've never had a young lady in the cottage afore,' he mused. 'Especially not one like her.' There was something about Sally that made him wonder. 'She has a look of . . . someone . . .' He had thought that from the first moment he saw her. 'She has a certain look in her eye . . . and the way she holds her head.' He began to think he was imagining it. 'Who knows? The mind plays funny tricks.'

Just then, the dog returned, dropping the stick at James's feet. He waited excitedly for it to be thrown again. Instead, James tucked the stick firmly in his pocket. Looking down at the old dog, who was panting hard, his tongue hanging out over his jaw, James told him sternly, 'I reckon that's enough running around for now. You're not so young as you used to be, you silly old fool.'

They walked back by way of the canal. 'Look there!' Pointing to the dark silhouette of a barge on its way into Blackburn, James thought how beautiful it looked. With its engines softly purring, it glided effortlessly through the night. 'Like a shadow on the water.'

Lingering for a while, he leaned against the broad trunk of a tree, head back and eyes closed when, for a few precious minutes, he let the world pass by, while he planned his future with Isabel. He would stay close to her; bide his time and learn the business inside out. Then he would build his empire, and keep her in the manner to which she had become accustomed. It all seemed simple, but he was no fool, and he suffered no illusions. The road that lay before him would be long and hard, and he would know many a setback before he earned contentment. Yet he was not deterred. Instead, he was stirred with excitement, impatient to take that first, unknown step.

Bemused, the dog sat on his haunches beside him, his faithful old eyes turned up to his master. As long as James was near, Jake was content. After a time, James looked down. 'Getting cold are you, old fella?' he asked. When the dog nudged up to him, he reached down to stroke his neck. 'You don't know how fortunate you are,' he told him. 'You live each day as it comes; you're fed and watered and taken out for a run, and you never need worry about the opposite sex—' He grinned. 'Though I've seen you giving that filly greyhound the glad eye afore now.'

Seeming to know what he was saying, the old dog looked away, his eyes searching the canal bank. James laughed. 'Seems like I've got it all wrong,' he said. 'Happen you *do* have a little heartache now and then, eh?' Tapping the dog on the shoulder, he urged, 'Come on then, old fella . . . let's see what's going on back at the cottage.'

As they wended their way back, James thought of Isabel. Day or night, she was never far from his mind. Since a boy he had known there would never be any other woman for him, and, as he grew, so his love grew, until now it lived and breathed inside him like the beating of his own heart. The possibility that she may never be his was like a numbing ache deep down in the pit of his stomach.

Once inside the cottage kitchen, James took off his boots and strung them by the laces over the backdoor nail; his coat was hung on the nail beside it. 'By! It's lovely and warm in here, after the chill outside.'

With the dog following, he went through the kitchen and into the parlour. 'Ssh!' Maureen put her fingers to her lips. 'Don't wake the lass, she's worn out.'

James's gaze went to Sally. Cradled in Maureen's arms, she was fast asleep. A sense of astonishment rippled through him; anger too. 'Why isn't she in her bed?' There was a sharpness in his voice that startled even him. It was an odd thing, but whenever he looked on this girl, she seemed to touch his heart in the strangest way. It had been like that back at the factory, even after he had sent her to his home. She had played on his mind, and now that she was here, he felt uncomfortable, threatened even, and he couldn't understand why.

'Don't make her too welcome,' he warned his mother, 'or she'll *never* want to leave.'

'Huh!' Maureen gave him a cursory glance. 'I thought you liked the lass?'

'Mebbe I do, mebbe I don't.' The truth was, he couldn't tell *what* he felt.

'You've come back in a bad mood, so you have!' Not for the first time, Maureen noticed how he seemed agitated when in Sally's presence. 'What's wrong with yer?'

'Don't know what you mean.' He did though.

Brushing over his remark, Maureen gazed down on Sally's quiet face. 'We were talking, and she fell asleep,' she explained, 'just like you used to do when you were a little lad.'

'What were you talking about?'

Seeming not to have heard, or choosing not to answer, Maureen asked softly, 'Do you think you could carry the lass upstairs without waking her?'

'I think I could manage that.'

Taking Sally gently in his arms, James followed his mother across the room. 'Let's hope she sleeps on 'til morning,' Maureen whispered. Opening the door for him, she held the lamp high. 'She's such a wee little thing, so she is.'

Guided by the lamplight at the foot of the stairs, and beckoned by the light emitting from the back bedroom, James made his way upstairs. Inside the bedroom, he laid her gently on the bed. Easing her legs beneath the covers, he drew the bedclothes up to her chin.

Twice he went to turn away, and each time he was drawn back

to gaze down on her sleeping face. 'What is it about you?' he murmured. 'Is it because I got one over on Leonard Mears . . . snatching you from him like that?' He smiled. 'It felt good, that's for sure.'

His gaze roved her lovely face: the small, straight nose and full, plump lips; her long, soft brown hair and that wonderful look of innocence. When he carried her upstairs just now, so small and helpless, he had felt protective of her, just as he had felt when he saw her for that first time. 'You *look* harmless,' he whispered, 'but you'll be trouble. I just know it.'

Gazing on her now, his feelings were in turmoil. Abruptly, he snatched up the lamp and hurried to the door. He turned and looked again, saying in the smallest whisper, 'I'll be glad when you're gone from here.' Though, as soon as the words left his lips, he regretted them.

Downstairs, Maureen had made two mugs of tea, and into each she had poured the smallest measure of whisky. 'Sit yerself down,' she said. Handing him the mug, she sat herself opposite. 'You didn't wake her up, did you?'

'No, I didn't wake her.' Again, that sense of irritability. 'She's sleeping like a bairn.' Stretching his legs before the fire, he settled down, his voice kinder as he murmured, 'When all's said and done, that's all she is . . . just a bairn.' He took a sip of his tea. Surprised by the tingle of whisky in his throat he gave a wry little smile. 'Funny tasting tea.'

Maureen confirmed his suspicions with a wink. 'Whisky,' she laughed. 'Just a drop to keep out the cold.'

It was always pleasant, the two of them resting beside the fire in that cosy parlour, with the contentment that comes from knowing each other well enough just to sit and be quiet, or confide the things closest to their hearts. They were more than mother and son; they were best friends, and that was a very special thing.

It was Maureen who spoke first. 'There's more to the lass than you think.'

'Oh?' Somehow James wasn't too surprised.

Maureen went on, 'She didn't ask me not to tell you, she just said she didn't want *him* to know.'

James sat up in the chair. '*Him?*' The way she said it made him think of Leonard Mears. 'Meaning who, as if I need ask?'

Maureen nodded. The best way to say it was straight out, so that's what she did. 'According to Sally, it seems Leonard Mears is her *father*.'

'What!' Shocked to his soul, James sprang out of his chair. 'Did she tell you that?'

'Aye, she did, and a lot more besides.' Leaning back in her chair, Maureen went on. 'Like you, I found it hard to believe at first. But I've had time to think on it, and I can see how the lass might be telling the truth. The man's a bastard, we all know that, and so why shouldn't he be enough of a bastard to father children outside his marriage?'

'Well, I have to admit, nothing he does would surprise me, but I don't understand. What was she doing roaming the streets, and why didn't she say anything when she came face to face with him?' Recalling the scene when those two met, he seemed to remember Mears seemed genuinely not to know her.

'Because he doesn't know her.'

Returning to his seat, James positioned himself so that he was looking his mother in the face. 'Tell me what she said,' he instructed softly. 'Every word, mind, don't leave anything out.' Wherever Leonard Mears was involved, he needed to know every small, incriminating detail.

Maureen told him everything. She explained how Sally had been fathered out of wedlock, and how Leonard Mears then paid his sister and her husband to take the child off his hands. 'But no amount of money could make his sister want the child,' she said.

'If it hadn't been for the kindly man who loved her like his own, Sally's life would have been a misery.'

'Then how come he let her go off on her own, wandering the streets like some vagabond?'

'Because he wasn't able to stop her, that's why.'

'And why not?'

Maureen explained how, after he died, Sally was left all alone. 'At the mercy of that wicked creature!' She told James what Sally had told her, how the lass was taunted about her beginnings, then beaten within an inch of her life. 'If it hadn't been for the neighbours, the poor lass would never have survived.'

While Maureen related the story, James sat with clenched fists and murder in his heart, and when she was done he was very still, very quiet, letting the full horror of it sink in.

After a while, he looked up. 'Why didn't one of these kindly neighbours take her in, I wonder?'

'I dare say they would have but she was so bent on finding her true father, she left to come north straight from the hospital. With his name and part of an address on that charred paper, she could only think to find him.'

'Aye, well, she found him right enough, and the bastard would have had her thrown in jail if I hadn't outwitted him.'

'But you see how it is, son?' Wanting a favour but half-afraid to ask, Maureen appealed to his sense of decency. 'You can understand how the lass must feel?'

James shook his head. 'To tell you the truth, Mam, I can't *begin* to understand.' Having been raised in love, he could only imagine what it must be like to be hated from birth, and then to find yourself alone and homeless when so young. 'I'll tell you this though, her coming here is bound to cause all manner of trouble.'

'In what way?'

'Think about it, Mam. Leonard Mears is a wealthy man. He's

also a very influential force hereabouts. If, as she claims, he is her real father, and he's treated her no better than he would a thief, she might take it into her head to fight him head on. What she knows about him is worth money. One whiff of this kind of scandal and his reputation is bound to take a turn for the worse.'

Maureen was adamant. 'She would never do such a thing. I've learned a lot about the lass tonight, and I can tell you this, it isn't in her to resort to blackmail.'

'I'm not saying she would, and neither of us could ever condone that, but there are other things to be considered.' His mind was working feverishly. 'If that girl upstairs *is* Leonard Mears' legal daughter, then surely she's entitled to the same considerations as his other children. Farming her out to his sister when she was a child can't change the facts.'

'You're right!' Maureen hadn't realised. 'And there's proof should it ever be needed.'

'You mean the agreement made between Leonard Mears and his sister?'

'Sally still has part of that letter, in Leonard Mears' own handwriting.'

'By!' James shook his head. 'If ever he finds out who she is, her life won't be worth a tuppenny piece.'

'Then he mustn't find out.'

'That's not for us to say, Mam.'

'Do you think she means to tell him?'

'Who knows what she's thinking?' He imagined she was a strong-minded little thing, or she would never have got this far. 'I'll talk to her in the morning, see what she has in mind.'

'James? I want her to stay.'

'I thought you might.'

'I'd like to see her get stronger. She's been through too much already, and now she's discovered what a monster her father is, God only knows where she'll turn next.'

'What does *she* say, about staying, I mean?'

'I think she would stay if *you* asked her.'

'Why me?' James was already beginning to regret having sent the girl here. 'Why can't *you* ask her?'

'I have, and she said no.'

'Then surely that's an end to it?' Though, in spite of his anxieties, he *was* concerned about Sally's welfare.

'It doesn't have to be.'

'Now you're talking in riddles.'

'She's taken to you, James, but for some reason she's got it into her head that you don't want her here.'

Embarrassed, James gave a soft laugh. 'What! Has she forgotten it were *me* who sent her here in the first place, after saving her from being taken by the authorities, I might add?'

'Then you *do* want her here?'

Agitated, he got up from his chair and began pacing the floor. 'It makes not the slightest difference to me whether she goes or stays.'

Funny, he thought, she's only been here a matter of hours, but already she seems to have made her mark. If she went now, the house wouldn't be the same without her, though whether that was for better or worse remained to be seen, he thought drily.

'Will you ask her to stay, son? For a while at least?'

'All right, Mam.' She was just a girl after all. 'If that's what you want.'

'It is.' Rising from her chair, Maureen told him, 'I like the lass, and I'd hate to see her take to the road again.'

'I'll get her to stay,' he promised. 'Don't fret yourself.'

Maureen smiled. 'After what she's been through, you'd think she'd be hard and bitter, but she isn't at all like that. She's got a lovely nature, and oh, she's such a helpful little soul.' Gesturing to the sideboard, she explained. 'She helped me wash the dinner things and put them away, and then we sat and talked some more. It's nice having a lass in the house.'

James gave her a fond look. 'Try not to get too involved, Mam,' he warned. 'A girl like that, she could be here today and gone tomorrow.' He could see his mother had already taken Sally under her wing, and he didn't want her hurt.

'She won't be gone tomorrow if I can help it.' In fact, Maureen was secretly hoping Sally might take his mind off the girl up at the big house. Then she remembered with a little shock – Sally was Leonard Mears' daughter too.

That night James couldn't sleep. Instead he stood looking out the window at the dark skies for what seemed an age. 'Leonard Mears' daughter!' He could hardly believe it. Like his mother, he wondered what the outcome of it all would be.

He thought it strange that Sally should turn up just now, the illicit daughter of his sworn enemy, and a real threat to the fabric of that family. He knew now why her features disturbed him. She had the look of Isabel, in the eyes and the way she turned her head. But then it wasn't so surprising, when Isabel was her half-sister.

Rising in the back of his mind was the idea that Sally's pretty blue eyes were softer than Isabel's, more giving somehow. Irritated with himself, he thrust the idea away. He needed to talk to Sally. He needed to hear her story at first hand. If what she said was true, then he had to warn her, guide her in the right direction, for he suspected she had no friends other than himself and his mother.

Oh, but she would have enough *enemies* if the truth was to come out. Not only her real father, but at the very least one of his offspring. Like his father, Jack Mears was a bad lot, obsessed with his father and growing from the same twisted root. Selfish and greedy, he would never allow an outsider to move in on his territory, especially if that outsider were to be entitled to part of his inheritance.

The girl needed protecting, James decided, or she'd be a lamb to the slaughter.

'It's strange all the same,' he mused aloud, 'that a secret and shameful part of Mears' past should find its way to me and mine.'

In that quiet moment, he was filled with an inexplicable sense of dread.

Chapter Seven

The following morning, James took Sally aside. 'Mam told me how you came to be here,' he said, 'and I'm sorry you've had such a terrible time. The truth is, you're very welcome to stay here for a time, if you want to, that is.'

'I'd like that.' Sally was thrilled. 'But only if you really want me to stay?'

'I've said so, haven't I?' There was something about her that got under his skin.

Fresh from a good night's sleep, Sally smiled at him through bright, young eyes. 'Thank you,' she said simply, 'I won't be a burden.'

'No, and you'd better not!' He smiled to soften his words. There was something else. 'Look, Sally, I think we need to talk. There are things you should be made aware of, for your own sake, you understand?'

Sally's smile fell away. 'You mean about my father?' Exhausted, she had slept the night through until dawn, when she suddenly awoke, her mind shocked into remembering. 'Don't worry about me,' she told James, 'seeing him the way he really is was just another setback.' She lowered her gaze. 'Now I wish I had never sought him out.'

'Like I said, we need to talk.' Shrugging on his coat, he strode to the door. 'Tonight,' he promised, 'we'll decide what to do.'

Maureen watched the two of them together and her heart was glad. She had always believed in fate. Ever since this lovely lass had come into their lives, she had hoped it might be for a special reason; that reason being to win James's heart. From now on, with each day that passed, she would pray for that to happen, and forget there might be repercussions of Sally being Leonard Mears' daughter.

For the next hour, the two women busied themselves. Maureen cleared and washed the breakfast things, while Sally set to, scrubbing the kitchen floor.

'I told you to leave that for me!' Maureen scolded. 'Or you'll be thinking I want you here to make a skivvy of you!'

Sally protested. 'I *like* doing it,' she said. 'My moth—' she stopped herself. 'I mean, Anne Hale, well, she never trusted me to do anything. She said I was useless, and that I should never have been born.' On that last note her voice trembled, and she fell silent.

Putting down her dishcloth, Maureen came across the room. Stooping to lay her arm across Sally's shoulders, she told her softly, 'She was wrong. You're certainly not useless, and I for one am very glad you were born.'

Sally looked up, the tears shivering on her eyelashes. 'Do you think I'm bad?'

'Good God, no!' Maureen understood what she was thinking, and was quick to reassure her. 'It doesn't mean to say that because you were fathered by a bad 'un, he bred that badness in you. It doesn't always work that way, sweetheart. A man can be the greatest musician in the world, and his child might be lucky if he can blow a penny whistle.' She laughed. 'Look at me and James! I can bake the best apple-pie in Lancashire, and he wouldn't know one end of a pie dish from the other.'

Sally laughed. 'I believe you.'

Hugging her hard, Maureen told her, 'You mustn't worry, child. I've known you for such a short time, but I can tell straight away there's no badness in you. You must take after your mother.'

Maureen had touched a sore point. 'I've often wondered who she was,' Sally said. 'I had hoped that when I found my real father, he might tell me, but I know now he wouldn't even give me the time of day.'

'Have you nothing at all to go by?'

Sally shook her head. 'I always thought my own parents raised me. I didn't know the truth until after the funeral, and all she said then was that my mother had been a streetwoman.'

'That doesn't mean to say it was true,' Maureen pointed out. 'From what you've told me about the old witch, she could have been lying. Or maybe Leonard Mears lied to her when you were handed over.'

'I was going to ask James if he might know how I could find out who my real mother was.'

'That's a good idea.' Giving her a nudge, Maureen pointed to the floor. 'You'd best get on, lass, or there'll be Lizzie banging at the door afore we know it.'

Mischievously, Sally reminded her, 'I thought you didn't want me scrubbing the floor?'

'Well, I've changed me mind, so get a move on and be quick about it, young lady!' Maureen had a thing about guests rolling up their sleeves, but somehow with Sally it was as though she was already one of the family.

Just as Maureen predicted, Lizzie turned up before they were finished. 'Ain't yer ready yet?' she called, her nose pressed to the window. 'It's gone eight o'clock. We shoulda been away down the road some ten minutes since.' Nosy as ever, it was only a moment before her quick eyes fell on Sally. 'Hello!' She gawped at Maureen. 'Who've you got there?'

141

'Wait 'til you're told, you nosy old baggage!' Maureen and Lizzie knew each other well enough to be rude.

A minute passed, during which Lizzie continued to stare at Sally, and Maureen got ready two baskets, one for her and one for Sally. 'She's coming with us,' she called out to Lizzie, who immediately came charging into the room.

'Who says?'

Canny as ever, Maureen asked, 'Do you want *me* with you?'

'Don't be so bloody daft, o' course I do!'

'Then Sally's coming too.'

While all this good-humoured bantering was going on, Sally stood in the background, trying not to laugh aloud when Maureen winked at her.

Lizzie came to have a closer look. 'She's nowt but skin and bone,' she declared. 'What use will she be?'

Maureen drew the old woman's notice to the kitchen flagstones. 'What do you think to my floor, Lizzie?'

Momentarily distracted, Lizzie looked down at the shining floor. 'By!' she gave a little click. 'That's the best I've seen 'em.'

'Well! I don't know whether to be insulted or pleased.' Smiling at Sally, Maureen explained, 'Because it were the lass who scrubbed the floor, not me.'

Suitably impressed, Lizzie turned to the girl. 'How old are yer, gal?'

'Nearly sixteen,' answered Sally.

'What name do you go by?'

'Sally.'

'Hmh! Sally what?'

'Just Sally.' She felt inadequate. 'You can call me Sally Hale if you like, but it's not my real name, and I don't like it anyway.'

Lizzie burst out laughing. 'You're a strange little bugger an' no mistake,' she cackled. 'But if it's not yer real name, and yer don't like it, happen I'll call yer just Sally after all.'

'Do I call you Lizzie?'

'You'd better! It's my name, ain't it? And what's more I *do* happen to like it.'

Snatching up one of Maureen's baskets she gave it to Sally, with an order: 'We've a long way to go, young 'un. So get yer best walking shoes on and be fit. All stragglers get left behind.'

'I've never been a pedlar before.' It was all new and exciting to Sally.

'There's allus a first time,' Lizzie told her, 'and you'd best work hard. No work – no wages.' She winked aside at Maureen. 'The lass don't look as far through as a blade o' grass,' she said. 'I hope I don't end up carrying the little snot home on me back.'

Sally had seen the wink, and was quick to reply. 'Don't worry about me keeping up with you,' she said. 'Just make sure you keep up with *me*.'

Lizzie screeched with laughter. 'Well I never!' Winking again at Maureen, she chuckled, 'By! You've got a cheeky little bugger there and no mistake!'

Maureen agreed; there was laughter all round. And a new friendship was bonded.

As they trudged along, full of talk and plans, Sally felt as though she had found a place at last.

At half past seven that evening James arrived home. 'It's been one of them days,' he told Maureen. 'Late deliveries and two men off sick.' He looked weary. 'I'm not sorry to be home, I can tell you.'

Maureen had the table laid and the food ready on the stove. 'Sounds like *we* had a better day than you.' Drawing his attention to the considerable pile of coins on the sideboard, she confessed with a grin, 'Sally sold more than me and Lizzie put together. When her own basket emptied, she'd come and take some of our produce. I tell you, son, if we'd had a wagon-load of stuff to sell, she'd have made us a little fortune.'

James was intrigued. 'Sounds to me like she's got a shrewd business head.' Then, in a softer voice, 'Happen she's her father's daughter after all.'

Fortunately Maureen didn't hear this latter remark. 'She's got such a way with her,' she said chuckling, 'and more energy than I can ever remember having, even at her age. By! The folks did love her. She'd chat and laugh and play with the young 'uns; she'd ask after their health and they took to her like a duck to water.'

Having washed at the sink while she talked, James now dried himself and slipped his shirt back on. 'Where is she?' He looked round the room. 'Collapsed in her bed, has she?'

'Not her!' Coming to stir the vegetables in the pot, Maureen informed him, 'She's taken Jake for a walk.' Funny, she thought, he didn't even notice the dog was gone, yet he noticed Sally wasn't here.

James was thinking the same. 'I should have known the old fella wasn't here,' he said, 'the way he pushes at me when I come through the door. I hope she doesn't take him too far. He has his limits these days.'

'She knows that.'

'How long have they been gone?'

Maureen glanced at the mantelpiece clock. 'I hadn't realised,' she said, growing concerned. 'They've been gone for nearly two hours. She asked which direction you usually come, and I said to wait near the market-place.'

Now they were both worried. 'I would have seen her,' James said. He was already putting on his coat. 'I'd best go and find her.'

'I can't understand it.' Maureen went to the door with him. 'I made sure she knew which way to go, and I told her if it starts getting dark, you make your way back smartish.' All the same she was beginning to fret. There were all manner of strange men about who might try themselves on a lone young woman.

Seeing how she was getting worked up, James took her by the shoulders. 'I'll find her, she'll not be far away, you'll see.' He remembered what Maureen had told him about their busy day. 'She's probably chatting to some woman and asking after her health.' His mischievous remark belied the anxiety inside.

Maureen smiled at that. 'Go on, son.' She urged him out the door. 'God willing, she'll be safe when you find her.'

Enthralled by the grandness of Corporation Park, Sally could not resist peeping through the gates. She stood open-mouthed at the huge lions' heads spewing torrents of water into the pools below. The main walkway was wide and clean, flanked on both sides by tall lamps that threw their light across the beautifully kept gardens. There were shadowy corners and tall, magnificent trees, and in the garish yellow lamplight the manicured lawns had a velvety sheen that took her breath away.

'Look at that!' Tugging the dog closer she gasped with delight. 'Have you ever seen anything so beautiful?' she murmured. 'It's just like wonderland!' Though Jake showed little interest as he cocked his leg up the wall.

Glancing down the street, Sally made sure there was no sign of James. 'Just a quick look round,' she promised herself, 'then we'll come back and wait for him.'

Once inside though, she wandered at will. Astonished and delighted by everything around her, she followed every little bypath, meandering in and out of surprising little places, and feeling like an intrepid explorer as she came upon new and exciting discoveries. 'It's scary and wonderful all at the same time,' she laughed, swinging round in horror when her laughter came back like a boomerang from the cliff-wall above her.

Losing all sense of time, she walked round the lake, and even sat awhile to watch the ducks. Then she scrambled up the bank, letting the dog loose for a few minutes on the high plateau, and watching him as he strolled about, scraping at the earth and looking for somewhere soft to lie. 'Tired are you, old fella?' she asked, going to sit beside him. From this spot she could see the twinkling lights of the town below. 'So this is Blackburn?' she muttered. 'I think I could settle here.'

Her thoughts alive with everything that had happened since she arrived here, it was inevitable that Sally's mind should turn to the future.

'Should I stay, or should I leave?' she asked Jake, but all she got for an answer was a soulful glance. 'It's no good looking to the man who fathered me,' she continued. 'He's no better than his sister. What then? Where shall I turn now?'

I have two choices, she decided. I can leave, take to the road again, and find a new life elsewhere – not an attractive prospect – or I can take up Maureen's offer and stay here. That way I'll already be able to earn a bob or two, and contribute to my keep, until I'm able to set up on my own.

She considered the two options. If she left, she'd be all alone again, and she had never found that easy. But if she stayed, she'd have a roof over her head, a warm bed, and good company. Maureen is so lovely, she thought. I feel I can talk to her about anything. As for James . . . She felt the warm blush creep over her face. James is very special, and he wants me to stay. He said so, didn't he? She thought about him for a moment or two when, beset with powerful emotions she hardly understood, she came to realise that she could fall in love with someone like James.

Suddenly, and so surprised by her own admission that she put her two hands over her face to stem the blush, she whispered, 'You might like him. But he thinks you're just a child, he doesn't see you as a woman, and maybe he never will.'

146

The odd thing was, Sally knew that almost overnight she had left being a child behind for ever. Instead she was a woman, with all the feelings and confusion that went with that. If you're staying because you want to win his heart, you could be heading for a fall, she warned herself. You can't *make* a man love you, however hard you try. Yet her instincts told her she must never give up. 'Maybe the day will come when he turns to you,' she mused aloud. 'Either way, you can't leave him behind.'

Breathing a deep, invigorating sigh, Sally came to a crucial decision. When it comes right down to it, you have *no* choice. Love him or hate him, this is where your real father is, and, according to Maureen, you have two half-brothers and sisters. Whether you like it or not, this is the only family you have. As for you and James . . . if you're meant for each other, it will all come right. If not . . . She shrank from the idea that it may never happen, saying to herself, 'Best not to think about that just now.'

After a while, she clambered up and, leading the dog ever so gently down the cliff-side, made her way to the bottom. Funny, she didn't recognise the path as the one from where she started the upward climb. Glancing up and down, she saw that the light was stronger if she turned left, and so that was the way she followed. It would be bound to take them back to the main gates, she decided.

It wasn't long before she had to admit she must have taken a wrong turn. 'We're back at the lake now,' she observed to Jake worriedly. 'I remember it was an uphill path to the lake.' Beginning to panic, she took a deep breath and calmed herself. 'Use your head, Sally. It stands to reason, if we came *up* to the lake, then we have to go *down* for the main gates.' It seemed simple enough.

Turning by the sand pit, she began her descent, only to find to her dismay that the narrow paths twisted and turned, until at last she stopped to take her bearings once more. 'We're lost good and proper now,' she muttered, 'and it's getting darker by the minute.' Fear took a hold, but she daren't shout for assistance, in case her cries reached the wrong ears. 'We'll just keep going down,' she decided, 'we're bound to come out in the open soon.'

As she broke through from the maze of footpaths, Sally gave a sigh of relief, because there, only a short distance away, stood what looked to be the park-keeper.

Having freed a swan from an illegal fishing line, he was now taking it back to the lake. 'Which way to the gates?' she asked. 'I'm supposed to wait for somebody there.'

In the lamplight, the old keeper took stock of her, thinking what a pretty young thing she was, and how he'd never let his daughter wander about at this time of a night, especially in a park this size. 'What are you thinking of?' he asked angrily. 'Have you taken leave of your senses?'

'What do you mean?'

'What I *mean* is – it'll be pitch black soon. You should know better than to be walking about here, and I don't care if you do have a dog.' He glanced at the old dog and tutted. 'Poor old bugger's worn out,' he said. 'Get off home with you, there are some very peculiar folk walks this park of a night.'

Coming closer he muttered, 'If I had my way they'd be locked up 'til they rot, bad lot, that's what they are, and they'd think nowt of draggin' you in them bushes over there.'

It was only now that Sally began to realise what terrible danger she might be in; in fact she wasn't even sure about the old park-keeper. 'If you'll just point me in the right direction,' she told him, 'I'll be away.' A bit quick an' all, she thought wryly.

'There's your way out, miss,' he said, pointing down the main walkway. 'If you'll wait a minute, I'll get this swan back to its mate, then I'll escort you out.'

As he walked off, Sally called out, 'Do I turn left or right to the market-place?'

His voice came back in an eerie echo, 'I've told you, wait 'til I get this swan back and I'll put you right.'

'Not bloody likely,' Sally muttered, and quickly took off in the direction he had pointed out. Sure enough, there were the main gates, and beyond them, civilisation.

As they came through on to the main road, Sally was greatly relieved. The lights were brighter, there were couples hurrying by, and all manner of carriages travelling up and down. 'Now then, old fella,' she murmured to Jake, 'am I to turn left or right?' All sense of direction had gone. 'Happen we'd best just sit here and wait.'

Realising the old dog was out on his feet, she thought to let him have a rest before they went any further. 'I know how you feel,' she confessed. 'My feet are aching an' all. I've never done so much walking all in one go. When I were living on the streets, I'd walk a bit and rest a bit, and it were all right. But now, what with peddling goods all day, then coming out here, I'm fair knackered, and that's the truth.'

When he looked up at her with forlorn eyes, she stooped to give him a cuddle. 'I'm sure he'll be along soon,' she said hopefully. 'We'll sit here a few minutes, then we'll see.'

The dog seemed to know what she was saying, because he promptly lay down. Stretching out his front legs he dropped his head as though it was too heavy for his body, then fell fast asleep.

The deeper he slept, the louder he got. 'Would you believe it!' Sally laughed. 'I never knew a dog could snore like that.' But she'd worn him out, and she was sorry for it. 'You sleep now,' she murmured fondly. 'If he's not here by the time you wake up, we'll set off back.'

With the night closing in fast and the cold with it, Sally drew Maureen's coat tight about her. Perching on the park wall, with the dog at her feet, she watched down the road, her eyes peeled for a sight of James, and her heart warming at the thought of him.

* * *

James was frantic.

Not knowing that Sally was in the park, he had been down to the market and back, and was now scouring the streets for her. Coming up Montague Street, he paused at the top, looking left and right. 'Where in God's name can she be?' Glancing across to the gates of Corporation Park, he witnessed what he assumed was a lover's tiff. The couple were struggling, and for a moment he wondered whether he should intervene.

When his attention was drawn to the dog, who was tearing at the man's trousers, his heart leaped. 'God Almighty!' At a run, he crossed the road and bore down on the attacker. As he did so, the man kicked out at the dog and sent him flying against the wall. Taking hold of Sally with one arm and covering her mouth with the other, he half-carried, half-dragged her towards the park.

With a cry of rage, James launched himself at the man and soon the two of them were fighting fiercely, the one wild-eyed and furious because he had been robbed of his captive, and the other cool but incensed, his every hard punch finding its home. 'You bastard . . . she's just a girl!' James meant to punish him, and punish him he did.

Taught a lesson he would never forget, the man took off, his nose bloodied and his face swelling by the minute where James's fists had found their mark. It would be a long time before he thought to have his way with some other innocent, unsuspecting woman.

Shaken and bruised, Sally had stayed beside Jake. 'He's hurt,' she said, her voice shaking, '. . . it's my fault.'

James gently examined the dog, who was quietly whimpering. 'All right, are you, old fella?' With a knowing, tender touch he moved his hands all over Jake's limbs. 'There's nothing broken,' he assured Sally, 'he's just had a shock, I reckon.' Cradling the dog's head between his hands, he tilted the face towards him.

'You're a silly old bugger, aren't you, eh? Fighting at your age, you should be ashamed.'

When Jake wagged his tail, Sally laughed through her tears. 'He'll be all right!' she cried. 'Oh, James, he'll be all right!' With her own ordeal over and Jake seeming to recover, she could no longer stem her emotions. Sobbing uncontrollably, she covered her face with her hands.

Deeply moved, James took her by the shoulders and eased her on to her feet. Drawing her close he told her softly, 'It's over now. You're both safe and that's all that matters.' Then he held her there, a wonderful warmth flowing between them. In that moment, James knew he would always take it on himself to protect her.

Yet even though he felt closer to her than before, he did not realise how deeply she had crept into the darker corners of his heart.

In the lamplight she gazed up at him. 'I would never have forgiven myself if he'd been hurt.'

James looked down at Jake, who was now contentedly nuzzling against him. 'Let's get you both home, eh?' Holding Sally there, looking into those soft blue eyes, James thought how very pretty she was and, for one inexplicable moment, he could not tear his gaze away.

Sally, too, wanted the moment to last. The warmth of his body lent a different warmth to hers, and it was like something she had never known before. His dark eyes were so mysterious, and yet she felt as though she had known him for ever.

The sound of a carriage approaching caused them to look up. 'You stay here,' he told her. 'Keep an eye on the old fella. With any luck, it will be someone I know and I might be able to cadge us a lift back home.'

As it happened, he was too late. By the time he turned, the carriage had already past. 'Well, we'd better start walking gently home.' Smiling, he glanced down at the dog. 'I'll get you there one way or another,' he promised, 'even if I have to carry you both on my back.'

Sally had no doubt he would if he had to.

The carriage rumbled on. 'You'll be the belle of the ball.' Leonard Mears sat facing one way, his wife and Isabel the other. 'I'm glad I chose the crimson fabric. Also the style I approved will suit you very well.'

Totally oblivious to the fact that they cringed at his every word, he continued in his overbearing, authoritative manner. 'I know you preferred the green gown, but you have to trust my judgement, my dear. With your beautiful bright hair, there is no other colour for you but the crimson.'

Seeing that Isabel seemed not to be listening, it was Frances who answered. 'You really need not have accompanied us, Leonard,' she said nervously. 'Isabel and I could have gone on our own. It doesn't seem right that you should have to give up your evenings and weekends attending the dressmaker with us, especially when you work so hard all day.'

'Quiet, woman!' The look he gave her would have been enough to silence someone far less nervous than she. 'It's *my* money that pays for all your dresses, and I have a right to decide how that money is spent. If it was left to you, God only knows what Isabel would be wearing. I have important people coming to the ball, and I want my daughter to look her very best.' Smiling at Isabel, he sought her approval: 'Nothing is too good for you, isn't that right, my dear?'

Isabel didn't hear him.

Peering from the back window of the carriage, she saw how James and the young woman had begun walking; he with his arm about her, and she nestling contentedly there. In the dark, James had obviously not recognised his employer's carriage.

She had seen James and the girl holding each other as the carriage passed and was shocked to her roots. If she imagined she could count on anyone, it was James. Now she felt cheated and betrayed. Her heart hardened. She would not forget. Neither would she forgive.

Chapter Eight

Robert had noticed the change in Isabel, and was deeply concerned. On this Monday morning he waylaid her as she went through to breakfast. 'You can tell me it's none of my business if you like,' he said, 'but . . . is there anything troubling you?'

'No.' Her features set unusually hard, she shook her head. 'Should there be?'

Taken aback by her defensive attitude, Robert wondered if he should leave well alone. 'I'm sorry if you think I'm prying,' he apologised, 'only, these past two weeks you've seemed different somehow. I can't quite put my finger on it, but there *is* something.' In a kind, brotherly gesture he touched her arm. 'I want to help, if I can.'

Dismissing his offer with a shrug, she seemed amused. 'Really, Robert, you do have a vivid imagination.'

Unconvinced, Robert persisted. 'Has Father been bullying you again?'

'No more than usual. But I can handle him. I always have.'

'And there is nothing troubling you?'

'Nothing whatsoever.' Her smile was shallow, her eyes harder than he had ever seen them before. 'If you don't mind, I'd like to go through now. Father will be sending out a search party if I don't soon show my face.'

Without waiting for an answer, she swept by, leaving Robert puzzled by her abrupt manner.

Hannah's voice interrupted his thoughts. 'I was listening,' she confessed. Clothed in a straight two-piece with small-heeled boots laced to just below the hem of her long dress, she looked as though she might be going on an outing. 'I'm like you,' she remarked, fiddling with her long fair hair. 'I think Isabel's got a bee in her bonnet about something.'

'About what?'

'She won't tell me. But she's fretting about something. I noticed it the evening she came back from the dressmaker.' Hannah prided herself on never missing anything.

'Have you *no* idea what's upset her?'

'No, but I'll tell you this.' Leaning forward she lowered her voice to a more intimate level, her face a picture of conspiracy. 'I think it has to do with a *man*!'

'What makes you say that?'

Blushing deep pink, Hannah grew coy. 'When a woman starts getting moody and irritable, there's *usually* a man involved.'

Suppressing a smile, Robert encouraged her. 'Oh? And why's that?'

Pouting sulkily, she assured him, 'Men just don't understand us women, that's all.'

Robert could hardly contain himself. 'Oh? And you'd know about that, would you?'

'Hmh!' Tipping her nose in the air, Hannah evaded his question. 'I'll find out what's ailing her,' she promised, 'but I probably won't tell you.'

From her place at the table, Isabel could see them talking together. Suspecting they were discussing her, she was relieved when her father banged the table loudly with his fist. It sent out a warning to both Robert and Hannah that he was on the warpath. 'Be late once more,' he warned them as they came

155

rushing in, 'and you'll go without breakfast for a week.'

Robert glanced at the wall-clock. 'We're not late, Father,' he observed, taking his place with dignity. 'I think both Hannah and I know better than to displease you in that way.'

The look his father gave him would have felled an ox. '*I'll* be the one to say whether you're late or not,' he snapped. 'In future, be at this table two seconds behind me, whatever time I choose to eat. Do you understand me?'

'Of course, Father.' Robert had long learned never to argue with him, for no one ever won a battle of words with Leonard Mears; he was always right, even when he was wrong.

Leonard Mears turned his attention to Hannah. 'Well?'

'Sorry, Father. It won't happen again.' It was fortunate for her that he didn't see the wink she gave Robert.

Impatient as ever, the master brought his fist down on the table once more. 'We're ready to eat,' he instructed the waiting housekeeper, 'and be quick about it! There's been enough time wasted already!'

As Mrs Flanagan hurried out, he patted his grotesque belly. 'Always start the day with a good meal.' His grin sickened everyone there. 'That's always been my motto.'

The meal was delivered and eaten in silence, though there was many a nervous glance passed across the table.

Hannah looked at Robert and Robert looked at Isabel, and he knew that, however much she might deny it, there *was* something playing on her mind: she was too far away, too picky with her food, and on the odd occasion when he caught her looking at him, he had the distinct impression that she really wanted to confide in him. He had given her every chance, so now it was up to her, though he suspected she would not allow him into her thoughts.

Isabel was a very deep person, not easily given to sharing her anger with anyone. And it *was* anger, he knew that. What he didn't know was how she had come to be so darkly angry. And if not with her father . . . then who?

Sensing an undercurrent, the ever-watchful Jack also glanced from one to the other. He saw the knowing looks pass between Hannah and Robert, and suspected that Isabel was at the root of it all. He had no idea what was going on, but he would make it his business to find out, and when he did, his father would no doubt be interested.

First though, he would follow his father's good example and wolf down a hearty breakfast. After that, he meant to be first at the factory, where he would knuckle down to the hateful job his father had shackled him to.

But he could bear that, as long as he knew that at some time in the very near future he might find himself in his father's favour to such an extent that he would be promoted to a higher level than his brother, Robert. That was his goal and, like his beloved father, he would let nothing stand in his way.

Quiet as always, Frances knew nothing of their conspiracies. All she knew was that every moment with her husband was more unbearable than the one before. Unable to look on him, she kept her head down, nibbling at her food and hating the pitiful existence she was made to endure. She listened to his disgusting animal noises as he dribbled and smacked at his food, and the need to see him dead was like a compulsion inside her.

But he wouldn't die, she knew that. Like all monsters, he would gobble everything in his path, growing fatter and stronger, until there was nothing and no one to knock him down. If only she had the courage, she thought. If only . . . Ashamed and frightened by her own destructive thoughts, Frances excused herself from the table. 'I'm not well,' she said, thinking how it was her own terrible, murderous thoughts that had turned her stomach.

Whatever the reason for her needing to get away, Frances

received no sympathy. 'You will leave this table when I say, and not before!'

And so she sat, quiet and still, forced to endure his company and wishing him dead with such hatred that her fists clenched so tight the nails drew blood.

Insensitive to his mother's discomfort, Jack concentrated on his meal, while Robert put down his knife and fork and let it be known that he had lost his appetite. Hannah was far too hungry to make such a grand protest, and, consumed by thoughts of James's betrayal, Isabel remained silent throughout.

Unmoved by the display of support for their mother, Leonard Mears leisurely finished his breakfast.

When at last he laid down his napkin, he turned to Isabel. 'I have a business meeting that will occupy me for a short while. However, I mean to cut it short. I shall return for you on the stroke of ten, so be ready and waiting.' He then nodded briefly and was gone, and the room seemed brighter for his leaving.

While Jack went at some haste after his father, Robert was the first to his mother's side. 'I'll help you to your room. You should lie down for a while,' he suggested. 'I'll get Mrs Flanagan to keep an eye on you.'

Frances graciously declined. 'There is no need,' she said. 'I'm feeling much better now.' The cause of her anxiety had already departed. 'You'd better go,' she urged. 'Don't give him an excuse to make you miserable.'

Robert's face grew grim. 'I don't intend going anywhere until I'm satisfied you're all right.'

He must have been satisfied because not long afterwards he left her in the capable hands of Eliza Flanagan. Isabel offered to stay with her, but her mother was adamant. 'He could be back early,' she warned. 'Go and make yourself ready. I'm quite recovered.'

'Where is he taking me, do you think?'

Reassuringly, Frances took hold of her hand. 'It could be to do with this ball he's so set on.' Her eyes lit up. 'It will be the first time we've had music and dancing in this house for many years and, I have to say, I find myself looking forward to it. Maybe he wants your opinion on something in particular. Don't ask questions, child. Just be thankful to get out of this house for a while.'

Anxious all the same, Isabel left to get ready. 'Don't you worry, miss.' A kindly soul, Eliza Flanagan followed her into the hallway. 'I'll keep an eye on her.'

After settling Frances in the conservatory with a pot of tea, Eliza satisfied herself that the household staff were busy at their duties before returning to the kitchen, where she and Cook helped themselves to a slice of cherry cake and a drop of sarsaparilla.

Having described the awful scene over breakfast, Eliza revealed, 'I don't know how the mistress puts up with him.'

'Because she ain't got no choice, that's why!' Cook had an answer for everything. 'He's her husband when all's said and done, but, I tell you this, Eliza. If he were mine, I swear I'd have to do away with him.'

Eliza thought of the part he had played in her own life. 'Somebody should,' she remarked softly. 'A man like that doesn't deserve to live.'

The remark was made with such feeling that Cook stopped chewing her cake to stare at the other woman. 'By! You said that as though you *really* meant it,' she said.

Eliza looked at her long and hard. 'Oh, but I did mean it,' she said. Nobody would ever know how much.

Bristling with authority and full of his own importance, Leonard Mears returned as he said he would on the stroke of ten.

Looking lovely in a cream-coloured flowing dress and waisted jacket, Isabel presented herself for inspection. 'You look lovely, my dear.' Proudly, he led her to the waiting carriage and helped her inside. 'We have a passenger to collect,' he informed her.

Intrigued, she asked where they were going, astonished when he replied that he thought it was high time she acquainted herself with his other great love.

Immersed in his work at the factory, James was not in the best of moods. For the past two weeks, he had tried desperately to catch sight of Isabel, but without any success. He was beginning to think she was deliberately eluding him, and it was driving him crazy.

Taking a moment to wipe the sweat from his brow, he looked up from the wheel he was finishing, and was riveted with shock, for there she was, standing before him like a figment of his imagination. 'This is Mr Peterson.' Leonard Mears' voice cut the air. 'A good man . . . does his job without me having to chase his tail from morning to night.'

Isabel was flanked by her father on one side and a young man on the other – tall and slim, he had a kind face and wore a well-cut suit. In James's opinion, he seemed far more interested in Isabel than in what he was being shown of the factory.

Puffed out like a bullfrog, Leonard Mears proudly took them from one stage of production to the next. With a knowledge gained only from years of experience, he explained the mechanisms of making a carriage and the importance of the right wood for the right task, though he was careful not to reveal too much; no businessman would ever do that.

Together with the young man beside her, Isabel was fascinated, asking all manner of questions and listening with interest; while James was filled with despair, for not once during the tour did she look at him.

'I can't imagine why Father would bring her here,' Robert told James, as the visitors made their way up the stairs to the office. 'But Isabel is his favourite and I expect he might want to show off his achievements to her.'

Jack was fuming. Intent on loading the trollies with wood, he squirmed with embarrassment when his father introduced him to the stranger as 'a young man learning the trade from the bottom up'.

All too soon the visit was ended. As she came down the stairs, Isabel turned her head to look at James. It was a long, cool look that shook him to the core and left him wondering what he could possibly have done wrong to deserve it. Stirred by the sight of him, Isabel was torn between love and hatred. One thing was certain: she could never feel the same about him. Not now. Not since she had seen him with his arms round another woman.

The day seemed to last an eternity to her. After a tour round the barrel factory, where her father went on at great lengths about how he had acquired the premises for a song when the merchant went broke, she found herself increasingly drawn into conversation with the young man her father had brought along. His father was a wealthy merchant, and as the only son, Adam Scarlet was set to inherit a fortune.

Unbeknown to Isabel, the two old friends had schemed to bring together their two children; not out of the goodness of their hearts, but out of greed and self-satisfaction. It was a business proposition. Nothing less. Nothing more. When it came to business, certain sacrifices had to be made, and these two young people were no exception.

Chapter Nine

While Sally ran ahead, Lizzie and Maureen walked behind, chatting about this and that, and enjoying the best sunny day they'd had for weeks. 'Look at the lass,' Lizzie chuckled. 'She makes me feel old.'

Laughing loudly, Maureen told her not to worry, because 'She makes *me* feel old, never mind about you.'

'She's coming on grand since she's been with you,' Lizzie observed, 'and she's such a pretty thing.'

'Lovely natured too,' Maureen told her. 'Nothing's too much trouble for her.'

'It's hard to believe she's Leonard Mears' daughter.' Lizzie knew it all. Trusting her implicitly, neither Maureen nor Sally had kept anything from her.

On Lizzie's comment, Maureen glanced nervously about. 'It's best not to say that out loud,' she warned. 'James reckons Sally's life could be in danger if Mears knew she was here. As far as he's concerned, she's far enough away never to hurt him or his. I don't suppose he's ever kept in touch with his sister and her husband. No doubt he dumped the child and his guilt with her, all those years ago. As you know, Lizzie, it's only by chance Sally discovered his identity.'

'Well, he'll never know her whereabouts from me,' Lizzie

promised, 'and neither will anybody else.' Maureen relaxed. Lizzie was always as good as her word.

But then she posed a question that had also been on Maureen's mind. 'Will the lass ever approach him with the truth, d'yer think?'

'God only knows,' she replied cautiously. 'But I'm sure if she ever did go to him with the truth, it would be for a very good reason.' Though, in all honesty, Maureen could not think of one good reason why Sally should put herself at the mercy of that man. 'She does respect James's opinion though. I'm sure if she ever thought about making such a move, she would talk it over with him first. I'm satisfied he would know how to advise her.'

Running across the field towards the River Ribble, Sally felt so happy she threw out her arms and twirled on the spot. 'Can we stop here and eat our muffins?' she asked. The muffins were fresh-baked by Maureen that very morning. Wrapped in muslin and curled in the corner of Sally's basket, they sent up a wonderful, irresistible aroma. 'I'm hungry.'

'Serves you right,' Maureen retorted, 'I told you to have a breakfast before we set out.'

'I wasn't hungry then,' Sally protested. 'Anyway, Lizzie's tired, aren't you, Lizzie?' Winking at Lizzie, she hoped the old woman might support her and, bless her, she did.

'It's so beautiful here.' Sally let her eyes feast on the view. This was her favourite place. Away from town, the countryside was like another world, with its rich green fields and bowing trees and willows dipping in the river. 'I could build a house here,' she told them excitedly as they settled themselves on the grass.

'Oh aye?' Lizzie loved to tease her. 'And what kind of a house would that be then, eh? A big, posh place with servants and chandeliers, I shouldn't wonder.'

Sally made a face. 'No, I wouldn't like that,' she answered. 'My house will be small and cosy, with a thatched roof and pretty windows, and an orchard, just like yours, where we could grow all our own fruit. I'd like a vegetable garden too . . . and a big lawn where the children can run about and have fun.' She stopped, realising with horror that she was letting her imagination run away with her.

Lizzie had listened and it was interesting to see how folks' dreams were all different; here she was wanting to expand her little business, and there was Sally talking about a house with an orchard and vegetable patch, and a lawn. 'Hey!' Tapping Sally on the shoulder, she asked in her kindly, blunt manner, 'These childer who'll be running about on that lawn . . .'

Sally was instantly on the defensive. 'What about them?'

'They'll be *yours*, will they?'

'O' course they'll be mine!'

'Aye? And who else's will they be?'

Glancing at Maureen, who was listening intently, Sally felt uncomfortable. 'Don't know what you mean, Lizzie.'

'Oh yes, yer do!' Lizzie was a bugger at the best of times. 'I'm asking who you've got in mind for their daddy.'

Embarrassed, Sally glanced nervously at Maureen, who was still listening intently. 'I haven't made up my mind yet.' Slightly flustered by the abruptness of Lizzie's question, Sally had no intention of answering it.

But there was only one man she could let father her children. One man she would ever love. And that was James.

They finished their muffins and were soon on their way again, Sally picking wild flowers and the other two resuming their conversation.

'Have you thought about what I said?' Lizzie took a minute to stuff a pinch of snuff up her nostril.

Sneezing with her as the snuff carried on the wind, Maureen switched the heavy basket to her other arm. 'If you mean about us going up in the world, I'm still not sure.' She had given it a deal of thought but it was a big step, and anyway, 'I think I'd rather carry on as we are,' she admitted. 'The more we sell, the longer we'll be out on the road. I don't know if I'd like that, working longer hours and taking on more responsibility. I like time to do the garden and there's allus sewing needed, and then there's James.'

'Aye.' Lizzie nodded affirmatively. 'I see what you mean, and you're right o' course. I must be an old fool even *thinking* about tekking on more work. I've got a gammy leg and a touch of arthritis in both me knees.' Sighing, she confessed, 'I expect it's to do with me getting older and more senile by the minute.'

'What's that supposed to mean?'

'There's not much time left for me to make me mark on this 'ere world, *that's* what it means.'

There was a sadness in the old woman's voice that touched Maureen's heart. 'Hey!' Drawing them both to a halt, she put her arm round her friend's shoulders. 'Don't talk like that, Lizzie,' she said. 'You've *already* made your mark, as you put it.'

'Why d'you say that, lass?' Rubbing the end of her nose with her hankie, she sneezed again.

'Think about it, Lizzie,' Maureen urged gently. 'Here you are, in your seventies. You grow flowers and vegetable produce, you tend the orchard and embroider the most beautiful doilies. As if that isn't enough, you make wicker baskets and fruit bowls, and then you sell it all by trudging round the countryside, fetching it right to folks' doors. How many other seventy-year-olds can lay claim to that, eh?'

Lizzie was thrilled. Laughing through her toothless gums, she gave Maureen a hug. 'You're right!' she cried. 'And, God willing, I'll go on for a few more years yet.'

Maureen felt guilty. 'All the same, if you're *really* set on expanding the business, I won't let you down, you should know that.'

Lizzie shook her head. 'You've made me see sense,' she said. 'There'll be no more talk of going up in the world.'

Yet, as they walked on, Lizzie felt downhearted. She had set her sights on having a 'barrer' with her name emblazoned on the side, and filling it with all kinds of goods. She had visions of it being painted in her own colours; she could see it now. By! and wouldn't it be grand ...

LIZZIE TAMWORTH

HOMEGROWN PRODUCE

and

HANDMADE WICKER GOODS

But it was not to be. She'd left it too late, and besides, when all was said and done, it was just a dream.

'I mustn't be greedy in wanting more,' she told herself. 'The Lord's been good, and I'm grateful for that.'

All the same, as they wandered over the hill to Widow Plessure's cottage, Lizzie couldn't help but feel the tiniest sadness that her dream would never come true.

It was a busy day, but enjoyable as usual, and as their baskets emptied, their pockets filled, heavy with the coins they earned. When at last their baskets were empty and their pockets full, they started on their way home.

'By! I'm that parched, me tongue's stuck to the roof of me mouth.' Lizzie said the very same thing every Friday. In fact, as she said it now, both Maureen and Sally mischievously mouthed it with her. 'What say we stop off and have a pint at yon pub?'

And, as always, that was exactly what they did.

Sitting outside on the bench, they supped their ale and rested their legs, and Sally felt as though she was one of the family.

'I fancy a meat and potato pie,' she said, and so they had one each; and so did the mangy dog who turned up at an opportune moment, then ran off again as soon as he'd filled his belly.

'Cheeky bugger!' Lizzie moaned, but as they continued on their way, all three were soon chatting and laughing, and planning a busy weekend.

'I mean to clean my windows and wash all the curtains,' Maureen announced.

Lizzie intended starting on her spring harvest. 'What have you got in mind then, Sally?' she asked.

Sally thought for a minute. 'I think I'll murder Leonard Mears,' she answered in a serious voice.

After that, they fell into a sober mood, with Lizzie glancing at Maureen with wide, wondering eyes. Until suddenly Sally burst out laughing. 'Why! You little sod!' Relieved, Lizzie landed her one across her backside. 'You really had me going there.'

Maureen didn't laugh. She had seen the look in Sally's eyes when she spoke of murdering her father.

And it was no laughing matter.

The weekend was wonderful.

At six o'clock on Saturday, Sally woke and threw open her curtains to a shining morning. 'James promised to take me fishing this afternoon.' She had hardly slept for the excitement of it all, though it wasn't the fishing itself that excited her. It was the idea of being with James, all alone, for the very first time.

Thinking she might impress him by being the first down to put the kettle on, Sally quickly dressed and ran down the stairs two at a time. 'By! It's enough to put a body off for the day!' joked Maureen who was already pouring the tea. 'Leaping down the stairs like that, at this time of a morning.'

Disappointed but trying not to show it, Sally gave her a hug. 'I thought you'd still be in bed,' she remarked casually.

'I might have had a little lie-in,' Maureen admitted. 'Lord knows I fancied one. But I've made up my mind to have all the curtains down today, and clean all the windows.' She glanced through the kitchen window. 'It's lovely out, and there's a good drying breeze, so I should be able to get the curtains back up today. Oh, but I'm not stopping there –' she had the spring fever – 'Tomorrow, I intend cleaning the house from top to bottom.'

'And I'll help you,' Sally promised. 'But I'm going out with James this afternoon, so I'll have to take a few hours off, if that's all right.'

Sensing her excitement, Maureen smiled. 'Course it is, you daft article,' she said. 'You go and enjoy yourself, and don't worry about work. I dare say it'll still be waiting for you when you get back.'

If the truth be told, Maureen was more excited about Sally going out with James than Sally was herself. Happen this would be the day when James saw her for the lovely young woman she had become, and not for the dirty, ragged lass he rescued from the streets.

Thrusting a thick slice of bread on to the end of a toasting fork, she handed it to Sally. 'The fire's well away now,' she said gesturing to the reddening flames. 'We'll have four pieces of toast while you're doing nothing if you please – two for James and one each for you and me.'

Sally got on with it, a smile on her face and a song in her heart as she thought of the day ahead. If only James knew how she felt about him, she thought. But he didn't, and she would never tell him, in case it ruined what friendship they already had.

It was twenty minutes past six when James came down, his hair still ruffled. He seemed to have his mind on far-off things. 'Are you all right, son?' Maureen suspected his quiet mood had something to do with Isabel Mears. 'You seem miles away.'

'I've got a lot on my mind,' he said. But that was all he would say.

'I've done you a grand breakfast, son.' Maureen put the plate before him: two poached eggs, three sausages and a rasher of bacon. 'Sally's just finishing the toast.'

Apologising, James pushed the plate of food away. 'Sorry, Mam, I couldn't stomach food right now.' Pouring himself a mug of tea, he smiled up at her. 'Happen Sally should eat it,' he said, loud enough for Sally to hear. 'She'll need to build up her muscles if she's coming fishing with me this afternoon. There are some big, fat trout lurking in that stream.'

'I'm really looking forward to it,' she said, blushing pink when he admitted, 'So am I.'

Maureen had been disappointed when he refused her food, but now, seeing these two smiling at each other, she was overjoyed.

Smiling together, she thought . . . fishing together. It may not be much, but it was a start.

On his way to work, James paused outside the Mears' house. There was no sign of Isabel and he didn't expect there would be.

For the briefest moment he stood there, his eyes drawn to a certain upstairs window. Once before, on a clear summer's morning, she had smiled at him from that very window. In his mind's eye he imagined her now, warm in bed, her beautiful long hair across the pillow. He had so much love for her – so much need.

He thought of the cold, cutting look she had given him when she came to the factory, and he wondered again what he had done to deserve it. Then, like the voice of his own conscience, his mother's warning whispered in his ear: 'Be careful, son. She belongs to the gentry. You're a novelty to her, that's all . . . summat to be used and cast aside.'

He sighed a long, deep sigh that touched his heart. 'Is Mam

right?' he murmured, his eyes focused on the window. 'Was I just a novelty?' What else could he think?

Yet, as he walked away, head down and shoulders stooped, he had not given up hope.

Unable to sleep, Isabel climbed out of bed. Going to the window, she drew back the curtains, almost at once catching sight of James as he strode away. As she looked, he slowed his stride and stared back; he didn't see her there, he was too far away. Even if he had, she would not have acknowledged him.

James had hurt her more than he could ever know. 'I thought you cared for me,' she murmured, 'but I was wrong. You're too frightened of Father to risk his displeasure.'

She watched him walk out of sight, before returning to her bed. She didn't sleep. Instead, she turned her mind to that other young man who had been so charming. Her father had told her he was invited to the ball. 'Maybe I was foolish not to look among my own kind,' she whispered sadly. 'I should have known better.'

Her gaze fell on the gown hanging over the wardrobe. It was a beautiful thing . . . vibrant with colour and with such a daring neckline she had wondered whether she might have the courage to wear it. Now she was determined. Not only would she wear it, but she would wear it the way a woman should, with pride in herself and her beauty, and with an eye to catch herself a 'suitable' husband.

'Adam Scarlet is not unpleasant to look on,' she recalled aloud. 'He comes of a wealthy family, and he seems to have taken a liking to me.' There was a hardness in her voice. 'What does love matter?' She had to get James out of her mind . . . out of her heart. It would take a while, but already she was planning a life without him.

* * *

The morning couldn't go quick enough for Sally.

With an enthusiasm that had Maureen gasping, she rolled up her sleeves and got stuck in. While Maureen washed the breakfast things, Sally mopped the kitchen floor. She then took herself upstairs to make the beds. Lingering in James's room, she stroked her hands down the sheet; it was still warm where she turned it back to straighten out the crinkles. When the bed was made, she sat on the chair by the window, letting her gaze rove round the room, and imagining him there. 'I'd give anything to share your life,' she murmured; 'to share your bed, and feel your strong arms round me.'

She hadn't forgotten that night, when he held her and they had looked into each other's eyes. 'That night, outside the park . . . I thought you might kiss me.' Her heart turned over at the memory. 'But then the carriage came and the moment was gone, but not for ever,' she secretly wished. 'Not for ever.'

No sooner had Sally helped Maureen to take down the curtains than James arrived home. 'Is it safe to enter?' He stood at the door, a slow, easy grin on his face. To all intents and purposes he was a man at peace, but inside he was in turmoil.

Maureen wasn't fooled. 'It's time we stopped for refreshments,' she told Sally. 'Afterwards, you and James can take yourselves off. It'll do you both good to get away from it all for a while.'

While James put the kettle on, Maureen and Sally went out the back door to shake the dust from their clothes. 'I never realised the curtains could hold so much of it.' Maureen clapped her hands to rid herself of the last clinging particles. 'God only knows where it all comes from.'

When they got back inside, James had the teapot on the table, and three small plates. Besides these stood one of Lizzie's wicker platters, covered with a pretty doilie and holding the fruitiest cake Sally had ever seen. 'I baked that while you were both fast asleep in your beds,' Maureen declared proudly.

'I left it for you to cut,' James explained. 'If I put a knife in, it's bound to fall apart.'

'*My* cakes don't fall apart!' Maureen retorted. 'There's a knack to cutting a cake . . . like this.' Giving a demonstration, she sliced three pieces – a large one for James, and two smaller ones for her and Sally. Moist and rich, the cake smelled and tasted delicious. 'There's more if you want it,' she told them.

'When you get time,' Sally asked, 'would you show me how to bake a cake like this?' If there ever came a day when James might see her as his wife, she would need to know these things.

Maureen understood. 'Course I will, lass,' she promised. 'I'll show you how to make a deep apple-pie too . . . James is very fond o' them.'

Letting the conversation flow over his head, James had his mind on other things.

Once the tea was drunk and the cake savaged, it was time to go. 'Have a good time,' Maureen told them. 'I wouldn't mind a couple of nice, fat trout if you can catch 'em.' She was very partial to a nicely baked trout, cooked in milk, with a coating of brown sugar.

'Right then.' Giving Maureen a kiss, James told her gratefully, 'That cake was one of your best. I don't suppose you could wrap a chunk for me and Sally to take with us?' When he gave a cheeky wink, how could she refuse?

She watched them leave: James with his fishing basket slung over his shoulder, and Sally almost running to keep up with him. 'You were made for each other,' she whispered with a smile, 'if only you could see it.'

Sally had never been happier. At times she was walking beside him, and then she was running. Twice they came to a ditch, and each time he put his arm round her waist and held her as he leaped across. When they cut through Farmer Lock's field, the bull took an exception to them and charged, head down, with fury in his red eyes. James picked Sally up as though she weighed nothing, and threw her over the gate, before following with great haste.

Though the breeze was chilly, the sun shone and the world was beautiful. All around them, nature displayed her glory in the guise of moorhens and wild geese, and rabbits that dared to run right across their path. The trees and hedges were budding up for spring, and already there were any number of bright yellow daffodils swathed over the banks. As they passed the lake, a heron soared past, and from somewhere in the woods came the sound of a starling in song.

As always, Sally was mesmerised. 'I love it here,' she told James. 'I hope I never have to leave.'

James glanced down on her eager face and smiled. 'You're a strange little thing,' he murmured. 'Why would you have to leave? You're a free spirit. You can go or stay. You don't have to answer to anyone.'

Something about the splendid loneliness and the desperation he wrought in her made Sally unusually bold. 'Will you miss me if I leave?'

Swinging his way round the tree, he softly laughed. 'I think I might.' Then he spoiled it all. 'If I'd had a sister, I'd have wanted her to be like you.'

Disheartened, but ever hopeful, Sally asked, 'Why would you want her to be like me?'

This time he laughed out loud. 'Because you're good company; you don't mind fishing, and because you have the prettiest nose.' Surprising her, he stooped and kissed it.

'James?' They were coming close to the stream now.

'Yes?' Taking the fishing basket from his shoulders, he swung it easily by his side. 'You mustn't chatter when we're fishing,' he warned, 'or you'll frighten them away.' He glanced at her. 'Sorry. What were you saying?'

'Do you think I'm pretty?'

Now it was his turn to be surprised. For a long moment he regarded her, strangely disturbed by a fleeting memory . . . of that night, outside the park, when he'd held her close. There had been something in her eyes, something very beautiful . . . He took a deep breath, answering in a casual voice, 'You're as pretty as anybody, I suppose.' Reluctant to continue this conversation, he put his finger to his lips. 'Ssh now. Trout are renowned for being nervous.'

They stayed for three hours, and every minute was a memory Sally would cherish for ever. James let her sit on the fishing basket. He set her up with a fishing rod and understood when she grimaced at the sight of a worm wriggling on the end of the hook. He didn't complain when she constantly tugged the keep net out of the water to see how the fish were doing, and he never chastised her when by accident she let one escape.

When, by some miracle, she felt a fish on the end of her line, James came to her aid, and between them they reeled in what James termed 'The biggest trout I've ever seen!'

At half past three, James decided it was time to pack up. 'It's a good half-hour's trek back home,' he reminded her, 'but we've had a successful afternoon.' Pointing to the submerged net, he said, 'It looks like Mam will get her trout after all, eh?'

Packing the basket, he didn't see how Sally was hell-bent on retrieving their catch. All he heard was a scream and the loud splash of water. When he turned there she was, up to her neck, and the trout taking off in the opposite direction. 'It was an accident!' Mortified, she thrashed about, trying to catch the trout as they slithered away. 'I slipped in the mud.' She was so miserable. 'Oh, James . . . I'm *really* sorry!'

At first James couldn't believe his eyes. He stared at her, and for one moment she thought he would bellow with rage, and quite rightly so. Instead, he smiled, then he grinned, and now he was roaring with laughter. 'I don't believe it!' he kept saying. 'I just *don't* believe it!'

It was a struggle to get her out. Her boots had sucked into the mud, and as he collected her into his arms, the weight of the water drew them both down. Eventually they were on the bank, wet to the bones and laughing so loud they frightened away all the creatures. 'I'm never bringing you fishing again,' James threatened. But he would. He hadn't laughed so much in a long time.

Maureen saw them coming. Sally had James's jacket on, and James had lost his fishing basket, and the two of them looked soaked to the skin. 'Whatever's happened?' Running out to meet them, she was horrified.

With a twinkle in his eye, James just shook his head.

'I fell in,' Sally confessed, 'and James had to get me out.'

Afraid they might catch their deaths of cold, Maureen ushered them both inside. She soon had the water boiling, and a set of clean clothes for each of them. James washed and changed in the outhouse, while Sally stripped in the parlour.

Later, over a hot meal and a drop of brandy which Maureen had been saving, they told her how it happened. 'So! I'll not get my trout after all?' she said. And the meal, like the day, ended in laughter.

But later, when the other two had fallen asleep in their beds, James paced his room. He and Sally had forged a wonderful bond today. But it was thoughts of Isabel that kept him awake.

Chapter Ten

Cook was all in a fluster. 'It's been years since I've done anything like this.' Groaning, she pushed back a stray lock of grey hair. 'I've been at it since four o'clock this morning, and all day yesterday, and that's on top of my ordinary duties.' Taking a tray of dainty pork pies out of the oven, she laid it on the cooling tray. 'I'm fair worn out,' she told Eliza. 'By the time this is all over, I swear I'll be a nervous wreck.'

Eliza Flanagan had helped all she could. 'Take a little breather,' she said. 'You've earned it.' Cook did look worn out: her face was all over pink, and her feet were beginning to drag.

When Eliza took Cook by the arm and led her to the table, there was no resistance. 'Now then, you sit there and I'll make a pot of tea.' Eliza turned to the two young things who were bustling about at Cook's orders. 'When you've finished what you're doing, I'm sure Cook wouldn't mind if you joined us.' She waited for Cook to give the nod, before telling them in a quieter voice, 'Make sure there's nothing left to spoil though –' she glanced meaningfully at Cook – 'or there'll be all hell to pay.'

The invitation brought a smile to their faces. 'Cor!' Polly Lampton saw Eliza take four fat muffins from the pantry. 'I don't know about Cook being worn out,' she muttered to her colleague. 'We've *all* been at it since four o'clock this morning.'

'Yes, but she's fatter and older,' said the other.

'Aw, she ain't a bad old devil,' answered Polly in a whisper, 'and she meks the best muffins in the world.'

When they were all round the table, resting their feet and filling their faces, the talk was of the forthcoming ball. Cook had more to say than most on the matter. 'In my experience, it's a sign that one o' the daughters is being sold off to a likely suitor.'

Polly dared to question her. 'What d'you mean, sold off?'

'I mean exactly what I say,' Cook informed her impatiently. She then silenced herself by stuffing a great chunk of muffin into her mouth.

Eliza had been deep in thought, but took a moment to explain. 'What Cook means is that usually, when a daughter is of an age, the father will scour about for a suitable young man for her. That young man will either be the son of a friend, or he'll be wealthy in his own right, or both. So, it would seem the master has decided it's time to marry off Miss Isabel.'

'I know all about what goes on,' Polly answered respectfully, 'but I've never heard it said they were being sold.' There was a look of shock on her face. 'I think that's terrible.'

'You're still a babe in arms, that's what you are!' Cook gave her a disdainful look. 'What else could it be, eh? When a man parades his daughter before all and sundry, looking to be rid of her . . . she's no more than a beast at market. He's looking to sell her, and that's a fact.'

'But what if she were to be in love with some other young man?' With Cook already in tatters, Polly was treading a very dangerous line.

'Dear me!' Cook was becoming exasperated. 'What a persistent little madam you are!' All the same, she explained, 'It wouldn't make no difference if she'd rather wed some other young man or not. If the master has his mind set on a particular

177

husband for his daughter, she won't have much say in the matter.'

'But Miss Isabel is his favourite, everybody knows that. Surely he wouldn't make her wed somebody she didn't want?'

Before Cook might explode, Eliza intervened. 'We shall have to wait and see, won't we?'

The ball was a glowing success.

In her beautiful crimson gown, with her shoulders bare and her long hair swept into a coil at the nape of her neck, Isabel took everyone's breath away.

Sidling up to her mother, Hannah complained, 'No one's interested in me.'

'You know what the evening is all about,' Frances gently reminded her. 'Your turn will come soon enough, and anyway, I've already seen a certain young man stealing a glance or two at you.'

Hannah could not hide her glee. 'Have you really?'

'Yes, and why *shouldn't* they look at you?'

Frances didn't have much in her marriage, but she was immensely proud of her two lovely daughters. 'You look so pretty,' she said. The blue dress suited Hannah's fair colouring. It brought out the vivid blue of her eyes too.

It was all Hannah needed. From then on, she smiled, and flirted, and captured the moment. And it didn't matter that Isabel was the star of the show, because, like her mother said, Hannah's turn would come soon enough.

Adam Scarlet was not allowed to monopolise Isabel. Woman enough to know that she was the focus of attention, she played the young men at their own game, until the one intended for her became increasingly anxious. He had been shown what might be his, and now he wanted her with every bone in his body.

When the evening was almost gone, and he knew he may not

have another chance to please her, he was the first to her side when the music started and quick to bring her a drink when it stopped. They danced like they were moulded for each other. The band played softly; they held each other close, and a spark of defiance made Isabel warm to him. 'You're a wonderful dancer,' she told him, and he, feeling giddy with the need to please, almost fell over as he twirled her round and round on the spot.

Leonard Mears was thrilled to see how well they were getting on. 'Look at that,' he told Adam's father. 'I do believe we've won the day.' And the two of them promptly began haggling over how they would use that piece of precious development land which straddled their two factories.

For many years the land had been split in half, though it was too small to be useful in two pieces. As one, however, it was worth a small fortune for development, though worth a great deal more as a business venture between the two men. If their children joined together in matrimony, the land too would be joined. There would be many options available once that happened.

Amongst the gaiety and the music, there was one quiet face that seemed not to enjoy the evening. Peering into that grand place from the doorway, Eliza Flanagan took note of it all. She saw the finery and the jewels and the smart turn of heels as the guests stepped lively across the floor. She saw how her mistress seemed almost to cower in the shadows whenever her husband glanced across at her; and she observed how the master and his crony whispered in the corner, making plans, building fortunes and ruining lives. Just like he had ruined hers! When she could no longer bear the sight of him, she turned and hurried away.

Upstairs in her room she took out the dog-eared photograph and gazed on it awhile. Cradling it to her bosom, she murmured, 'He'll pay for it. Maybe not today or tomorrow. But one day . . . soon!'

* * *

'You're very beautiful.' Sliding his arm round her waist, Adam drew Isabel from the dancefloor. 'It's so warm in here,' he told her. 'Do you think anyone would miss us if we went outside for a breath of air?'

Isabel told him she liked the idea. 'Besides, the only one who might object is Father, and he's too busy making deals to worry about what we're doing.' Sometimes she hated him. Sometimes she pitied him. Other times she admired him with a passion.

Excited, Adam grabbed a bottle of wine and two glasses. 'Let's get out of here,' he said.

'You go first,' she suggested, 'while I get my wrap.'

Sneaking off like thieves in the night, they were noticed only by Frances, who turned away and pretended she hadn't seen. If she ignored them she would be in trouble. If she brought them to his attention, she would *still* be in trouble. So experience had taught her that when in doubt, she should pretend ignorance.

Outside, Adam drew Isabel's wrap about her. 'Are you cold?'

'No,' she answered, giggling, 'but I think I've had too much wine.'

He stroked his hand down her bare arm. 'You're trembling.'

'I know.'

'Would you rather go back inside?' He prayed her answer would be no, and it was.

'We could go to the summer-house,' she suggested in a fit of the giggles.

That brought a smile to his face. 'Lead the way.'

'Follow me.' Taking his hand, she started running, laughing when she tripped against the rockery. 'Whoops! Mustn't crush the daffodils.'

'I'd better take a stronger hold on you,' he said, and did so; much to her amusement.

In the summer-house, they danced to the soft strains of music floating over the air from the open windows of the house. 'I think you're the loveliest thing I have ever seen.'

'Only think?' Giving a loud hiccup, she clamped her hand over her mouth. 'Oh dear! I'm not used to the wine.'

They danced a moment longer, enjoying the music, enjoying each other, and at that particular moment all alone in the world.

Mesmerised by her beauty, he looked down into those rich blue eyes and was lost. 'You do realise our fathers mean to throw us together, don't you?'

'I know.'

'What do you think about that?' He stroked her hair. 'Don't you find it nauseating?'

'Do *you*?'

'On the contrary. But you haven't answered *my* question.'

'I find you splendid company.' She giggled like a schoolgirl. 'Handsome too, and a wonderful dancer. You'll make someone a fine husband.'

'Not you though?'

'Maybe. Maybe not.' She loved to tease.

Reaching down he took up the bottle of wine from where he'd placed it on the floor. When he reached into his jacket pocket he discovered one of the glasses in fragments. 'You use the other glass.' Picking out the bits of broken glass, he placed them all together under the wooden seat, then, handing her the whole glass, he filled it to the brim. 'Cheers, my beauty!'

Isabel raised her glass. 'Cheers!' While she sipped from the glass, he took a great swig from the bottle.

They had a moment of giggling, then a moment of being serious, and now he grew amorous. 'I think I'll make love to you,' he said, and she, laughing, answered, 'I think you might.'

Warm and cosy, her senses affected by the wine, Isabel felt his body on hers. His hand sought out her most private parts, and there was no turning back. Her emotions were a mingling of regret and excitement; regret because it wasn't James who was holding her; excitement because this was her very first time. 'Don't hurt me,' she said, half hoping he might decide to stop, though he didn't.

Laying her on the hard wooden seat, he lifted her skirt and drew down her undergarments, and slid himself into her with apparent ease. There was a flicker of pain, then the strangest feeling as he began moving backwards and forwards, faster and faster, until she felt her senses bursting. His too.

When he withdrew, gasping on top of her, she felt wicked, but wonderful. She felt she had punished James but, in doing so, she suddenly realised she had cheapened herself. But if she was cheap, it was James's fault! For the wrong he had done her.

Unable to sleep, James had taken to the streets to clear the chaos in his mind.

Inevitably, he was drawn to the Mears' house by the sound of music on the night air. He'd heard of this party from Robert and Jack at work. The lights were on all over the house; there were people laughing and some, slightly drunk, had even taken to singing.

It was when he swung away that he saw Isabel running through the garden. His heart fell to his boots when he saw she was with a man.

Hand in hand they made their way back to the house. He had his arm round her and they paused several times to kiss.

Suddenly, she turned to see him there, and her eyes widened with astonishment. Then, in the cruellest way, she slid her arms round the young man's neck and kissed him lingeringly. As she drew away her smiling eyes looked over his shoulder at James's shocked face.

Shaken to his soul, James strode quickly away. If he had entertained hopes of her wanting him, he had no illusions now.

'You've been a bloody fool!' he told himself angrily. 'A blind, stupid fool!'

But it wasn't anger that ran through him. It was a sense of loss. He had loved her . . . *still* loved her.

And as far as he could see, in spite of what she had done, nothing would ever change that.

Chapter Eleven

Hannah noticed it first. 'What's wrong with you, Isabel?' Standing at the door of the bathroom now, she made a face at the sight of her sister, retching and groaning over the sink. 'That's three times you've been sick in the mornings.'

Isabel was not in the mood for Hannah's chirping. 'Go away, Hannah. Leave me alone.' She felt like death on a bad day.

Hannah gave a sly little grin. 'I heard Cook telling Mrs Flanagan about one of the maids where she used to work. Apparently she was sick in the mornings too, and it turned out she was having the master's baby. They sent her away bag and baggage, and she was never seen again.'

'Shut up, Hannah!'

'I hope *you're* not having a baby. Father would strangle you with his own bare hands.'

Suddenly, Hannah was caught by the shoulder and spun round. 'That's dangerous talk, my girl!' White-faced and horrified, Frances had heard every word. 'Go downstairs,' she ordered angrily. 'At once! And don't breathe a word of this,' she said quietly. 'If I hear you've spoken to anyone about your sister being sick, you will answer to me.'

Realising there was more going on here than she knew how to deal with, Hannah fled downstairs. She sat at the breakfast table with such a sullen face that Robert told her jokingly, 'It's a wonder you don't turn the milk sour.'

Leonard Mears ordered them to stop chattering and get on with their breakfast. Addressing Hannah, he asked, 'Where on earth is your mother, child? I sent her for Isabel almost ten minutes ago!'

'They're talking.'

His face reddened with anger. 'Talking?' He threw down his napkin. 'Go and fetch them. Now!'

Eager to be gone, Hannah was out of the room in a moment. Rushing up the stairs, she peered in at the door of Isabel's room, to see her mother cradling her sister, sobbing, in her arms. 'Father sent me,' she explained nervously. 'He says you're to come . . . now!'

'Tell him we're on our way.' Frances dared not refuse.

When Hannah was gone, she quietly voiced her suspicions to Isabel. 'That night at the ball . . . when you went outside with Adam Scarlet, did you . . . do anything?' It was difficult for her to talk like this, but she feared the worst. 'Tell me straight, Isabel,' she said. 'I can't help you if you hide the truth from me.' Though she wasn't sure she could help in any event.

Sitting across the bed from her, Isabel remained quiet, head bowed and feeling so ill she just wanted to lie down and never get up again. Hannah had already stated what she herself had feared, and now her mother was asking what happened on that awful night. God! How she wished she had never led him on, and she *had*, there was no doubt about that.

Growing impatient, Frances spoke in a firmer voice. 'Isabel! Did you and that young man get up to mischief?'

Isabel looked up, her eyes swimming with tears. She didn't need to say anything. The answer was in her face for all to see.

Realising the truth, Frances covered her mouth with her hands. Oh, dear Lord, it was the worst thing. The very worst. How could she tell her husband? What would people think? Fear made her shiver, and instead of her comforting her daughter, it was Isabel who had to comfort her.

'It'll be all right,' she promised. But she couldn't see how. All she could see was shame and punishment ahead.

Knowing Isabel had no one else to turn to, Frances soon regained her composure. 'You get back into bed, and don't worry about your father,' she said. 'I'll make him understand you're too ill to come down.'

Relieved, Isabel wiped her eyes. 'What am I going to do?'

Frances shook her head forlornly. 'First we have to make sure. After that, we'll know what must be done.' Shaking her head chastisingly, she told her, 'What in heaven's name were you thinking of?'

Isabel couldn't bear to look at her. 'I'm sorry, Mother,' she said, her shameful gaze downcast.

Disgusted and pitying, Frances was torn two ways. 'I'd better go,' she decided, 'or he'll be on the warpath.'

As Frances came into the room, his cruel eyes sought her out. 'Where is she?'

Isabel is too ill to come down.' Fear rippled through every fibre of her being. 'I've told her to get back into bed.'

'Ill?' He had a way of staring that made her tremble. 'What do you mean . . . ill?'

'She must have caught a chill, I think. I'm sure it's nothing serious.'

Dabbing the remains of yolk from his chin, he replaced the napkin and stood up. 'I shall go and see her.'

Horrified, Frances assured him, 'Better not. She's sleeping soundly.'

Amazed at her mother's protest, Hannah gave a frightened little gasp. Bracing herself for an almighty scene, she was relieved when her father seemed not to have noticed. Another time Frances would have been punished for daring to reply in such a way, but her husband had a great deal on his mind this morning, not least of which were his imminent plans for Isabel's future.

The idea that she was ill had made him uncomfortable. 'Hmh!' He stared at Frances, his mind feverishly working. 'Very well. As it happens, I do have an extremely busy morning ahead of me, but I'll get away early. You look after her. Call the doctor if needs be.' That said, he was swiftly gone, out of the room and out of the house in no time at all.

In the wake of his leaving, there was a moment of quiet, before Robert asked, 'Would you like me to call in and alert the doctor? It wouldn't be too far out of my way.'

Frances graciously refused. 'Sleep is best for now.' She looked on his kind, honest face and thought how, if she could turn to anyone, it would be Robert. But just now she dare trust no one, and the knowledge of Isabel's secret was a truly terrible burden.

Jack was not interested in Isabel, or anyone else for that matter. All he cared about was himself, and right now he was feeling very pleased. His father had just informed him how – for reasons he did not care to discuss – he had hired a new man to labour in the factory. Therefore, Jack was to move back upstairs to the office, where he must pay particular attention to Robert's way of working. He would listen and learn, and do as he was told, because he would not get a second chance.

Wrongly believing it to be a reward for working well on the factory floor, Jack meant to show his father that he was a better man than his brother. In his mind, he was already scheming and conniving. If he could topple Robert, there was no limit to what he might do.

When they were gone to their respective places of work, her two sons to the factory, and her younger daughter to her studies,

Frances gently woke Isabel and told her to get ready for an outing. 'This is our chance to visit the doctor without your father knowing. Quickly now. Pinch some colour into your cheeks and meet me downstairs.'

For the first time defying her husband's orders that they must not leave the house without his permission, Frances instructed the trap to be made ready.

Through the library window, Hannah was curious to see her mother giving orders to the groom. Making an excuse to the governess, she stole a moment to find Isabel, who was just emerging from her bedroom.

'What's happening?' she demanded excitedly. 'Is it to do with you? Are you *really* having a baby?'

When Isabel looked at her, in a certain sorry way, she gasped aloud, her mouth wide open with shock. 'She's taking you to the doctor, isn't she? She daren't have him here, in case he tells her out loud and the servants hear?'

Isabel put her finger to her lips. 'Ssh! They'll hear *now* . . . unless you lower your voice!'

'Oh, Isabel!' Curiosity had gone and in its place came a terrible fear. 'Oh! What about Father? Oh, Isabel, he'll go crazy!' Terrified by her own thoughts she burst out crying. 'He'll whip you, Isabel! He'll whip me too, I know he will.'

For the second time that morning, Isabel found herself comforting someone else, when it was her who needed reassuring. 'Look, we don't know what's making me sick,' she told Hannah in a whisper. 'It might just be something I've eaten. We won't know until I've seen the doctor.'

They went downstairs together, and when she set off in the trap with her mother at the reins, Isabel glanced back to see Hannah at the library window. 'He *won't* whip you,' she murmured. 'I won't let him.'

* * *

It was confirmed. Isabel was with child.

The doctor was as certain as he could be. The child must have been conceived on the night of the ball. He calculated the birth to be around the end of the year.

On the way back, both women were silent, each ravaged by what the doctor had confirmed.

'Now I have the awful task of informing your father.' Frances didn't even know how to start.

Isabel was adamant. 'Let me tell him, Mother,' she pleaded. 'I'm the one who's brought shame down on us, and I'm the one who should take the brunt of his fury.'

For the first time in her life, Frances was in charge. 'When your father comes through that front door, I want you to go up to your room, and turn the key. You're not to come out until I tell you . . . not for anything. Do you hear me?'

Isabel had never been afraid of her father, and she was not afraid now. 'Please, Mother . . . let me tell him.'

Frances was unmoving. 'I asked . . . did you hear me?'

Isabel nodded. 'Yes, Mother,' she answered, 'I heard you.'

'Then do as I say.'

Reluctantly, Isabel agreed.

It was four-thirty when he came home.

Isabel had stood vigil by the window for the last hour. When she saw his carriage draw up, she quickly stepped back from the window. Waiting until she heard the front door slam, she then went quickly across the room and turned the key. That done, she returned to the bed, where she sat very still, her eyes turned towards the door, and her ears tuned to every sound.

Bumptious as ever, Mears came into the drawing room where Frances was sitting on the couch, fretting over what she might say. How she might tell him, and what awful consequences might follow.

'Where is she?' Obviously irritated, he went to the dresser where he poured himself a large whisky. 'Nothing's gone right today!' he snarled. 'I'm surrounded by idiots.' Throwing the liquid down his throat he pressed his lips together and sighed, 'That's better.'

'Leonard?' Since returning from the doctor's, Frances had been out of her wits. 'I have something to tell you.'

Staring at her disapprovingly, he took a moment to wipe his mouth. 'Can't it wait?'

'I think you should sit down.' She herself stood up. It was too disconcerting with him towering above her like that.

Remaining where he was, he began to realise something was dreadfully wrong. Suddenly his face fell and the colour drained away. 'Oh, my God!'

'Oh no!' Realising he believed Isabel had taken a turn for the worse, she told him, 'She's fine . . . well . . . I mean . . . she's not *ill* exactly.'

Relieved, he closed his eyes, his chest swelling with an intake of breath. 'Not ill exactly . . . what the devil are you talking about?' All day he had been negotiating the best deal he had envisaged in a long time, and for one dreadful minute he had seen it evaporating before his eyes. 'If she's not ill, what then? Stop stuttering, woman, and get on with it!'

Frances took a deep breath. Mustering all the courage she had, she began, 'The night of the ball . . . Isabel and that young man—' Her throat seemed to close up with terror.

'Adam Scarlet, yes?' He frowned. 'A fine couple, I thought. Yes? What about them?'

Frances gulped. 'You recall they went into the gardens for a time?'

'I remember.' He had seen and chosen to ignore that little rendezvous.

She had to get it over with. 'Isabel tells me they went into the summer-house—' The words stuck in her head, and she couldn't get them out. Suddenly they tumbled one over the other, and she couldn't control them. 'This morning, I took her to the doctor's and it was confirmed . . . she's with child . . . *his* child.' A choking sob escaped her. 'I'm sorry, I just don't know how to deal with it.'

As the truth sank in, he was visibly shaken, his fists clenched and his breathing erratic.

Terrified, Frances waited for the backlash. When it came, it was with such fury that she had no defence. The blows rained down on her until she thought he would kill her. He was like a mad thing. 'You . . . went out!' His scream was deafening, then eerily quiet. 'You left this house without my permission?' Incensed because she had defied him, he knew no mercy. 'If she's a slut, it's because you've set her a good example!'

On and on he went. In the kitchen the servants heard him screaming and kept themselves confined there; Hannah, too, heard him as she came up from the garden. Fearing she would be thrashed as well, she ran to the summer-house and crawled into a corner, where she hoped he would never find her.

Upstairs, Isabel knew she would have to intervene. This was her fault, and her mother was taking the punishment. She couldn't let that happen. Quickly now, she went down the stairs, her fear like a cold anger inside her. Throwing open the door, she challenged him, her voice quiet but assertive. 'Leave her alone!' Her mother was stooped before him, her hands across her head and the blood trickling between her fingers.

For one peculiar moment it was as though the scene was frozen in time; he turned, his fist raised in the air and his face twisted in fury. He remained like that for what seemed an age, looking at Isabel and trying to remember what he had been told.

In that moment when Isabel ran across the room to comfort

her mother it seemed to jolt him awake. With a cry, he spun round and brought his fist across Isabel's head with such force that it knocked her sideways. 'You filthy *slut*!'

Defiant as ever, Isabel stared up at him. It seemed to have a sobering effect. Gesturing towards Frances, he told his daughter, 'Clean her up. Then the pair of you report to my office. Quickly, damn it!' One last, disgusted glance, a shake of the head, and he was gone.

It was Eliza Flanagan who came first on the scene. 'It's all right, miss,' she told Isabel, who was still reeling from the blow. 'You sit down, I'll see to her.' She left then, and was only gone a minute before she returned with a bowl and toiletries to bathe Frances's face. She also had a cold wet cloth, which she told Isabel to place across her face where he had caught her with his fist. 'The skin isn't split,' she told her, 'but you'll have a nasty bruise, I've no doubt.'

A few moments later, both badly bruised and subdued, they reported to his office. 'Come!' The low, gruff voice was forbidding. Gingerly, Frances opened the door and went in. Less humble, Isabel followed.

With the pair of them standing before him, he remained at his desk, turning his pencil over and over on the desktop, before eventually addressing them. 'I hope I don't have to say how shocked I am at your behaviour,' he told Isabel. 'I always believed you had dignity. I saw you as a real lady, while others could never hold a candle to you. Now I can hardly bear to look on you.'

To make his point he glanced down at the desk before he continued in the same reprimanding tone. 'You have let me down badly. Indeed, you have let this *family* down badly. I can never remember a time when a Mears created such shame.' Except for himself, and he was not about to reveal that.

Throwing caution to the wind, Frances sought to protect her

daughter. 'Isabel is very sorry about what happened. She was plied with wine and it went to her head. It will never happen again.'

'I don't give a bugger about whether it will happen *again*!' he snapped. 'It's happened *now*. And I have to decide what's to be done about it.'

Isabel saw the glint in his eyes, and was quickly on the defensive. 'I won't let you take the baby away, Father.'

Humoured, he laughed aloud. 'Oh, you *won't*, won't you?'

With downcast eyes she remained silent.

'It is up to *me* what will be done with this child, and it is up to *me* what will be done with you.'

The brief ensuing silence was almost unbearable for the two women. Presently, he got from his chair and began pacing. It was a while before he spoke and when he did, it was with a delighted grin that astonished them. 'Right!' His face was pressed so close to Isabel's that she could smell the whisky on his breath. 'So you have made up your mind to be a mother, have you?'

'Yes, Father.'

'Ha!' Her answer was music to his ears. 'Then you must now make up your mind to be a *wife*!'

At this Isabel stared at her mother, and her mother stared at him. He, however, went on totally oblivious to their reaction. 'I have been doing some serious thinking and can see only one possible satisfactory solution.'

With gusto he swung round to beam on them again, excitedly pacing the floor, hands behind his back and looking for all the world like a frog in a suit. 'You and Adam Scarlet will be married without further ado, and I shall arrange for the wedding to take place at the first possible moment. Now get out!' he told them. 'You disappoint me.'

In there, in front of her husband, Frances had kept her dignity.

Once outside the door, she visibly sagged, her face white and drawn. To the side of her temple and on the lower part of her neck, the skin was red and bruised where he had brought his fist down time and again. Isabel saw how weak she was, and helped her to her room.

'I'll be all right,' Frances told her. 'Leave me now. Let me sleep awhile.'

'I'm so sorry, Mother.' Isabel thought she would never forgive herself for not having gone down earlier, but, for the first time ever, she had been afraid to face him.

'This young man, Adam . . . do you love him?'

Isabel took a moment to answer. 'I'm not sure,' she said. 'I don't know if it's wise to love *anyone*.' Not when you could be hurt, like she had been hurt by James.

'Do you imagine life with him might be miserable?' Like hers had been, she thought bitterly.

'I hope not.' For reasons known only to herself and James, Isabel had already turned towards Adam. 'I do *like* him,' she confessed. 'But I hardly know him.' It was a terrible admission, especially when she was carrying his child.

Frances despaired. 'I did so hope you would find a man you might be happy with,' she sighed, thinking how some people paid heavily for their mistakes, while others spent all their lives wicked and sinful, and were never made to pay the price. 'But maybe . . . just maybe, there is a chance that you and this young man will be good for each other after all.'

'I hope so, Mother.'

Now that the decision was made and she was to be given in marriage to Adam Scarlet, she was suddenly afraid. After all, what did she *really* know about him?

The woman hardly ever smiled. She was hard-faced and unpleasant, and he suspected she could be a nasty character. But she did have a few saving graces. These being that she was well-dressed and dignified and, most important of all, possessed a very healthy bank account.

Her married name was Anne Hale; he knew that from her application to open an account. He also knew she had reverted to using her maiden name. 'Good morning, Miss Mears, and how are you today?' As always, she had come to his counter. He liked to think it was because he went out of his way to make her feel special, when in actual fact she was quite ordinary, except for the amount of money she owned. 'That's a very pretty hat you're wearing, I must say.'

Anne Mears, as she now liked to be known, did not return his smile, though she did return his greeting. 'I would like to withdraw ten shillings.'

He chatted while he worked and, as always, she seemed to warm to him. 'You're looking very well,' he told her.

'Thank you,' she replied, 'and so are you.'

He lowered his voice. 'Have you decided on the matter you and I discussed the other week?'

'You mean the tearooms?'

'Yes. A chancy business venture, I thought.' He smiled hopefully. 'I've been thinking about it, and I'm sure you yourself might still be turning the idea over in your mind.'

'I must admit, I haven't altogether given up the idea, in spite of your good advice.' Having got rid of her old life, she was now ready to do something useful with her money; preferably to double it.

'That's what I thought.' His pleasant, fleshy face lifted in the most attractive of smiles. 'Look, Miss Mears, I have an idea.' Leaning across the counter he lowered his voice. 'In these matters it is usually a good idea to undertake a certain amount of investigation, if you know what I mean?'

Suddenly, she had glimpses of Sally cowering in the corner,

while the whip tore open her skin. Alarmed, she clutched at her throat. 'What exactly are you saying?'

'I'm saying you and I should set up surveillance on these tearooms. That way I can assess the flow of customers, and advise you better.'

Sinking with relief, she smiled nervously. 'If you like.' For one awful moment she had imagined *she* might be under investigation.

'Good!' He hadn't realised it would be so easy. 'Shall we say midday on Saturday? I can either collect you from your address, or I can wait at the tearooms for you to join me there. Whichever is easier for you.'

Already regretting having agreed, but still greatly relieved that she had misunderstood his words, Anne told him curtly, 'If you really think the exercise is necessary …?'

'Essential, I should say.'

'Then I would prefer to meet at the tearooms.'

'Good! It's settled then. We shall meet at the tearooms at midday on Saturday . . . day after tomorrow.' Adding in a businesslike manner, 'We shall see how suitable a business venture it might be.'

'Is there a fee to be paid?' She was always frugal with her money.

'Not at all, Miss Mears. It's all part of the bank's service.'

'Thank you. It's good of you to give up your time.' With a curt nod of the head, she took up her ten shillings and departed.

As she went out the door, the clerk smiled to himself. 'Gently gently, catch a monkey,' he muttered.

Anne Mears was a perfect catch. From her application to open an account here, he had discovered all he needed to know.

Since her husband's demise, she was all alone in the world – no family, no ties; and not once, since she had been coming to the bank, had he seen her with a friend or colleague. The haughty

Miss Mears apparently preferred her own company, which suited him down to the ground.

More importantly, every penny in her considerable bank account was deposited in her own name.

Chapter Twelve

Two days after Isabel's pregnancy had been confirmed, Leonard Mears drew the servants together; assembled in the drawing room, they looked a sorry sight. The parlour-maid was shaking like a leaf, fearing she was facing the sack; her colleague did her best to hide behind Cook, until the master told her 'Stand up straight and look at me!' Red-faced and itching to get back to her kitchen, Cook shifted from one foot to the other, thinking she knew what this was all about, but not being altogether sure.

Tall and dignified, Eliza Flanagan stood apart from the others. She had no doubt whatsoever what this was about, and when the master began addressing them, her suspicions were satisfied.

'My daughter is to be married on Easter Saturday,' he said. The two young maids glanced nervously one to the other; it was fortunate for them he was pacing the floor and did not see.

He halted and went on, 'I have no doubt you have heard certain things said in this house.' His piggy little eyes narrowed to slits as he warned, 'All of you are in a position of trust here, and as you must be aware, I am a man of influence in all corners of the North. Should it *ever* come to my notice that there has been the slightest breath of scandal concerning this family, I shall root out the culprit and see to it that this same person will never work again – whether it be in a house of importance, or the lowest hovel in the land.'

Satisfied that they understood his meaning, he continued. 'Moreover, I shall make it my business –' here he glared at them, his finishing words slow and deliberate – 'to have that person severely punished.'

When he was done, he dismissed them. 'I urge you all to bear in mind what I have said.'

When they were gone, he stood for a moment by the doors, fists clenched and head bowed, hoping he had frightened them into a vow of silence. Certainly, as they filed back to the kitchen, not one of them spoke. Cook led the way and, like little ducks, the young maids followed. Eliza Flanagan paused by the stairs, where her curious gaze drifted back to the drawing room. 'Shame and unhappiness seem to follow you wherever you go,' she muttered. There was such hatred in her heart at that moment, she could almost taste it.

When she arrived in the kitchen, there they sat, nervous and silent. Her heart went out to them. 'There is no need to be worried about your positions here,' she assured them. 'We all know what's going on in this house, and he is quite within his right to ask for our silence. But that is all! We owe him nothing else. Every one of us earns our keep, and if we were to leave tomorrow, I am quite sure the mistress would send us away with glowing references.'

The parlour-maid looked up with sorry eyes. 'Hmh! That ain't what 'e just said.'

'Maybe not, but it's what *I* just said. The only thing you have to remember is to keep your tongue between your teeth and don't be tempted to gossip. Every family has a right to its dark secrets.'

They all looked at her, thinking they knew what she meant. In truth, they had no idea.

* * *

James was devastated. When the news leaked out that Isabel was to be married, he could hardly believe it. Oh, there was talk – there was always talk – that the courting had been short and the wedding too soon. Some said she was rushing it along to get away from her domineering father. Others said the father himself had engineered the marriage for business reasons.

It was common knowledge that Leonard Mears had long wanted to buy that valuable piece of land straddling his carriage factory and the warehouse next door; he owned half of it, and Adam Scarlet's father owned the other half. It was said there were two marriages going on here. One between the men, and the other between their unsuspecting offspring.

Maureen felt for her son, but deep down she wasn't sorry the Mears girl was getting married. 'Maybe he'll realise she was never meant for him,' she confided to Sally. 'I've feared all along that he was reaching for the moon.'

But Sally knew what James was going through, because she was going through the very same. He wanted Isabel. Sally wanted him. There was bound to be heartbreak along the way.

The days sped by. On the Friday before the wedding, it was rumoured that the occasion would be the biggest and most glamorous for years. Women talked about what she might wear, and how she would fashion her hair; and how many bridesmaids were planned.

In the alehouses, the men muttered into their pint jars about how the young pup would regret it when there were a dozen brats running round his arse.

Every tradesman hoped he would be involved at some point, and as the day drew near, the excitement mounted.

Since that day when she and James had gone fishing, Sally had grown to love him more. She watched him leave of a morning, and waited for him to come home at night. She stayed down with him in the evening after Maureen had gone to bed, when, easy in each other's company, they would talk and laugh. Once when he was feeling low, he confided in her how he felt about Isabel, and how he couldn't understand why she had turned away from him the way she did. He was unhappy, and it showed in his slow smile and the dark, brooding eyes.

Sally felt his unhappiness, and her heart broke.

On this Friday evening before the wedding, he was deeply agitated.

'Will you look at him?' Drawing Sally from her washing-up, Maureen pointed through the window to James. 'He's been at it ever since he got home,' she said. 'He's painted the barn and replaced the broken window there; he's fixed the wheel on the cart and cleaned out the coal cellar. And now he's chopping enough wood to last 'til I'm ninety!'

Exasperated, she wiped her hands on her pinny and sat herself down at the table. 'He's making me that nervous,' she admitted, 'I'm like a cat on hot bricks.'

Sally lingered at the window, her gaze focused on James; stripped to the waist he made a fine sight. The sweat glistened on his skin, already tanned from what sun there'd been this early. He was well-built and immensely strong, and now as he swung the axe high above his head, the thick, deep muscles on his arms and back rippled like a mighty tide coming in.

Helpless to comfort him, Sally could only imagine how desperate he felt. The girl he loved was getting married tomorrow. And he was handling it the best way he knew how. Turning from the window, she looked at Maureen. 'There's nothing we can do . . . is there?'

''Fraid not, lass.' Gazing up at Sally with forlorn eyes, Maureen shook her head. 'I've seen it coming,' she said, 'but he wouldn't listen. All he could see was her and himself . . . man and wife. Now he knows I was right and it doesn't give me any pleasure.'

'He'll be all right,' Sally answered, 'once it's over and everything begins to get back to normal. You'll see.'

Maureen nodded. 'Make us a brew, will you, lass?'

While Sally bustled about doing that, Maureen went to the pantry and took out one of her chunky apple-pies. Grinning, she remarked with a wink, 'I reckon we've earned a few minutes' break, don't you?'

'James, too?' Sally treasured every minute near him. 'Shall I call him in?'

'You can if you like, lass,' Maureen said, 'but I wouldn't count on him coming in just now.' He had been out there since early light. Right now she suspected he didn't want people round him, not even her and Sally.

All the same, Sally went out to him. 'Will you come in and have a brew with us?' she asked. 'Your Mam's got an apple-pie ready.' Keeping her fingers crossed behind her back, she waited for his answer.

Slicing the axe into the wood, he paused, his back still bent with the flow of the axe. For a moment it looked as if he might accept her invitation, then he looked up, his dark eyes filled with pain. She wasn't surprised when he said softly, 'Later, Sally. I'm not in the mood for company just now.'

'I should imagine he's got things to sort out in his own mind,' Maureen told Sally. 'I know from experience you need to be alone for that.'

Sally nodded. She knew all about that too. All those long, lonely months on the road, alone and afraid . . . She'd had more time to think than was good for her; what might have been; how it all turned out; wondering what the future would be now. It had been a nightmare. And it still wasn't over.

She told Maureen as much now. 'I thought when I found my

real father, everything would be all right,' she confessed. 'But it's worse. Before, I was angry that he'd abandoned me like that. I wanted to see him, to hear him say he was sorry and that he had always wondered about me. I needed him to tell me all sorts of things . . . things that would make me forgive him for what he did. Now, after meeting him, and realising what kind of man he is, I don't want him for a father.' She smiled proudly. 'The man who raised me was so different . . . kind and generous. I couldn't have had a better father.'

'Then you must be grateful for that. When the anger comes, remember him, and in time the bad feelings will pass.'

Sally thought about that for a minute, but she knew different. 'The trouble is, I ruined his life.' She had not forgotten what Anne Hale had told her. 'You see, I came between him and his wife, until, in the end, all he had was me. I didn't realise. How could I?'

'It wasn't your fault, child.'

'No. It was *his*! Leonard Mears has a lot to answer for.'

'Well, I'm afraid the devil takes care of his own, so I've no doubt he'll continue to prosper.'

Sally's pretty features hardened. 'He mustn't be allowed to. Now I want him hurt, like he hurt me, like he hurts *them*.' In spite of the way that the woman had disfigured her, Sally had come to realise that Anne Hale was also a victim. Dark, dangerous emotions swept through Sally. 'A man like that has no right to walk God's earth.'

'That's not for us to say.' Frightened by the look in Sally's eyes, Maureen wondered how deep the scars had gone. 'You've done so well,' she told her. 'Since you've been here, I've seen you blossom. Please, Sally, trust me. The best thing you can do is to put him out of your mind altogether. Nothing good ever comes of revenge.'

In spite of her tender years, Sally understood. 'I'm not looking for revenge,' she answered quietly. 'I just want him to know the pain and suffering he's caused. I want him to realise what a terrible coward he is. I have to tell him how it was. I don't want him for a father,' she promised. 'I'll visit him just once, for the first and last time.'

Maureen had hoped this would never happen. 'So? You've made up your mind to see him then?'

Sally gave a half-smile. 'I *have* to,' she said, 'or I'll never know any peace.'

'You want him to tell you who your mother is, don't you?'

Sally nodded. 'I'm haunted by it. I don't believe she was a whore off the streets. I think it more likely she was a poor servant girl he had his way with.'

'Think, Sally.' Maureen tried to dissuade her. 'If he didn't tell his own sister and her husband, what makes you think he'll tell *you*?'

'I won't give him any choice.'

Maureen paled. 'Oh, now, Sally!' She gave a groan. 'If you're thinking of blackmailing him, I beg you to forget it. Leonard Mears is not a man to be threatened.'

'We'll see.'

'And if he throws you out?'

'He won't.' Never had she been more determined. 'I think it's time he knew his daughter – the one he gave away. The one he was ashamed of. It's also time I knew the name of my mother. I have a right.'

Briefly they lapsed into silence. Then Maureen wisely lifted the conversation by drawing Sally from her dark thoughts. 'At least one of his daughters will be getting out from under his feet.' Pouring them each another cup of tea, she went on, 'I reckon the whole town will turn out to see her in all her finery.' Rolling her eyes she could imagine it. 'By! It'll be some wedding, that's for sure.'

'I don't even know what she looks like.' Sally was curious.

Suddenly Maureen clapped her hands. 'I know!' Excited now, she suggested, 'Let's you and me go to the house tomorrow morning . . . happen we'll tek Lizzie too.'

Sally was in two minds, but her curiosity got the better of her. 'I'd like that.' Struck by a pang of jealousy, she pushed it away. This was her chance to see the woman James was suffering for.

Maureen leaned forward. 'Not a word to James now,' she warned. 'I don't want him knowing.'

Sally understood, and the conversation ran on to other things. But even while she talked with Maureen, her mind was on James and Isabel Mears. Herself too. Love was a strange, painful thing, and Sally couldn't help but wonder how this unhappy situation would end.

All night long, Sally heard James pacing the floor downstairs.

Startled when there came a tap on the bedroom door, she sat up against the pillow. 'Who's there?'

Maureen's voice came back: 'It's me. I can't sleep.'

Barefoot, Sally ran to the door and let her in. 'Neither can I,' she said, closing the door behind Maureen. 'James hasn't gone to bed yet. He's been pacing the floor all night.' She glanced at the bedside clock: it was almost four. 'It'll be dawn soon,' she said, 'and he's had no sleep.'

Maureen yawned. 'James is a sensible man. He'll get over her. Once Isabel Mears is married he'll realise she was never for him.' She sat down on the edge of the bed. 'Well, that's what I'm praying for,' she confessed, 'because if he *doesn't* get her out of his system, it will drive him crazy.'

Suddenly, the front door was heard to quietly close. 'Gracious me!' Running to the window, Maureen peered down to the street. 'He's gone out. What the devil is he thinking of . . . taking off at this time of a morning!'

From behind her, Sally watched as James strode away, hands in his pockets and shoulders hunched like he carried the weight of the world on his back. 'I expect he needs to distance himself from it all,' she said. 'I know how he feels. Sometimes, when I was on the road, I used to get as far away from people as I could, just to think and clear my mind.'

'Well, I can't see as how either of us will get any sleep now.' Maureen drew the cord of her robe tight about her. 'It strikes chilly at this time of morning,' she said. 'You get back to bed. Try and get some sleep if you can. I'm going down to get a fire started.'

She was halfway down the stairs when she heard Sally pattering behind her. 'I thought you'd be glad of the company.'

Maureen smiled to herself. 'Come on then, lass,' she said, 'I'll light the fire. You put the kettle on the stove.' The day would be here soon enough.

Just as Maureen predicted, it seemed the whole town had turned out for the wedding.

They gathered outside the big house, waiting for the bride to appear. The women's chatter was lively as bees round a honey-pot, while the men stood back, smoking and laughing, brought there by a natural curiosity for the rich and infamous.

'I'd like to see me try and marry our Rosie to some man she hardly knows,' said one. 'What! I'd get the length of her tongue and no mistake.'

His friend had other ideas. 'It's how the gentry go on, ain't it?' he remarked knowingly. 'And I'll tell yer this: if I thought I could make a killing and end up rich, I'd marry off both me daughters and me wife as well.' He laughed aloud. 'Only trouble is, they're so bloody ugly, nobody'd have 'em!'

That set them all laughing, until suddenly the cry went up. 'They're coming out!' Everybody strained forward to catch a glimpse. After all, it wasn't every day a gentry wedding took place; especially one which involved the daughter of the most hated man in Blackburn.

Inside the splendid hallway, Isabel made ready. 'I wish I wasn't so nervous,' she told Hannah; but it wasn't nerves. It was doubt . . . and the doubts had been getting stronger with the passage of time. 'Oh, Hannah, I hope I'm doing the right thing.'

Hannah, who looked lovely in a cream brocade dress with a flouncing hem, was practical as ever. 'You should have thought of that.' The smallest bit jealous, she had not altogether forgiven her sister. 'Besides, Adam is good-looking and rich, and he adores you. So you've nothing to worry about.'

Lowering her voice, Isabel confided, 'I don't love him.'

'So why did you let him do it to you?'

'I was silly with the wine.'

'That's no excuse.'

'I was angry too.'

'Who with?'

'Never you mind.' Things were bad enough, she thought. There was nothing to be gained by bringing James into the conversation.

Frances pushed her way forward. 'Right . . . maid of honour first.' She began fussing and fretting, until chastised by her husband.

'Step aside,' he told her. 'You're getting in the way.'

Obediently she stepped away, and he drew Isabel to the back. 'You stay with me,' he told her. 'We'll make a grand departure, show these peasants how it's done.'

Isabel visibly squirmed. 'I told you I didn't want a grand wedding,' she said. 'I would much rather have had a quiet affair.'

'Nonsense! You're the daughter of Leonard Mears, and you deserve the very best. It's expected of us . . . you must understand that.' Smiling down on her, he said softly, 'You look beautiful. What's more, your secret is safe, and soon enough now you'll be wed, and no one any the wiser.' His gaze strayed to her stomach. 'Sometimes these things are a blessing in disguise.'

When she looked at him, astonished, he jolted her arm. 'Don't let me down,' he told her. 'Be proud. Look them in the eye.'

A few moments later, they emerged from the house to the gasps of onlookers. 'Oh, doesn't she look grand,' one woman cried; another threw rice, and others stood with open mouths. The men took it all in their stride before making their way to the alehouse to down a few well-earned jars of best ale. 'To toast the happy couple,' they said. It was as good an excuse as any.

Outside the church the people waited. Inside the many guests softly talked. Hannah and the two smaller bridesmaids, daughters of business colleagues, toyed with their flowers and got chided by Frances. Looking unusually pretty in a pale green matching gown and jacket, she constantly glanced towards the doors. 'Hurry up,' she murmured beneath her breath, 'let's have it done with.' She could not rid herself of the feeling that here, today, was a tragedy unfolding.

When the carriage arrived and Isabel got out, a wave of shock went through the crowd. They had never imagined how beautiful she was. Her chestnut hair was set off to perfection against the white veil. Figured with silk and shimmering in the sunlight, the dress resembled something from a fairy tale.

As she walked up the aisle, her father smiled beside her. Isabel smiled too, though in her heart she had already begun to despise Adam Scarlet.

When the service was over, the congregation all followed the bride outside. With the formalities done, they made their way to their carriages. The crowd surged forward to get a closer look, among them Maureen and her two friends. 'By! I bet this lot cost a pretty penny.' Lizzie hated to see money spent in such a way. 'That wedding gown will never be worn again, and it won't be long afore them lovely flowers are upside down in the midden.'

Maureen remained silent. She had come here out of curiosity. Now, with her curiosity satisfied, she was ready to leave.

Having been pushed and carried by the women who had surged forward for a better look, Sally stood a short distance away. From here, she could see the bride as she went to her carriage, and she understood how James could love her. Isabel Mears was incredibly beautiful, in a way that *she* never could be.

Mesmerised, she watched every move. She saw how Leonard Mears guarded his daughter, and for one inexplicably mad moment, she almost cried out, 'Look at me! I'm your daughter too!' But common sense prevailed. Besides, she no longer wanted him as a father. He was her enemy now.

Being in a position to see Isabel's face as she climbed into the carriage, Sally was amazed when she smiled down on her. That's my sister, Sally thought sadly, and she doesn't even know me.

Isabel then looked up, seeming to flinch with surprise. Intrigued, Sally followed her gaze, and was astonished too.

Standing back from the crowd, James had seen everything. He had seen her arrive and go into the church. He waited until she came out, and now he was witnessing her leaving. It was a painful thing but he had to be there. All night he had promised himself he would not come here, but when morning came he could not keep away.

Now, with Isabel's eyes on him, his heart turned over. 'I love you,' he mouthed, and *both* young women read his lips. Full of regret, Isabel looked on him a moment longer before being ushered into the carriage, from where she deliberately averted her gaze. Sally's eyes stayed on James. But he didn't see her. Instead, he briskly turned and went from there. As the carriage rumbled by, he was gone. And only Sally had witnessed what had passed between them.

There followed an evening of wining, dining and dancing to the best band money could buy. Adam held his wife as though he would never let her go, while aching to be alone so they could make love to their heart's content.

Leonard Mears shook hands with Adam's father on 'a deal well done'. Delighted to have brought the matter of their children to a conclusion, they now arranged to finalise their plans with regard to the jointly owned land.

When the cake was cut and the toast to the newly-weds given, Adam escorted his bride up to the hotel room, where they had arranged to change for their journey to the South of France for a two-week honeymoon.

Adam tried to take her in his arms.

'No!' Isabel drew away. 'Not here, Adam. Not while they're all waiting downstairs.'

Reluctantly, he let her go. 'All right,' he grudgingly conceded. 'But you'll have to make it up to me when we get to France.'

A short time later they appeared ready to leave. Isabel looked stunning in a blue outfit and large-brimmed hat.

Inevitably there were whispers. 'It's curious how quickly this wedding was arranged, don't you think?' gossips said.

'Time will tell,' one large lady remarked, knowing they would all wait with bated breath for the truth to emerge.

Adam led his new bride out to the carriage. As Isabel climbed up the steps, she realised she had left her purse behind in the hotel.

'Feather-brain,' Adam teased, and ran back inside to retrieve it.

Isabel settled herself into the seat. Startled by a tap on the window she leaned forward to see who was there. It was beginning to rain and, with the raindrops spattering against the window, she couldn't quite see. Intrigued, she sat right up to the edge of the seat and peered out.

Standing there in the darkness was a young woman. White-faced and thin, she was looking up at Isabel. She had a child beside her and a babe-in-arms. There was no one else around. Isabel wound down the window. 'You shouldn't be standing in the rain.' She wondered whether she ought to invite her inside the carriage. 'Are you in trouble?'

The young woman seemed not to have heard. 'I've come to warn you,' she said.

'Warn me?' For some inexplicable reason, Isabel felt threatened.

'It's *him*.' The young woman gestured towards the hotel. 'He's a bad lot. You'll need to watch him, miss. He's a clever bastard.'

Suddenly the other door opened and Adam clambered in. 'Damned weather!' Unaware of the stranger outside, he handed Isabel the purse. 'Ready, driver, on you go.' Banging his fist on the roof of the carriage, he settled himself in. 'Go as quick as you can,' he called out. 'We've lost enough time as it is.'

Turning to Isabel he advised, 'Brace yourself. We'll have to go at some speed if we're to catch the early-morning ferry.' Smiling warmly, he added, 'Not that I'm blaming you. You're a woman after all. I expect I'll have to get used to you forgetting your purse.'

As the carriage surged forward, the rain sprayed in through the window. Quickly, Isabel closed it. In that split second, she caught sight of the young woman again. Standing in the same spot, she held her children close, her long dark hair dampened by the rain, and her soulful eyes following the carriage.

Disturbed by the encounter, Isabel turned to her new husband. 'Did you see that young woman just now?'

Adam drew her close. 'What young woman?'

'The one standing back there in the rain.'

Curious, he glanced through the back window. It was only a fleeting moment, but he saw her and was clearly horrified. 'She didn't approach you, did she?' He made an effort to keep his voice calm, even though he had obviously been shocked to his roots. 'I asked . . . did she approach you?'

Something about his manner warned Isabel not to confide in him. 'Why? *Should* she have done?'

He didn't answer. Suddenly his ardour was cooled. For a time he sat quite still, one arm round her, the fingers of his other hand gently tapping the seat, thinking.

Seeing how he reacted, Isabel too was subdued. The warning reverberated in her brain – *'He's a bad lot . . . You'll need to watch him.'*

Maureen and Sally had been home for hours before James showed his face. He had a bite to eat, then took Jake out for a walk. 'James is best left alone while he's like this.' Maureen knew him too well.

They watched him go, throwing sticks for the dog to retrieve, and striding out as if he might never come back. 'He hasn't said much about the wedding, has he?' Sally had her nose pressed to the window, but with the night and the rain, she soon lost sight of him.

Maureen was scrubbing the pans. She paused, deep in thought for a moment. 'Even as a lad, he kept things close to his chest,' she answered. 'He'll talk it through when he's good and ready, I'm sure. Or he won't say a word, and that'll be the end of it.'

She smiled. 'I remember years since, he found this injured owl in the barn – a cat or a fox had been at it – and it were in a bad way. Well, he fetched it indoors and nursed the poor little thing for days. In the end it died and you could see he were heartbroke. But he never said a word. He just got through it all on his own.' Turning to Sally, she assured her, 'He's nobody's fool. However much he loves that lass, he'll come to realise it's all for the best.'

James returned with his dog eventually, but went out again almost immediately. He didn't say where he was going. Eventually Maureen put down her darning. She stretched and groaned. 'It's been a long day, lass. I'd best get off to my bed afore I seize up.' Giving Sally a concerned look, she told her, 'Happen *you* should get away to your bed an' all.'

Unsure, Sally lingered. 'What about James?'

'He'll be back. Don't you worry your head on that.'

Sally's worried glance shifted to the door. 'Where do you think he's gone 'til this time?'

'Who knows?' Seeing Sally's concern, Maureen put an arm round her shoulders. 'Come on, lass,' she said, 'he won't want us sitting here waiting for him to show his face. Why! This very minute, he might be standing out there in the cold, waiting for us to get away to our beds, so he can come in and be on his own.'

Realising Maureen knew him better than she did, Sally allowed herself to be persuaded, though she did argue, 'I'm not really tired.' Having said that, no sooner had she laid her head on the pillow than she was fast asleep.

In the early hours some distant sound woke her. Going to the window she looked out. At first she couldn't see anything; the clouds had covered the moon to send a shadow over everything. A moment passed and then there he was, just standing beside the barn. 'James!' His name sprang from her lips. With her heart beating wildly she threw on her shawl and ran downstairs. Letting nothing stand in her way she ran through the kitchen and out to the yard.

He was nowhere to be seen. Suddenly, she heard a sound coming from the barn. Picking her way over the rough ground, she followed the uneven path to the door and looked inside, but it was too dark to see.

She called softly, 'James, it's me . . . Sally.' Her voice trembled. 'Are you in there?'

Seated on a half-split log, James had been deep in thought. Now though, on hearing her call, he glanced up, and what he saw sent a dark thrill through his senses.

Silhouetted by the moon, Sally made a wonderful, ghostly sight. With her long, fair hair flowing in the breeze and the shape of her legs naked through the flimsy nightgown, she stirred all manner of emotions in him. Anger amongst them that she should have invaded his quiet time here. 'Go away, Sally . . . please.'

Now that she knew he was in there, Sally would not be sent away. 'It's not good for you to be on your own,' she said, coming forward. 'Let me sit with you, James . . . just for a little while,' she softly pleaded. 'I won't be in the way.'

She was halfway in when two strong arms grabbed her by the shoulders. 'You *are* in the way!' he snapped. 'If I'd wanted company, I'd have come in when you and Mam were downstairs.'

Turning her round, he would have sent her out, but she clung to him and he was afraid to hurt her. 'Please, Sally.' His face was dangerously close to hers, his dark eyes enveloping her. 'Just leave me be. We'll talk tomorrow, I promise.'

Neither of them knew when it happened or how, but suddenly he was kissing her, and she thrilled to his touch. His hands moved over her body and the need rose in him like a tidal wave. Tenderly, he drew her to the ground.

The lovemaking was wonderful.

Sally felt his nakedness cover her smaller frame. She felt the need in him, and though she suspected it was a need for another woman, it didn't seem to matter. Not then. Not when he was holding her to him like that.

Right there, with the warmth of hessian sacks beneath her

buttocks, and the warmth of the man above her, Sally gave herself to him. It was the first time she had given herself to any man. And she was proud that it was James. In taking her innocence, he had taken her heart. There could never be any other man for her. But then, Sally had known that all along.

When it was over and he helped her to dress, she could see he was ashamed. He opened his mouth to say something, and she put a finger to his lips. 'Ssh!' Smiling with a wisdom far beyond her years, she told him softly, 'It's me that should be sorry. You asked me to go, and I didn't.'

His face wreathed in anguish, he took hold of her. 'What I did was unforgivable. How can I ever make amends?'

'By never referring to what happened here tonight,' she answered. 'As far as I'm concerned, it's already forgotten, and you don't have to say anything.' The smile faded. 'I understand . . . really I do.'

With dignity she gathered her shawl about her shoulders and left. Behind her, she could hear the sound of fist against wood. He blames himself, she thought. But it was no more his fault than hers.

Chapter Thirteen

It was June. For days now the sun had blazed down relentlessly. Nearing the fourth month of pregnancy, Isabel was already feeling heavy and uncomfortable. The heat affected her mood, and the moods grew darker with the passing days.

Frances had seen a terrible change come over her daughter these past weeks. Twice a week, on Mondays and Thursdays, Isabel would visit. Today was Thursday. As always, the two of them would sit in the drawing room, chatting about this or that, and never discussing the more important issues.

Today though, Frances spoke her mind. 'You worry me,' she said. 'I had hoped you might be content, but you're not, are you?'

Isabel looked away. Getting up from her chair she wandered to the fireplace, where she stood, gaze downcast, her thoughts troubled.

Frances looked at her daughter's sorry face and her heart ached. Isabel was so changed, it was a pity to see. Dressed in a gown of burgundy, with her chestnut hair swept back, she was as lovely as ever, and the roundness of her figure suited her. She looked well in herself, but so sad – so incredibly sad.

Presently, Isabel turned to face her mother. 'I don't know what to do.' Her voice was so soft, Frances only just caught what she said.

Gesturing to the chair opposite, Frances urged, 'Come and sit down, child.'

Hesitantly, Isabel returned to her seat. 'I didn't want to burden you,' she told her mother. 'You have enough to contend with.'

'Who else have you to confide in, if not me?'

'No one.'

'Well then?' Frances had known there had been something wrong since Isabel and her husband had returned from their honeymoon in France. 'Is it to do with the baby?' She sincerely hoped not.

'No. Dr Lucas says the baby is coming along fine.'

Relieved, Frances smiled. 'That's wonderful.' She was so looking forward to being a grandmother. 'I know it isn't money,' she said. 'Your father settled a considerable amount on you after the wedding. Adam's father bought you that beautiful big house on Park Street, and you have money in your own right.' She made a little sound, almost like a sigh. 'It must be strange to have your *own* money. That's something I've never had. Your father pays the wages and measures all the household bills to the very last penny. I've always had to justify what I want whether it be a new sofa or a personal undergarment.' Oh, what bitter regrets she had.

'You don't need to go begging to *him* for every penny,' she reminded her. 'Not now. Not any more. If you want money, you only have to ask. I've told you before.'

Reaching forward, Frances took hold of Isabel's hands. 'I know that,' she acknowledged. 'But I don't need money.' What I need is to be rid of *him*, she thought.

'I understand what you're saying, Mother.' Isabel smiled at her, but it was a sad smile. 'You can have all the money in the world, but it doesn't bring happiness.'

'But you have your freedom, don't you, child? I mean you're not kept under his thumb, the way your father keeps me?'

'No.' Letting loose her mother's hands, Isabel leaned back in the chair. 'I have my freedom at long last.'

'So? It isn't the baby, and it isn't money troubles.' Scrutinising her daughter's face, she knew at once. 'It's *Adam*, isn't it?' Horror flickered across her features. 'Oh, dear God! Don't tell me he's taken to beating you?' That would have been the hardest thing. All these years she had suffered at the hands of her own husband, and to have it happen to her daughter! She daren't even think on it.

'He's never laid a hand on me in violence,' Isabel admitted. 'But he's done far worse, and I can't forgive him.' She had not meant to discuss it with her mother, but the truth was too close to being spoken to stop now. 'I wonder why he married me at all,' she said. 'I suspect he's seeing other women. Even on our honeymoon, he couldn't help but make eyes at every attractive woman who crossed his path.'

Visibly relieved, Frances told her, 'Men are like that, child. It's something us women have to live with.' But when she heard Isabel's next words, her smile dropped away.

'It isn't just that, Mother . . . though that in itself is bad enough. Adam has another family. I'm sure of it.'

White-faced, Frances sprang to her feet. 'Another family?' She shook her head disbelievingly. 'Are you saying he bigamously married you?' That would mean her daughter was living in sin, and the child would be born a bastard. It was too much. 'Answer me . . . is that what you're saying?'

'No!' Isabel was shocked. 'I don't believe he's already married, but I'm sure he's hiding something from me.'

'But do you know it for *certain*?'

'No, I can't be certain,' Isabel confessed. 'But there is something I can't explain.'

'What is that?'

Isabel told her mother about the night they were leaving for their honeymoon, and the young woman who came to the carriage. 'She was younger than me . . . a pretty thing. She had a small child beside her, and a babe-in-arms. She told me to watch him . . . that he was a bad lot.'

'Did you ask her what she meant?'

'There was no time . . . Adam came back and we were quickly on our way. But I asked him if he'd seen her, and he looked out the window. She was standing in the rain, watching us leave. He knew her, I'm sure of it. He had the look of guilt all over him.'

'I don't believe it!'

'It's true, Mother . . . those were the exact words she used . . . "You'll need to watch him . . . he's a bad lot." That's what she said.'

Frances glared down on her. 'I don't care what she said. I just can't believe he would do anything so terrible.' Falling into her seat, she pleaded with Isabel. 'Think about what you're saying, child. Adam Scarlet is a fine young man from an old respected family. Can you really believe he's married to this sorry creature . . . or that he's fathered her two children? You have jumped to this conclusion without any evidence.' She threw out her arms in exasperation. 'How can you ever imagine he would marry you illegally, risking a prison sentence apart from everything else?' She was adamant. 'No! Never! I will not believe it. Not for one minute!'

Not for the first time, Isabel wondered if she had got it all wrong. 'I did say I couldn't be certain,' she answered quietly.

'You must be wrong, believe me. And the sooner you get this dangerous idea out of your head, the better. Good God, child! You've only been married a matter of weeks, and here you are, harbouring these shocking suspicions without any real cause.' Fear for Isabel made her spiteful. 'How do you think you can make a success of your marriage if you're so quick to condemn him like that? I want your word that you will not mention this to anyone, especially not to your father; especially when it seems to me the whole thing is nothing more than a fabrication of your imagination.'

'I'm not so sure about that, Mother.' Isabel had thought long and hard about it, and the more she dwelt on it, the more she believed there was something very underhand going on. 'What about that young woman? Why would she approach the carriage like that? Why would she say those things? And why did Adam look so guilty?'

'Like I said, you let your imagination run away with you. After all, it's understandable. You were only just married, excited too, I expect, and you're with child. The mind plays strange tricks when you're with child. What with one thing and another, you misread the situation . . . misheard the young woman maybe. As for Adam, he wasn't looking guilty . . . he was worried in case you missed the ferry across to France.' Pleading with her eyes, she murmured, 'It can't possibly be what you think.'

In that moment, with her mother's eyes on her, and that tremor in her voice, Isabel realised her mother was afraid – afraid of what her husband might say, afraid she might be at the wrong end of his fist if he found out.

Eager to put her mother's mind at rest, Isabel nodded in agreement. 'You're right, Mother. I must have misread the situation, just as you said.' Smiling brightly, she promised, 'I was being very silly. So now I shall put it out of my mind altogether. You'll hear no more of it.'

Frances actually laughed aloud. 'Ha! Good girl, I knew you'd see sense.' Quickly moving on to other, mundane matters, she hated herself for the coward she was.

Two days later, on Saturday morning, Isabel was wandering about Blackburn market; it was a practice her new husband might have frowned on if he'd known. Certainly her father would have had all kinds of fits . . . 'What!' he would scream. 'A daughter of mine buying her wares from a market stall?' But the idea of this being an illicit pleasure only made Isabel enjoy the experience all the more.

'Morning, dearie, what can I do for yer?' The stallkeeper had served this fine young lady before and come to like her. She wasn't proud and standoffish like many another of her kind.

Besides, she had recognised Isabel as Leonard Mears' daughter, because she had seen her go into church as a bride, and seen her come out again . . . like something out of a fairy tale, she'd been. It was a memory she was never likely to forget.

'I've got some lovely lace,' she teased, slithering the pretty stuff between her work-worn fingers. 'Make it meself, I do,' she said. 'An' I can promise you, you'll not find a more pretty lace this side o' London.'

Reaching out to take it from her, Isabel felt the quality. Fine and delicate, with a spidery pattern, the lace was exquisite. 'I'm having a cradle made,' she told the interested woman, 'and this might be just the thing to finish the hood.'

The deal was made. Isabel paid the asking price and was about to drop the wrapped lace into her purse when she noticed the woman looking beyond her to something else. It was a strange look . . . a warning look. Of the kind a conspirator might use.

Intrigued, Isabel glanced round and was shocked. Not too far from where she was standing, a young woman was hurrying away. There was a small child alongside her and another in her arms. Though the woman had her back to her, and the babe in arms was older now, Isabel knew straight away. It was the woman who had come to the carriage that night. The woman who had warned her about Adam. She had to talk with her. She needed to know the truth.

In a minute she had taken after her and once the young woman knew she was being pursued, she began running, urging the child on foot to go faster and faster. They weaved and dodged through the stalls until, somewhere down a back alley, Isabel lost sight of them. 'Damn!' Exhausted, she leaned against a wall, her hand on her side, stroking the discomfort there. The child was moving inside her, and she could hardly get her breath.

Suddenly the young woman appeared at the far end of the alleyway. '*Ask him!*' she called out. 'Ask him about Ruby, a silly, trusting girl who served at his father's table. Ask him about his two sons and why he's turned his back on them.'

As quickly as she had appeared, she disappeared, and Isabel could only stand and watch. Distraught, Isabel made her way back to the carriage, her mind on the stranger. '*Ask him!*' she had said. And that was exactly what she meant to do.

On her way home, she went over every detail of that disturbing incident, talking to herself, asking questions. 'Was she lying?' Part of her wanted to believe that. The other part knew they were not lies but the truth. She had seen the way Adam made up to the women. Why shouldn't he have made up to one of his father's servants? It happened all the time. And yet there was something sinister about this. Even if it was true one of the children was his . . . why would Adam have kept the relationship going and have fathered a second? It didn't tie in with the antics of a spoiled rich boy.

Though Isabel dreaded the prospect, she knew the only way was to confront him.

Arriving at Park Street she waited for the driver to help her down. 'Thank you, Michael,' she told the kindly man. 'I won't be needing you any more today.'

Going inside the spacious hallway, with its winding stairs and plush carpets, she glanced around. 'I'd give it all up for contentment,' she murmured. Contentment was something she had not yet found.

The housekeeper, Mrs Palmer, was there very quickly. A

short, round creature, she had a smile that seemed to envelop her face. 'I'll take your cloak, ma'am,' she said, laying it across her arm. 'Is there anything else you might need?'

'I've had a busy morning,' Isabel replied wearily. 'I think I'll have a rest now. Be sure to wake me in half an hour.' That should give her time enough to compose herself before confronting him.

With that, she went upstairs and into her room. Lavishly furnished, with the best that money could buy, it meant nothing to her. The house was a surprise from her father-in-law, prepared down to the last detail while she and Adam were away on honeymoon.

If it had been of her choosing, she would have had simpler, serviceable furniture and prettier things. Even then, it would have made little difference, because this great house and all its contents did not feel like home. Here, she was lonely, but never alone. She hardly ever had time to think, before someone was asking after her, or calling with their silly gossip, and often Adam would bring his colleagues back and she would be obliged to entertain. There was no happiness here. No privacy. No time when she could be herself. In fact there were times when she would have preferred to be locked in her father's watch-tower.

As was often the case, Adam stayed out longer than he had promised. It was early evening when he found his way home. 'I got caught up in one of Father's lectures,' he lied beautifully. 'But I'm home now, so you can tell me all about your day.' When he came across the room to kiss her, she remained stiff and unyielding. 'It's been a hell of a day, I can tell you. Father got on his high horse about waste and expenditure, and I was made to endure a full hour of his rantings.' Oblivious to her discomfort, he poured himself a strong drink and sat down on the sofa. 'And what has my lovely Isabel been up to today then?'

Unmoved by his sweet talk, Isabel moved away. He had this

Josephine Cox

nauseating way of patronising her, as if she was three years old, or senile.

Sensing her mood, he smiled knowingly. 'Oh, I see? It seéms we're not in the best of moods. So? You've *not* had a very good day either, is that it?' As if he cared.

'I want to ask you something.'

'Is it important? I had a mind to look up an old friend.'

'Yes, Adam, it *is* important.'

'Then ask away.'

Taking a deep breath, Isabel felt her every limb trembling. Nevertheless, she had come this far and would not be deterred from what she must do. In a clear, firm voice she asked him, 'Do you know a young woman by the name of Ruby?'

Though his heart almost stopped, he managed to convey indifference. 'Not that I remember. Why?'

'She claims to have been a servant in your father's house.' Her probing gaze never left his face.

'There have been many servants in my father's house. Am I expected to know all of them by name?' This time he was not so assured of himself. Instead, he was deeply disturbed by her knowledge of someone he would rather pretend did not exist.

Sensing his guilt, Isabel persisted. 'She has two sons . . . quite young they are. She's small and pretty, with long dark hair.' Still her gaze never wavered. 'You must remember her?'

Squirming beneath her cool gaze, he laughed nervously. 'This is beginning to sound like an inquisition.'

'I saw her again today.'

Fear leaped into his eyes. 'What do you mean . . . you saw her again?'

'The first time I saw her was on our wedding day . . . you were inside fetching my purse. She tapped on the carriage window and told me . . . *things*.'

'What kind of things?' Turning his head sideways he peered

224

at her from the corner of his eye. 'What did this slag say to you?'

'She said I was to ask you if you knew her and that you had turned your back on your own flesh and blood.' The words came out in a frantic rush. 'Are they *your* sons, Adam?' Her heart was pounding. 'Are you married to that wretched girl?'

Leaping out of his chair, he took her by the shoulders and shook her. 'Are you mad . . . listening to some crazy drunk who should never be allowed to walk the streets?' Thrusting her away, he seemed to lose control, his voice rising to a screaming pitch. 'Your father was right. You're not responsible enough to be let out on your own. From now on, you will stay within the confines of this house. It seems I've been lax, but now I see I'll have to assert my authority. You give me no option but to keep you on a tight budget, and I shall instruct Michael he is not to drive you anywhere. Your freedom is at an end. From now on, you must consult me at every turn.'

Isabel stood firm. He didn't hit her. She knew he was not that kind of man. Instead, he tried to shift the guilt. It didn't work.

'You haven't answered me,' she said boldly. 'Was she telling the truth?'

In that moment he came closer to hitting her than at any time. His fists clenched and unclenched by his sides and his face drained of colour. In a quiet, shaken voice, he told her, 'You have accused me of marrying you when I already had a wife. Do you mean to see me in jail? Want rid of me, do you? Is that what all these lies are about?'

Leaning forward he lowered his voice to a whisper, the merest of smiles playing round his lips. 'I should be careful if I were you,' he warned. 'I might think you're losing your mind. And if that were the case, I would be well within my rights to have you committed.'

From the look on his face, Isabel could see he meant every word. Yet she still looked him in the eye, daring him to answer the question she had put, more convinced than ever that everything the young woman had said was true.

He glared at her a moment longer, admiring her defiance yet afraid of her. The thought of the truth coming out was terrifying. Adam had heard rumours of what kind of a man Leonard Mears was. It would be very unwise to get the wrong side of him by falling out with his precious daughter.

Suddenly, he raised his head and backed away. 'It's all lies,' he said confidently. 'The woman you spoke with is obviously out for money. To my mind, there is only one way to deal with blackmailers.' With his fists still clenched, he strode out of the room.

A moment later, Isabel heard the front door slam. Shaken by the confrontation, she stayed in her room a moment or two longer. 'What now?' she mused. 'I've accused him, and he's denied it all. So, what now?' In the wake of his threats, she began to wonder whether it had been wise to raise the issue at all. Deep down though, she knew it had been the right thing to do, and now she must see it through. 'I have to find her! I must get to the truth.' With her mind made up, she started downstairs.

She was almost at the bottom when she heard his carriage draw away. Running the last few steps she hurried to the hallway window. As the carriage sped by, she saw him there . . . grim-faced, he sat hunched inside, obviously a man with a purpose.

And Isabel had no doubt what that purpose was. 'He's going to see *her*,' she whispered. 'To threaten her . . . like he threatened me.'

Summoning a maid, she instructed, 'Tell Michael I want my carriage . . . quickly now.' And while the maid scurried off, Isabel got herself ready.

Michael wasn't his usual cheery self; helping her into the carriage, he confided worriedly, 'I'm wondering if I've done anything to upset you, ma'am?'

'Why would you think that?'

'Just now, the master left a message with Nancy that I was to report to him the minute he got back. Nancy said he wasn't in the best of moods . . . if you don't mind me saying, ma'am.'

'You've done nothing wrong,' she assured him, 'and you have nothing to fear. You have my word on that.'

Visibly relieved, he nodded. 'That's good to hear, ma'am.'

Isabel described to him where she had last seen the young woman. 'I know the very place,' he told her. 'Me and the missus lived there some years back. That were afore we took our separate ways o' course.'

'I may have to leave you waiting at the mouth of the alley,' she told him. 'I can't be sure you'll get the carriage through.'

'Aw, it's no problem,' he answered. 'Now the *master's* rig . . . being bigger an' all . . . I dare say you'd never get that through them narrow alleyways. *This* little darling though –' he smiled confidently – 'I'll get her through anywhere.' Patting the carriage, like she was his favourite child, he confided to Isabel, 'The master would have summat to say, I'm sure, if I left you wandering them alleyways of a night-time.'

'A cobbled alley near the market,' she told him as they started off. 'I seem to recall there was a pawnshop on the corner.'

'I recognise the place,' he said. 'Lord knows I've been made to use that pawnshop many a time. But that was afore I came to work for the master and yourself.'

As good as his word, he went straight to the alley she had described. 'I'll go slowly,' he said, edging the horses over the cobbles. 'If you happen to spot the person you're after, give a shout and I'll stop straight away.' Isabel had told him she was searching for an old nanny who was reported to have fallen on hard times.

They went down the alley and back up again, and Isabel's hopes faded; there was no sign of the young woman and no sign of Adam's carriage. Had she been wrong? she wondered. Had he gone on another errand altogether?

Michael suggested they should extend their search. 'This is a maze of alleyways,' he explained. 'She could live in any one of them. Just because you caught sight of her at the top end of this one doesn't mean to say she lives here, does it?'

Isabel agreed, and so they came out of the bottom alley and took a wide circle, starting at the outside and working their way in.

As the darkness closed in, and they were almost back where they started, Isabel gave a shout. 'There!' Halfway down the alley, and parked as far away from the lamplight as possible, was a carriage.

The carriage could have been Adam's, but without going closer, she couldn't be sure. 'Wait here,' she said, and was quickly out of the carriage and running down the alleyway. The closer she got to the carriage, the more certain she was.

Inside the house, Ruby feared for her life. Having first called at the alehouse to soothe his wounds, Adam had found her right where he left her, just a year or two ago. 'You lying whore!' With his hands on her throat he pressed her to the wall. 'I paid you good money to forget I ever existed. Now that it's all gone, you think you can crawl out of the sewers and threaten me, do you?' Squeezing her throat until her eyes bulged, he sneered in her face. 'Well, you couldn't be more wrong. Before I'll let you ruin my life, I'll see you dead . . . the brats too. They mean nothing to me.' Turning his head he glanced towards the bedroom. 'In there, are they?' he demanded. 'Sleeping the sleep of the innocent, are they?'

The woman's frightened eyes opened like saucers, her voice painfully distorted as her throat was squeezed through his fingers. 'Don't . . . hurt . . . them ...'

Chuckling, he dragged her through the curtain that hung across the doorway. Peering in the candlelight, his eyes were drawn to the mattress on the floor, and the two small figures huddled together there. 'Well now!' Ignoring her muffled cries, he pulled her roughly across the room, until both of them were standing over the mattress. 'No . . . No!' She saw the murder in his eyes and was terrified.

Laughing aloud, he kept her secure with one hand, while with the other he reached down and plucked the smaller child from its bed. When the child cried out, momentarily startling him, the woman dropped to the mattress and covered the children with her own body. 'I don't mean to ruin your life,' she pleaded. 'I love you, but I need money . . . your sons need food and clothing, and there is no one but you. Please . . . Adam . . . I'm sorry. Leave us alone, and I'll go away. You'll never hear from me again …'

Her pleas turned to sobbing when he snatched her up by the hair; with the drink inside him he had a manic strength she was helpless against. 'I'll make *sure* I never hear from you again.' Throwing her aside his gaze enveloped the crying children. 'I want you out of my life for good . . . *all* of you!'

Reaching into his pocket he took out a small, dark object. 'I want you to watch first,' he whispered madly. 'Then it'll be your turn.' Cowering in the corner, she had hoped that once he had struck the fear of God in her, that would be enough and he would leave. But now, realising with a rush of horror that the object he had taken from his pocket was a gun, she covered her head and face, waiting for the inevitable.

Something, some deep instinct, made her look up, and her heart froze. He was pointing the gun at her babies! With a cry of horror, she ran across the room, arms out with the intention of protecting them.

Taken unawares, he suddenly swung round and fired. The woman slowly crumpled before him, her eyes wide open, shocked as they focused on his face. With all her remaining strength she grabbed at his legs, trying to topple him, to make him hesitate, anything to save her babies, and all the while her life's blood trickled away. She didn't grieve for herself though. All that mattered were her babies. And he had them at his mercy!

'It's too late,' he told her. 'You should have thought what you were doing.' With a vicious kick he sent her sprawling. Deliberately, calmly, he then turned the gun on the children. 'I must have been mad not to rid myself of you long ago!'

When she came into the room, it took only a split second for Isabel to see what was happening. 'Dear God! No!' The piercing cry seared his senses. As he turned she launched herself at him, taking him unawares. Intent on wresting the gun from him, she fought like a wild thing, but he was strong, out of his mind, and the fight was fierce.

There was a moment of triumph, then a resounding shot. He smiled into her face. 'You should have left well alone,' he murmured. His smile fading, he fell to the floor, one arm buckled beneath him; the other across the mattress at a peculiar angle, as though he was cradling his sons.

Having heard things they would rather not, the neighbours had locked themselves inside. Now, in the ensuing quiet, they crept out to see. Gathered round the door, they saw only what their eyes told them. And that was Isabel holding the gun and, lying at her feet, two dead people. 'God help us!' Nervously, one old woman crept forward to take the children. 'What have you done?' Her face trembled as she first looked on Isabel, then at the blood spattered everywhere. 'Oh, child!' She had lived a long time and never seen such carnage. 'Whatever have you done?'

Michael came running in, having reluctantly decided to leave Isabel's carriage unattended when he heard the shots and saw the neighbouring doors opening. 'What's going on?' he demanded.

'Ma'am, are you all right?' His eyes then fell on the crumpled bleeding bodies – and the gun in Isabel's hand.

At the door, an old man made the sign of the cross. 'She's killed them both.' Tugging at the old woman's shawl, he urged, 'Come away. Keep the children safe.' Turning to address the gathering, he urged someone to 'Fetch the police . . . quickly!'

Part Three

1889

THE TRIAL

Chapter Fourteen

The trial of Isabel Scarlet shocked the whole nation.

People's opinions were divided. Some swore that Adam Scarlet deserved what he got, and his lover with him. Others claimed that Isabel had taken a terrible revenge; she had robbed two innocent children of their parents, and should swing from the end of a rope for her crime.

During the trial, which spanned many weeks, the rigours of prison life and the terrible uncertainty took its toll on Isabel. Succumbing to a debilitating infection, she lost her unborn child, and seemed to have no concern whether she herself lived or died.

In a packed court, the tragic story unfolded. The tale was riveting, some observers coming every day to catch all the developments. Maureen, Sally and James came when they could, though their motives were different from those of the gossips.

The young woman was named as Ruby Shillman. Having worked at the Scarlets' home as a girl, she had been seduced by Adam – a swaggering, immature young fellow. Later, when it emerged that she was carrying Adam's child, his father took control. After buying her silence, she was chased away, with the instruction that she should say nothing, and never again show her face in the area. Adam, however, had taken a liking to her. He discovered where she was living, and the relationship was resumed.

The consequence of this was the conception of yet another child. At this point, Adam chose to distance himself from her, but not before paying out yet another bundle of money to buy her continuing loyalty.

Now, during the trial, his father explained how 'My son was a good man. He had committed no greater sin than many a young man before him.' Turning to Isabel, he pointed a damning finger. 'If anyone is guilty here, it is this woman, Isabel Scarlet!'

Genuine tears filled his eyes. 'By her hand alone, my son lies in the churchyard, and now she stands before you today . . . labelling *him* a murderer. She claims that *he* ended Ruby Shillman's life, but she lies! It was me who sent that young woman away . . . me who paid the price for his foolish, boyish behaviour. He and I argued about my harsh punishment of her. You see, my son had warm feelings towards her. He wanted to protect her.'

Here he paused, remembering. 'He would *never* have murdered her. Anyone who knew my son will tell you . . . there was no malice in his heart. He was a good son, and I had every reason to be proud of the man he became.'

Turning to Isabel once more, he pointed an accusing finger, 'In a jealous rage . . . in front of those innocent children, she killed that helpless woman. And for no other reason than that he was there, with the mother of his children, she killed my only son.'

He paused, the whole courtroom hanging on his every word. 'My son is guilty of the slightest misdemeanour; that of loving someone while too young to shoulder that responsibility. Yes, he made her with child, not once, but twice. Yet he lived to regret that, as possibly many here among us might have done.'

Bowing his head, his voice dropped almost to a whisper. 'A small sin . . . created out of love and immaturity.' Looking up, he faced them with humility. 'No man deserves to die for such an insignificant thing.' Overcome with grief, his voice cracked, and he could go on no more.

Isabel's father had hired the finest legal defence in the land. Yet, as the lawyer stood up to question one witness after another, it was obvious he had a mighty task to perform if he was to save her from the hangman's noose.

White-faced and visibly trembling, Frances Mears was called to the witness-box.

She told how her daughter had confided in her that Adam had ogled other women on their honeymoon. She described how a certain young woman, now known to be Ruby Shillman, had approached her even as they left for their honeymoon to warn her about her husband. From that day on, the incident had haunted Isabel to such an extent that she insisted on discovering the truth about the relationship.

Frances explained how her daughter was a kind and generous soul, who had been driven to the limits of her endurance by the inconsiderate and humiliating behaviour of her husband; and all this while she herself was carrying his child. In tears, she told them what her daughter had told her. 'She did not shoot the woman. When the gun went off and Adam died, it was an accident.' Wringing her hands in despair, she pleaded, 'In your heart of hearts, you cannot punish her too severely for that.'

There then followed a succession of other witnesses: members of each household; people, too, who had heard or seen anything which might add weight to the proceedings.

The most damning evidence of all came from Isabel's own household.

The housekeeper told how, on the day of the killings, she had witnessed a fearful row between the master and mistress. 'I was passing the bedroom, sir . . . so I didn't hear it word for word. Oh, but it were a terrible thing, sir . . . such anger.'

Known for her honesty and forthright character, Mrs Palmer had served in Adam's father's house for many years. When he married, she was transferred to his house at Adam's request. 'I knew him as a boy, you see, sir,' she remarked, smiling fondly, 'smacked his little behind many a time for turning the linen cupboard inside out looking for his lost toys. Oh, but I were proud to serve him and his new wife. It were a beautiful house, and I took the very best care of it . . . almost as if it were my own.'

When instructed to keep to the point and describe exactly what she had heard on that day, she paused to take control of her emotions before continuing. 'The master was very upset, sir,' she revealed. 'Something the mistress had said made him lose his temper, and he was always such a quiet boy, never prone to fits and starts of that kind.'

When prompted again, she resumed her telling. 'Well, as I recall, the mistress said something to him, and he asked if she was mad. At that point, I buried my head in the linen cupboard to count the number of clean towels there . . . it was my day for taking stock of what needed replenishing, if you see what I mean, sir, and I was embarrassed to be so near when they were fighting like that.' Again, she was told to keep to the point.

'I quickly finished what I was doing, then rushed by their room as softly as I could.' Taking a deep breath, she revealed, 'It was then that I heard the master tell her, "Your father was right! You are not responsible enough to be let out on your own." That's what he said, sir. And he sounded extremely concerned.'

It was a shocking revelation, but it would not be the last of its kind. Isabel's own brother Jack did nothing to help her cause. 'It's true she's always been a wild, rebellious creature. Father has found it necessary to shut her away from time to time. I often wondered if those periods of isolation might affect her mind.' He made a show of pleading for her: 'Though I cannot bring myself to believe she's capable of murder.' But the harm was done and he knew it. Isabel had always held first place in his father's affections. Now, if she were to be imprisoned for many years, he stood a better chance of being first.

There were those who desperately tried to put her case and show her for the kind, humane creature she really was.

Her parents were at their wits' end, and Hannah cried as she told how Isabel would never hurt even the least of creatures. 'She badly tore her own hands when rescuing a rabbit from a snare . . . and once, she was bitten while parting two fighting dogs. If she says she didn't hurt Adam Scarlet, or that woman . . . then you have to believe her. Such an act is not in her nature.'

Wretched and afraid, Robert corroborated her story. 'Hannah is right,' he finished. 'Our dear sister Isabel is no murderess.'

When Isabel herself described the events of that night, she told the story with a clear, honest voice that held the courtroom in a hushed silence. She described how Ruby Shillman had approached her on the night of their wedding, and how she had later confronted Adam with that knowledge. 'He denied it, of course . . . threatened to have me put away.' In a quiet, dignified manner, she confessed, 'I did go looking for him that night, just as Michael described. I needed to catch them together. I had to be sure, but not to hurt him . . . never to hurt him. All I wanted was for him to tell me the truth.'

Taking a moment to compose herself, she went on, 'I was in the yard, when I heard raised voices. One of them was Adam's. As I was going up the stairs I heard what sounded like a gunshot.'

Closing her eyes, she relived that terrible moment when she came into the room. After a moment she was able to describe it: 'There were neighbours peeping out of their doorways as I passed. I opened the door and went in. At first I didn't realise what had happened, then in the half-light I saw my husband. He was holding a gun to the children. There was the woman, lying on the floor and blood everywhere.' Swallowing deeply, she made herself go on. 'I ran at him . . . tried to snatch the gun out of his hand, but he fought so . . . the gun went off . . .' Her voice rose with emotion. 'I didn't mean it to happen,' she cried out. 'It was an accident! A TERRIBLE ACCIDENT!'

One by one the neighbours were called. With fear in their eyes, they peeped at Adam's father, a powerful and influential man, and their courage failed. Yes, they heard the rowing, but could not say exactly what the row was about. Yes, they saw Isabel Scarlet, though they didn't know who she was, or why she was there, nor that she was hunting for her husband.

In the summing-up, it was pointed out by the defence that the gun that fired the fatal shots belonged to Adam Scarlet. Questions were put: 'Why had he gone there carrying a gun? Wasn't it with the sole purpose of shooting this woman who could finish his marriage? A woman who could go on blackmailing him for the rest of his life? You heard the neighbours . . . they were rowing. Why was that, do you think? Was it because he was warning her off, and she threatened to tell?'

The prosecution lawyer answered, 'The row could have been about anything, and we must not draw the wrong conclusions. What we must examine closely are the facts as we know them.'

He argued that it may well have been Adam Scarlet's gun, but it was not *he* who took it to the house that night, but his wife. 'It was *she* who went there with murder in her heart. She had searched for her husband and found him with another woman . . . the mother of his children. I want you to think about that.'

Allowing the argument to sink in, he walked from one side of the courtroom to the other, his eyes on every face of the jury in turn. 'In a jealous rage she shot them both dead; she was seen standing over the bodies with the gun still in her hand. Her guilt was there for all to see. Innocent? No! Isabel Scarlet killed two innocent people. She must be made to pay the price for her evil and wicked crime.'

The price was devastating.

When the verdict was read out, there was an audible gasp right around the courtroom.

Knowing she had told the truth, Isabel had hoped they would believe her. Now, pale with shock, her heart sinking and her hopes dashed, she faced the judge.

In his black cap and gown, he made a formidable sight. His slow, resonant voice echoed in her ears, yet she heard only ten solemn, terrifying words: '. . . *you will hang by the neck until you are dead* . . .'

Up in the gallery, James leaped to his feet. 'She's innocent! For God's sake . . . can't you see . . . she's INNOCENT!'

His screams caused uproar. Suddenly he was being bundled from the courthouse. Shaken and crying, Maureen and Sally ran after him.

Behind them the doors burst open and people came running out. 'She's got what she deserved,' they shouted, and went away laughing and cheering.

Inside the courthouse the mood was very different. Frances Mears and her husband sat very still, unable to believe what had happened here. They didn't speak. They could not look at each other. Instead, they waited. Quietly and with dignity. Broken-hearted, Robert sat beside his mother, holding her hand and giving her strength. Hannah was apart, eyes staring at the judge's bench, as though waiting to see him come back and say it had all been a mistake, that Isabel was innocent and could go home with them.

Jack, too, was deeply shocked. He had not wanted this. All he wanted was for her to be locked away, long enough for him to gain affection in his father's eyes.

Adam's parents remained a moment longer. As far as they were concerned, justice had been done here today. With a wary glance at Isabel's family, they made their way out. For the briefest of moments the two men looked at each other. There was nothing to say.

Chapter Fifteen

In the weeks following the trial, shock turned to anger and then to despair.

Good money following bad, Leonard Mears did his utmost to save his daughter from the hangman. Appeals were put and rejected, and as each day passed, hope faded.

'There must be a way!' James and Robert had been drawn closer by the tragedy and spoke of it often. On this particular Monday morning, James paused in his work to confess the torment on his mind. 'We can't abandon her. There has to be something we can do.'

Robert had known for a long time. 'You love her, don't you?' He spoke softly, out of the hearing of the other men.

Drowning in guilt, James merely nodded.

'My father is doing all he can,' Robert told him. 'It's a pity he didn't do more, sooner.' There was a world of bitterness in his voice.

When James looked up, curious at his words, Robert explained, 'As you know, Isabel went to my mother and told her how she suspected Adam had another family. Days before the killings, my mother revealed all this to my father, but he wouldn't listen. Instead, he accused her of never really wanting Isabel married, and attempting to discredit that "fine young man".'

'Why would he do that? Isabel has always been his favourite. I would have thought he'd have confronted Adam . . . moved heaven and earth to find out the truth?'

'Ah! But the truth is . . . money and profit have always come first, even above Isabel. He was obviously afraid his partnership with Adam's father might be affected if he stirred up muddy waters. So, to protect his own interests, he kept his mouth shut, and the whole thing came to a head.' Clenching his fists one into the other, he murmured, 'It should be *him* going to the hangman, not Isabel!'

James was astonished. He had never seen Robert so agitated about his father, though it was understandable, given the circumstances. All the same, he was shocked at the raw hatred in Robert's voice.

But for now he had his own troublesome thoughts. 'Did you find out why they won't let me see her?'

Robert gave a wry little smile. 'Father has arranged that no one should see her; not her brothers and sister, and certainly not Mother. He claims to be the only one who can keep her calm.'

'That's wicked. I know she would want to see her family. I hope she would want to see me.'

'I'm sorry, James. But I will say he's doing all he can to free her. No man could do more.' With a sorry shake of the head, he turned and left.

Like James, he believed that the best thing was to throw himself into his work, and pray it would all come right in the end.

Sally wanted so much to comfort him, but she didn't know how.

She asked herself how she might feel if it was James who was facing the hangman. The mere thought was so terrifying that she couldn't even begin to imagine how he was affected by it all.

'If only he'd show his feelings,' Maureen said one day when she, Lizzie and Sally were doing their rounds with the baskets. Skipping over a stream, Maureen waited for the other two. 'But he won't, and that's the trouble. He just pretends it's not happening, and if you speak to him about it, he seems to close his mind.'

Lizzie understood. 'It were the same when my old mammy were ill,' she revealed. 'I couldn't imagine life without her, so I pretended everything were fine. Then one day it weren't fine, and I thought the world had fallen in on me.'

Sally listened but made no comment. Her mind was on James. Only on James.

It was a hot September morning, and the baskets were heavy, yet they had decided not to stop until all the wares were sold.

Changing route, they made their way to the hamlet of Samlesbury, where they sold half their goods along the way. 'By! That's better.' Swinging the basket easier now, Lizzie suddenly burst into song. Then stopped just as suddenly, when she realised this was no time for singing.

After a short walk to the tram-stop, they caught one into Blackburn town and hawked along the side streets. Caught off guard, Lizzie threw a fit when a snotty-nosed boy made off with a bunch of carrots from her basket. 'Thieving little swine!' she yelled after him. 'You'll have a sore arse an' no mistake, if I catch up with yer!'

Seated on a chair outside her door, a busty fat woman was feeding her bairn. 'Hey, you!' Stuffing her ample breast back into its blouse, she shouted, 'Stop yer bawling an' swearing, yer silly old biddy.'

Lizzie took offence. 'Who the devil are *you* talking to?'

'I'm talking to *you*! That poor little lad yer screeching at . . . well, he ain't got no mam nor dad, an' you begrudge him a few lousy bloody carrots. Shame on yer. Anybody'd think he'd made off with the bleedin' crown jewels!'

Shamed bright pink, Lizzie hurried off. 'How was I to know 'e ain't got no mam nor dad?' she asked the other two. 'The little buggers all look the same to me.'

Maureen told her not to worry.

Sally made her laugh out loud when she held up a miserable-looking bunch of baby carrots. 'At least yours have gone to a good home,' she chuckled. 'Mine have wilted in the heat. I shouldn't think any self-respecting donkey would give 'em a second glance.'

Behind them, the lad crept up on the fat woman. ''Ave they gone, Mam?' he whispered, cuffing his runny nose.

'Aye, they've gone, lad. You're safe enough now.' Her flabby chops lifted in a cheeky grin. 'Get them carrots skinned and chopped,' she said. 'By! It's been a while since I tasted a fat, juicy carrot.'

A short time later, when the produce was sold and their feet ached so they could hardly put one before the other, Lizzie suggested they should make their way to the old cottage. 'We ain't been there in a long while,' she said, 'and I'm curious.'

Sally was curious too. 'What's this old cottage?' she wanted to know.

Maureen explained. 'Some time ago, we were making our way back from Darwen, when we stumbled across this beautiful little place . . . had an orchard and everything. But it were derelict . . . not a soul in sight.' She smiled at Lizzie. 'We used to sit and take a rest there, didn't we, Lizzie?'

Lizzie suggested they should make their way there now. 'We'll finish that jar o' sarsaparilla off. Hey! Happen the trees are full of rosy apples an' all,' she said, licking her lips. 'We could sell a few an' eat a few.'

'And why not?' Like Sally, Maureen thought it was a brilliant idea. 'That's if there's no one living there now. It's been some time since we went by that way.'

As it turned out, there was no one living there. The cottage had sadly deteriorated, but the orchard was bursting at the seams. 'By! Look at this!' Excited, Lizzie rushed about, filling her basket and pockets with ripe, tasty fruit: pears, apples and plums for the taking, and no one to chase them out.

Smiling at Lizzie's antics, Maureen bided her time. Seating herself near the cool of the stream that ran at the side of the overgrown garden, she took off her shoes to splash her swollen feet in the fast-running water.

Sighing blissfully, she leaned back on the tree trunk and closed her eyes. As always when she was quiet, her thoughts went to James. 'Don't let it destroy him,' she asked some unseen power. 'And, oh . . . that poor lass . . . what a terrible thing. But none of it her making, thank God.'

A moment later, she took off her pinny and spread it over the grass. That done, she took a bulky muslin bundle from her basket. Unrolling the jar of sarsaparilla and three small earthenware cups, she half-submerged the jar in the stream, between a boulder and the bank, so it would not be swept away. Here it was lapped by the clean, rushing cold water.

While that was cooling, she set the earthenware cups on the pinny and alongside them three large, misshapen muffins. 'Come on, you two,' she called, 'afore the insects take a fancy to your nibbles.'

Leading Sally back to the fold, Lizzie couldn't help but chuckle. 'A chance would be a fine thing,' she said naughtily. 'It's been a long time since anybody took a fancy to me nibbles.' Maureen told her to behave herself, and tuck in.

Sally was besotted with the cottage. 'How come it's empty?' she asked, taking a bite of her muffin. 'It's such a pretty place.'

'We wondered that,' Maureen replied, 'so we made it our

business to find out. Miss Lockhart, who you already know –' she pointed to the big white house in the near distance – 'she said as how it were owned by the squire for a time. He then sold it to a young doctor who planned to live in it after he wed his sweetheart. Sadly, on the night afore the wedding, she were run down by a carriage and four.'

Lizzie took up the tale. 'That were fourteen years back, and the cottage has stood empty ever since. He won't sell it nor rent it out, and he won't live in it. Now and then he wanders down here and sits by the stream, quiet like . . . just thinking.'

Sally thought that was such a sad tale, and Lizzie agreed. 'But he had his sweetheart for a time,' she said philosophically. 'Some folk never know what it's like to be in love.'

After they'd eaten, Sally wandered over to the cottage. For a time, she stood outside, looking up and imagining how it might have been different. With pretty curtains at the window and the door open to let in the sunshine. There could have been children, a dog maybe, and lots of laughter. Oh yes, lots of laughter. A cottage like this should be wrapped in happiness.

She peered through the windows. It was dark in there, with cobwebs and destruction everywhere. But, from what she could see, the rooms were beautifully furnished, with fine, expensive furniture; the deep inglenook was filled with vases of the remnants of long-dead flowers, and the table set for two. A wedding breakfast – she let her imagination run riot – or maybe a quiet evening for two young lovers.

'Come on then.' Maureen's voice cut through her thoughts. 'It's time we were on our way.'

As they went, Sally glanced back at the cottage several times; with its peeling paint and holey thatched roof, it made a sorry sight. 'Such a waste,' she murmured. In her heart, she would have loved a cottage like that . . . her and James . . . together. That was all she wanted out of life.

* * *

That evening, Sally and Maureen were sitting in the garden, waiting for James to come home from work, so they could all have a meal together.

'How old is Lizzie?' Sally asked.

Leaning back on the rustic bench, Maureen looked up, covering her eyes to shade herself from the sun. 'I'm not sure exactly,' she answered. 'In her seventies though.'

'I thought she looked really tired today.'

Maureen laughed. 'She weren't the only one neither . . . them baskets seem to get heavier and heavier.'

Observing how Sally was pushing backwards and forwards on the tree swing, she thought how like a little girl she seemed . . . slim and small, with her long hair flowing behind her, and those bright blue eyes. But she was no child, Maureen knew. For here was a woman who had already run the gauntlet of life. Going on sixteen she might be . . . but in her short life she had known more hardship and pain than many a woman twice her age.

'I was just thinking.' Putting her feet to the ground, Sally stopped swinging.

'Oh?' Maureen smiled. 'And what were you thinking about?'

Sally took a moment to answer. Whatever thought came to the forefront of her mind, there were others at the back – dark, frightening thoughts which she daren't acknowledge . . . of James and Isabel. And the awful, uncertain way of things.

Like always she pushed these dark thoughts away. 'Why didn't you and Lizzie ever get that barrow?'

Maureen felt guilty. 'Because I talked her out of it, that's why,' she said. 'And to be honest, she didn't need much persuading. You see, to justify the purchase of a barrow, it would mean selling more produce . . . and seeing that neither of us could grow or make enough on our own, we'd have to buy more produce in. It would mean a lot of work and commitment, and I don't reckon neither me nor Lizzie are up to it. The way we are, we carry what we can, and what we make is our own. Do you see what I mean?'

Sally did see. But she had a plan. One they might *all* benefit from.

A short time later, with the sun going down and the evening turning chilly, they went inside. 'He gets later and later.' Maureen glanced up at the clock. 'Look at that,' she groaned, 'half past eight already, and he's still not home.'

Sally understood. 'He needs to be on his own,' she said. 'He has a lot to think about just now.'

Maureen gave a long, deep sigh. 'Aye, you're right, lass,' she conceded, 'but I would have thought at a time like this, he might look to his family.'

Sally shook her head. 'It doesn't always work like that.' And she should know. Look at the times she had wanted to confide in the man who adopted her, and didn't, in case he too felt her pain.

The table was set and the food ready when James walked in. 'Something smells good, Mam.' He always said that. It gave her comfort, tonight particularly.

'It's your favourite – steak and mushroom pie.' Giving him a smile, Sally kept her distance. Since their all too brief, precious moments of love together, she had felt wary of him, unsure of herself.

His dark gaze studied her for a long moment. 'Hello, Sally,' he murmured, 'looks like you've caught the sun.' In her eyes, he thought, and in her lovely smile.

Maureen explained. 'The lass is never out of it, that's why. Me and Lizzie walk in the shade, while she runs across the field in the full glare of the heat. Then, when she gets home, she's out there on that swing you built . . . face to the sun and loving every minute.'

James looked away, his mind assailed by other, more desperate matters.

By the time he was washed and changed, the meal was on the table. Maureen dared to ask, 'Have you heard anything, son?'

James slowly, thoughtfully, shook his head from side to side. 'Nothing hopeful.' He looked her in the eye. 'Robert says it looks real bad.'

After that, they all seemed to lose their appetites. Though, for his mother's sake, James made an effort to eat as much as he could before pushing away his plate. 'I'll be outside if you want me,' he told them.

When he was gone, the two women sat for a minute, lost in their own thoughts. Sally's frightened voice broke the reverie. 'They won't really hang her, will they?'

'Who knows what they'll do, lass?' Maureen saw hope disappearing with each day. 'Two people were killed . . . they found her standing there with the gun in her hand. If you ask me, it won't matter what else is said . . . folks will believe the worst of her now she's been sentenced, whether she's really innocent or guilty.'

'Do *you* think she's guilty?' It was the first time she had asked Maureen to make a judgement like that.

Taking her plate, Maureen scraped all the leftover meat on to it. She then took the plate across the kitchen and emptied it into the dog bowl; much to the delight of Jake, who had been lying in his basket, feeling sorry for himself. At this time of night he was usually taken for a walk, but something was happening, and he sensed it.

Coming back to the table, Maureen gave her answer. 'I think the lass were caught up in something not of her making,' she confessed. 'But *somebody* has to pay for the lives of those two souls and as she's the only one left to tell the tale—' Grimacing, she held out her hands in a futile gesture. 'Feelings are running high, lass, and there are powerful people concerned here. As to whether she'll be made a scapegoat, well now . . . your guess is as good as mine.'

On that sombre note she and Sally cleared the table and washed the dishes, and hardly a word was spoken the whole time. When the work was done, Sally put on her coat. Fastening the lead around the dog's collar, she told Maureen, 'I'll just go as far as the meadow. Let him walk off his dinner,' she grinned, 'especially as he had more than the three of us put together.'

'Aye. Go on then, lass. But don't you go any further than the meadow. It's too dark to be wandering far.'

Sally was as good as her word. She went as far as the meadow and back, and when she saw the lamp lit in the barn, she hesitated for only a moment before making her way there.

James was standing by the door. Unbeknown to her, he had watched her leave the house and then waited for her to return. 'Thank you for taking him out,' he said, ruffling Jake's head, 'though I would have taken him later.'

Sally lingered. 'Do you need some company?'

'What I need is peace of mind.'

Hesitating, she had to ask, 'Is there really no hope?'

He held her gaze for a moment, as though he wanted to say something but didn't know how.

Sally wasn't all that surprised when he changed the subject. 'Have you decided what you'll do?'

'What? You mean . . . whether I'll stay or not?'

He shrugged his shoulders. 'Something like that.'

When the dog began to pull on the lead, she unfastened it and let him wander into the barn, where he settled down on a sack. 'I think I'll stay,' she answered. In fact her mind was made up. She and Maureen had talked about it, and it seemed the sensible thing to do. Especially when she had this wonderful plan already formulating in her mind.

'Why?'

She was puzzled. 'Why what?'

'Why do you think you'll stay?'

Hesitating, it was on the tip of her tongue to say, 'Because I love you, and want to be near you.'

But common sense prevailed. 'Because I love it here, and Maureen asked me to stay on. And for the first time in a long while, I feel wanted . . . *really* wanted.'

'And that means a great deal to you, does it? To be wanted?'

She looked into his eyes and for one wonderful, unforgettable moment, saw her own future there. 'Isn't that what any of us need?' she replied softly. 'To be wanted?'

'I suppose.'

'Besides, I'm earning my keep now, but it's not enough. I have plans, you see . . . plans that I think Maureen will approve of.'

Her excitement made him smile. 'Plans, eh?' The smile slid away and in its place came a look of regret. 'We *all* make plans at one time or another. But they don't always happen, do they?'

Mortified, she felt ashamed. 'I'm sorry,' she apologised, 'I'm letting my tongue run away with me.'

To her astonishment, James covered her hand with his. 'Have you decided what to do about your father, your *real* father?'

'I'm not sure, but, one way or another, I think he should be punished.'

James laughed, but it was a grim sound. 'Hmh! You're not the only one who thinks that.'

'He has to pay for what he did to me . . . and to his own sister. He took away everything she had, ruined her marriage, ruined her life. He made her the monster she became.'

Sally had given it a great deal of thought. 'The more I think about Anne Hale, the more I realise what a terrible strain she was under.'

James had never had any doubt. 'That man destroys everything he touches.'

'I'd better go.' Suspecting his mind was on Isabel, she felt out of her depth. 'Your mam will wonder where I've got to.'

'Thank you, Sally.'

'What for?'

'For your company.'

'I only wish I could do more.' Like give you my love, she thought . . . like make you happy.

'I'm glad you're staying,' he said. 'It's good to have you around.'

Feeling closer to him, she dared to ask, 'Do you think everything will be all right, for Isabel, I mean?'

'I only wish I knew.' His voice was charged with emotion. 'It's out of the hands of ordinary folk. All we can do now is wait for the outcome.'

When she called the dog, he told her, 'Leave him, Sally. I'll bring him in later.'

As she went towards the house, he gave a long groan. 'Dear God!' Wiping his hands down his face, he closed his eyes and leaned his head against the timber frame. 'Where do we go from here?'

There were two women in his life. One was a friend; but the other he loved with every fibre of his being. And, for a time, God help him, he had not recognised the truth of it all. But now he knew. He had known for many weeks. Long before this terrible tragedy unfolded, he had prepared himself to tell her of his love. Now though, with everything the way it was, how could he?

Especially when he had been so certain he could never love any woman but Isabel.

* * *

The following week, the worst kind of news was given out.

Isabel Scarlet was to pay the heaviest price imaginable. There was to be no reprieve.

'Oh, it's true right enough.' Slicing his knife through a pork-knuckle, the butcher boned and folded the joint. 'There are to be no more appeals for clemency. I had that Mrs Thwaites in, whose husband works at the prison. Tomorrow morning at half past eight, she'll swing from the gallows, and that's an end to it.'

Shocked to her soul, Mrs Daley dropped her purse in a fluster. 'Oh, dearie me!' She was a sweet old soul with no heart for violence. 'And I was beginning to hope she might be spared.' Making the sign of the cross, she hurried from the shop.

'Poor litle bugger.' The butcher paid mind to his next customer. 'I wish I hadn't told her now,' he said. 'She's such a gentle little thing.'

Mr Pearson was not so gentle. Reaching up to collect his tripe, he spoke his mind like the blunt, honest fellow he was. 'As far as I'm concerned, Isabel Scarlet's punishment could have been nothing *less* than a hanging!' With that, he dropped his coins on the counter and marched off to tell all and sundry the news.

It had already reached those who mattered through official channels.

Leonard Mears flew into a rage, then he went so quiet his household briefly feared he might have done away with himself.

Comforted as always by Robert, Frances cried bitter tears. 'It's all my fault,' she sobbed, but Robert told her she had been the best mother possible.

Hannah locked herself in her room and wouldn't come out, and Jack drank a whole bottle of wine, keeling over with the last dregs.

* * *

Distraught, James walked the hills and valleys. Throughout the trial and afterwards, he had felt it would come to this. 'Always the innocent,' he told the skies. 'Lambs to the slaughter.'

He desperately needed her to know that he had not forgotten, that she was still on his mind and in his heart. But not like before. That was over the day she slipped another man's ring on her finger. Only he hadn't known it then. Not straight away.

It was late evening when he returned home. 'Have you a sheet of writing paper and pen?' he asked his mother. 'There are things I need to write down.'

Bringing the items from her own drawer, she placed them before him. 'Are you all right, son?' she asked tenderly, her eyes red with tears.

His answer was to clasp her to him and hold her there for a while. When presently he let her loose, he was too choked to speak. Instead, he nodded, and she understood.

As Maureen moved away, he looked up to see Sally gazing on him; she too had shed a tear for someone she never knew. For James too, for she believed he loved that tragic young woman, and her heart went out to him.

He bathed in her gaze a moment longer, then, when she looked away, disturbed by events, he thanked his mother again for the materials, and taking them to his room, began to write.

My dearest Isabel,

I don't know what to do, or how to comfort you. When the news came through, it was like a stab to the heart.

I tried to see you, but they wouldn't let me. You were never out of my mind or heart, and however long I live, you will never be far from my thoughts.

There are all kinds of love, Isabel, and I have loved you in every way. Now, when you must call on all the courage you have, please remember me, as I remember you. Think of the dreams we shared and the secret smiles when nobody knew . . . and nobody ever will.

It was our time. Tomorrow will be your time, but you are not alone, my lovely. I will be there to hold your hand and make you brave.

God bless you, Isabel. Be proud as you are innocent. And you must never be afraid.

My thoughts are with you to the end.

James.

When it was written, he folded his arms over it and sobbed pitifully.

When the sobbing was done, he put the letter in his pocket and left the house. Turning in the direction of the prison, he quickened his steps . . . striding out – a man with a purpose.

On arriving at the prison gates, he pressed himself into the shadows and waited. The vigil was long and uncomfortable. But he knew if he waited long enough, his reward would come. It came in the shape of Robert.

Making sure first that Robert was alone, James dashed out of the shadows and waylaid him. 'Give her this, please,' he begged, folding the letter into Robert's hand. 'It's all I can do.'

In the lamplight, Robert's tears were like tiny drops of silver running down his face. 'I don't know how I can face her,' he said. 'Oh, James. What am I to do?'

Placing his two hands on the other man's shoulders, James shook him hard. 'Be brave,' he said; 'brave and strong . . . as she must be.'

His proud words hit home. 'You make me feel ashamed,' he whispered. Then he was gone, clutching James's letter tight in his fist.

James was to learn later that Isabel had read his letter and, because of it, was ready to face the day. 'Tell him it's all right,' she said. That was all. But for James, it was enough.

The following morning, the crowds gathered outside, some praying for her soul, others hard and unyielding. But when the great clock struck the half-hour, the praying stopped and the silence was awesome. Then the crowd began to disperse and drift away.

It was all over.

Chapter Sixteen

The house shone from top to bottom. 'By! I'll not know the place by the time you've finished!'

Rolling out the dough on her kitchen table, Maureen had been watching Sally for a while. 'My ornaments are sparkling; the windows are so polished I could be forgiven for thinking there ain't no glass in 'em, and now . . . well.' Casting an eye over the fire range, she couldn't believe it. 'It looks brand new, does that.'

The old range had seen its best days, and though Maureen kept it clean, Sally had gone further. First she scraped it down to its base, then blackleaded it, and now was bringing the shine through with a dubbing cloth. 'Are you pleased though?' Sally had been up since five o'clock, and hadn't stopped 'til now. 'You don't mind me going through your house like a dose o' salts, do you?' she asked worriedly. 'Only, I felt restless, so I thought I'd set my hand to something.'

Maureen laughed. 'Well, you've certainly done that, my girl!' Clapping her hands together to shake off the flour, Maureen rolled the mound of dough into a muslin rag, then left it there to rest a while. 'I thought you were going into Blackburn market today? You allus like to do that on a Saturday.' Sometimes Maureen went with her, sometimes she didn't.

'I thought about it,' Sally confessed, 'then I decided I couldn't do with being squashed in a crowd.'

Maureen could understand that; especially since the hanging, when the whole world seemed to have gathered at the prison gates. 'Come on, lass,' she urged, 'wash the muck off your hands. I reckon we deserve a brew, don't you?'

Sally didn't argue. In fact she felt so hungry her stomach was turning somersaults. 'I'll make the tea,' she offered. Softly singing, Maureen went to the pantry and took out two currant teacakes.

When they were seated at the table, enjoying a well-deserved break, Maureen told her, 'I'll be glad when Christmas has come and gone and the new year arrives.'

Sally had a mouthful of teacake, so didn't answer.

Maureen chatted on. 'No, I shan't be sorry to see the back of the old year, an' that's a fact.' Scooping the currants from her plate, she popped them into her mouth. She was quiet for a minute, her mind going over all that had happened. Taking a swig of her tea, she asked Sally, 'What's mekking you so restless then?'

'I'm not sure.'

'You've been that fidgety lately –' A frightening thought crossed her mind. 'Hey! You're not planning to leave us, are you?'

Sally smiled. 'I've been thinking . . . about James. Do you think he'll ever forget her?'

'Ah!' Now Maureen knew why Sally had been so restless. 'It's *him* that's on your mind, ain't it, lass?' she queried. 'You think he'll never come round to noticing you . . . in the way you want, I mean. Am I right?' She knew Sally was head over heels in love with her son, and was delighted. But she also knew that James had a fair way to go before he could clear his mind of Isabel.

260

'I love him so much, I can't think about anything else.' These days Sally felt she could confide anything in Maureen.

'Awe, I know how you feel, lass,' Maureen told her. 'I've known almost as long as you've known yourself. But it's all a bit raw just yet . . . only three weeks to my reckoning.' Fondly patting Sally's hand, she offered a measure of hope. 'Give him time and he'll begin to see above the clouds.'

'Do you think he'll ever come to love me?'

'Well now—' Maureen gave one of her knowing smiles. 'Do you know what I *really* think, lass?'

Sally shook her head.

'I think he *already* loves you, but doesn't know it.'

Her remark brought a smile to Sally's face. 'I'd better get on,' she said, blushing bright pink. 'I've to polish the quarry-tiles at the front door yet.'

'An' I'd better get the hotpot bubbling. Your man will be in afore too long.' Glancing at the clock, she noticed it was nearly midday. 'These days he seems to get home when he should, and not four hours later.' It was a good sign, she thought.

Sally was still on her knees buffing the quarry-tiles when James came up behind her. Pausing a moment, he observed how deeply she was engrossed in her task. Jake lay content beside her, and occasionally she reached out to tickle his belly. 'You're a lazy old thing, aren't you, eh?' she'd say, and the dog would wag his tail like a young pup.

James thought it was the loveliest scene. He thought, too, of how much he loved her. But he couldn't tell her. Not yet. There were things he had to get out of his system first. Besides, how was he to know if she felt the same way?

After a few minutes he stepped forward. 'By! I'm half afraid to walk on them tiles,' he teased, ruffling her hair.

Sally told him he'd better step over them.

Sitting back on her haunches, she let herself enjoy the moment.

He had ruffled her hair. It wasn't much to sing about, she thought. But it was the first time he had laid a hand on her since that night in the barn. 'It's a start,' she murmured. 'Maybe Maureen was right. Maybe the clouds are shifting at long last.'

That same night, Leonard Mears drank himself stupid, like he had done every night since his daughter was lost to him.

'You can't go on like this.' Seeing how weak he really was, and hating him more by the minute, Frances was bolder these days. 'I know how you feel, because I feel the same,' she told him. 'I know you miss her, and so do I, but we have to try and move on with our lives or it will drive us insane.'

'You bloody fool!' Staring through pink, bulbous eyes, he laughed out loud. 'She's gone, and she's not coming back, I know that.'

Frances didn't understand him. 'Then what's wrong with you?' His violent mood swings were worse than she had ever seen.

Downing the remainder of his drink, he went into a sulk. 'My grieving's done,' he muttered. 'It was none of my fault, and I'll not hear anybody say it is.'

Lying, Frances tried to console him. 'Nobody's saying it was your fault.'

Seeming calmer, he peeked at her out of the corner of his eyes. 'Tad Scarlet is determined to finish me.'

Frances was astonished. He had never discussed business with her before. 'How can he do that?'

'We had an agreement to join in partnership and build a factory on that site . . . a partnership that could have brought rich returns. Now he's not only reneged on the agreement, but he's gone and sold both his piece of land *and* his factory to one of my biggest competitors – a carriage-maker by the name of Bill Carter.'

'But what does that matter? This Bill Carter can't harm you, can he? You're too established.' Frances never did understand the way of business.

'You don't know anything, do you?' Sneering, he made her feel insignificant. 'For years I've been just a whisker in front of Bill Carter. He builds good carriages, though I'd never admit it to anyone else. But you see, he's been struggling in a back-alley warehouse, with hardly room to swing a cat. All the bigger sites are long gone. Now though, thanks to Tad Scarlet, he's acquired a prime site on the canal front. Not only will he be increasing his output and undercutting my prices even more, but he'll be right there alongside me, watching everything I do.'

Drink and anger addled his senses. 'This is all *her* fault!' Slamming his empty glass into the wall, he cursed. 'My own flesh and blood! I wish to God she'd never been born.' Bowing his head, he cried like a baby. 'Why couldn't she have left well alone?'

Disgusted, Frances left him there, steeped in drink and self-pity. 'Fit for nothing.' She closed the door on him. 'It's *you* who should never have been born.'

From her vantage point, Eliza Flanagan watched Frances go up to her room; she heard her lock herself in, and was satisfied the mistress would not come out again this side of morning.

Softly, she returned to her own quarters, but she didn't sleep. Instead she waited for everyone to retire for the night, then lingered by the door, occasionally peeping out, making certain there was no one about.

When the clock struck midnight, she made her move.

On tiptoe, she went nervously towards the library. 'This might be my only chance,' she murmured as she went. 'The way things are going in this household, who knows how long it will hold together?'

Already, Robert was planning to move into a place of his own, and since his father seemed to be losing his grip, Jack was easing himself into the driving seat. Hannah had always been unpredictable, but now she was deliberately rebellious, a constant worry to her poor mother.

Then there was this business with Adam Scarlet's father. Oh yes! Things were sliding down a very slippery slope.

Not so surprisingly, the situation suited Eliza's purpose well. With the master drunk most evenings, he might be easier to work on, and tonight, unusually, both sons were out. Hannah was fast asleep; Eliza knew that because she had taken her a mug of cocoa earlier, and already the girl was out to the world.

As she stood before the library door, her heart was thumping. She was afraid, yet her fear was nothing when compared to her purpose for being there. 'I want my daughter,' she whispered, 'and he's the only one who knows where she is.' In her mind's eye she could see the tiny bairn that was torn from her sixteen years before. Suddenly, the courage rose like a tide inside her.

Carefully, she tapped on the door. When there was no answer, she undid the top four buttons of her blouse, leaving the swell of her breast exposed. Loosening the clip from her hair, she let her long brown hair fall about her shoulders.

Then she opened the door and looked in, half-expecting to be bawled out, and pleasantly surprised when she was not. With a smile, she closed the door, and took stock of the situation.

Sprawled on the settee, Leonard Mears had his eyes closed. On hearing the click of the door closing, he opened one eye and glared at her. 'Who the devil's that?' He appeared confused.

'Eliza, sir.'

Both eyes opened. 'Eliza?'

'Eliza Flanagan, sir.'

Rolling over, he observed her for a moment, his eyes drawn to the loose folds of hair that tumbled over her shoulders . . . and then to the milk-white skin of her breasts. 'What do you want?'

On quiet footsteps she went to stand before him, in her sweetest voice saying, 'I've come to see if there's anything you want before I go to bed.' Her smile was slyly suggestive.

Thrilled, he dragged himself to a sitting position, his lustful eyes again on the rise of her breasts. 'Look at yourself, woman!' The grin spread over his features like an evil shadow. 'My God! You're half-naked!'

Feigning shock, she swiftly pulled her blouse together, but left the buttons undone. 'Oh, I am sorry, sir,' she apologised breathlessly, 'only I was preparing for bed when I heard the mistress go up, and I wondered if you were all right.'

He opened his arms. 'Come here!'

'Oh, I can't do that, sir,' she said coyly, tantalising him all the more. 'I know all about you.'

His eyes opened wide. 'Oh, do you now?'

'I worked with a girl called Sadie . . . oh, a long time ago. She knew you, sir. And she thought you were just wonderful.'

Preening himself, he chuckled, 'Wonderful, eh? In what way?'

Knowing she had him hooked, Eliza gave the best performance of her life. 'She told me how you and her—' Lowering her gaze, she shyly giggled. 'I'm sorry, sir. I'd better go.'

When she turned to go, he called out an instruction: 'Fetch me that whisky bottle . . . on the desk, there!'

With her back towards him, she raised her eyes in gratitude. Going to the desk, she took the bottle into her hand and returned to the settee. 'Will that be all, sir?' she murmured, her eyes smiling down on him, as she handed over the bottle, leaning forward just low enough to tantalise him with her unbuttoned blouse.

Grabbing the bottle with one hand, he reached up with the other. 'I didn't realise you had such a fine figure.' Undoing the rest of her buttons, he began to tweak her nipples. 'You shouldn't hide your goodies behind that dull uniform, you know.'

'No, sir.' Leaning forward she made it easier for him to fondle her breasts.

'How many men have you had?'

'Lots, sir.' She knew that was what he wanted to hear. 'Sadly, none of them was very special in bed.'

'Do you think *I'm* special?'

'I don't know, sir. But my friend Sadie said you were the best she ever had.'

'This Sadie . . . how do I know her?'

'She was the parlour-maid at a big house in Preston . . . your father's house. Don't you remember, sir? Said she'd met you when you visited.'

'Sadie?' His brain was too addled. 'Hmh!' Taking a deep swig of booze, he pulled her down to him. 'I think I'll take you here and now. What do you say to that?'

'What if I said no?'

He laughed. 'It wouldn't matter. I'd take you anyway!'

Pushing his hand up her skirt, he forced open her legs, groaning when she seemed to slip away from him. In a slurred voice he ordered, 'Take off your drawers.'

Slowly, provocatively, she lifted her skirt. 'Sadie never got over you,' she murmured. 'She always loved you, did you know that?' Sadie was Eliza's real name. But she had changed it when coming to work here.

'Lots of women have loved me.'

'Not like her though.'

'They were after my money . . . every one of them. But they didn't get it. I'm no fool.' Quietly smiling, he never took his eyes off her lower body. 'Hurry up, woman!' He was visibly sweating; whether it was with drink or desire, Eliza didn't know, but she did know one thing – she was not leaving this room until she discovered what had happened to her baby daughter.

When she let her skirt drop to the floor he gave a little whoop of laughter and lunged forward. Grabbing her thighs he rocked her off balance and the two of them went tumbling to the carpet. 'You little vixen!' Rolling her over, he ripped off her blouse and bent his head to her breasts, his wet mouth covering her nipple and sucking like a greedy infant. Between her legs she could feel his member hard against her, his hand tearing at her underwear.

Nauseated by his touch, she wondered how she could ever have loved him, let alone have borne him a child. 'I'll do it,' she said, pushing his hand away, 'I don't want you to tear my clothes.'

Raising his head he laughed in her face, his pink, drunken eyes looking into hers. 'I never knew you were so attractive,' he whispered, patiently waiting for her to slide him in.

Taking her time, she asked softly, 'Did you think Sadie was attractive?'

He was silent for a moment, his mind going back, his memory beginning to return. 'Sadie?' He took a deep breath, which seemed to swell his stomach and suffocate her. 'Ah! *She* was the one. Bloody slag . . . could have got me into all kinds of trouble.' With an almighty thrust he was there, his voice becoming one long moan, and his grotesque body writhing with ecstasy.

Now, too intent on satisfying himself, he wouldn't answer her questions. Until, with a little scream of delight, his ardour burst inside her. Rolling away, he lay there for a moment, drunk out of his mind, and too weakened to get up.

Afraid he might go to sleep, she shook him. 'Wake up.' When he opened his eyes, she asked softly, 'Was it better than with Sadie?'

In his confused mind, all he could see was his sister . . . and the daughter he had disowned long ago. 'Sadie was a fool! She should never have let herself get with child.'

Relief etched itself on her face. 'The child,' she said. 'What happened to her?' Her memory took her back and it was almost too much to bear – only minutes after she gave birth, the men had burst in and taken her baby. The tears rolled down her face as she shook him again. 'What happened to the child?'

He looked up at her . . . at her terrible distress, and he knew!

Softly crying, she asked again, this time without pretence, 'Please . . . tell me where my child is now?'

Shaking her off, he went crazy. 'Get off! Get away from me! The child is dead!' Sometimes he even believed his own lies. 'It was for the best.'

Giving her an almighty push, he sent her halfway across the room. Desperately trying to stand, he floundered, lost his balance and fell, the drink flooding his senses.

Eyes closed and body twisted, he lay there – dead or unconscious, it didn't matter to the watching woman. 'You devil!' she whispered. 'You wicked, cruel devil!' She watched him as she dressed, the loathing like cold steel inside her. 'You'll pay for what you did,' she murmured, passing his inert form. 'If there is any justice, you'll be made to burn in hell!'

Outside, someone listened. Now, having heard everything, the figure scurried away.

In the early hours he began to stir. Everything that had gone before was now lost to him: the crude coupling with Eliza; the mention of Sadie and her lost child – all blotted out by the drink.

Shaking his sore head he wondered how he had come to be half-undressed; a glance at the stained carpet told him. 'You've pissed yourself, you silly old bugger.' Fastening his trousers, he saw the half-empty bottle on the settee, and the other emptied on the floor.

Chuckling, he picked up the half-empty one and took a swig from it. 'Hair of the dog,' he laughed, and flung it back down, oblivious to the fact that it spilled out all over the seating. 'I need my bed,' he mumbled. 'Got to rest my bones.' He waddled out, leaving the door wide open.

Stumbling and tripping, he made it up the stairs. But he didn't make it to his room; instead, he fell in a heap outside his bedroom door. Hearing a noise, Frances looked out and saw him there. 'I don't care if you never wake up again,' she murmured, and going inside, locked her door.

It was almost an hour later when Robert came through the front door. Leaning heavily on his shoulder was his brother, Jack. 'You're a damned fool, Jack,' he hissed angrily. 'Just look at you! Have you no more sense than to get tangled up in a fight like that?'

Bruised and bleeding, Jack had no regrets. 'I won't let them talk about Father like that,' he grouched. 'What do *they* know? It wasn't his fault! If only she'd known how to keep her mouth shut, none of it would have happened.'

'Shut up, Jack . . . or I might wish I had never come looking for you.'

Knowing his brother too well, and acutely aware of how badly Robert had been affected by Isabel's death, Jack did as he was told.

Being careful not to make too much noise, Robert got him up the stairs and into his room. There he dipped a towel into the ewer and roughly washed the crusted blood from Jack's face and neck.

When at one point Jack opened his mouth to cry out, he stuffed the towel in it. 'No noise!' he warned grimly. After that, Jack was still while Robert cleaned him up the best he could.

'Now get some sleep.' He eased him on to the bed. 'You can clean yourself up properly tomorrow. And be quiet! I don't want the whole house awake!'

'Don't keep giving me orders!'

'You've got a choice, Jack. Either you be quiet, or you can spend a night out in the cold.' He glanced towards the window, his meaning very clear.

'Hmh! It won't always be like this . . . with you telling me what to do and what not to do!' Peeved, Jack glared at him through swelling eyes. 'Father won't live for ever, and then *I'll* be the boss. He knows you blame him for what happened to Isabel, and he won't forgive you for that. He's biding his time . . . waiting for me. Soon he won't trust you to run things any more.'

His bloodied face lifted in a mischievous grin. 'He'll change his will and leave it all to me. Huh! I'll bet he's done it already. Your days are numbered, Robert,' he taunted. 'You wait and see if I'm not right!'

Ignoring his ramblings, Robert smiled. 'Good night, Jack.'

'Bugger off!' Sulking, Jack turned over.

Robert lingered by the door, waiting for Jack to settle before leaving him there.

To get to his own room, Robert had to pass his father's room. In the half-light, he almost tripped over him. 'Drunk again!' Disgust coloured his voice.

There had been times when he, too, could have lost himself in the booze, but it wasn't the answer. Going on . . . living your life with your eyes to the future. That was the only way to put it all behind you. It was hard though, even when with every day that passed the horror of it all seemed less crippling. But it would never be forgotten. *Never!*

He stood there for a moment or two, his eyes on that seemingly lifeless, misshapen figure; even from where he stood, Robert could smell the booze. 'You're no good,' he murmured. 'You think you're strong and clever, but you're none of those things. You're a cruel, selfish creature, with a stone for a heart, and an insatiable appetite for money . . . prepared to sacrifice anything to that end.'

Touching him ever so gently with his toe, he watched as the roll of fat on his face twitched and shivered. 'Jack said I blamed you,' he whispered, 'and he's right . . . I do. You've been like a canker at the heart of this family for too long. It should be *you* lying in the cold ground, not Isabel.'

Thick, desperate emotion rose in his throat. 'She didn't deserve what you did to her. But it's over now. She's out of your reach.'

He stayed a moment longer, staring down at his father and wondering how he came to be. Shame and anger flooded his senses until he could watch no longer. Without a backward glance, he hurried away to his much-needed sleep.

For a long time, his father lay there, unmoving, until the cold began to penetrate his bones and startled him awake. Scrambling up, he stood against the wall, keeping his balance and angry that he should have been left there through the night. 'Spiteful bitch!' Cursing he made his unsteady way to his wife's room. When he pushed on the door and it didn't open, he began yelling. 'Open this door . . . or I'll break it down!' Banging his fist on the door, he threatened all manner of retribution.

White with fear, Frances opened the door. 'What's wrong?'

Pushing his way in, he took hold of her by the shoulders. Shaking her fiercely, he spat the words in her face. 'Bitch! You left me out there . . . curled up in the cold like a stray dog. What the devil d'you mean by it?' Holding her tight with one hand, he brought the other one hard down on her face. When she whimpered, he pushed her to the floor and took off his belt. Folding it between his fists, he raised it high above his head. As it came swishing down she turned, crying out when the sharp belt-buckle sliced across her shoulder. Glancing up fearfully she saw the rage in his eyes, and prepared herself for the worst.

Down the hall, Jack was in a deep sleep.

Hannah woke, but made no move. She was too afraid, too much of a coward.

Robert was woken by the one, faraway cry. Sitting up in bed, he listened intently. When only silence greeted him, he lay down again. 'I expect it was Jack having a nightmare.' He smiled. 'That should teach him not to top up on Dutch courage and take on two twice his size.'

In the servants' quarters, only Cook realised what was happening. Her room was nearest to the main stairway and, because she was a light sleeper, she had heard it all many times before. Other times she would lie in her bed, turning restlessly and trying not to be stirred by it. Tonight, though, she couldn't rest. Getting out of her bed she paced the room, agitated to the point of being wide awake. 'You're a bad man,' she murmured. 'A bad, bad man.'

After a while, she returned to her bed and closed her eyes, letting the tiredness wash through her. After all, she had a very busy day tomorrow.

Just as the dawn was breaking, Leonard Mears emerged from his wife's room. Dressed only in his undergarments, he carried his shirt and trousers over his arm.

Still intoxicated from the booze and exhilarated by the more recent events, he began laughing to himself – softly, insanely – unaware that he was being stalked.

As he ambled past the stairway, the follower lunged forward. All it took was a gentle push and he was tumbling down the stairs out of control – over and over, bouncing and leaping from step to step, like the barrels he made, when they went rolling down the chute. His head smashed on the banister as it went, leaving little damp pockets of blood behind. Astonished and shocked he cried out, but the cries froze in his throat.

From the top of the stairs, his attacker watched. Until at last the falling figure came to a halt at the foot of the stairway. Sighing, the figure turned away. The deed was done. Twisted and broken, Mears lay there all alone, eyes wide open. He hadn't liked to be left in the cold, but it didn't matter any more. Leonard Mears didn't matter any more.

* * *

Clambering out of her bed, the parlour-maid feared she might be late. 'Get the fires lit or the master will have yer guts for garters,' she muttered to herself, running about dressing. 'Cook'll be after yer any minute an' Lord help yer if everything ain't right.'

Splashing her face with cold water from the bowl, she shivered. 'Must be a better way to earn a crust,' she complained. 'First up, last to bed, and nothing but baggy eyes to show for it.' Looking into the mirror she put out her tongue. 'Ugh! What a 'orrible sight!'

With her hair rammed under her mob cap and her pinny on inside out, she picked up the lamp and crept softly away. 'Don't you disturb Cook,' she warned herself, 'leastwise, not 'til you've got that range going. When the kitchen's warm an' cosy, *then* yer can fetch her from her bed.' She gave a long, audible shiver. 'Lucky old sod . . . an' there's me has to brave the cold like a good 'un!'

Lighting the lamps as she went, she began humming a little melody. As she turned towards the stairway, the melody ended and she stood, frozen to the spot, her eyes scouring the bundle at the foot of the stairs. 'What can that be?' Coming closer she blamed all and sundry. 'There'll be the devil to pay if anybody trips over it and hurts themselves . . . honest to God, some folk can't be bothered. Master Jack, I should think, he's allus leaving things lying—' Now she could see and the words faded on her lips.

The first flush of wonder melted into curiosity; then horror as she realised. 'Oh . . . OH!' Like a flowering blossom her face opened, her eyes rolled in her head and the voice which had been singing only moments before rose to a shrill, piercing scream, going on and on, as if it might never end. Suddenly the whole house was awake.

When Robert found her there, she had her hands covering her

face. The screams had broken into uncontrollable sobbing, and she was so rooted to the ground he had to wrench her away.

'See to her,' he told Cook, who had run out like the rest of the household. Realising after a brief examination that his father was past all help, he quickly took charge. 'Mrs Flanagan, get everybody away, there's been a terrible accident.' As she moved away, he called to her. 'Bring me a towel. Quickly!' The sight of his father's eyes staring up at him was more than he could bear. But he could not close them. Even if his life depended on it, he could not bring himself to close those accusing eyes.

Ushering them all into the kitchen, Mrs Flanagan glanced back. There was no compassion in her heart. Only hatred. And a bitter regret that all her hopes of finding her daughter had come to nothing.

When they were all seated round the table, with Cook recovered enough now to make them a hot, soothing drink, Mrs Flanagan hurried back with a towel. While Robert respectfully covered his father's face, Frances sat on the top step, shaking and shivering, her gaze downcast and her face set like stone. He was gone now, and she needn't be afraid. But she was afraid. She would always be afraid.

Crouched on the floor, Hannah remained half-hidden behind the banister. She had seen, and now she didn't want to look any more. In her short life she had seen too much and knew too much, and her tortured mind was desperately trying to shut it all out.

Seemingly unaffected, Jack stood at the top of the stairs, legs apart and arms behind his back. With his bruised face, he looked even more damaged than his father.

When Robert looked up, Jack was smiling. 'Jack!' His voice shattered the silence. 'Mother and Hannah . . . get them away from here!'

Satisfied that Jack was doing as asked, he then set about sending for the authorities.

'Tell them to come quickly,' he told the groom. 'Tell them Mr Leonard Mears has fallen accidentally to his death.' His words reverberated in everyone's ears . . . 'Tell them Leonard Mears has fallen accidentally to his death.'

Sweet words.

But they were not true . . .

Chapter Seventeen

It was half past eight on a cold November evening. Having sold all her hot chestnuts, the old woman cleaned her barrow and prepared to go home. It wasn't far . . . over London Bridge, then down alongside the Thames, and she was almost there.

Carefully, she wended her way through the Christmas shoppers. 'Too early yet to think about Christmas,' she muttered, drawing her coat tightly about her. 'Two days before, that's time enough for me, and even then I ain't got nobody to shop for . . . just meself. A little fat chicken and a mince pie, that'll do me.'

She smacked her lips. 'Oh, an' a drop o' good brandy . . . enjoyed in front of a cheery fire. What else would anyone want?' She was a simple soul with simple tastes.

Sometimes singing, other times quietly chuntering to herself, she ambled along. Nobody took much notice of her, except to smile at her eccentricity. She took even less notice of them. If they weren't buying her chestnuts she had no need of them.

Knowing it was more sheltered there, she took the path alongside the river. It was warmer too, and quieter. But the barrow seemed to get heavier as she went along, and she wasn't as young or strong as she used to be.

Taking a moment to rest, she sat on the cold, hard bench to get her breath. Manoeuvring the barrow so she had the handles closer to her, she kept one foot on the wheel. 'Let any bugger try and run off with it,' she muttered, 'an' they'll be in for a shock.' Reaching into the tray, she drew out a long leather truncheon. 'This'll give 'em a headache, I'll be bound.'

Chuckling to herself, she fought with her shawl for a minute before plucking an old pipe from its considerable folds. Laying the pipe down beside her, she indulged in another battle with the shawl before a moment later withdrawing a box of matches. 'Just a puff or two,' she promised herself. 'Then it's off home at the double.' She chuckled at her misguided optimism. She had never been anywhere at the double in the whole of her uneventful existence.

But with a life or death drama unfolding only an arm's reach from her, all that was about to change.

Settling back on to the bench, she drew on her old pipe, her face a picture of bliss as she puffed away. Soon she was softly humming again, her old eyes skimming the water and thinking how lovely it all was at this time of an evening.

A short distance away, Anne Hale stood by the bridge. Melting into the scene, she leaned against a pillar, her troubled eyes looking across the same stretch of water as the old woman. But their thoughts were very different. Where one saw a familiar scene and loved it for its beauty, the other saw it as a means of escape.

For a long time she stood there, her mind playing out a picture . . . of herself falling into the cool, dark depths of the water. There would be peace there, and maybe forgiveness.

Her desperate whispering gentled through the evening air. The name, one which had haunted her for too long, escaped in a sigh: 'Sally.' Oh, how she wished she could turn back the clock. 'Sally . . .' Over and over she murmured the name in her fevered mind, hoping somehow the girl might hear. 'I'm sorry …'

Further away, the old woman sat up, her ears pricked. 'What

was that?' There were all kinds of sounds alongside the Thames, and she knew every one. But something . . . the softest of cries . . . had disturbed her.

Peering first one way and then the other, she let her gaze cut through the familiar things, searching for something different. At first she didn't see the woman climbing on to the parapet, but then she did, and her heart stood still. 'Oh, my God! Whatever is she doing?' But it was plain to see what that desperate creature meant to do.

With no thought for her precious barrow, or the old sock filled with her day's takings, the old woman threw down her pipe and ran as fast as her fat little legs would allow. 'No!' Her voice went before her. 'Don't do that! Please . . . Yer mustn't do that!'

Breathless and afraid, she stopped short of where Anne stood. Teetering on the edge, one arm steadying herself by the pillar, she told the old woman, 'Go away. I don't want you to see.' In her miserable life she had caused enough pain to others, and now she had to make amends.

'I ain't going nowhere 'til you come down off there.'

There was a long, agonising silence, with the old woman crossing her fingers behind her back, and Anne wanting to jump . . . to end it all, yet knowing real fear. The kind of fear she had inflicted on Sally.

'Please, lady . . . come down.'

Turning her sorry eyes, Anne looked at her and the old woman knew she was losing the argument. At any minute the stranger would let go of the pillar and there would be no saving her.

She tried another tack. 'All right, lady, if jumping in that water ends all your troubles, I reckon I'll jump in with yer!' Without further ado, she hitched up her skirt and began climbing.

It worked.

'No! Get down!' Terrified she might be the cause of the old lady drowning, Anne pleaded, 'Get down, please.'

Ignoring her, the old woman kept up her pretence, making a bother of getting her fat little frame up the parapet, yet keeping her feet in the same hole all the time. She hated heights and had a horror of water. Any minute now, she feared she might faint and fall in the river without meaning to.

'All right! All right, I'll come down.' Inching herself along the parapet, Anne clasped both her arms round the pillar to steady herself.

The old woman warned her, 'Just remember, if for any reason *you* happen to fall, I'll be sailing through the air behind yer.' Though the idea sent her weak at the legs.

When Anne was down, and the old woman too, the pair of them clung to each other. 'What in God's name were yer thinking of?' the old woman wanted to know. 'Surely things can't be that bad you want to drown yerself.'

Shaking uncontrollably, from cold as well as fright, Anne allowed herself to be led back to the bench. When the old woman screamed out, she almost leaped out of her skin. 'Me bleedin' barrer!' Dropping Anne on to the bench, she ran about, arms waving. 'The bastards 'ave tekken me barrer!'

Dropping herself beside the startled Anne, she moaned, 'The thievin' bastards! *And* they've got more than they bargained for . . . 'cause all me bleedin' takings were in that barrer.'

Mortified, Anne comforted her. 'It's my fault,' she apologised, 'but I'll make amends.' All she ever wanted was to make amends; to Sally more than anyone. 'Look! I've got a wealthy brother. You might even have heard of him . . . Leonard Mears, the carriage-maker. He owes me more than he could ever repay—'

'What?' She observed how poorly the other woman was dressed, and how undernourished. 'You's not saying *you* lent him money?'

Anne shook her head. 'No, not money,' she answered softly, the awful memories flooding back. 'It's another kind of debt. I'll

279

ask him for enough money to buy you another barrow and replace your takings.' Shivering, she folded her arms about her to keep out the cold, her voice fading to a whisper. 'I'm sorry.'

The old woman realised how this one could catch her death of cold if they weren't very careful, then all her persuading would have been for nothing. ''Ere!' Taking off her shawl, she put it round Anne's shoulders. 'I'm fat as a walrus,' she laughed. 'You need this more than I do.'

'I *will* get you another barrow,' Anne promised, '*and* recompense you for your takings. Tell me how much you need, and where you live, and I'll bring it to you as soon as I can.'

'Oh aye! An' the minute me back's turned, you'll climb up on that parapet an' throw yerself off it!' She prided herself on her knowledge of human nature.

Anne smiled, a sad little smile that touched the old woman's heart. 'I won't do that,' she promised. 'Not now.'

Because *now* she meant to find Sally and ask her forgiveness. 'There are other reasons I need to see my brother. I didn't have the courage before, but I do now.' Lowering her gaze she murmured, 'He has a great deal to answer for.'

The old woman was intrigued. 'This brother of yourn . . . has he ever harmed you?'

'Me . . . and others.'

'Then I'll not have you going begging to him on my account!'

'It's something I have to do. Though I didn't deserve it, you saved my life.'

'I'd have done the same for any poor soul.'

'Me going to my brother should not concern you,' Anne explained. 'It's been a long time coming. Besides, like I said, he owes me a great deal.'

'Are you some kind of a lady, come on hard times?' The way Anne spoke, the fine long fingers and clear skin, made her think that way.

'Hmh!' Anne couldn't help but smile at that. 'I don't know your name, or what you do,' she said curiously, 'but I do know you are more of a lady than I could ever be.'

'The name's Libby.' Shaking Anne's hand, she told her, 'I sell hot chestnuts. I ain't rich, and I ain't no lady, but I hope I've been blessed with a kind heart.' Glancing down the street, she shook her fist. 'Though if I ever catch up with them thievin' buggers, I'll knock their bleedin' lights out!'

When she heard Anne laugh out loud, she laughed too, and soon the sound of their laughter echoed over the river. 'We'd best be off,' Libby roared, 'or we'll have every duck on the river awake and quacking!'

Easing Anne to her feet, the old woman began propelling her along. 'You'd best come home with me,' she insisted. 'What you need is a good meal inside yer, an' a warm bed. I ain't fancy, mind, an' you sound too posh fer the likes o' me . . . but you're welcome to share what I've got. Rich or poor, troubles and misfortune touches us all, an' that's a fact.' And she should know.

Anne didn't protest. Libby's was the first friendly voice she had heard in many a while, and it was wonderful. 'Thank you,' she muttered. 'I do appreciate your kindness.'

They made an odd sight, one thin and tall, the other short and round; one refined, even in distress, while the other was coarse and comical – sturdy and reliable as the ground they walked on.

Reaching up to hold the shawl across Anne's bony shoulders, Libby led her along at a steady pace. 'This brother o' yourn, where does he live?'

'In the North.'

'Wealthy, you say?'

Anne nodded. 'He's got more money than he'll ever need.'

'An' is it *money* troubles that you've got?'

'Along with everything else.'

The old woman gave a wry little grin. 'Hmh! It sounds to me like there's a man at the bottom of it all!'

Anne smiled down on her. '*Two* . . . as a matter of fact.' Her estranged brother and the new man, who had glibly taken her for everything she'd got.

'*Two* men, eh?' Libby snorted. 'Then all I can say is, you're a greedy bugger for punishment.'

Helping Anne over the cobbled road, she asked, 'If part o' yer troubles is money . . . why ain't yer asked that brother o' yourn to help afore now?'

'Because I was afraid to.'

'I see.' The old woman had to think about that. 'An' are yer not afraid *now*?'

Anne shook her head. 'Not now.' Now, thanks to this little person, she had got her mind and her priorities in order. 'You'll get back everything you've lost because of me,' she reaffirmed. 'You have my word on it.'

'If you say so . . . but I'll not starve in the meantime,' she answered. 'I've still got the old pram I used afore, an' I can use it again.'

'It might take me a while, but you must trust me. I'll be back.'

'There ain't no rush. I'd rather you got yerself strong first.'

The little woman had taken a liking to this sad creature. 'Look 'ere, it's just over six weeks to Christmas. So long as I've got me barrer back in four weeks' time, I'll be happy, 'cause that's when folks come out shopping in their droves,' she went on. 'It's when I make the biggest killing,' she revealed. 'I stoke up the fire, then not only do they buy more chestnuts, they cluster round the barrer to keep warm.'

Shivering, she gleefully rubbed her hands together. 'If it's as cold as it is tonight, I'll be happy enough,' she said, ' 'cause the colder it is, the more I sell.'

Feeling the night air cutting through the shawl, Anne only

now realised how the little woman must be feeling the chill. Lifting her arm, she wrapped the shawl around the two of them. 'I'm being selfish,' she apologised. And, with a cheeky grin, Libby agreed.

Glad to be under the shawl, Libby regarded her with critical eyes. 'So you've a few weeks yet, dearie,' she said. 'Besides, I reckon you'd do well to stay in one place for a time, so's I can fatten yer up.'

'So you think I need fattening up, do you?' Anne was enjoying the banter. She had been alone for so long, she had almost forgotten how to communicate.

'What!' Tutting loudly, Libby ran a disapproving look over Anne's frail figure. 'Look at the state of yer!' she cried. 'You're not as far through as a bleedin' sparrer! Right! First things first,' she declared affirmatively. 'A good stew with plenty o' fat dumplings, then yer can tell me all about it. If yer want to, that is?'

Anne had no doubts. She felt that here was someone she could trust. Oh, to unburden herself of everything that had happened over the years . . . she would especially tell her about Sally and the shocking things she did to that innocent girl. And she would tell her all about the man who had persuaded her from her own home . . . brought her here to a place she didn't know, and then deceived her. Now she had no home, no money . . . And no friends except this dear soul beside her, she thought gratefully.

Misunderstanding the other woman's silence, Libby thought she had overstepped the mark. 'I'm sorry,' she apologised, 'happen I've gone in front of meself. If yer don't want to stay, and yer don't want to talk, that's all right by me.'

'No!' Anne suppressed the troublesome thoughts. 'I'd like that,' she said. 'Thank you.'

'Things will get better, you'll see.' Libby was relieved. 'It's a sure fact they can't get much *worse*!' She gave a gruff laugh.

'Not when you're ready to turn yerself into a meal for the bleedin' fishes, they can't!'

Anne had no way of knowing if things would get better. But they would certainly change. She would make sure of that! And she would have no difficulty finding her brother.

But how to find Sally? That was the thing . . .

Sally had kept the secret well.

On this fine Sunday morning in the blacksmith's yard, she practised as she had practised many times during the past month. 'How am I doing?' She felt confident, and it showed.

'You're a natural, I've said that from the very first.' Proud as punch, the blacksmith stood hands on hips as Sally trotted round on the grey gelding. 'You sit well, and you've got firm hands, without being too sharp.' He beckoned her in. 'Right. Let's see you take horse and wagon down the lane once more. After that, I'll have taught you all I know.'

Sally jumped down. 'It's just great!' she said, her blue eyes shining. 'I feel like I'm on top of the world up there.'

He laughed. 'You look like a pimple on a haystack,' he said, 'but you're a good little rider, I'll give you that.'

'I don't suppose I'll be doing much riding,' she confided. 'Remember I told you . . . the idea is to have the horse and wagon so we can expand the business. Lizzie had talked about it, but Maureen said it would all be too much trouble. So I've taken it on myself, and now I'm just hoping they'll be pleased.'

'The last time you came, you were in a hurry to get to some meeting,' he recalled, 'to arrange a contract, you said.' He remembered how he'd laughed about that after she'd gone.

'With Mr Hawkins, the merchant, that's right.' Sally had never envisaged being a businesswoman, but now she found it all seemed to come naturally. 'You see, most of the goods we sell are what Lizzie and Maureen make themselves. Maureen bakes the scones and muffins; Lizzie does embroidery, doilies and such. Then there's the produce she grows in her allotment. There's also the wicker things: baskets, fruit bowls, and all manner of lovely stuff . . . she's even got Maureen and me doing it now.'

'It sounds like a regular little industry.'

'Maureen and Lizzie needn't worry about the merchants, paperwork and all the other stuff,' she said. 'I'll do all that.'

He looked at her with renewed interest. 'You're nobbut a lass,' he said. 'How do you reckon to deal with grown men – hardened businessmen at that?'

'I'm *not* a lass,' she answered, and something about her made him believe he had her wrong. 'I can deal with the businessmen, though I'll admit some of them chased me away from their factories. But I persevered, and in the end I managed to draw up an agreement with Hawkins, the merchant. Not only will he supply us with whatever goods I choose to take from his warehouse, but he will take back whatever isn't sold by the end of the week. That way, we only pay for what we've sold, and we make a profit without taking too many risks.'

He laughed aloud. 'Well, I'm blowed!' He knew Hawkins, because he shod his horses and kept his wagons repaired. 'If you've managed to screw a contract like that out of Hawkins, you've got my admiration.'

'Oh, it works both ways,' she said.

'How's that?' His admiration of her was growing by the minute.

'Well, like I told Mr Hawkins, I shall take only the goods I feel we can sell, so I don't expect any returns and, if it all goes as planned, the business may expand even further, so then we'll be buying more and more from Mr Hawkins.'

'And what if the other two aren't interested in expanding the business?'

'Then I'll do the work, and they can take a handsome cut.' She would always look after them. 'After all, it's their business, not mine, so I'll be guided by them. And if there ever comes a time when they don't want to be involved, I'll make sure they always get their fair share.' She laughed. 'But I don't reckon Lizzie will ever stop,' she said. 'Like Maureen, she can do as much or as little as she likes. Either way, they'll be looked after, you can count on that.'

'Well, you're a surprise to me, I can tell you that,' he admitted. 'Most young women can't see further than the next fella . . . or which frock to wear at the dance.'

Sally was quiet for a minute, her mind going back over the years. 'Things like that have never mattered much to me,' she answered thoughtfully. 'There have always been more serious matters to contend with.'

'And now here you are, buying a horse and wagon.' He shook his head in wonder. 'I've never seen anyone take to riding the way you have.'

'I'm glad I came to you.'

He gave a wide, satisfied grin. 'Aye, an' so am I, lass. So am I.'

As they led the horse to the wagon, he peered at her from the corner of his eye. 'Are you *sure* you've never ridden before?'

Sally had already explained. 'We lived in a town, with no call for riding, and anyway, money was tight. My mother used to say I cost more than I was worth, so I can't see how she would ever have agreed to me having a horse. The only horses I ever got close to were the big shires from the brewery.' She turned to the horse and nuzzled its nose. 'But they were much bigger than you, weren't they, Clancy, old fella?'

'Aye, an' they'd need to be.' The blacksmith had shod many a brewery horse. 'They need muscles like elephants to pull them brewery wagons, you take it from me.'

With the wagon already prepared, it took only a minute to

hitch the horse to it. 'Now remember what I've told you,' he reminded her as she climbed into the driving seat. 'He's a sensible fella, and like as not he'd never do anything silly. But horses are animals of flight and there's any manner of things that could trigger them off.'

'I'll remember.'

'Right then. Off you go.'

Clicking her tongue, she tapped the reins gently against the horse's rump. When he moved forward, she could still hear the blacksmith issuing instructions from behind. 'Stay alert,' he called. 'Don't let him have too much of his head, or he might get the idea he's in charge.'

He watched her down the lane and he watched her back, and was delighted. 'I'm proud of you,' he said. 'Proud of *me* too, 'cause I've taught you well . . . even if I do say so myself.'

Exhilarated, Sally flung her arms round the blacksmith, almost knocking him off balance. 'Oh, I can't tell you how excited I am.' She laughed. 'I just know Maureen and Lizzie will be thrilled . . . and Lizzie won't have to stop every two minutes to rest her weary legs.'

Unbeknown to Sally, James was on his way from the timber merchant's. At this particular point he had to cross over the hill overlooking the blacksmith's yard. When the sound of a woman's laughter filtered up to him, he instinctively glanced down and saw her there. Sally! Surprised and curious, he drew the wagon to a halt.

A closer look showed her with her arms round the blacksmith's neck. For a minute, he couldn't understand it . . . what was she doing there? Why did she have her arms round his neck? Jealousy took a hold. What the devil was she playing at? As he started down, he could hear the conversation and suddenly it all became clear.

Emptying her purse into his hand, Sally told the blacksmith, 'It's all there, just what we agreed . . . the price of the horse and wagon, and the horse's feed until Christmas Eve.'

'You've done well,' he said.

'I don't know how to thank you,' she replied. 'You've taught me to ride and handle a wagon, all without anybody finding out.'

'Aye, well, it's been a pleasure. I only hope your two friends are as excited about it as you are.'

'Thank you, Mr Taylor.' Another quick embrace and she was ready to leave the same way she came, on foot across the hills.

Smiling, James watched her climb the pathway from the forge. 'What are you up to now?' he murmured fondly.

The smile faded. It was strange how a man could love two women at the same time, in different ways. 'Oh, Sally,' he whispered, 'I only wish I could tell you how I feel, but first I have to close the door to one room before I can go into the other.'

Slowly, carefully, he turned the cart back on to the main road. 'But what if she turns me away?' he mused. 'What then?' He didn't even want to think about it.

Part Four

CHRISTMAS 1889

REVELATIONS

Chapter Eighteen

'Christmas Eve already!' Maureen could hardly believe how fast it had come round. 'But I'm all ready,' she said proudly, glancing at the table, where varieties of food were in different stages of preparation. 'The goose is stuffed and ready for the oven, my Christmas pudding has matured nicely, and all the cake needs is icing.'

She turned her attention to Sally, who was seated at the table, stringing together paper bows to decorate the parlour.

Still in her dressing-robe, Maureen stood with her back to the window, quietly sipping her tea and watching her. Sally had brought sunshine and laughter into this house. The prospect that one day she might move on was always a worry to Maureen. But she was a great believer in fate, and in her heart she knew how James and this lovely young creature were meant for each other. But she would not interfere. It was not her way.

Feeling Maureen's eyes on her, Sally glanced up from her task. 'What did you say? Sorry . . . I wasn't listening.'

Maureen laughed. 'No, I can see that,' she said. 'I was just saying how the cake needs icing.'

'*I'm* doing that, aren't I?' Sally reminded her. 'The way you showed me, with Lizzie's holly leaves and pretty decorations?'

Maureen nodded. 'When you've finished stringing them paper

bows together, I'll help you decorate the parlour, then we'd best get on with the food.' She glanced at the clock over the dresser. 'It's half past seven already,' she observed with a fright. 'I've been up a full hour and done nothing.' Smiling to herself, Sally took no notice. If Maureen stopped dashing about for two minutes, she had a guilty conscience.

'By! There's so much to be done.' Gulping down her tea, Maureen rushed over to the oven, where she opened the door and looked in. 'I can't understand why this range is taking its time getting hot,' she groaned. 'I'm waiting to get the goose in the big oven, the pork can go underneath in the small oven, and while it's all cooking I'll get on and make the mince pies and sausage rolls.'

'With me helping,' Sally reminded her. Tying the last paper bow to the string, she pushed her chair away and stood up. 'Right, that's another job done!'

Maureen followed her into the parlour, where the cheery fire lit the room with a glow. 'I'm glad James was up early to light the fires,' Maureen commented. 'There's nothing worse than getting up to a cold house, especially on Christmas Eve.'

'He's been gone a long time.' Sally had deliberately got up early to see him, but he'd already gone. She needed his help in keeping the surprise she had planned.

'He's probably sitting at the top of the valley, thinking about this and that,' Maureen answered quietly. 'But you know him. He's a bit of a loner these days.'

Past events crossed both their minds. Isabel, then her father, and now the alarming rise of Jack in his father's shoes. But neither of them remarked on it.

'I so much wanted a white Christmas.' Dismissing the darker thoughts, Sally pulled a chair out from under the dining-table, and carried it to the far corner of the room. Here, she took off her shoes and stood on it. While Maureen held the tag end of the decoration, Sally secured the other end to the picture-rail.

'I reckon you'll have your white Christmas.' Maureen looked out at the snow-laden skies. 'Either tonight or tomorrow morning, the heavens will open, you'll see.'

When the last decoration was put up and looking pretty, Maureen returned to the kitchen, while Sally put the finishing touches to the tree, which, like the parlour, was small, though it was a perfect shape and looked so pretty with its paper balls and coloured trinkets. 'There!' Satisfied, she replaced the chair and returned to the kitchen, where Maureen was already sliding the pork into the lower oven.

For the next hour, they worked like beavers. The meat was in the oven, the cake iced and decorated, thirty mince pies made ready, and when Sally asked why so many, she was told, 'They'll be gone before bedtime tomorrow, and I'll be wishing I'd made thirty more.'

When the kitchen was at last in order, the house tidied, and the pantry bursting, Sally made them each a fresh brew of tea. Sitting at the table, they talked of Christmas, and how Lizzie would be spending the whole day with them, as she'd done for many years past.

The conversation drifted to James and his work. 'Do you think Jack Mears will cause much upheaval at the carriage works?' Sally asked.

'As much as he can, I'll be bound,' was Maureen's considered opinion. 'He's as bad as his father ever was. Give him time and he'll come to be worse, I'm sure of it.'

'But what about Robert?' Sally wondered. 'I thought *he* had the ruling hand?'

'Really, it's Frances Mears who has the ruling hand,' Maureen answered, 'only she doesn't know the first thing about business and, if she's got any sense, probably wants nothing at all to do with it.' She sighed. 'I'm afraid it'll have to be decided between the two brothers, God help us!'

'What about Hannah?'

'Hannah is too young to be taking on the business yet, but I fear she's neither use nor ornament.' Maureen felt sorry for the Mears lass. 'What with her sister, and then her father, dying in such circumstances, she seems to have gone right off the rails.' She recalled a conversation she'd overheard between the postmistress and a customer. 'Apparently she's taken up with all manner of dubious characters – laughing and singing through the streets at all hours of the night.'

'Do you think it would help if I went to see her?' Sally had been wondering about that for some time.

Maureen was amazed. 'I had no idea you were thinking along those lines,' she said. 'I thought you decided you wanted nothing to do with the Mears family?'

'I don't, but if Hannah is going off the rails because she's lost her sister, maybe it would help for her to know she's got *another* sister . . . well, a half-sister, but at least we're about the same age, and she might be able to talk to me . . . about . . . things, if you see what I mean?'

'That's for you to decide,' Maureen told her. In her heart she hoped it would end there. To her mind, things were best left as they were, and nobody any the wiser.

Sally shrugged. 'It was just a thought.' She studied Maureen's troubled face. 'You don't think I should, do you?'

'I think that, even with Leonard Mears gone, that family is still a danger.' She deliberately added, 'Especially to you, lass.'

Sally listened to her as always; she trusted Maureen. 'Maybe it wasn't such a good idea after all,' she said, and pushed it all to the back of her mind.

* * *

It was quarter to ten when James returned. 'We thought you'd fallen down a hole, never to be seen again,' Maureen quipped. 'Still, happen the mince pies might have lasted longer with you not here to pinch them every five minutes.'

Sally and he smiled at each other. 'I see you missed me then?' he asked teasingly, ducking when Maureen threw a lump of leftover dough at him.

'I hope you and Jake aren't trailing mud and God knows what all over my clean floor!' she warned.

Grabbing the dog into his arms, he made for the door. 'I don't know about me and Jake.' He grinned. 'Look at the mess *you've* caused.' The dough had landed, splitting asunder in all directions.

When he made a hasty exit, Sally followed him. 'That's it!' Maureen's voice rang out behind. 'Leave me to clear up the mess, why don't you?' But she had a smile on her face as she did whenever she saw the two of them together.

In the barn, James wiped the dog's feet while at the same time listening to Sally. 'The horse and wagon is a present for Lizzie and your mam,' Sally explained. 'But I have to collect it before midday today.'

James listened as she told him all about her plan, and at no time did he let on that he had seen her there. 'A horse and wagon, eh?' he said, seemingly surprised. 'That's an odd sort of present.'

Sally explained the reasoning behind it. 'Now that I've struck a deal with the merchant, we only pay for what we sell,' she finished, 'so, you see, it's a golden opportunity.'

'What I *see* is a young woman with a head for business,' he admitted proudly.

Momentarily downcast, Sally wondered aloud, 'Maybe I've taken something from my father's side of the family after all.' For that brief moment she felt disgusted with herself.

James went to her. 'Hey!' Looking down into her eyes he told her sternly, 'There's no such thing as inheriting an eye for business. In my experience it's character and circumstance that make and mould what you do in life.' Chucking her under the chin, he added kindly, 'Besides, there isn't an inkling of Leonard Mears in you . . . not in any way, shape or form.'

Her bright smile returned. 'About the horse and cart, will you help me?'

'Depends.' Now he was teasing her again.

With her insides trembling beneath his easy smile, she focused on the matter in hand. 'I don't want them to know yet,' she said excitedly. 'I need to hide them until the morning.'

'I'm sure that can be arranged.'

'Thank you, James. I knew you'd help me.' Instinctively, she reached up to kiss him fleetingly on the cheek, afraid to show her deeper emotions. 'I have to go.'

'What?' He hadn't quite realised she meant right away. 'You mean you're going to collect them now?'

'As soon as I change my boots.' The ones she had on were for round the house and garden. They weren't suitable for a long trek.

'Give me a minute, and I'll take you.'

'No.' Putting up a staying hand, she told him, 'I'd rather do it all myself.' She had saved the money, found the horse and cart and done a deal with the merchant. This last little stretch was easy.

'Independent, eh?' He gazed on her for a moment, holding her there. 'I'm very proud of you,' he said. 'What you've done can't have been easy.'

'I planned it all well beforehand.' It was strange talking to him like this, when all she wanted to do was fling herself into his arms.

'Are you confident enough to drive a horse and cart?'

'The blacksmith thinks so.'

His smile enveloped her. 'Then who am I to argue?'

'One other favour?'

'I knew it.'

'I should be back in about an hour. Will you watch for me?'

'Of course.' Didn't she know he would spend every minute watching for her?

'When you see me coming over the hill, will you make sure Lizzie and your mam are well out of the way?'

'I'll bundle them both up and throw them in the cellar. Will that do?'

She laughed heartily. 'As long as you remember to lock the door.' It was so good to see him getting back to his old self.

'I thought you were in a hurry?'

'I am!'

'Well then, you'd best get yourself off. And I hope you've got a good excuse ready for Mam, because you know what she's like. She'll want to know where you're going and how long you're likely to be.'

Maureen thought she was mad. 'Going for a walk in this weather?' Glancing out the window, she gave a warning, 'Don't go too far, lass. I don't want you caught out in a snowstorm.'

Dressed in her heavy shawl and thick boots, Sally started out.

Deep in thought, James watched her from the barn.

When she had gone from his sight, he lingered there. Isabel was strong in his mind. Sally was stronger in his heart. 'Life is a funny thing,' he told Jake. 'Just when you think you've got it right, it gives you something else to think about.'

'Come on then, old fella.' He began his way back to the house. 'We've got a job to do. Sally says we're to keep them out of the way, and we will. But I'm beggared if I know *how*.'

'Whatever's the matter with you, son?' Maureen had noticed how restless he was. 'You're like a cat on hot bricks . . . one minute pacing about, the other staring out the window.'

He looked up at the clock. 'I was watching for Sally.'

'She's only been gone half an hour.' With a sly little grin, she asked, 'Why don't you go out and meet her, if you're that worried?'

'No. You're right. It was just . . . I thought she'd been gone longer, that's all.' Half an hour! It seemed like an eternity to him.

'I'll tell you what you can do.'

'What's that?'

'You can take this to Lizzie.' Replacing her hot iron on the trivet by the fire, she filtered through her pile of ironing and took out a brown blouse. 'Tell her I've darned it the best I could, but you can still see where she tore it on the fencing.'

'How come you're doing Lizzie's darning?'

'Because Lizzie's best at some things, and I'm best at others, that's why.' Thrusting the garment into his hands, she told him, 'Take Jake with you. I don't know what's wrong with him, but he's mooching about the same as you are and the pair of you are making me nervous.'

'Come on, boy!' Sally wouldn't be too long now, he thought, but, thanks to his mam, an idea was already forming in James's mind.

Going straight into the barn, he checked that everything was ready . . . a stable for the horse and a corner for the cart. 'Then all we have to do is keep Mam away from here 'til tomorrow morning.' Leaving the great doors open, he made his way to Lizzie's cottage.

Coming round by the shed, he saw something out of the corner of his eye. It was Sally, just a speck in the distance, but it was her all right. 'We haven't got much time,' he told Jake. 'I've got an idea, but you have to do your bit or it won't work.' With the dog staring up at him, he finalised the plan in his mind, then he bent to the dog and whispered in his ear. 'So, you play your part,' he finished, straightening up. 'And Sally will have that horse and cart in the barn before anybody realises.'

Just as he had feared, Lizzie was already on her way to see Maureen. 'I'm wondering what I can do to help,' she said. 'It don't seem fair to leave it all to yer mam.'

Stuffing the blouse in his pocket he suggested, 'I'll walk along with you. As a matter of fact, she asked me to collect a few things from the shed.'

'Can I help?'

'If you like.' It was what he had hoped for.

Manoeuvring Lizzie inside the shed first, James stayed at the back. 'See that bundle of string on the shelf there?' he called out. 'She wants that to truss the goose up for tomorrow . . . oh, and can you see a big baking tray? It's been here since last New Year, and now she's after using it again . . .' He knew Maureen had already dug it out and at that moment it was in the oven holding the joint of pork.

'I can't see it.' Rummaging about, Lizzie turned the place upside down.

'I know it's in here somewhere. But look, leave it. You go on in, Lizzie. She's waiting for this pan. I'll run it in, then I'll come back for the baking tin.'

Lizzie offered to take the pan, but he refused. 'It's too heavy for you.' Empty or filled, the pan was a big cast-iron thing that was almost impossible to carry. Maureen had thrown it out ages ago for that very reason. 'But you go in, Lizzie,' he prayed she wouldn't, 'and I'll come back for the baking tray.'

Just as he thought, Lizzie wouldn't hear of it. 'Tell yer mam I'll be in when I've found it,' she said.

Promising to be back in a matter of minutes, James winked at the dog. 'Do your stuff,' he whispered, and Jake's ears pricked with excitement.

Putting the pan down in the back porch, James looked to

where Sally was already halfway down the valley. 'Come on, Jake,' he muttered, 'don't let me down now.'

Suddenly he could hear Lizzie's voice raised in anger. 'Get out of the way, you silly old bugger. What's got into yer?'

Rolling his eyes to heaven, it was all he could do not to laugh out loud. Suppressing the laughter, he threw open the kitchen door and called for Maureen. 'Mam! You'd best come quick!'

'What's the matter?' Wiping her hands on her pinny, Maureen came rushing to the door. 'What's all the yelling about?'

'It's Jake!'

Going at a run down the path, he led her to the far end of the garden, well out of sight of the barn and Sally. 'He's got poor Lizzie pinned in the shed . . . he won't take any notice of me!'

Sure enough, as they rounded the corner, there was Lizzie trying desperately to get out of the shed, and Jake baring his teeth at her.

'I can't think what's got into him.' Feigning anger, James commanded, 'Get away, Jake! Come to heel!' Normally, when he said that, the dog was rigidly obedient. But not this time. This time he straddled the doorway, and dared anyone to go near him.

When Maureen gave him the same order, he barked fiercely, making her take a step back. She couldn't believe it. 'I knew there was something wrong,' she said. 'He was mooching about in the kitchen . . . getting under my feet and acting strangely. In fact the *pair* of you were acting strangely.'

Secretly, James was thrilled. Jake was playing his part to perfection. 'You keep trying . . . keep talking to him,' he told the women, 'but don't get him too worried. I'll go and fetch a chunk of meat . . . that might do the trick.'

By the time he got to the barn, Sally was coming softly up the hill. 'Quickly,' he ushered her inside, cart and all. 'You take his harness off, while I see to Jake . . . oh, and make sure you keep these doors closed.'

Taking a moment to glance critically at the horse and cart, he asked, 'Did you do the choosing?' When she answered yes, he delighted her by saying with conviction, 'You've got a good eye for quality.'

As he went away at the run, she came to the door, at once aware of Jake's frantic barking. 'What's wrong with Jake?'

'Nothing a juicy titbit won't put right,' he laughed. 'And a certain nod from me.' He thought he had better go and rescue Lizzie. 'But I'll tell you all about it later.'

Chapter Nineteen

Anne stood by the carriage door, waiting for the train to shudder to a halt. On her journey from London, she had tried to avoid a certain elderly gentleman who had insisted on sitting beside her and talking the whole way.

He came up behind her now. 'I can't think why I ever agree to travel on Christmas Eve,' he moaned. 'But what can I do? My sister is the only family I have left, and she does like me to stay overnight for Christmas morning. If she'd had her way, I'd have been up here first thing this morning, but, as I told her, as long as I'm there for Christmas evening, isn't that all that matters?' He glanced through the carriage window at the growing dusk. 'I don't like being about in the dark,' he said. 'I shall get a cab straight up there . . . before the night closes in altogether.'

Leaning forward with unwelcome intimacy, he addressed her softly. 'It'll be pitch black in no time,' he observed. 'I could always ask the driver to make a detour and take you to your destination first. Would you like that?' It was painfully obvious that *he* certainly would.

'No. Thank you all the same.' Realising by his accent he was not from these parts, Anne had not asked him about Leonard Mears, but she did so now. 'I'm going to see my brother,' she said. 'Leonard Mears . . . are you familiar with the name?'

Pursing his fat lips, he shook his head. 'No. Sorry, I can't recall that name,' he answered. 'But I've lived away from these parts for so long, it's a wonder I can remember the way here.'

When the train came to a halt, Anne hurried away, thankful to leave him behind. Quickening her pace, she slowed only when she came out on to the boulevard. After the closeted air inside the train carriage, the cold took her breath away.

'Winter's arrived good an' proper.' The woman was about Anne's age, tall and well-built. She looked to be prosperous in spite of her common-sounding manner.

'It seems that way,' Anne remarked, 'it does seem much colder up north, I think.'

The woman laughed; it was a raw, raucous laugh. 'You could say that,' she answered, 'but then it all depends on whether you've got a man to keep you warm.'

When Anne gave her a curious look, she laughed again. 'I know what you're thinking,' she said. 'You're thinking how can a common cow like me be wearing expensive clothes and carrying fine luggage.'

Before Anne could have apologised for giving that impression, the woman went on, 'And you'd be right. What's more you'd be right in thinking I get it from pandering to men who've got more money than sense. *They* earn it . . . I spend it. I've learned to be very good at that.'

It was obvious to Anne that the woman was a highly paid prostitute. Another time, in another life, she might have hurried away. But now: 'Each to their own,' she said. 'Who am I to judge?'

The woman was astounded. 'Well, I never. I would have put you among the snooty devils who make my life a misery. But here you are, turning all my past experiences upside down.'

'Life is a good teacher and we all make mistakes,' she said. 'Some more than others.' And me more than most, she thought wryly.

The woman looked at her for a moment, thinking how haggard she looked. Being a connoisseur of people, her imagination ran away with her. She had seen the dregs and she had seen the best, and she knew this thin, pale woman had been through the mill.

Now, when Anne turned to half smile, the woman asked politely, 'Would you like to join me in a cup of tea and a muffin?' Nodding to the café across the boulevard, she added, 'I know that place well, and I can heartily recommend it.'

Anne was more interested that she had some local knowledge. 'So you know this area well, do you?'

The woman nodded. 'I've lived here all my life. I know every street, pub and church . . . and most of the *men* too.' Her lewd laughter echoed in the air. 'But we mustn't say too much about that, must we?'

Anne decided that here was her chance. 'I'm looking for someone in particular,' she admitted, 'I wonder if you might be able to help me?'

'If *I* can't . . . nobody can!'

Without warning, she cupped her hand under Anne's arm and propelled her across the cobbles. 'I'm not partial to discussing matters out in the cold,' she said. 'We'll find ourselves a cosy little table and talk over a pot of tea. Much more civilised, don't you think?'

And what could Anne say but 'Thank you, that would be nice'?

Intrigued by the rapturous welcome the woman had received from the waitress, Anne commented, 'It's obviously not the first time you've been here?'

Leaning back in her chair, the woman took a silver cigarette case from her purse and, plucking out a cigarette, she lit it with a slim gold lighter. 'That's because I *own* this place,' she said, lazily drawing on the cigarette. 'This is my latest acquisition. I have another in Blackpool, and one in Preston.'

When the tea arrived, she stubbed out the cigarette and gave the ashtray to the waitress for removal. 'A woman has to plan for the future,' she confided. 'You never know when the good times might come to an end.' Pouring for them both, she enquired, 'Now then, who's this particular person you're looking for?'

Accepting the tea with thanks, Anne explained, 'It's my brother. I know he's lived in Blackburn these many years, and I have an idea he might still be here. You understand, we haven't seen each other in a long time and now, for reasons I won't go into, it's imperative I find him.'

'I see.' Sipping her tea, the woman regarded Anne through inquisitive brown eyes. 'This brother of yours . . . what's his name? What does he do exactly?'

'When last I knew, he was making quite a name for himself in the building of fine carriages. He supplied carts and wagons. As far as I know that was his main business.' She took a deep breath, hoping against hope that the woman might recognise him. 'His name is Leonard Mears . . .'

The woman almost choked on her tea. 'My God! I knew your brother . . . very well . . .' She dared not say any more about their relationship. 'But, my dear . . . I'm afraid . . .' How could she tell this sickly woman that her brother had died in a shocking accident, and that his daughter had been hanged for murder?

'You actually *know* him?' She thought that at last her journey might be almost at an end, with only Sally to find and peace to make with her.

'Where will I find him, can you tell me?'

Uncomfortable beneath Anne's eager smile, the woman fidgeted, wondering how she might break the news. 'Oh, my dear!' she said hesitantly. 'I don't know what to say. I would have thought, being his sister and all, that they might have informed you. After all, you do have a right to know—' That said, she was lost for words.

Anne sensed her dilemma. 'Whatever is it? Please don't be afraid to tell me.'

'It's bad news, my dear.' She decided to tell it all. 'Some time back, his daughter . . . Isabel, well, she was tried and convicted on a charge of murder . . . oh, there were them as said she was innocent, and there were them as said that justice was done, but how do we know?'

Reeling from the news, Anne demanded, 'Are you telling me his daughter was –' she could hardly bring herself to say it – 'are you saying she was . . . hanged?' Her voice faded to a whisper.

The woman nodded. 'She was . . . caught at the scene, with the murder weapon still in her hand.' Seeing how Anne had leaned back in her chair, her face altogether drained of colour, she said kindly, 'What can I say to console you?' She wished now she had never struck up conversation at the railway station. 'Did you know his daughter well? I mean, you said you hadn't seen your brother for a long time.'

'No.' Though shocked to her roots, Anne rallied a little. 'I hardly knew his family at all.' Never wanted to either, she recalled bitterly.

'Ah, well, in one way, I suppose that's a blessing.'

'What of my brother?'

'He took it very hard. Out of the four children, it was said he loved her the most.' Reluctant to go on, she cast her gaze to the table, her fingers nervously toying with the corner of the cloth.

'You have more bad news for me, haven't you?'

Encouraged by Anne's calm voice, the woman looked up. 'When it happened, the murder and everything, your brother took to the bottle more than usual. There was a terrible accident

. . . he fell down the stairs . . . and . . .' She could say no more.

Anne knew straight away. 'He was killed, wasn't he? That's what you're trying to tell me.'

'Yes, he was. It was a very bad fall, d'you see?' She tried to soften the tragedy with explanation, but the news was as devastating as it could be.

Anne took a deep breath. 'His wife – Frances, as I recall – and the other children, do they still live hereabouts?'

'As far as I know.'

'I don't suppose you happen to know the address?'

The woman thought for a moment, then shook her head. 'I've an idea they have a big house somewhere near Samlesbury, but I can't be certain.' Without meaning to, she let slip a snippet of information. 'Leonard always came to me. I never really knew where he lived, not altogether.'

'It sounds as though you had a close relationship with him.' Memories rose in her mind, disturbing memories she would rather forget.

Wary now, the woman dismissed the inference. 'You don't want to hear all that,' she said, 'not with him being gone, and your brother and all.'

Thanking her for her valuable help, Anne stood up. 'Samlesbury, you say?'

'That's right, dearie.'

'Is it far?'

'About five miles or so by road . . . you'll find a cab right outside of here, I'm sure.'

When Anne lingered a moment longer, her gaze fixed on the other woman's face, she asked, 'Was there something else, dearie?'

With thoughts of Sally strong in her mind, Anne found the courage to voice her suspicions. 'It's obvious to me that you and my brother had a liaison of a kind,' she said quietly. 'Tell me . . . did you ever have a child by him . . . a daughter?'

The other woman need not have answered because the shock and humour on her face told its own story. '*A child!*' She fell back in the chair as if she'd been poleaxed. 'I've had many a man over the years,' she said, 'and I'm not ashamed to say it, but I've never had a child and never wanted to. I've been too clever to get caught like that.'

'Thank you anyway.' With that, Anne hastily took her leave.

As usual at nine o'clock, Frances was relaxing in the drawing room when the housekeeper entered with the tray.

'Are you awake, ma'am?' Setting the tray on the small table beside her mistress, Mrs Flanagan took the opportunity to peep round the chair, startling Frances. 'I'm sorry, ma'am,' she apologised, 'but I thought you might be asleep.'

'Just dozing,' Frances replied, squaring herself up in the chair.

'Are you all right, ma'am?'

'As right as I shall ever be, I suppose.'

'Your bed is ready when you are,' Mrs Flanagan told her. 'I've sent Peggy up with a warming pan. She has instructions to move it every fifteen minutes until you retire.'

'Thank you, but I'm not ready for my bed just yet.'

'Would you like me to pour?'

'Please.' And while the housekeeper poured her tea, Frances chatted like she had never chatted before. 'What's the world coming to?' she murmured. 'First my daughter, then my husband.'

'It's hard, ma'am, I know.' Surprised that the mistress should confide in her this way, Mrs Flanagan didn't know whether to excuse herself or stay. 'Life is very cruel.'

'Do you think my Isabel could really murder her own husband . . . and that woman?'

'It does seem hard to believe, ma'am.' She wasn't quite sure what she ought to say.

'I do miss her, you know.'

'But that's only natural, ma'am.'

The tone of her voice changed. 'I don't miss *him*!'

When Mrs Flanagan remained silent, Frances turned to look at her. 'That shocks you, doesn't it?'

'No, ma'am.' Hatred flooded her heart.

'He was a bad man, you must know that?'

Again, Mrs Flanagan thought it wiser to remain silent.

'You and everyone else . . . you must have heard him . . . night after night . . . treating me as if I was a streetwoman for the taking.'

'Yes, ma'am.' There was no use denying it.

'Did you think I was a coward?'

'At some time or another in our lives, we are all of us cowards.'

'Did you never marry, Eliza?'

'There was a time when I thought I might get married, but no, I never did.'

Eliza thought the mistress must be very lonely, for here she was calling her by her first name, and telling her things that no mistress should tell her housekeeper. Moreover, she had guessed the truth, though it was not unknown for the courtesy title of Mrs to be used by senior domestic staff who had remained unmarried. 'How did you know, ma'am? That I never married?'

'Just a feeling. Somehow, Mrs Flanagan never suited you, though how you chose to be addressed never mattered to me. All I know is, you have proved your worth time and again . . . especially of late. To tell you the truth, I don't know how I could have managed without you here.'

'You do yourself an injustice, ma'am.'

Their conversation was interrupted by the sound of the front doorbell. 'I can't imagine who that could be at this time of night.' Frances was in no mood for visitors.

Excusing herself, Eliza hurried away to answer the door.

A few moments later, she returned. 'It's a lady by the name of Anne Hale, ma'am.'

The name rolled back the years. 'Hale?' Frances stared into the fire, all manner of images dancing there. 'I do believe I knew someone by that name.' But it was no use trying to remember. These days she could hardly recall what happened yesterday. 'You had better show her in.' Sitting upright, she prepared to receive her visitor.

'Please . . . go in.' Eliza ushered Anne Hale inside, thinking what a strange visitor she was, with her dowdy clothes and sallow face. There was an aura of sadness, almost despair about her. Maybe she was owed money, Eliza thought. But if that was the case, she should think herself fortunate, because she could never be owed what Eliza herself was owed. Not if she lived for a hundred years.

When her visitor lingered, unsure, by the door, Frances waved an impatient hand. 'Come in . . . come in and sit before me.' In one way she would rather be left alone with her thoughts. In another she was glad to have someone to talk with, though Eliza had proved herself to be more of a friend than she had ever anticipated.

Overawed by the grandeur of her brother's home, Anne did as she was bid, but with great respect towards her hostess, and nervousness. She had come here to ask after Sally, and as Sally was the result of an affair outside marriage, this was a very delicate situation.

When Anne was seated, Frances discreetly took stock of her, her curious gaze going from the small black-stockinged feet and the well-worn shoes, to the limp feathered hat and the way she constantly twisted her gloves in her hands.

'Do I know you, my dear?' Frances could not rid herself of the feeling that she and this woman had met somewhere before. A long time ago, maybe . . . when they were younger and life was not so cruel.

All the way here in the cab, Anne had promised herself she would be as discreet as possible, so as not to cause her brother's widow more pain and anguish than necessary.

Now she agonised as to how she might go about such an arduous task. Should she say right out that Sally was her husband's daughter by another woman? No! Well then, should she lie and say she was looking for her *own* daughter? Of course not! How could she say that, and at the same time explain why she was here, in this house?

Sensing her reluctance to speak, Frances urged, 'You must state your business. What is it you want of me? Why are you here?' Suddenly she had her suspicions. 'Were you one of my husband's women, is that it? Have you come to extract money from me with a hard-luck story?' Agitated, she sat bolt upright, staring at Anne. 'Out with it!' Frances demanded. 'Why are you here?'

On the verge of lying her way out of there, and giving up the whole idea, Anne swallowed her fear and determined to give her answer in a calm voice. 'I'm sorry, Mrs Mears, but I'm looking for someone. I had hoped you might be able to help me.'

Frances was visibly relieved. 'So you are *not* one of my husband's women?'

'I most certainly am not.'

'Who is it you're looking for?'

'A girl I raised from a child.'

'I see. And might I ask why you think I can help?'

Frances's eyes flickered nervously and Anne could see how disturbed she was. Knowing she had already suffered two severe blows, how could Anne deliver another?

'Well?' Frances couldn't take her eyes off the visitor, convinced that she knew her, but unable to recall where from. 'I'm waiting to hear what you have to say.'

Losing her nerve, Anne stood up. 'I'm sorry,' she stuttered, 'I seem to have made a mistake.'

'Sit down.'

'I shouldn't have come here. I'm sorry.'

'*I know you, don't I?*'

Anne had been so sure she could carry it off without giving too much away. Now, though, she was lost as to what to do. It all seemed so futile, so cruel – all her life, the raising of her brother's child, the crumbling of her marriage and the cruelty she had inflicted on two innocent people – it was all too much for her to bear. Why had the barrow woman rescued her? Why hadn't she left her to drown as she had planned? It had taken so much courage to climb up there on that parapet . . . one more minute and it would all have been over.

Looking at her, Frances began to remember. It was the face; she remembered it as a proud, regal face. Now it was sharp and pinched, as though it had known great distress. Of course! '*Anne!*'

Hearing her name, Anne turned. Now she looked into Frances's eyes, and realised her identity was revealed. Relief and horror surged through her. She tried to speak, but the words wouldn't come.

Suddenly, her whole body was shivering. The tears began as a hard, painful lump in her throat and then they were tumbling down her face. All the pain was washed away with them.

In a moment she felt Frances's arm round her. 'Come and sit down, my dear,' she said. 'I think we need to talk.'

Having resettled her visitor in the chair, Frances rang for Mrs Flanagan. 'Bring fresh tea,' she said, 'and sandwiches . . . perhaps a slice of Cook's fruit cake.' With an intimate smile, she let Mrs Flanagan see that she had a very important visitor, and one they must be kind to.

When the two women were settled, Frances gently spoke her mind. 'You're Leonard's sister, aren't you? I met you many years ago,' she recalled. 'Only the once . . . when your brother and I were married.' She cast her mind back. 'I never saw you again. Leonard said you and he had never got on . . . that you were difficult, and that I should have nothing to do with you.'

With the tears subsided, Anne had to smile. 'He said that, did he?'

'At the time, I believed every word he said, but, as the years went on, I began to realise that he chose his words carefully . . . a mantle to camouflage the truth.'

'He was right though. We never did get on. You couldn't get close to Leonard, and it wasn't long before I stopped trying.' She smiled, easier now the truth was out; not the *whole* truth though – that was yet to come. 'We were always destined to go our separate ways.'

'He was a bad man . . . he used people, I'm sure you knew that?'

When Anne looked astonished, she quickly reassured her. 'He's gone now, and it's a strange thing for me . . . I was so domineered, you see? He was so overpowering. Now there seems to be a void . . . it's unnerving. Oh, I *am* grieving, my dear. But not for him.'

A hardness came into her eyes. 'You see, my husband . . . your brother, was partly to blame. He arranged a marriage between our elder daughter and the son of his business colleague, all for profit of course. He would sell his own soul if it made a profit. The marriage went wrong, and ended in tragedy.' Her voice broke. 'Forgive me, I tend to be rather emotional these days.'

Mentally composing herself, she confided, 'I don't regret *his* passing at all. It's *her* I miss . . . my dear Isabel, such a lovely girl.'

Anne knew all about greed, and loss and regrets. 'I'm sorry,' she murmured. 'It must be hard for you.'

Just then, there came a tap on the door and Mrs Flanagan entered. Seeming oblivious to her presence, Frances continued. 'I must apologise for thinking you were one of his women,' she said, 'only I know what he was like, and I know he cheated on me many, many times.'

'I understand how you might have mistaken me.' She glanced at Mrs Flanagan, who was preparing the tea plates. 'Yet you remembered me . . . after all this time.'

'I remember the important things,' Frances revealed, 'and since he's been gone, it's all become clearer in my mind. You see, you tend to go over and over these important things until every little detail is etched in your mind.'

Aware of Mrs Flanagan, Anne was cautious. Lightening the conversation, she asked, 'I imagine your other children give you great comfort?' Taking the cup and saucer from Mrs Flanagan, she gave her a courteous little smile.

For a long moment, Frances seemed deep in thought, not even aware that her own cup and saucer had been put down beside her. After a time, she said in a quiet, knowing manner, 'What about your own daughter? Does she give you comfort?'

'My own . . . daughter?' The cup and saucer trembled in her hands. 'I wasn't aware you knew I had—'

Frances interrupted, 'Like I say, my dear . . . everything is very clear in my mind now. I remember, Leonard was greatly agitated. I suspected it had to do with a woman, but I could never be certain. He had been unfaithful so often, I had learned to accept it. But this time it seemed different, so one night, when we were staying at his father's house in Preston, I had him followed . . . oh yes, I know it was not the correct thing to do, but

I had to know! I couldn't have him getting too serious with this woman, and leaving me. I was used to living in a certain style by this time, and I was not prepared to lose all that.'

She went on quietly, 'Unfortunately, I never did find out who the woman was, I only learned there was a liaison. In the end, she went the way of all the others.'

She paused, going through the pictures in her mind. 'It must have been seventeen years ago, or thereabouts.' She smiled, a smile that was both serene and forgiving. '*I was told he brought the baby to you, my dear.*'

She had no idea the shock her revelation caused, not only to Anne but to the other woman . . . the woman whose identity Frances had tried to discover all those years ago.

'But then, you were his sister. In an odd sort of way, he did the child a kindness by bringing her to you instead of taking her to the workhouse, which he could so easily have done.'

She studied Anne's face with interest, wondering what havoc Leonard had caused in doing what he did.

When Anne again looked in Mrs Flanagan's direction, Frances realised her discomfort. 'It's all right, Eliza,' she said, 'you can leave us now.' So engrossed in her visitor had she been, she hadn't noticed how shocked and pale Mrs Flanagan had become.

'Thank you, ma'am.' Excusing herself, Eliza could never remember how she got herself out of that room without stumbling over. Her heart was pounding and every nerve in her body screaming.

Outside, she collapsed against the wall, her voice whispering over and over, 'The child was mine. *My* child! *My* daughter!' Joy mingled with anger. But he said the child died? Was he lying? Anne Hale's words had seemed to imply the child had lived. Dear God, how could she find out? She listened at the door, but the wood was so thick and the voices so low she could hear nothing clearly. With her duties done, she escaped to the kitchen; everyone else was in bed, so she had no fear of being seen there.

Pacing the floor, then looking out the window, then listening outside to ensure that the visitor had not yet left, she grew frantic. 'I'll follow her,' she muttered, all else but her child gone from her mind. 'I'll follow her . . . tell her the child was mine, and that I must know where she is . . . whether she's safe and well . . . or whether she was ever told about me.'

Excitement mounted, then despair took over. She could not sit still – pacing the floor, waiting and watching. 'I'm so close to knowing,' she muttered. 'So very close!'

Presently she heard them emerge from the drawing room.

Creeping into the hallway she saw them there, the visitor and the mistress. 'You have my address,' Anne Hale was telling Frances. 'Please . . . if there is anything you can find out, anything at all, please let me know, and I'll be on the first train back. I just have a suspicion she may have come north – have found out this is where she came from.'

'I shall do all in my power to find this young woman,' she promised, 'and of course, you must realise, this may well have implications for my own children?'

'And, with respect, I hope *you* understand, she must not be made to suffer for the accident of her birth.' Anne recalled the incident all too well, and to her shame. 'There was an unfortunate occasion . . . before we went our separate ways, when I blurted out the manner in which she was brought to me.'

'You should not blame yourself for that.'

'I was not as kind as I might have been, and now, given the opportunity, I would so much like to put things right between us.'

'We'll find her, my dear, don't worry.'

'I feel you will.' Frances had given her confidence. 'Thank you for your time. I'll wait to hear from you, and hope for good news.'

'I shall do my utmost, that's all I can say.'

Eliza was devastated. There was little use in following the visitor. How could she tell her where the child was when she didn't even know herself?

'Eliza!' The mistress's voice startled her thoughts.

Quickly, she gathered her wits and hurried out. 'Yes, ma'am?'

Frances was in a state of great agitation. 'I imagine you heard all that?'

The innocent remark made Eliza flush with embarrassment. 'No, ma'am! It isn't my habit to listen in on conversations.'

Frances assured her she meant no such insult. 'I want you to take this letter to my solicitor first thing in the morning.'

'But it's Christmas Day, ma'am.' She began to wonder whether Frances Mears was finally losing her mind. 'The solicitor won't be at his office on Christmas Day!'

'Mr Parnell is a personal friend as well as my legal adviser. The address on the envelope is his *home* address. I have no doubt he will get on to this urgent matter right away . . . Christmas or not, I promised that poor woman I would do everything in my power to find the girl, and I mean to keep my word.'

'Yes, ma'am.'

'When Master Robert comes in, I want to see him straight away.'

'Of course.'

'And I hope he won't be too long, because I'm very tired.'

'Like I said, ma'am . . . your bed is ready when you are.'

'I wouldn't sleep. Not until I have spoken with my son.' She gave a wry smile. 'Leave me now. But remember . . . the moment he comes in.'

Outside in the hallway, Eliza gazed at the letter. After a moment she pressed it close to her heart. 'I had thought never to see her again,' she murmured, her face a picture of happiness, 'especially after the lies *he* told me. If the mistress says she'll find her, then she will.'

At long last, she had something to hope for.

It was an hour later when Robert arrived home from celebrating Christmas with some friends he would not see the next day. 'The mistress wants to see you right away,' Eliza informed him. 'She won't go to bed until she's spoken with you.'

Robert had never known his mother to stay up so late, and he said so now. 'Have you any idea what it's about?' Like his mother he felt he could trust Eliza implicitly.

'All I know is . . . she has had a visitor.' And that was all she had a right to say.

'Right! Thank you, Mrs Flanagan.' He went straight to the drawing room. Eliza heard him say, 'Are you all right, Mother . . . only Eliza said you wanted to see me the moment I came home.'

'Oh, Robert! Thank goodness—'

When the door closed and the voices became muffled, Eliza took herself to the kitchen, where she made a nightcap. She had hardly put it to her lips when she heard the front door open and close. A moment later, Jack poked his head round the kitchen door. 'Where are they all?'

Flustered as always in Jack's presence, Eliza stumbled to her feet. 'Miss Hannah is spending the night with a friend, sir.'

'And the others?'

'In the drawing room, sir.'

'Hmh.' He thought for a moment. 'If anyone wants me, I'll be in the library.' With that, he strode away.

A moment later she heard the library door softly open and then close. 'Jumped-up little nobody!' she grumbled. 'Thinks he's master in this house already! Too much like his father, that's the trouble!'

It was a good half-hour before Robert emerged from the

drawing room, his mother with him. 'Get some sleep,' he told her gently.

'You will tell Jack and Hannah, won't you?' she asked again. 'I know I should tell them myself, but I'd rather you did that.' She sighed. 'Besides, I expect they'll be after me soon enough when they realise what this implies.'

'Don't worry, Mother.' Robert could see how the past events had taken their toll on her. 'Please . . . leave all this to me. I'll deal with it.'

He kissed her good-night and watched her go up the stairs.

Seeking Mrs Flanagan out, he addressed her in a serious voice. 'Mother says she gave you a letter?'

'Yes, sir.' Eliza took the letter from her pocket. 'I'm to deliver it first thing in the morning.'

'It's very important.'

'Yes, sir . . . I do realise that.'

'Then I can trust you to guard it well?'

'With my life, if needs be.' This letter was the most precious thing she had ever been charged with . . . apart from the child itself.

He smiled at her sincerity. 'I'm not sure Mother would want you to risk life and limb.'

'All the same, sir.'

He had often wondered about Mrs Flanagan. He wondered now. 'You're a good woman,' he said. 'My mother is very fond of you.'

'And I'm fond of her.'

'I believe Hannah is staying with friends tonight?'

'Yes, sir, but she will be home early in the morning.'

'And Jack?'

'He's in the library.'

'Trying on Father's shoes for size, is he?' Smiling, he added, 'It's all right, Mrs Flanagan, you don't have to answer that.'

He found Jack in his father's seat, his feet up on the desk. Smoking his cigar and drinking his whisky, he looked every bit the businessman. 'My! My! Wouldn't Father be pleased to see you following in his footsteps?' Entering the library, Robert closed the door behind him. What he had to say was for Jack's ears only.

'It's only a matter of time before I take over,' Jack boasted. 'Hannah's just a girl, and you're not big enough to take it all on.'

'You think it will be that easy, do you?'

'There are two obstacles to overcome . . . you and Hannah. I think that should be easy enough.'

'What if there was another?'

'Such as?'

'Such as . . . *a sister we didn't even know about.*'

'You're talking in riddles.' Sitting up, he took another swig of whisky. 'If you've something useful to say, get to the point. If not . . . bugger off and leave me alone.'

Rushing across the room, Robert snatched the bottle out of his hand. 'If you can get your addled brain together for one minute, I have something to tell you.' Smelling the booze on Jack's breath, he said with disgust, 'Perhaps tomorrow might be a better time . . . when your brain is clearer.'

Realising it must be something important for Robert to lose his temper like that, Jack began to take notice. 'My brain is clear enough,' he said, and to prove that he was all attention, he slid his feet from the desk and leaned forward. 'Well? I'm waiting.'

Tempted to leave it until tomorrow, Robert hesitated. This was important, and unfortunately, as his mother had so rightly pointed out, Jack had as much right to know as Robert himself did. 'Do you remember that young woman you found in Father's shed?'

'At the factory? Yes, I remember . . . brown hair . . . scruffy vagabond type. Thieving little bastard. What about her?' When

Robert hesitated, he raised his voice. 'I asked . . . what about her?'

'I have an idea she may well be our sister . . . our *half-sister* I should say.'

Jack's face opened in astonishment, then it crinkled into a grin. 'You're in fine form tonight. What is this . . . some kind of a joke?'

Slowly, Robert shook his head. 'It's no joke,' he answered. 'Mother had a visitor tonight . . . a lady by the name of Anne Hale. And if she's a surprise to you and me, she was just as much a surprise to Mother.'

'What was her business here?'

'She's our long-forgotten aunt . . . Father's sister.'

'What?' His father had never spoken of a *sister*!

'She came to ask Mother if she would help in finding her missing daughter.'

'Why in God's name would Mother want to do that? Especially if the woman hasn't been in touch all these years?'

'Because the girl she's looking for isn't her *real* daughter.'

'Now you *are* talking in riddles!'

'She was given custody soon after the child was born. It was *Father's* child . . . got by some woman he was having an affair with. He tempted his sister and her husband with money, then foisted the child on to them. He turned his back on them, Jack!' Robert thought that was typical of his father. 'The reason we didn't know about her all these years was because Father didn't want us to . . . though of course Mother knew the child existed.'

Jack's face reddened with rage. 'You're a liar!'

Ignoring his protests, Robert continued, 'Apparently, the arrangement – if you can call it that – caused a great deal of trouble in that family. Consequently, when the husband died, the sister turned on the girl. She blamed her for the waste of her own life. When the girl ran away, there was a change of heart, and now it seems our estranged aunt is searching for her . . . wanting to mend their relationship.'

'I don't want to hear any more. Get out!' Banging the desk with his fist, it might have been Leonard Mears sitting there.

'The girl's name is Sally.' Robert let that sink in before going on. 'I can tell you . . . the girl hiding in the shed was of the same name. She was not a vagabond, as you thought. In fact, she is now staying with James's family . . . making a name for herself in the world of business . . . so James informs me.'

Thoroughly enjoying himself, he went on, 'Apparently, she's got a shrewd head on her shoulders.' Stepping forward, he leaned over the desk to look into his brother's face. 'Now then, Jack –' his voice was soft, inferring – 'wouldn't it be a turn-up for the books if *this* Sally happened to be the same Sally who ran away? The same Sally who was delivered to Anne Hale as an infant?'

From the look on Jack's face, he knew he had hit home at last. 'Yes, that's right! The young lady staying with the Petersons could well be Father's daughter. Another sister for us, Jack. Wouldn't that be wonderful?'

'You're mad!'

'Maybe. Maybe not. We shall have to see. But one thing is certain. Don't get too suited to Father's chair. There might well be another contender for it.'

Leaving Jack dazed by the news, Robert bade him good night and went to his room, where he thought over the night's events. 'It all begins to fit,' he mused. 'I think maybe it's time I paid a call on James . . . and his friend.'

He had seen a light in his mother's eyes tonight, and it gave him hope. Maybe this girl would help Mother out of her pain. From the way James talked of her, it seemed she did not inherit Father's wickedness. He slept well. There was no conscience or malice in his heart. Unlike his peevish brother downstairs.

For a time, Jack stayed in the chair, his thoughts in turmoil. Suddenly he started laughing. 'You old bastard! Sowing seeds where you've no right.' His admiration for his father was endless. 'And why not? Who are they to say what you can and can't do? They've got no idea. Leonard Mears is a legend. He can do what he likes, and to hell with the rest!'

He lapsed into a moment of silence. Then, covering his face with his hands, he sobbed like a baby. 'I miss you, Father,' he cried. 'Nothing's the same without you here.'

Snatching the bottle he took a long, crippling swig. 'They're all fools!' Almost choking on the mouthful of booze, he began giggling. 'Did you hear what he said . . . about her being a contender for your chair?' The idea was preposterous!

He took another, smaller swig, his brain suffocating, his voice slurred almost to incoherence. 'Your . . . other son thinks I'm . . . a waste of time, but I'll show him. It won't be long before . . . he's out on his ear . . . I can promise you.'

Getting up from the chair, he made his unsteady way to the door, then out into the hallway and up the stairs, always in danger of falling backwards, but able just to hold the banister and steady himself. At the top, he paused to look back, his eyes following the stairs down, as he recalled what had happened.

It was a long moment before he murmured harshly, his face twisted with grief, 'They think you fell. But I know different, isn't that so, Father?'

Unable to undress, he lay on top of the bed, his mind filled with dangerous, disturbing thoughts. 'This . . . bitch, Sally . . . she'd better . . . not make trouble,' he burbled, drifting into a fitful sleep, 'or, so help me . . . she'll be sorry . . .'

Too excited to sleep, Sally had been up since early light.

'What the devil is she up to?' Maureen and Lizzie were closeted in the kitchen, where they'd been ordered to stay.

'And no peeping!' James reminded them sternly, when Maureen began her way to the window. 'You're to wait here, just like she said.'

Lizzie was like a child. 'I can't wait to see this very special present,' she chuckled. 'The lass has been out there for a good half-hour by my reckoning.' Testing James, she urged mischievously, 'Go on! You can tell us. Yer know what it is. I saw you going into the barn when I were on my way 'ere this morning.'

'I *do* know what it is,' he admitted, 'but I've had my orders, the same as you.' Sally was a force to be reckoned with when she put her mind to it. 'So you'd best resign yourselves to waiting here until she's good and ready for you.' And, much to his amusement, Sally had posted him there to make sure of it.

As he spoke, Sally's voice sailed into the room. 'All right, James. Make sure they don't peep 'til I say!'

With the two women laughing and giggling, enjoying every minute, James led them out to the porch. 'Keep your hands over your eyes,' he warned. 'Wait until she tells you.'

They could hear the odd rattle and shuffle, and for the life of them they couldn't imagine what she had planned, then suddenly she was telling them, 'Right! You can look now.'

When they uncovered their eyes, it took a minute to focus. 'Oh, my Lord, will yer look at that!' Maureen clapped her hand to her mouth in astonishment. Lizzie laughed out loud and jumped on the spot, and James shared in their delight.

'She's been planning it for weeks,' he told them, and in a minute everyone was crowding round the horse and cart.

'Oh, lass, it's beautiful!' Lizzie's eyes swam with tears, while Maureen hugged Sally so hard she couldn't breathe.

Both horse and harness were groomed to a deep, rich shine, and the cart was spick and span as could be. The work and love she had put into it all was there for them to see. 'I'll take you for a ride, if you like.' Sally couldn't wait to show off her new driving skills.

It didn't take much persuading. 'Mind how you go now,' James helped them up, 'and don't be out too long. The weather's about to turn any minute.'

Sally asked if he'd like to come along. 'This is *your* day,' he told her proudly. 'Go on, Sally. Show them what you've been up to these past weeks.'

As she went off, chatting and laughing, and occasionally glancing back at him, his heart swelled with love. 'You'll have to risk telling her,' he murmured. 'One more night lying awake fretting over it, and you'll be fit for nothing. I'll tell her today,' he decided.

With his heart more at peace than for a long time, he gave a sigh. Then he looked up at the skies and smiled. 'It's funny how things turn out.' Thoughts of Isabel came into his mind.

But then he had been a boy, with a boy's wild and fanciful dreams.

Now he was a man, and his dreams were real.

The groom was terrified in case he got the blame. 'I swear to God I couldn't stop him! He took the stallion and rode out of the yard like a crazy thing.' Stuttering, he finished lamely, 'I'm sorry, sir, but . . . I reckon Master Jack had had a drop or two an' all . . . if yer know what I mean?'

Robert laid no blame on this man, and told him so. 'Bloody fool! He's a danger to himself in that state!' He had little choice. 'I must go after him.'

In a matter of minutes the gelding was saddled. While Robert took off after his brother, the groom ran into the kitchen. 'One sane, the other mad as a bleedin' hatter!' he told Cook. 'It's not over yet . . . not by a long chalk it's not!'

Cook made little comment. She had her own troubles.

Sally was coming up the hill when she saw him; one minute a dark speck on the horizon, and suddenly there he was, his horse straddling the road before her. He peered at her as if he knew her. Almost at once she recognised him, and her heart sank. It was Leonard Mears' son . . . the one who had locked her in the shed. 'You're in my way!' she pointed out angrily. 'Please . . . let me by.'

He stared more intently, his piercing gaze cutting through her; then he threw back his head and laughed. 'My God! Think of the devil, she's sure to appear!'

'Let me pass!' Sally's voice shook with anger. 'Or I swear I'll drive straight through you!'

Surprising her, he reined the horse aside. 'Of course.' His smile was pure evil. 'I can't imagine why you should think I *wouldn't* let you pass?'

Cautiously, she urged the horse forward, passing him without another glance except from a safe distance, when she turned to see him still standing there, watching her with hostile eyes.

'Who the devil's that?' For a minute there, Lizzie had been very frightened.

Maureen had seen him before. 'That's Leonard Mears' son, if I'm not mistaken.'

Sally said nothing. Instead, she took the narrow lane towards home. Clicking the horse into a trot, she glanced back once more, afraid he might pursue . . . greatly relieved when she saw that he was gone.

Maureen looked up at the sky. 'James is right,' she observed. The snow had held off for too long, and now the skies were fast darkening. 'We'd best get home.'

Sally had only briefly glanced up when out of the corner of her eye she saw the horse and rider bearing down on them. 'Dear God!' Shouting for the others to hold on tight, she tried desperately to turn the horse away, but Jack Mears had murder in his heart and would not be denied his victory.

Galloping straight at them he veered away at the last minute, laughing when both horses were spooked. Though he managed to control his own, he delighted in the fact that Sally was having difficulty.

Again and again, he charged at them, forcing her this way and that until, to her horror, the wagon wheel caught in a deep rut, throwing her completely off balance. She could hear Maureen and Lizzie screaming. 'Hold on!' she kept yelling, but, inexperienced as she was, it would be only a matter of time before the whole thing went over. 'Whoa, fella . . .' Suppressing her own fears, she tried desperately to calm the frantic horse.

When, almost immediately, Jack Mears came at them again she could do nothing. In his terror the horse reared in fright and, breaking from his harness, sent the wagon over the bank and down, tumbling over and over until it finally shuddered to a halt at the foot of the valley.

The ensuing silence was awesome. Looking down, Jack Mears was well pleased with his day's work. Softly, a little afraid, he stole away.

Waiting at the cottage, James began to grow concerned. 'What the devil does she think she's playing at? I warned her the weather was about to turn!' Outside, the snow was already beginning to settle.

Donning his coat and boots, he set out after them, as always going by way of the narrow lane which cut across the moors and down by the main road. With Jake at his heels, he quickly covered the ground . . . every inch of the way keeping his eyes peeled for a sight of them.

Coming over the rise, he noticed how the bank was ripped up. The road was strewn with harness, and a short distance away a grey horse, still wearing its bridle, backed nervously away on his approach. When James recognised it as the one Sally had brought home, his every instinct warned that something terrible had happened.

Calling her name, he ran back to where he had seen the bank ripped up. Rushing from one place to another, he found slivers of wood from the wheels, and further away one of the wheels itself wedged against a tree. Hardly daring to think, he ran to the edge of the rise and looked down, his heart turning over at what he saw. 'Oh, dear God!'

The wagon was on its side, and clearly visible beneath were the insensible bodies of two women. Further away, caught up in shrubbery, lay another figure, face down and oddly twisted. James knew straight off. 'Sally!' His desperate cries echoed over the valley.

Running and leaping, he prayed as he went. 'Don't let them be dead!' he pleaded. 'Please God, don't let them be dead!'

He came to the wagon first.

Quickly and gently he examined the two women, who were each badly hurt, he could see. He found his mother to have a pulse, though he couldn't be certain about Lizzie. Beneath the wagon they were partially hidden from the elements, but the wind was bitter and their shawls offered little protection against the cold. Gathering their shawls tight about them, he took off his jacket and covered them as best he could. 'I'll get help!' he kept saying. 'I'll get help!'

Approaching Sally, he hardly dared look at her – she lay so still and lifeless. 'Don't take her from me now,' he murmured, 'not now . . . when I know how much she means to me.'

Gingerly, he reached down and put his fingers to her neck. Faintly, *very* faintly, he could feel her heart beating. 'Thank God!' he groaned. 'Oh, thank God!'

* * *

After scouring the countryside for his brother, Robert was circling round once more, this time going by way of the lane and the high rise above the valley.

He didn't see the wagon at first, but then something else caught his eye and caused him to look down into the valley. It was only when James saw him and began shouting that Robert realised who it was.

By the time he got to the bottom, James was running towards him. 'There's been an accident!' he yelled. 'For God's sake . . . get help!'

Part Five

1890

GOING HOME

Chapter Twenty

It was the second of March 1890. Today was a very special day, because at long last Sally was going home.

Looking especially pretty in a red dress and jacket, with her little portmanteau beside her, she kept vigil beside the hospital window, her eyes glued to the lane and her heart bumping for joy.

'Look at that!' The two nurses had grown so fond of Sally, they didn't want to see her go. 'The ward will not be the same without her bonny smile,' said one.

'But we have to be glad she's going home at long last,' said the other. 'There was a time when none of us held out much hope for her.'

'It won't be the last time we see her, though, will it? Don't forget we're invited to the house-warming once she's settled into her new home.'

Suddenly, Sally was hobbling down the ward. 'He's here!' she cried, her face glowing with excitement. 'I have to go now.' Kissing each of them in turn, she went to wait by the door. 'James is coming for me,' she murmured, her eyes stinging with tears of joy. 'James is coming for me!'

When he rounded the stairway she almost fell into his arms. 'I've been watching for you all morning,' she told him, and they held each other for what seemed an age.

Now, as he looked down into her face, he murmured lovingly, 'We have a very special stop to make on the way.'

'I know.' The happiness shone out of her.

At the church, they were all there, anxiously waiting. 'You're sure everything was all right? I mean . . . the doctors did say she was fit and well, didn't they?'

Maureen smiled. 'Everything's fine, Eliza,' she said. 'You know yourself what the doctor said . . . Sally is as strong as an elephant. Once she's home she'll come on in leaps and bounds. He told you that, didn't he? So give over worrying yourself into the ground, for goodness' sake!' She had grown very fond of Eliza.

'They're here!' Eliza cried, and the two of them rushed forward. The minute James helped her out of the cab, they threw rice and flowers and everyone laughed. It was a day everyone had feared they might never see: Sally and James's wedding day.

Inside the church, Sally's gaze kept wandering to where Eliza stood. Eliza smiled back. Over the past months a bond had grown between them that would never again be broken. 'I lost you all those years ago,' Eliza had told her at the infirmary, 'but I will never lose you again.'

Outside, the photographer called them all together; it was a small but very important gathering. Sally with her new husband, then Maureen and Eliza . . . the mother she had longed to meet, and now had come to love and understand. These were her people. She needed no others, except maybe one who could not be there.

'You didn't mind me wanting a quiet wedding, did you, James?' she asked on the way to the cab.

'Whatever you want is what I want too,' he promised, and gave her a long and wonderful kiss to prove it.

As they all four climbed into the cab, Sally caught sight of a familiar figure walking down the lane towards them. The nearer the figure got, the more Sally's heart pounded. At first she thought she must be imagining it, but then as the woman came closer she knew it was not her imagination.

'Hello, Sally.' Anne Hale was different – somehow softer and kinder of face. 'I asked them not to tell you . . . you were so ill . . . and I was so afraid.' Lowering her gaze, it seemed as if she might lose her nerve. But then she looked at Sally and her eyes were filled with tears. 'I know apologies are meaningless after what I did to you,' she confessed, 'but can you ever find it in your heart to forgive me?'

Astonished, Sally looked to Maureen, then to Eliza, and finally to James. They all knew. It was there in their faces. She didn't speak, because she didn't know what to say. Then James nodded, and she knew what must be done. Turning to Anne, she told her, 'I didn't understand . . . but now I've come to realise how hard it must have been, and yes, I forgive you, in the same way you must forgive me for bringing such misery into your life.'

At that moment, Anne opened her arms, and Sally went to her, the past forgotten.

While Eliza and Anne struck up a friendship, James and his family slipped away for a moment to pay a visit to a dear old friend. 'I'll never forget you, Lizzie.' With great tenderness, Sally laid her bouquet of flowers on Lizzie's tombstone. Maureen told her old friend what a wonderful day it was, and how she wished she had been there to see it. 'She's here,' Sally assured her. 'I can *feel* her all around.' And somehow that seemed right.

Sally's new home was the cottage she had seen on her travels with Lizzie and Maureen. Renovated and bursting with sunshine, it was a happy, welcoming place. 'I'd like two children, a boy and a girl,' she told James.

Over the years she got her wish . . . of a sort. First she had a boy, the image of James; then another boy who had the look of

Maureen, with fiery red hair and a temper to match. Then she gave birth to a girl, with a smile to light the heavens. 'She looks like you,' James told Sally, 'and I'm the luckiest man on God's earth.'

Sally was content. Later, when the children were older, she and James meant to expand his newly formed merchant business. 'With you behind me I can't go wrong,' he declared proudly.

Rich or poor, they were destined to be happy.

Frances Mears sold the business, giving Jack enough money to set up on his own abroad, where he was not known and where he could avoid jail and cause the family no more distress, while she and Robert went on a long Mediterranean cruise. 'When we get back, I have a mind to build a fleet of merchant ships,' Robert told her. And, though it was not for many years to come, he did just that.

The house was sold too, and Frances intended finding a more modest home when she returned, where she and Hannah, who was at finishing school, could live in peace.

While the other servants found places in the various big houses, Cook sought a quieter life.

Waiting for the train, she befriended a young stray cat. 'Hello, you,' she chuckled, giving it part of her sandwich. 'Happen the two of us should take up with each other,' she said. 'I need someone to talk to . . . someone to confess my sins to.'

When it rubbed against her, seeming to adopt her for its own, she smiled; a sad, resigned sort of smile. 'I would never hurt you,' she promised. 'You're so gentle and harmless. Not like the master I once had.'

Just then the train whistle could be heard. 'Not a sound now!' Scooping up the kitten, she placed it in her cavernous tapestry bag. As the train drew in, she tickled the kitten under its chin. 'Like I was saying . . . Leonard Mears was such a bad, wicked man . . . *who could blame me for pushing him down the stairs*?'

Chuckling to herself, she climbed on to the train where, finding a seat in a quiet corner, she contemplated her sins.

'Yer a bleedin' natural!' The fat chestnut seller laughed aloud. 'I'm buggered if yer won't soon be selling more chestnuts than yours truly!'

'It's not so bad once you get used to it, is it?' Anne Hale even had her own barrow now.

'Hot chestnuts! Come an' get 'em!' Anne's voice echoed along the Thames.

Much water had gone under the bridge in more ways than one, she thought.

But, like Sally, she had never been happier.

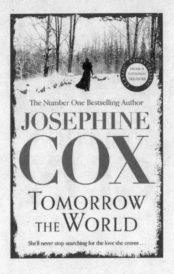

Don't miss Josephine Cox's other bestselling family dramas

LET IT SHINE

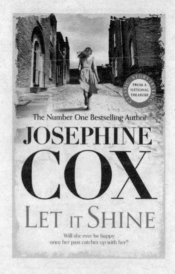

A dramatic and enthralling family drama of love, loss and second chances.

Ada Williams once believed money and power would bring her happiness. But now she is all alone except for her greedy son Peter, who waits only for the day he will inherit her fortune.
Ada, however, has a different plan altogether.

She enters the lives of the Bolton family, living just a few miles away in Blackburn. The Boltons may be poor – but the love they share means they can overcome almost any adversity. But no one could have foreseen the shocking events of Christmas night, 1932, which split the family asunder, leaving Larry crippled and the twins, Ellie and Betsy, in a foster home. Events that Ada Williams, even after all these years, will never forget . . .

978 1 0354 0933 4

HEADLINE

An unmissable treat from bestselling storyteller Josephine Cox

JINNIE

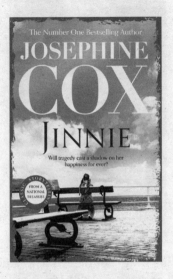

Past tragedies cast a menacing shadow on the happiness of two families . . .

Ten years ago, Louise Hunter's life was torn apart when her husband, Ben, killed himself; her brother-in-law, Jacob, was murdered; and her sister, Susan, abandoned her new-born daughter. Louise remains haunted by guilt over the one night she spent with Ben's friend Eric, and refuses to return Eric's love. But after adopting Jinnie, she finds new happiness – until Susan decides she wants Jinnie back.

Meanwhile, Adam and Hannah, whose mother was killed with Jacob, are on the run. What Adam witnessed on that dreadful night has put them all in danger, but their beloved grandmother knows that one day they must return to the place where it all began . . .

978 1 0354 0930 3

HEADLINE

Unforgettable stories from a national treasure . . .

MISS YOU FOREVER

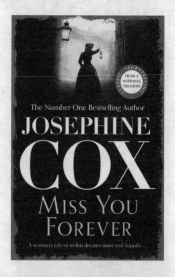

A spellbinding drama of hidden lives and lost love.

One winter's night, in the coalhole in her yard, Rosie finds a woman sheltering there who has been severely beaten by thugs.

At a glance, Kathleen looks like an unkempt, aged vagabond who tramps the roads carrying all her worldly possessions in a grubby tapestry bag. Her only friend is the mangy old dog who accompanies her; the sum of her life is in the diaries she zealously guards. Yet close up, Rosie can see that Kathleen has a gracious beauty – the look of a respectable lady of means.

In hospital, fighting for her life yet moved by Rosie's care and compassion, Kathleen entrusts the diaries to her, urging her to read them. There, in the soft glow of the lamp, a heart-rending tale of stolen dreams, true love, heartache and loss unfolds. A tale that, somehow, must have a happy ending . . .

978 1 0354 0926 6

HEADLINE

Lose yourself in Josephine Cox's magnificent novels

LOOKING BACK

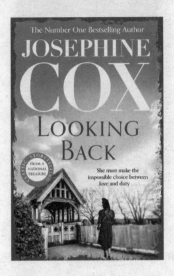

A heartbreaking story of love and sacrifice . . .

When Molly Tattersall learns of a stranger's visit, she is filled with fear. And only a short time later, her mother disappears, leaving behind a letter in which she asks Molly to take care of her five siblings. Molly's wayward father rejects his responsibilities, forcing Molly to make a choice between the young man she has given her heart to and the family she adores.

Molly realises that, however, hard it may be, she must put the children's happiness before her own. It is the cruellest decision of her life, with heartbreaking consequences. Only one thing is certain: Molly's life will never be the same again.

978 1 0354 0934 1

HEADLINE

Don't miss Josephine Cox's magnificent family dramas

BAD BOY JACK

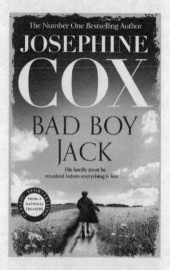

Can he find his children before everything is lost?

Unable to cope with raising his children alone, Robert Sullivan abandons three-year-old Nancy and seven-year-old Jack to those he believes can provide them with a better life. However, he quickly has a change of heart and goes back for them. But on the way there, he is involved in a horrific accident.

Jack and Nancy are placed in the brutal regime of the Galloway Children's Home, where Jack's fiery temper lands him in trouble. Clinging together, the children find themselves at the mercy of the corrupt Clive Ennington.

As Robert recovers in hospital he is determined to reunite his family. But soon he realises the terrible consequences of his cowardly actions, and wonders if he will ever see his children again . . .

978 1 0354 0932 7

HEADLINE